Tiamat's Nest

Tiamat's Nest

Ian S. Bott

Dark Sky Press

Published by Dark Sky Press, an imprint of Ian S. Bott,
Writer and Artist
Visit our website at www.iansbott.com

Book Design by Jim Bisakowski
Cover illustration by Ian S. Bott

Library and Archives Canada Cataloguing in Publication

Bott, Ian S., 1960-, author
 Tiamat's nest / Ian S. Bott.

Issued in print and electronic formats.
ISBN 978-0-9937242-2-0 (pbk.).--ISBN 978-0-9937242-3-7 (html)

I. Title.

PS8603.O9183T53 2015 C813'.6 C2015-902315-7
C2015-902316-5
Printed in the United States of America
First Edition: August 2015
10 9 8 7 6 5 4 3 2 1

To Megan and Matthew,
May we always remember
that we don't inherit the world from our parents,
we borrow it from our children.

Acknowledgments

Many thanks to the community at CritiqueCircle.com for helping me lick this puppy into shape, and especial thanks to beta readers Teresa Cypher, Delores Lowndes, Misha Gericke, and Tony Raine.

CHAPTER 1

It was barely eight in the morning, and Professor Charles Ainsley Hawthorne was already having a bad day. He'd just watched six billion people live. People who should have died.

Charles scowled at the screen lining one wall of his office. Animated charts and diagrams spanned the full five-meter width of the room, a dancing profusion of data, lines and arcane symbols. The simulation mocked him with a myth of a prosperous history that had never happened.

It had gone off the rails.

Again.

He closed his eyes, ground his knuckles into his eye sockets, and counted slowly. Calming his heartbeat, Charles poured a cup of tea and turned back to the screen looking for some flaw in his reasoning. If he couldn't produce publishable results, and soon, the Oxford University council would pull his meager funding, but he couldn't see a way to cross this impossible gulf between simulation and miserable reality.

Anger sparked. The cup flew across the room. Splashes of tannin hid the evidence of yet another failure. Charles blinked away the waking dream, and reassured himself that the antique china cup, an heirloom from another age, was still intact.

He relaxed his grip on the handle and set the cup down on a sideboard with only the hint of a rattle. Trembling fingers sought out the flat panel sound system hanging above it and the opening bars of Sibelius' Fifth filled the room like the first winter daybreak on the northern frontiers of New Denmark.

A section of the screen cleared to reveal a tanned face framed by black hair.

"Evening, Terry." Charles glanced at the assortment of clocks on his antique mantelpiece, picking out the one labeled 'Alaska'. "I wasn't going to trouble you this late."

"Morning, Professor. I got an alert from Typhoon's monitor." A frown creased Terry's face. "Shit!"

"Succinct as ever, Terry."

"What happened this time?"

"That's what I hope you can tell me."

"I'm running out of ideas, Professor. I've spent all term tightening up the simulation. We've reached the point where there has to be something wrong with the theory itself."

"The theory is sound," Charles barked. He caught Terry's eye and moderated his tone. "Sorry, but it's passed test after test, except this one. I honestly thought we'd have something to report by the end of term, some insight into the biggest turning point in human history."

"Billions of people died. That's fact." Terry could recite the well-worn argument by rote. "If the theory fails to account for it then guess which version of history I'm listening to."

"There has to be something else." The room around Charles seemed to darken. Terry's face blurred, and Charles felt for something solid to hold on to. "Latency again, or intruders ..."

"I've stitched up our plenum tighter even than Homeland Security!" Terry chewed his lip. "But I'll check we haven't got rats in the basement again."

Charles gave a weak nod. Terry was right, they were close to a dead end.

But they weren't there yet.

⁕

Tin Man scanned his surroundings once more for signs of intrusion. Still immersed in the audio-visual senses of his avatar, he could feel his real world pulse racing. He steadied his ragged breathing. Hell, there was no physical effort in moving around in virtual space, but after that mad chase through the global network under-layers it felt like he'd run a marathon.

How the heck did they fetch up here? Every zone he'd ever seen was dressed with some visual props to feed to his locked-in senses, even if it was nothing more than a bare wire frame grid. In this zone, he seemed to hang in an unfathomable void. The emptiness around him sucked at his senses. It wasn't blackness. Even the black of space, the usual measure of emptiness in the real world, would have been a comforting *something* in comparison, but this was a complete absence of visual stimulus of any kind.

Disoriented, Tin Man hastily returned his gaze to the only features in this unworld: his two companions, and the machine interface which one of them was systematically opening up. "C'mon, Moonshadow," he whispered. "Let's get one more layer between us and that ... that ..."

"Tiamat," said Pink Marie. "She has a name, remember?"

"Sure, Pink. Tiamat. Whatever. That was too damned close."

"Whassup?" Pink teased. "Afwaid big bad dwagon will hear you?" She prowled around Tin Man and Moonshadow, cupping taloned fingers to feline snout in a pantomime show of projecting her voice. "Tiamat! Tiamat!" she called.

"Shut the fuck up, Pink," Moonshadow growled. "Genius trying to work magic here."

Pink sobered and twitched the tip of her tail. She scowled and slumped to the floor-that-wasn't.

"And keep a good lookout," Moonshadow continued. "We're still on a game, and you're still our watchman."

Pink's scowl deepened. "Can't. None of my scanners are working here. I'm blind."

Tin Man shuddered. "All the more reason to move on."

"I think if she was going to follow us, she would have by now." Moonshadow looked up from the swarm of glowing symbols he was busy manipulating. "Your first brush with Tiamat?"

Tin Man nodded. "I've heard enough stories, but never ran into her before."

"Jeez, Moonie," Pink sneered, "you have to pick a noob for our flagman?"

Moonshadow gazed at her, his bearded face barely visible beneath his hooded cloak. For a moment Pink looked on the verge of protesting further, then she shrugged. Moonshadow rarely needed more than a glance to enforce his leadership.

Tin Man let out a silent breath, but Pink did have a point. He was relatively new and they'd been assigned a tricky target. The Chilean Police Academy was known for its tough stance on hackers, and for ingenious booby traps to mess with unwelcome visitors. Planting a subtle watermark on their public-facing logo, his job on the team, would take innate caution bordering on paranoia and an obsessive attention to detail. Qualities he'd been chosen for.

"If you're sure we're safe," Tin Man asked, "why are you still hacking?"

"To see what's on the other side." Moonshadow turned his attention back to the interface, a metallic pod splayed open like the petals of a large and slightly sinister flower. "This plenum's a strange one. Our clan records show it's been hacked before but they're really sharp on closing the loopholes. I was able to get us through that first quarantine layer no problem, but they've changed the locks on these inner layers. May as well make use of the time while we wait for the coast to clear."

"Good job the outer zone was still open, then. Tiamat almost had us."

Pink sniffed. "You really need to loosen up, Tinny. What's the worst that can happen?"

"Sure, none of this is real," Tin Man said. He tried not to stare at Pink Marie's impossibly generous bust filling her pink leotard, flouting the normal laws of physics. "It's all just photons in crystals in some cloud server in a basement somewhere."

Moonshadow looked around sharply. "But if the wrong construct gets hold of your avatar, it can dump audio-visuals into your head that'll give you nightmares for weeks."

"So what?" Pink pouted, leaped to her feet and prowled the unbounded confines of the quarantine zone once more.

"Some of that shit can screw you up for good in the *real* world."

"Aww, Moonie, you don't really believe that bull, do you?"

Moonshadow didn't answer. He returned to his work.

The silence lengthened.

Eventually he looked up again. "I never listened to the stories you hear around the game zones. Everyone seems to know someone who knows *someone* who supposedly got caught by Tiamat and was never seen again."

"Just stories."

Piercing yellow eyes stared at Pink from the depths of his hood. "Remember Chewie? Or Martingale?"

Pink frowned and pursed her lips. Feline whiskers twitched.

"I was there."

"Tiamat?"

Moonshadow nodded. "Bit like tonight, except we didn't find a secure shelter like this."

"You never told me." The pout this time was half-hearted.

"I saw Martingale once more, a few days later. Just briefly. He wasn't himself, and he signed off in a hurry. Never saw him again."

"But we don't know who they were in real life. How'd you know anything happened to them?"

Moonshadow shrugged. "All I know is they ain't been back."

He turned back to the interface. With a wave of his hands, the metallic petals closed. "C'mon then! You're anxious to put another zone between us and Tiamat? Let's go!"

Tin Man looked around and saw that a new portal had opened up behind him. He hurried through, followed by Pink and Moonshadow. "How long are we going to spend exploring?" The adrenaline was wearing off, and he was now getting anxious about remembering the directions he'd been given to complete their assignment. Plus he had real work to do, deadlines to meet, if he expected to eat and pay rent this week. He hadn't planned on being out this long.

"Tiamat never stays put for long," said Moonshadow. "When she realizes she can't follow us, she'll be off chasing one of the others. All we have to do is wait a while, then we can leave and get back to the game."

"Or exit," Pink added, with a sly glance at Tin Man. "If you've had enough."

Tin Man was thankful his liquid metal avatar couldn't reproduce the hot flush creeping over his cheeks. It had indeed occurred to him that this might be an ideal opportunity to exit virtual space safely. He pictured those agonizing moments of helplessness, of vulnerability, while your avatar dissolved and the cloud reclaimed its footprint. Games rooms protected you from interference the moment you started the exit sequence.

This was not a games room. Moonshadow had drummed this into him, voice low but insistent. "You need to leave yourself quiet time to exit fully. At least three seconds. If any half-decent security agent snags even the residual image of your avatar, it can trace your umbilical back to point of entry."

"That means they got your real life ID, kiddo," Pink had added. "If you get caught in some bigwig corporate plenum, expect a knock on the door from some slack-jawed friendly types reminding you of your civic duty."

But to run now? Fear of capture faded, eclipsed by thoughts of losing face. Tin Man was steadily building a reputation amongst the gamer clan, a reputation enhanced when the legendary Moonshadow invited him to team up for an infiltration game far from the safety of the regulated zones. A reputation that would be shredded if he turned tail now.

Of course! They were testing him! They must have deliberately run into Tiamat to see what he'd do. And, he had to admit, scared shitless as he was, the adrenalin rush had been phenomenal.

"What the heck is this place?" Moonshadow's voice was filled with awe.

Tin Man stopped and studied his new surroundings for the first time. They had emerged from behind a pillar into a space that reminded him of pictures he'd seen of old-fashioned railway stations. Ornate columns supported a vaulted ceiling of iron and glass. Grey clouds scudded overhead, and rain drummed convincingly on the glistening panes.

There were no tracks or trains. Instead, rows of displays divided the floor, showing moving graphs and diagrams, rolling text, and tables of figures.

In the centre of the vast space, a globe hung in mid air, spinning slowly. Looking up at it, Tin Man recognized the outlines of the continents, but the poles were covered in sheets of white. Around the equator, the words 'August 2083, pop. 8.7 billion' glowed in orange fire.

While he watched, 'August' changed to 'September'.

"What's this?" Tin Man said. "Somebody's idea of alternate reality?" The brilliant white of the poles unnerved him.

"Dunno, but I've never seen so many quarantine layers outside of government plenums," said Moonshadow, "and just look at all this monitoring gear."

Pink signaled for quiet. "Someone's coming," she hissed.

CHAPTER 2

Charles paced his office, alternately glaring at the offending wall still dancing with data from his failed experiment, then gazing out the windows across The High, Oxford's one main street. Buildings opposite glowed in the morning sun, muted by subtle tinting in the toughened perspex. A lonely car cruised past, briefly masking the murmured conversation of a few passers-by beneath his window on the shaded side of the street.

Terry's profile still showed on Charles's screen, but his eyes were vacant, withdrawn. Terry preferred to work in full audio-visual immersion, senses slaved to the online world in a way that gave Charles vertigo.

Last day of term tomorrow, then he'd be traveling. The thought cheered and chilled him equally. His eyes lingered on familiar surroundings that he'd be leaving, however briefly. The wall screen and sound system were latter-day intrusions into a room that could otherwise have been a historical vid setting. He ran his fingers over worn spines of books crowding creaking shelves. Old friends. Comforting ...

For the tenth time that morning alone, Charles reviewed his plans. Public transport schedules, all legs of the journey accounted for and contingency plans laid in case of weather delays. Travel bag already packed—he fought the compulsion to unpack it yet again to double-check the contents. No perishables left in his meager larder, and there was his instruction to his landlady to cancel water deliveries for the next two weeks ...

Charles sensed the rising panic and channeled it instead into anger at his own weakness. He was going to see his daughter and grandson again, after far too long, and his deep-rooted fears would not stop him. *Their winter freeze will be thawing now.* He wondered how Krisgaarde had changed in the years since his last visit.

He would see soon enough. Meanwhile, aimless musing was not helping the immediate problem. He had a class to prepare for this evening, the last before the Easter break. He'd hoped this last run of the simulation would give him worthwhile results to present, from which he could devise vacation assignments for his students. Disappointment gnawed at him.

Suddenly decisive, Charles thumbed the handheld which nestled in the pocket of his lightweight safari jacket. A new vista overlaid his vision, his office still visible through a shadow world from the global ether. His eyes picked out the forecast pages from the Oxfordshire Public Services plenum.

Weather clear for the next two hours.

That'll do.

He called out, "Get some sleep Terry. Pick it up in the morning. I need some thinking time."

Eyes still glazed, Terry waved vaguely in his direction to acknowledge that he'd heard.

Charles clattered down two flights of stairs to a dim hallway at street level. Faded wallpaper, antique lamps, and the worn wooden staircase with balustrade polished by centuries of use, jarred with the gleaming plastic of the inner porch door at the end of the hall. The door swished open as he approached, and sighed closed behind him. Sand crunched underfoot as he crossed the few meters to the armored street door. He ignored the row of storm capes and face masks hanging from pegs on the wall and stepped out into the street.

The mid-morning heat of Oxford gripped him.

He strode along The High and turned into an alley alongside Oriel college, automatically steering himself to make best use of the available shade. The pristine walls of Oriel contrasted with the sand-blasted remains of Merton across the street. When most of England turned to storm-wracked desert, some places could afford polymer shielding. Many could not.

His shoes clacked on the hard-baked dirt of Christchurch Meadow. A faint burnt tang in the air pricked his awareness; there'd be a storm before too long, but the sky above was still clear. No immediate danger. Besides, too many lives depended on the weather forecasts for them to make mistakes.

A few minutes' walk brought him to the Head of the River pub.

The handful of newcomers to Oxford often puzzled over this name. They didn't know their history. Water had flowed near here once—Charles barely remembered the muddy trickle from his boyhood—and a bridge had stood by the pub once, long since swamped by drifting sands.

Charles knew his history. That was what got him into this profession in the first place. History that he was trying to understand, that he was trying to recreate in his simulations.

History that stubbornly refused to repeat itself.

The inside of the pub was cool and quiet. Charles nodded to a group sitting in the far corner as he made his way towards the stairs. He recognized three from the faculty of agricultural science, and an assistant from his own faculty of anthropology.

Charles paused at the entrance to the upper lounge, choosing a quiet table to work at.

"Morning, Professor," a woman called from behind the bar.

"Good morning, Sam. Pint of Norwegian, please."

Charles collected his drink, and settled near the double doors opening out onto a narrow deck encircling the upper level of the pub. Sun streamed across the table, tinted to a mellow amber.

Hmm. About this class. Charles took a sip of pale beer and closed his eyes. *Three third-year students from the North American Alliance. Smart kids, too.*

An idea began to form in his mind.

Charles took the handheld out of his pocket and thumbed it into life.

He spoke in a low murmur, barely audible a foot away. Jaw and retinal implants formed a seamless whole with the handheld, picking up subvocalized speech and echoing back the text of his notes in front of his eyes.

Frequently, his eyes would focus on a section of text while his fingers squeezed coded instructions through the molded grip of the handheld. Editing, rearranging, rewriting.

Charles was absorbed in preparations for his students when a tiny thundercloud flashed on the edge of his vision. On reflex, he squeezed the handheld. Information unfolded across his view, confirming the earlier forecasts. *Right on time.*

He cleared his sight and rubbed his eyes, peripherally aware of the pub's few customers already standing, finishing drinks, and making ready to leave.

The bartender strolled through the lounge, singling out the one or two patrons still seated. "Strength four, twenty minutes. Expected to last three hours," she called as she went. "Not a biggie, but lethal grit content. Shutters down in fifteen, so make your minds up, folks."

She lingered near Charles's table. "How about you, Professor?"

"Best line up another, please." He drained his glass. "And your lunch menu. I'm in no hurry today."

————♦————

Moonshadow pushed Pink Marie and Tin Man into a corner behind a display console. "Someone with a Samurai avatar," he muttered. "He was checking the displays. I don't think he saw us."

"What now, Kemosabe?" asked Pink.

"Hope Tiamat's lost interest. We need to get out of here. Meet back in the games room and have another crack at that assignment." Moonshadow eyed both of them. "Assuming you're still up for it?"

He didn't wait for an answer. "Okay, listen. This zone's set up with habitat props, which usually goes hand-in-hand with some variation on standard physics rules. He might not notice us if we stay quiet and out of sight."

"That's good, right?" Tin Man asked nervously.

"Depends." Moonshadow looked around. "This is a work area, not a games room. Functional. Might not enforce normal rules. And who knows what extra surveillance he might have." Yellow eyes speared Tin Man. "And if it *is* close to standard, the downside is that an exit invokes housekeeping which might trigger alarms. And it might be disabled altogether, and we might be limited to fixed portals to get out."

"So, can you tell?"

Moonshadow shook his head. "Regardless of physics or surveillance, best not to try to exit from in here. If it's anything like the corporates we'll just ring alarm bells." He pointed across the aisle back the way they'd come. "When I give the signal, run for the portal where we came in and get the heck out of here. Find somewhere outside this plenum to exit."

He reached into his cloak and handed each of them a slim booklet. "I've copied all the keys I used to get in here. Portals usually only restrict incoming movement, but you never know around here."

He peered around the end of the display board.

"Go," he hissed.

Pink sprinted across the open ground towards safety.

Tin Man followed. He glanced over his shoulder to see Moonshadow turn. In the distance, a Samurai warrior also turned towards them. "Go, Pink, go!"

Pink was already slipping through the portal into the first quarantine zone.

Tin Man followed.

While Pink opened the next portal Tin Man looked back.

There was no sign of Moonshadow.

They bolted through the open portal.

"Stop!" someone shouted from behind.

"Keep going!" Tin Man roared. Pink fumbled with the key to the next zone.

Shit! How many zones were there?

"Last one!" The final portal opened. Pink shrieked and recoiled into Tin Man. A golden serpent's head forced its way into the opening. Clawed legs and beating wings followed, seeming to fill the nothingness.

"Tiamat!" Tin Man yelled. "Pink, this way!" He turned. His way was barred by the Samurai.

Screw this! He tried to exit.

Nothing happened.

He tried to move, but couldn't.

A roar from behind him rattled his senses.

CHAPTER 3

The roaring wind peaked and died away to a dull rushing sound, punctuated by the occasional clatter of grit against the armored shutters shielding the window at Charles's side. He looked around, brought out from his thoughts by the sudden lull, but the clock on the wall told him that the storm was still far from spent.

"Finished there, Professor?" The bartender must have seen him surface back to the real world.

Charles glanced down at the dregs of leek and potato soup in front of him, and nodded. He stretched and yawned. *Another beer? Best not. Even if it is end of term.*

"Mind if I join you Charlie?"

Charles jumped and twisted around in his seat. "Gwen! Didn't see you come in. How long have you been sitting there?" *Inane question! The pub's been shuttered for the last two hours.*

Gwendolyn Stoppard, Professor of Computation, grinned a slow, predatory grin that had been known to give first year students nightmares. "Didn't want to disturb you," she said, sliding over to a seat at Charles's table. "I know you can only focus on one thing at a time."

Charles ignored the customary barb. "You could have messaged me to say you'd be in Oxford in person. To what do I owe the pleasure?"

Gwen hesitated. "This will probably be the last time. Our faculty base has been in Aberdeen for years now. We've held our end of term meetings here purely out of tradition, but Malachi feels it's time to cut ties with the mothership."

The words doused Charles's lunchtime wellbeing like a cold flannel.

"The last of the faculty will have moved out by the end of Trinity term. I thought I'd tour my old stomping grounds one last time." Gwen sniffed and glanced around the pub. "Let's face it, it's a short tour."

Charles quashed a spark of anger. Gwen was right, yet ... "This is my home you're talking about."

She gave him a pitying look. "You need therapy."

Charles snorted. "Tried it. Overrated." He sighed. "So Computation's finally joining the exodus."

"The only surprise is that we've held out for so long. Oxford University is a global village. Has been for decades. The name will live on long after the town."

"There's two sides to that coin," Charles said. "Our networked lives mean there's nothing to keep anyone physically here; it also means that here's as good as anywhere." He recognized the innate stubbornness in his thinking, and shuddered at the psychological ties that kept him here. The intellectual in him recognized the futility. He'd have to face facts sooner or later.

But not yet. "Well, I'm glad to see you." He steered the conversation towards more comfortable territory. "I think Terry might need some more help from your faculty. We're still hitting problems, not sure if it's security or latency. You know we're trying to run massively parallel simulations with time-sensitive interconnections ..."

Gwen held up an admonishing finger to stem the flood. "It wasn't co-incidence. I thought I might find you here."

When Charles put on his best poker face and cocked an eyebrow, she pouted. "Okay. Terry tracked your handheld for me."

"I'm going to have words with that man," he growled. Then he paused, catching Gwen's uncharacteristically serious demeanor. "You were trying to find me."

"Needed to talk before you take off." She leaned forward, her voice little more than a whisper.

Charles watched her long and garishly-painted nails drumming the tabletop.

"Charles, I don't know how much longer Computation can keep helping you on this project."

'Charles', not 'Charlie'? This is serious.

"Our resource budget is meant for practical disciplines, like engineering, weather, genetics ..."

"The university council still maintains an allowance for speculative research," Charles said. "Everything's above board. They approved the Typhoon project at the outset—"

"A small plenum to set up a small simulation, that's all. You're meant to do all the actual work yourselves. If Malachi knew how much we were helping Anthropology, of all things, he'd have my hide."

Fingernails still clacked. *There's more to it than that.* "I didn't want to put you on the spot, Gwen. We've been careful to cover our tracks. Do you think Malachi suspects any connection?"

Gwen shook her head. "Terry's been great at formulating problems in the abstract. And they've all been fantastic computational challenges to put to the students." It looked like she was about to say more, but she pressed her lips into a thin line.

The hands stopped fidgeting. Silence lengthened.

"I've heard rumors that the university council might pull funding from Typhoon altogether."

"Malachi?" A cold knot twisted Charles's stomach. He'd crossed swords with the elderly head of Gwen's faculty before.

"And he's talked a lot of the Fellows around to his way of thinking. Charlie, this project's a resource hog, and no sign of producing results."

Ouch! But fair. "I thought there'd been some spin-off from the problems we got you to look at."

"Weather simulations certainly got a boost, but I can't admit to Malachi where we got the stimulus from." Long fingers twisted on the tabletop. "That's not the point. I'm not worried about some students' time. They were good assignments. But Charlie! He's been digging into where our computing budget goes. Typhoon was only meant to be a small-scale workspace, but it now accounts for a huge slice of the university's infrastructure. I can't keep that hidden."

———◆———

Tin Man sat in darkness. Or, rather, his real body sat while his visual senses floundered in the darkness of his avatar's world.

And silence.

Sweat tickled his spine despite the chill in his apartment.

He waited.

Waited for … what? What did Tiamat do to people she caught? Spook them with nightmares? Sights … sounds … fed straight into his head through retinal and jaw implants. You can't close your eyes to it, can't block your ears.

Several times, his fingers had squeezed the sequence on his hand-held that would cut all connections to his avatar and return him fully to the real world.

But each time he had stopped short at the final commit.

Curiosity held him back.

It might be scary, but it couldn't be physically harmful. The implants had built-in safety limits that would stop short of any dangerous stimuli. It could be no worse than watching a graphic vid, and he was sure he could handle any visions Tiamat could throw at him.

Dammit, he'd spent months creating this avatar, and two years establishing his online persona. There was so much time, effort, and history locked up in that virtual self, no bloody rogue games construct was going to take it away.

So he waited.

Nothing bad continued to happen.

Tin Man pondered his options.

He'd already found that he couldn't simply exit virtual space. Nothing unusual in that. Many corporate plenums required you to enter and exit through approved portals, so his avatar was trapped where it was.

More seriously, he couldn't hibernate the avatar and regain the use of his senses. It was not responding to any of the usual commands, and refused to relinquish its coupling to his sensory implants.

That was worrying.

How could it have gotten frozen like that? Standard zone protocols didn't allow that to happen. But then, Moonshadow had already noted that this was *not* a standard kind of zone.

Tin Man swallowed a sour knot of anger. *Get over it! That's the risk of trespassing outside the safe zones.*

Cutting the connection completely was a last resort. Once the umbilical was severed, he'd never find the connection to his avatar again, lost in the vastness of inner space.

There was a way, he was sure, that you could rescue a frozen avatar, providing you still had some sort of a connection to it. But Tin Man didn't know how to go about that. He'd have to find someone, one of the other gamers, to ask about that.

And to do that, he needed ... an avatar.

Crap!

Gamers only knew each other by their online personas. *Never* real world ID's.

But the germ of a plan formed as Tin Man thought through the obstacles. He was sure he could hibernate his handheld. Just enough to keep hold of the umbilical while freeing his senses. He'd need to configure a new handheld to his implants. Not a problem. He'd need a new avatar to seek help with. But no time to customize it properly. Could he really show up in the games zone with an obviously off-the-shelf persona?

Tin Man felt his cheeks reddening in the darkness. It felt like walking into a shopping mall naked. He'd never regain face with the clan after that. He might as well abandon his avatar and start over.

Is that all that Tiamat does? Is that what happened to Chewie, and Martingale, and others? Did they simply lose their avatars? Maybe they were still around in the games zones, under new identities, too ashamed to reveal their past history.

Light glimmered.

Tin Man tensed. Sweat-slicked fingers keyed the first part of the escape command in readiness.

CHAPTER 4

"So, in summary, Typhoon is a full and working embodiment of the theorems of Krupp and Moresby." Striding the width of his office, hands clasped in the small of his back, Charles was in full-on lecture mode. The didactic pleasure dispelled the gloom of Gwen's warning. Four more pints of Norwegian pale ale also helped.

He turned to the wall screen where his three students gazed back at him from the other side of the ocean. Most classes were held in virtual classrooms but Charles insisted on old-fashioned teleconference-style meetings where he could see real faces. He studied his students for their reactions. If they understood the importance of what he'd just said, their jaws should have hit the floor.

A beer-induced glow mellowed Charles's disappointment when jaws stayed firmly in place.

His students knew his lecture style by now, and would know this was their time for questions and discussion. While he waited, Charles poured himself a cup of tea and played his usual guessing game. Would it be Michael first, with an attempt at a put-down or one-upmanship? Michael thought he knew it all. It was Charles's professorial duty—no pleasure involved—to enlighten him. Or would Lauren chime in with some gushingly positive observation? No. If she was going to do so, she would have by now.

That left Serena The Enigma. Her white pudgy face was screwed up in concentration. Most of the time she seemed little better than a Third Class student, yet she showed rare flashes of genius, pulling disparate facts together in breathtaking leaps of insight. She always waited for one of the others to speak first.

Michael Stokes cleared his throat, large teeth flashing yellow against dark skin. Charles mentally awarded himself a beer for guessing right.

"Everyone gave up on Krupp and Moresby forty years ago. They were just an intellectual curiosity."

Charles suppressed a flash of irritation at Michael's dismissive manner. "Krupp and Moresby gave the world a calculus of human interaction—"

"With mathematics so dense nobody's ever proved the theorems or solved the equations." Michael delivered his killer blow and leaned back, running one hand through his afro frizz.

"Their work is abstract," Lauren said, "but it's beautiful."

Right on cue, Lauren. Charles chalked up another beer.

"And lots of real-life examples *do* fit the equations," Lauren continued.

"Which proves nothing," Michael said.

"But Professor Hawthorne said he'd proved their theorems."

"He said nothing of the sort."

Charles eyed Michael and held up a cautioning finger to forestall the student's customary tide of scorn. "Lauren, I chose my words with care, do me the courtesy of listening with equal care." Charles was normally happy to let discussions, even heated debate, run their course, but this evening he felt time pressing. "I said Typhoon is an embodiment. A model, not a proof. Nor have I found any general solutions to the equations. I'm not a mathematician, and better men than me have sunk their careers on those rocky shores."

Charles took a deep breath. *Patience!* This was the first time he'd discussed the purpose of Typhoon with anyone other than Terry. Even Gwen's students, who'd solved many of the computational challenges, never knew what they were really working on. "People have analyzed many historical events and shown them to be partial solutions, but it's easy to show that a given answer fits the question. Now, for the first time, we can walk the other way down that street and use the theorems in earnest to forecast global human behavior."

Now he had their undivided attention and interest. "I've plugged in starting conditions from every well-documented epoch in human history. From each of those snapshots in time, Typhoon has successfully played out subsequent events over the course of many years. That is clear support both for the theorems and for the computational approach."

"Can it really predict the future, Professor?" asked Lauren.

"Course not," Charles barked. "What a question. Haven't you been listening? I said Typhoon closely *modeled* big chunks of history, but only in broad-brush terms. It doesn't predict localized events, such as the twin towers. Furthermore, you have to manually correct for inherently unpredictable disturbances, such as technological breakthroughs or natural disasters. For example, starting from the nineteen-twenties, Typhoon foresaw the start and the general course of the second world war, but it couldn't see the atomic bomb coming."

He sucked air through his teeth and ran his fingers through his hair. "Let's try again. Twin towers. Good example. Big, dramatic event. Turning point. But it was a specific event and Typhoon doesn't do that."

He scanned the wall screen, looking from face to face. "However, Typhoon *did* calculate that cultural tensions would produce a catastrophic event within a two-year time bracket, and it identified the main players and subsequent wars. At the time it came as a shock, a bolt from the blue to people living back then, but Typhoon saw the signs."

"That's a significant result," said Serena. "You haven't published anything yet, so what's the catch?"

Charles gave her a wry smile. Her insight was spot on. "I said I had success from every epoch. That wasn't entirely true." He paused, enjoying the moment of rapt attention. "Running from the nineteen-nineties to the twenty-forties, I tried to make sense of the political and corporate reactions to environmental catastrophe. First Rio, then Kyoto, then Copenhagen went nowhere. That was no surprise, but after that Typhoon goes right off track. When you factor in the political and economic impact of events like hurricane Jenny, the Arctic sea ice collapse, and the thawing of Siberian permafrost, Typhoon insists that humanity rallies. The Skeptics should have been revealed for the charlatans they were."

"They were ... eventually." Michael's usual self-confidence wavered.

"But too late to help. The planet crossed avoidable tipping points in all its major climatic systems. World population crashed from nine billion to three, fighting over the habitable margins at the edges of deserts." Alerted by three pairs of wide eyes regarding him with alarm, Charles moderated his voice and calmed his breathing. In a more conversational tone, he continued. "Typhoon says none of that happened. So, why the widening gulf between model and reality? Typhoon goes from outstanding success to outright uselessness over a few decades. Why? Terry and I have looked at this problem every which way for the last two terms."

Serena sat back and folded her arms across her chest. The look on her face said she knew what was coming. Charles struggled to keep his expression deadpan. "Your vacation assignment is to develop some new approaches to solving this riddle. You are coming at it with fresh eyes, and I am looking for some fresh ideas. You will collaborate on this, and you will be marked as a group."

The students eyed each other for a few moments. Eventually Michael broke the silence. "What have you already tried?"

Aah, good! Faced with collaboration, rather than competition, Michael the Practical was awake at last. "There's a complete project history in Typhoon's archives, but I'll give you some hints. Contamination? We've had our share of unwanted intrusions, and we've taken measures to keep them out. Temporal integrity? The simulation is fiendishly difficult to keep together. We're already looking into that. No marks for rehashing the obvious. I'm looking for new angles to explore."

"Any more positive hints, Professor?"

"Well, some thoughts. Have we overlooked some cultural factor in the model? Maybe some technological advance that hasn't been given enough weight? On another tack, what if we've hit some kind of boundary condition or phase transition? Populations were communicating faster and becoming ever more connected throughout the early twenty-first century. Maybe we crossed a threshold and Typhoon isn't strong enough to model it accurately. Or maybe the theorems we're working with break down at some point." Charles felt his heart race as he spoke. "If we uncovered something like that it would be a career-making discovery."

And then screw you, Malachi, and the rest of the council!

"You can sign on to Typhoon's external interface using the token I've just sent you." Charles eyed the patchwork expanse of displays spread across his office wall, half-obscured by the teleconference windows. "But you probably need to be at a faculty building to make the most of it. Or, if you prefer using an immersive avatar," his mouth twitched briefly, "you can enter through any university portal."

While the students pondered his instructions, Charles wandered over to the window and looked out into the street. Despite Gwen's warning he suddenly felt giddy with optimism. Until he'd put it into words just now, he hadn't appreciated how many stones still lay unturned. Oh, his students would get their assignment grades, whether they turned up anything useful or not, as long as they worked together and applied good science. Regardless of what they unearthed, he and Terry would have their work cut out for them next term.

Orange lights flashed in the twilight. A muted rumble outside marked the passage of an unmanned sweeper clearing sand driven in by the afternoon's storm.

V ision returned.

Tin Man faced not the half-expected unimaginable nightmares, but the expressionless mask of a Samurai warrior.

"What?" In speaking, Tin Man found that his avatar was once more under his control. He looked around, recognizing the cavernous, rain-spattered glass vaults.

The Samurai seemed unfazed by the inane utterance. "Seems I need to set better fences," he muttered.

There was Pink, and Moonshadow, both standing and moving their limbs experimentally like they, too, had just been freed from virtual captivity.

The Samurai gazed long and hard at the three of them. "Gamers!" He spat the word like a curse. "You're free to move, but only within prescribed limits. And if you want to exit with your avatars intact I need good answers to some questions."

He turned his back on them, gazing at one of the displays, as if daring them to try to escape. *He has control in this environment.* Tin Man glanced at Moonshadow, who gave a tiny shake of his head. Pink sat down, cross-legged on the floor.

The Samurai glanced back over his shoulder and grunted. "What do I do with you?" He didn't seem to expect an answer to this, and nobody offered one. "I should have deleted your avatars straight off. That's what my boss would have said. No point going to the authorities. We're just an impoverished department in a cash-strapped university. We have no clout."

He turned to face them. "But I'm a curious guy, and unanswered questions don't bug me half as much as unasked ones. Let's start with a simple question. This is a highly secure zone. You didn't just wander in by accident, so what are you doing here?"

When no-one answered, he snarled, "Don't mess with me. You have no idea what I already know. I need to hear it in your own words."

"We were hiding," said Moonshadow. He looked around at Pink and Tin Man. For the first time, Tin Man thought he looked slightly lost. Unsure of himself.

The Samurai peered close. "This was no part of any of your games. You were running scared. What from?"

Moonshadow's shoulders sagged. "I know it sounds weird, but there's a construct out there that gamers sometimes run into. It's bad news."

"He saw it," Tin Man said.

"That?" The Samurai gestured, and a golden dragon filled the air between them.

Pink shrieked and back-flipped to her feet, looking ready to run. Moonshadow grunted, but held his ground.

The dragon, frozen mid-lunge, rotated slowly so they could all get a good look. A sinuous body rippled with power beneath iridescent scales. Individually, their color defied analysis, like a film of oil on amber, but overall the beast shone a lustrous reddish-gold. Translucent wings cupped virtual air, and razor-tipped talons stretched to snag invisible prey. So far, so dragonlike. But the eyes! As they swung into view, they appeared little more than flat black discs, vacant and lifeless. But as Tiamat faced Tin Man full on, for a moment, they seemed like portals to a limitless void, empty yet all-seeing. He felt them strip away the veneer of his avatar and pierce him in the darkness of his apartment. *I know you!* The sensation was overwhelming.

"Why are you so afraid of it? This whole world"—the Samurai's arms swept in a wide circle, encompassing everything around them—"is nothing more than an arcade game to you. No connection with any-thing real. Nothing to cause you any harm."

"If she gets hold of our avatar—" Tin Man ventured.

"Pah! Bytes in a bit bucket? A few hours of time invested in your precious *personas*?" Tin Man recoiled under the Samurai's scorn. "Do you still have a roof over your head? Food in the larder? This has no connection to anything of *real* importance."

"People vanish," Pink blurted.

The Samurai paused. Tin Man waited for more scorn, but the Samurai simply waited.

Pink looked to Moonshadow for support.

Moonshadow sighed. "It's just gamer talk, wild stories, but too many to ignore. Practically everyone knows someone who was with someone who got caught. Their avatar gets trashed, and they don't come back."

"Why don't you keep backups?"

"Some do, but why bother? Mostly it's an expense we can do without, and there's no real danger of getting deleted. Even the corporates aren't a threat. Enough got sued back in the sixties, when they got aggressive with intruders, that these days they either prosecute or release you. And if they do get nasty, they want to keep your avatar intact to use its bread-crumbs as evidence. Then, either the courts force them to turn it back over to you, or you've got bigger problems to worry about."

"So, Tiamat grabs you, you lose your avatar. What's the big deal?"

"That's the point. Nothing much. Sure, you have to start over, it's a pain in the ass, but it's no big deal. Yet nobody knows of anyone who's ever returned."

"That's what scares people," Pink said. "Everyone's got so spooked by Tiamat, and we're all crapping ourselves to hear what really happens." She paused. "And just think, with all the mystery around her, if anyone *did* come back to talk about it ..."

"... Major bragging rights." Moonshadow finished Pink's train of thought. "Impossible to resist. Yet nobody's ever come forward. *That's* what scares me."

"Hmmm." The Samurai seemed to absorb everything they said. From his impassive mask, it was impossible to tell what he thought of it all. His avatar stood, immobile, for ages.

Tin Man pictured a real person, somewhere in the world, pacing the floor while he thought. To a gamer it became second nature to mimic your real or imagined actions through the controls of your handheld. More, the virtual world offered possibilities not constrained by conventional laws of physics. Newcomers had to make a conscious effort to perform gymnastics unheard of in the real world. To an accomplished gamer, thought and virtual deed became one, utterly subconscious.

He hadn't quite reached that stage yet but he could tell, by how an avatar moved, how expert was its owner. This immobility was something unexpected, as though the person behind the Samurai simply didn't care how his avatar looked. Such indifference was unnerving.

"So, I'm convinced that you honestly believe there's something to fear here." The Samurai came to life as suddenly as he'd stopped. "That is not my concern. Here's what's really eating me. That dragon, Tiamat, wasn't like any avatar or games construct I've ever seen. Firstly, I don't think it was a pure construct. I'm sure there was some guiding intelligence behind it."

Moonshadow nodded slowly. "I'm glad to hear you say that. I've often thought it, but never been sure. It's kind of a gut feel. I've played games, with human and machine players, and I can always tell the difference. This thing, though, I can't make up my mind."

"Okay, but secondly, it wasn't like any avatar I've seen. I caught you three easily enough, but Tiamat wasn't affected by my isolation trap."

"Yeah, how did ..." Pink started to say. She subsided as the Samurai turned to her, eyes glittering from the depths of his mask. "Okay, okay. You're asking the questions."

The Samurai grunted. "But thirdly, and oddest of all ... well, let me show you and see what you think." He waved at the dragon, which abruptly came to life. It seemed to be in flight, reaching for something, when it reared up arching its back. It thrashed around as if in pain, then it splintered into shards of golden light and was gone.

It all happened too quickly for Tin Man to follow, but Moonshadow leaned forward eagerly. "That wasn't a normal exit."

"Too right it wasn't. You already know you can't exit from that zone anyway." He gave Tin Man a glance. "And it wasn't any regular kind of shutdown either. I spent an hour trawling the zone logs. Housekeeping had no record of anything that matched Tiamat."

"What do you mean? You've got a record of her right here."

"Superficial structure only. But did you see how it disintegrated?"

Moonshadow nodded.

"All we were seeing was some kind of epiphenomenon."

Tin Man was glad to see that Moonshadow looked as baffled as he felt.

"There were structures interacting with the plenum environment, but there were no underlying code or data structures for housekeeping to clean up."

"That's impossible!" Pink said.

Moonshadow frowned. "Everything here is code and data." His voice held less certainty than his words. He kept looking at the space where the image of the dragon had disappeared in such a baffling manner.

"You see my problem," the Samurai said. "I have an important experiment to protect from unwanted influence. Until I can show otherwise, this thing is a threat. We need to get a closer look."

"What do you mean, 'we'?" Pink blurted.

"Exactly what I said." The Samurai put his hands on his hips. His chin jutted forward as he thrust his face close to Pink's. "Feel free to abandon your avatar here if you don't like it."

He stood, immobile once more, lost in thought. "So ..." He finally turned and acknowledged them again. "You say this beast, this Tiamat, chases gamers?"

"It's a known hazard whenever you leave regulated zones," said Moonshadow. "Tiamat seems to prefer the unoccupied inter-plenum zones. I've never heard of her showing up in a managed and secured environment, but she can lurk in the infrastructure layers underneath."

"Does she always appear?"

Moonshadow shook his head. "It's always a risk, but you never know when you'll run into her."

The Samurai straightened, seeming to have reached some private decision. "This is how it's going to work. First, we're going to swap real life contact information."

Pink gasped. Moonshadow made a low growling noise.

"And don't go whining. Screw your gamers' code. You screwed with mine when you broke in, so now it's my way, or nothing." He looked at each of them in turn. His Samurai mask, not bound by real world constraints, was subtly animated. Right now it wore a 'don't fuck with me' expression that brooked no argument.

"I'll get the ball rolling. I am Doctor Terry Quan, a Fellow at the university of Oxford, England, though I work from my home in Fairbanks, Alaska." He reached into his armor and pulled out a jet black ball the size of a baseball. He tossed it into the air. It stopped, hanging in mid-air between them, and unfolded to reveal both online and real world identification details.

Moonshadow gave a disgusted snarl, and cast a threadbare scroll to the ground. It stopped just short, and unraveled up into the air. "George Matthews, warehouse manager, Sydney, Australia."

Tin Man glanced at Pink, who had her arms crossed tight over her bosom. Her whiskered snout was curled in a pout. He sighed and pinched at his liquid metal chest, plucking off a gleaming teardrop. When he threw it into the air, it splashed outwards, as if it had hit a solid surface, and spread into a thin film of silver, etched with writing. "Joseph Wong, White Horse. Technical journal editor."

Pink hesitated.

"And, of course, I *will* be checking," the Samurai growled.

He probably already has. He had time to. Tin Man wished he'd cut his connection while he had the chance. Then he remembered Moonshadow's warnings about getting caught. It had already been too late the moment the Samurai had set his traps.

Pink scowled and flung a white rose, which unfurled and expanded, joining the constellation of images hovering between them. "Trudy Lundquist, Tromso, Norway. Why is this necessary?"

"Several reasons." The Samurai grinned. "First, to see if you were stupid enough to lie to me. On your way in here, you already walked through a trap that gave me more information than you can imagine. Your service accounts aren't as secure as you'd like to think they are."

Moonshadow gasped.

"Now you know I mean business. I need your help, but it's going to take some setting up. I'm going to let you go, for now, but I can be confident now that you'll be back here when I tell you to be."

Tin Man couldn't speak for the others, but he'd already decided that it was probably easier to go along with whatever this Samurai wanted, for now, anyway.

"And finally, insurance." The mask seemed to wink at Moonshadow. "If this Tiamat is as bad as you say, we can check up on each other. If one of us gets caught, the rest of us can find out what really happens. You might get something out of this venture after all."

He gazed at each of them in turn. "Do we have an agreement?"

The three gamers glanced at each other, then acknowledged.

"Then let's hunt us some dragon."

CHAPTER 6

T in Man paused, heart pounding despite the lack of real exertion. He risked shifting his grip on his two-fisted handheld so he could wipe his palms. When this gig started for real, he'd need all the control he could get.

Pink Marie smirked. She must have noticed the tell-tale wobble of his avatar and guessed the reason. "C'mon, Tinny, think what yarns you can spin back in the game zone when this is over."

"Why do *we* have to be the live bait?"

" 'Cos that's what the Samurai said, dumbass, and we're his bitches until he says otherwise."

Tin Man grunted.

"Besides, who'd you rather have standing ready to spring the trap and haul our asses out when we lure Tiamat in?"

Pink had a point. This Terry guy—Tin Man grimaced at the thought, it felt fundamentally wrong to know someone by their real world name— seemed to know his stuff, and Tin Man was confident Moonshadow wouldn't let Tiamat get her claws into them.

At Terry's insistence, the three gamers had spent long into the night plundering the gamer clan's records of encounters with Tiamat. Terry charted her appearances on a vast and detailed diagram of the major zones and interconnections of the decentralized global network. After hours of painstaking work some hot spots started to emerge—regions of activity where she most often appeared.

The rest of the night had been spent laying plans, building the trap, and rehearsing their movements for this fishing expedition.

Despite the lack of sleep, Tin Man was now alert, pumped with adrenaline. It was time to move.

Pink and Tin Man sidled through a garish thoroughfare, a long-abandoned commercial zone now empty of traffic, reachable only by those who still knew where to find it. Zones like this were a favorite with gamers, affording them unwatched places from which to jump to forbidden territory. Tin Man often came this way to reach the game zones, but that was not where they were heading today.

With a flourish, Pink opened a maintenance portal. She gave her striped tush a provocative wiggle, and somersaulted through the opening. Tin Man shook his head, and followed.

After the neon brilliance behind them, with its pristine images still advertising decades-old fashions, this maintenance layer was stark. A sky blue wire frame grid hung in emptiness, providing a three-dimensional spatial reference. Nothing gathered dust here, but the darkened panels of unused displays gave a convincing illusion of decay.

Pink's yellow eyes glowed in the emptiness. "Ready?"

Tin Man took a deep breath, and nodded. "We're both ready," he muttered for the benefit of Terry and Moonshadow, who were waiting back at Typhoon's back door portal and listening on the private chatline they'd set up for themselves.

The next zone led to one of the hot spots on Terry's charts, as good a place as any to start the search for Tiamat. Tin Man hoped she'd bite, and fast. The irony was not lost on him after spending his gaming career careful to avoid such encounters, but this seemed the quickest way to get the Samurai off their backs.

Before Pink could open the next portal, they both jumped at Moonshadow's hoarse cry over the chatline. "She's *here!*"

"Tiamat's showed up at Typhoon." Terry's calmer tones intervened. "Change of plan. We're leading her into the trap and you need to get back here to close it."

"And snap it up." Moonshadow spoke softly, normal poise resumed, but he couldn't keep the edge out of his voice.

Tin Man was already pounding through the virtual labyrinth, following the path they'd mapped out to bring him and Pink back to Typhoon. He'd rehearsed his moves for utmost speed, picturing himself running with Tiamat in pursuit. This wasn't how it was supposed to work. She was now ahead of him, not behind, but a stream of curses over the chatline gave fresh urgency to his movements.

He was dimly aware of Pink following close behind. He was more acutely aware that this was never part of the plan, and he had no idea how to work the trap. Live bait didn't ask such questions.

A howl of anguish jarred him. A spot between his shoulder blades crawled.

"We've lured her into the trap, but she's got hold of Terry," Moonshadow panted. "I'm going to try something. Whoever's driving her is in for a shock."

"My eyes," Terry moaned. "It burns."

Tin Man waved the grips of his handheld, urging his avatar onwards. He pictured Moonshadow and the Samurai grappling with the giant golden dragon. Memories of those dead eyes chilled him. Whatever it was that Tiamat did to captured avatars, and to their owners, they were about to find out.

"Not *that* way!" Pink Marie yelled as Tin Man was about to leap through the next portal.

"Crap! Thanks, Pink." In his haste, Tin Man was following the route to the bitter end. He would have blundered right into the trap along with the others.

Embarrassed and disorientated, he followed Pink into the executive zone Terry had created to manage the trap. Tin Man stared in dismay at the spread of controls and displays cobbled together in haste last night.

Parts of the panel resembled the manual controls of an aircraft. Another display was eerily reminiscent of the Glasgow traffic control grid he'd seen in an engineering article he'd helped to edit. Sleek retro styling clashed with brass-bound steampunk contrivances, culled from a dozen resource libraries and repurposed for their utility rather than usability.

Flickering lines and bars danced above a row of gauges, showing intense but indecipherable activity in the trap. "Damn these tech-heads!" Screams and roars over the chatline battered Tin Man's senses. "What do we do?"

"Just freeze the damned zone!" Moonshadow's voice was a strangled yelp.

Pink Marie reached past and slapped a large red button in the middle of the patchwork mess. The schematics stilled. A row of status lights ceased their rainbow dance and blinked a steady gunmetal grey.

"Oh, great! Any idiot could have done *that*!" Tin Man snarled into the abrupt silence. "Now what?"

"What? I froze it like the man said."

"Do you know how to drive this heap?" Tin Man gestured to the makeshift controls.

Pink shrugged.

"Nor do I, and the only ones who do are now frozen in there, so how the heck are we supposed to get them out?"

"Oops." Whiskers drooped.

Tin Man gazed glumly at the panels. "Boundary handshakes ... footprint stats ... housekeeping tree ..." he muttered. "Crap! I was so freaked about deliberately bumping into Tiamat, I was kinda focused on the escape route. I wasn't paying attention to the rest of Terry and Moonie's instructions, and it was all over my head anyway."

"Look," said Pink, "everything in the trap is frozen in place, held in suspended animation like the Samurai did to us when he first caught us. Terry and Moonie can wait, and so can whoever's behind Tiamat. They're not going anywhere, so calm down. No pressure now. We'll figure it out."

"Pink, one wrong move could wreck everything. I can't make sense of half these controls, and I wouldn't even know where to start."

"First we seal the zone, like so." A cloaked arm reached past, startling Tin Man.

"How'd you manage that?" The avatar standing next to him was recognizably Moonshadow, but subtly different. Less well-formed, it seemed. Did Tiamat inflict some damage?

"Easy, I configure the zone boundaries there, and there—"

"You know what I meant. How did you get out?" Understanding dawned. "That's not the same avatar."

Moonshadow smiled, a shadow of movement under his hood. "Oh, you poor noob!" His amused tone took the sting out of the disparaging epithet. "I've hacked my handheld. An open secret amongst us old timers."

"What sort of hack?" Pink's eyes lit up.

"Adds some non-standard buffers between me and my avatar. It was designed to make an umbilical more difficult to trace if your avatar ever got caught by some security creep. An added benefit is that I can unhitch my implants from my avatar if it gets frozen."

"And you have a spare avatar set up."

"Not quite as well-tailored, but loaded and ready to use." While he talked, Moonshadow's fingers flew over the controls. He held up a hand, scanning the panel with a ferocious intensity. Apparently satisfied, he glanced at Tin Man. "Time to see what we've got. I've found the footprint of our avatars. I can partly unfreeze the zone and let them out while keeping Tiamat trapped."

He caressed the controls, then let out a deep breath. "Now, I need to retrieve my property."

The second-rate Moonshadow vanished, to be replaced moments later by the original version. "Phew! I've been in some online fights, but that was not good. I can understand someone tangling with Tiamat not wanting to come back for more."

The Samurai staggered into sight. "What? Sorry, my ears are still ringing, and I'm half blind."

"That shouldn't be possible," Tin Man said.

"You ain't been around long enough," Pink muttered.

Tin Man thought for a moment. He knew some of the gamers had a 'dangerous' reputation. He took a guess. "You know some handheld hacks that can override someone else's implant safeties."

Moonshadow growled, "If I wanted, I could dump enough into your head to cause permanent nerve damage." He shook his head, looking bemused. "I pulled out all the stops when that bitch got her claws into Terry, but it only seemed to goad her on. She's got some serious hacks."

"What do you mean?" Tin Man asked. "What did she do?"

Moonshadow grimaced. "Imagine staring into the sun, unable to close your eyes." He hesitated, and glanced at the dazed Samurai. "I've got some counter hacks that helped me deal with the overload, but it's obvious Terry's not a gamer. I wonder if he's gonna be okay."

The Samurai bumped into a control panel, then froze. "I'm unhitching myself for a minute," he muttered. "Need something for the pain."

"Listen," Moonshadow whispered to Pink and Tin Man, with a sidelong glance at the dazed Samurai, "this stays between us, right?"

With a tingle, Tin Man realized that the mighty and self-assured Moonshadow was distinctly uncomfortable. He spoke to Pink, but his words were meant for Moonshadow. "I'm still a *noob*, but I guess hacks like this are un-gamerlike?" That they were illegal was not even an issue, of course. Gamers delighted in living on the wrong side of real world laws, but their own code was sacrosanct.

"Sure." Moonshadow snorted. "Deacon would have a hissy fit if he found out."

Tin Man winced at the contempt with which Moonshadow referred to the unofficial leader of the gamers.

"Yeah, I can handle him. I never use any hacks gaming, but some folks out there will give me a hard time if they find out."

"What do we do about the trap?" Tin Man asked. After a renewed flurry of activity, the monitors had grown suspiciously quiet again.

Moonshadow eyed the panel. "Whoever's behind Tiamat will have worked out they can't do anything. This is Terry's show. We wait."

At last, the Samurai came back to life. "Better. Don't think there's any lasting damage, but that's a new one for the archives."

He checked the panels one by one. "I don't know exactly what we've captured, but I had recorders logging everything from the moment you guys set off. There's a lot of data to analyze, but right now I want to talk to whoever is behind that thing." He flexed his fingers. "Okay, let's see what we've got."

The Samurai's confident air dissolved in a stream of invective.

Tin Man, Moonshadow, and Pink Marie peered over his shoulder at the screens.

The trap was empty.

CHAPTER 7

The plane plunged. Charles clenched his teeth and squeezed his eyes shut, fighting the bitter taste that clawed at the back of his throat.

Eyes still closed, he activated his handheld. Visual signals flooded his awareness, contradicting his inner ear. *Bad enough when the room is still!* Charles tried to ignore warning signs from his gut and looked for the regional weather status.

He just had time to see that they were flying between two violent storm systems that were descending over the top of Scotland into the maelstrom of the North Sea, then he hastily shut off the handheld and fixed his gaze on the rain-lashed horizon.

At last the heaving in his stomach subsided enough to tear his eyes away from the window. He fumbled in his pocket for the off-the-shelf travel sickness pills he'd picked up in Glasgow. For a few moments of frustration Charles tried to remember the dosage instructions and calculate the hours since his last dose, then he gave up the effort. The effects of a miscalculation could hardly be worse than what he was already suffering.

He glanced towards the cabin attendant. Something in Charles's expression must have betrayed his misery because the attendant unstrapped himself from his seat and reached into a locker at the front of the cabin. He worked his way down the aisle, holding onto seat backs for support in the lurching aircraft, and squatted alongside Charles.

The attendant glanced at the packet half-crushed in Charles's fist. "Not very effective, are they, Professor? You going to be driving or operating machinery in the next ten hours?" When Charles shook his head, wincing at the resurgence of nausea, the attendant popped the lid off a small tube and dropped a pink gel capsule into his hand. "Let it dissolve under your tongue."

Charles complied. The urge to vomit started to ease after a few minutes, despite a series of gut-wrenching swoops and shudders. Gesturing out the window, Charles mumbled, "Is this normal?"

"Pretty typical for this time of year. We get one storm after another brewing in the Atlantic and sweeping around towards Norway. And don't worry about the craft, it can stand a lot more than this."

"Really?"

The attendant smiled. "We'd be bouncing off the ceiling long before the aircraft took any damage. If this was an uncrewed mail run, it would happily drive straight through that storm out there."

As he spoke, the cabin intercom hissed into life. "My apologies for the rough ride, ladies and gentlemen," a woman's voice announced. "As you may have noticed, we're flying close in between two storms. We're making a dash for a corridor due to open up north of Iceland, which should give us a smooth passage the rest of the way north to New Denmark. If you can put up with the discomfort a little longer we'll be on the ground in Isfeldt roughly two hours sooner than if we'd skirted around that westernmost storm."

The attendant stood, clapping Charles on the shoulder. "Hang tight, Professor. We've got another fifteen, maybe twenty minutes in this turbulence, then we get into clearer skies."

Charles looked around the cramped cabin at the handful of other passengers. A couple at the back seemed to be dozing, while their three children waved clenched fists in the air, shrieking in delight, eyes unfocused as they immersed themselves in some interactive game.

Double handhelds? I have enough trouble using one hand at a time. How do they manage it?

"Professor?" A young woman across the aisle was looking at him. Her voice held hope and excitement.

Charles gazed back at her, dredging his memory for some flicker of recognition.

"I'm sorry." The voice was heavy with a European accent. "I heard the attendant call you 'Professor'. Just on the off-chance, would you happen to be Professor Morrow?"

Charles shook his head. "Professor Charles Hawthorne, Oxford University."

"Oh!" Her face fell slightly. "Genetics? Or engineering?"

Here we go. "Anthropology." Charles had long ago resigned himself to the instinctive contempt that his chosen profession invoked. He never spoke of it to strangers unless pressed, and rarely wasted time justifying the discipline.

She struggled to conceal her disappointment. "That's interesting. We have little call for ..." she seemed to be casting around for the right word, "... *academics* in New Denmark."

Charles just smiled and inclined his head. In refined academic circles, the gesture might have appeared gracious. The effect was spoiled by a lurch that had him clutching the armrest.

"I'm sorry. I am being rude." She wedged herself against the seat in front and leaned across, holding out a hand. "Katrine Lind. Electrical engineer."

Charles hesitated, then took her hand. "Pleased to meet you." She seemed disappointed rather than hostile, and some companionship would be a welcome distraction.

⸻ ◆ ⸻

Joseph Wong took another pull straight from the bottle of cheap bourbon he'd hurried out to buy. He almost never touched alcohol, let alone hard liquor. It dulled his thinking. Right now, that was what he wanted. "Fuck it all, Pink, I was *talking* to him when it happened!"

"Shit, calm down, will you, Tinny?"

It felt strange, hearing a heavy Scandinavian accent so different from her online voice. Joseph, a.k.a. Tin Man, realized he still had much to learn. Everyone tailored the heck out of their avatar's appearance but he had never bothered to alter how he sounded.

"It must have been a shock, I know that, but how does this change anything?"

The sultry tones helped Joseph to distance himself, to separate the online world from the real. He was talking to an online acquaintance, but this was a very real world problem, trying to find the whereabouts of a friend. "Have you found any news reports yet?"

"Starting to pop up." Pink whistled. "That was some transit pile-up. The worst that modern Sydney's ever seen. Any word from Moonie?"

Joseph shuddered. After their failed attempt to trap Tiamat, he'd had enough. Whether or not the Samurai would agree to release them, he wanted no more of this madness. It would help if the three of them were in agreement before their next meeting in the Samurai's lair.

It had been difficult enough, violating every gamers' precept, to contact Moonshadow in person to discuss their next move. His reluctance was eased by an equal reluctance to re-enter the immersive online world just yet. So in the end he used a simple low-tech voice line, handheld to handheld, and tracked down George Matthews, a.k.a. Moonshadow, on his way to work. They talked for a minute, then Joseph heard him and many others in the background scream in pain and fear. Then deathly silence.

The bourbon had been a necessary evil before daring to try Pink Marie.

Pink was right. This changed nothing. They'd done what the Samurai had asked up to now but the game had changed. They were finished with him. If he felt like chasing after them, so be it, but their part of the agreement was over.

"Still not answering. I'll keep trying." Crap, he was not thinking straight. "Even if he got out unhurt, they'd likely take everyone in for check-ups. It could be hours before he's in contact. Who knows where he might be?"

"You're right. He'll be in touch when he can."

In the awkward silence, Joseph wondered idly whether her figure in real life in any way resembled that of her avatar. Without the fur, of course.

"So, what now?" Pink's voice was quiet, emphasizing the physical distance between them.

"We rendezvous as agreed. With or without Moonie. We tell the Samurai that we're through with his games. You with me?"

"Abso-fucking-lutely."

———— ◆ ————

Smooth asphalt offered a haven of stability for Charles's reeling senses. He breathed deep and nearly choked as the chill air seared his lungs. Pulling on the thermal overcoat Sylvie had bought for him on his first and only visit here, he scanned the milky blue sky arching impossibly vast overhead. No sandstorms here. He'd forgotten how fresh and clean the air smelled.

The rollercoaster flight already seemed little more than a fading memory, and his mind felt light as thistledown. *Must find out what was in that pink capsule. Danged good stuff!* Pangs of homesickness, for familiar warmth and ochre hues and the huddle of timeworn buildings, would begin their siren calls all too soon, he knew. But this was a time for greeting, for joy.

A low rumble rose to a whoosh behind him. Charles turned, nearly overbalancing, to see a tiny craft bullet into the sky and dwindle to a speck in the emptiness. A small mail plane, fully automatic. For a moment, he tried to orientate himself to see where it was heading, then quickly gave up.

He turned back more carefully and paused to let the horizon settle. The straggle of passengers ahead of him had almost reached the administration building, dwarfed by the hangars, workshops, and warehouses lining the runway. They must have been here decades now. Old by the standards of this newly-claimed country, but still shiny and brash compared with the tired antiquity he was used to.

A sign on the side of the building in English and Danish read "Isfcldt International".

Barely through the door of the terminal building, a fleeting peripheral glimpse of movement left Charles no time to brace himself. Familiar perfume enveloped him. He staggered to keep his footing as he returned his daughter's hug, then held her at arm's length. "You grow more beautiful with each passing year." Even beneath her red winter jacket, Charles could see she still kept herself well in shape.

"You're aging gracefully, too, Dad." Sylvie smiled, but eyes betrayed concern. She was counting angiomas again.

Charles tried to head off the customary health lecture. "My aim has always been to age *dis*-gracefully, as you very well know, my girl."

Before she could argue, he looked past her shoulder, scanning the small crowd of passengers and greeters mingling with airport staff. Sylvie's husband, Aaron, loitered near the back. Charles pushed past to greet him, hand outstretched. A young boy peered from behind Aaron.

"Ben! My God, you've grown."

Ben's eyes widened. He shrank back behind his father.

"Say 'hello' to Poppa, Ben." Sylvie gave an encouraging smile. To Charles she said, "Eighteen months is a long time for a five-year-old."

Charles crouched down so his eyes were on the same level as Ben's. "I guess I'm bigger than I look in telecons, eh?" He grinned, and framed his face with thumb and forefinger of each hand. "This better?" He stuck out his tongue.

Ben giggled.

"Come on," Charles said. "You want to ride on my shoulders?"

Aaron collected Charles's baggage and led them through the fast-emptying concourse and out the far door.

"New truck?" Charles pretended to admire the gleaming monster looming over him on soft, fat tires. His own cloistered life held little use for motorized transport, but machinery in all its mystery was the lifeblood of frontier nations like this.

Aaron grunted as he hoisted bags into the trunk. "The farm is doing well now."

Charles lifted Ben up into the cab, and climbed after him. Goosebumps crawled up Charles's neck as he settled into a seat. Nothing to do with the cold. "And still fully manual, I see."

Aaron grinned, slipping behind the wheel. "And still as safe as any of your British vehicles, Professor. I've seen the roads in big city centers and *that* scares me far more. Maybe you need computer guidance to keep things moving safely, but we have not the traffic to trouble us."

"Even Isfeldt is hardly a busy metropolis, Dad." Sylvie strapped in next to Aaron.

Icy fingers kneaded Charles's stomach. Ghosts of glory past. "Neither is Oxford."

CHAPTER 8

I n the end, Charles decided, the drive wasn't that bad after all.

At least the truck didn't cavort in three dimensions, leaving him feeling like he and his stomach had parted company. On his journey north, Charles had felt comfortable enough in the bustle of Glasgow, its vehicles flashing past with centimeters to spare, hurtling through intersections in a perfectly-choreographed tapestry of movement. But that was with computers in control, with reflexes measured in microseconds. With a human being at the wheel, Charles barely stopped himself from flinching every time a vehicle passed in the other direction. It was fifteen minutes before he took note of the width of the highway with generous clearance between vehicles, and began to relax.

The highway outside of Isfeldt arrowed straight to the horizon, edged by mounds of snow greyed by traffic-churned slush.

Despite the nearly empty road, Aaron didn't seem to be in any hurry. Soon, Charles found his eyes flicking from side to side. It took him a while to put words to his uneasiness. "I can't see anywhere to shelter. What happens if there's a storm?"

"We slow down," said Aaron.

Sylvie laughed at Charles's shocked expression. "Aaron has never seen an English storm."

Charles grimaced. "Where I come from, an approaching storm has everyone fleeing top speed for the nearest shelter."

"Here," said Aaron, "biggest problems from storms are visibility and debris on the road. Truck is built for rough terrain, not for speed."

"Yet, here you have a brand new road, clearly built for speed."

Aaron looked sidelong at Charles, then roared with laughter. "You're messing with me, Professor." He subsided to a rumbling chortle. "New road, yes. Three years now. Good surface so it will last. Take more traffic."

"We're opening up the western land, beyond Krisgaarde," said Sylvie. "Each year, we improve the road network so we can get materials out and produce back more easily."

The land ahead began to climb. The highway hugged the contours, sinuous grey winding through rust-colored tundra splashed with white. A turn in the road opened up a distant vista of vivid cobalt. The Indhav. Greenland's inland sea. The largest freshwater lake in the world.

The nearer landscape caught Charles's eye. "Looks like we've slipped back into winter." As the road snaked down the far side of the hills, it etched a deepening furrow into a white blanket covering the tundra.

"This is why Isfeldt was settled first," Sylvie said. "Hot springs behind us keep that side a few degrees warmer. Life is harsher further west, but we're working on it. You'll see." She and Aaron exchanged smiles.

Krisgaarde appeared to have changed little in the last five years. The same rows of buildings lined the street as they passed through.

Five years. Sylvie and Aaron had lived here back then, when Ben was born. When they were still trying to raise funds for their farming venture. Charles tried to remember which side street led to their old apartment.

Five years. It had taken the birth of his grandson to draw him from the comfort of his Oxford home. They'd visited him in England twice since, but seeing Ben now, Charles realized how much he was missing. He really would have to deal with his fear of travel.

Whatever was in that gel capsule seemed to have helped. He cursed himself for not getting the name of the drug from the attendant, but at the time he'd been too absorbed in restraining his stomach contents. Some of the attendant's warnings came back to him, though. What to expect when the drug started to wear off. Dizziness, anxiety ... Charles could already feel his pulse starting to race and his vision swimming. He turned his attention back to the winter landscape, trying hard to enjoy the novelty of it and to share his daughter's enthusiasm for the progress they'd made.

This is what he'd come out here to see. His family first and foremost of course, but more than that, to witness first hand the opening of a new frontier.

Beyond Krisgaarde, it soon became clear that the truck was as much at home on packed snow as on asphalt. They drove another twenty minutes through fields of white, then Ben tugged at Charles's sleeve. "Hjem." He flashed a dazzling smile. A steel arch towered over the road, holding a gleaming sign with scarlet lettering: Johansinge.

The buried road led them another two hundred meters to a row of large, windowless sheds on their left. Blue corrugated sidings gave them an industrial look. *Hard to imagine this being home.* The thought ambushed Charles. The yearning for sun and sand and buildings steeped in history threatened to drown him.

"Look, Poppa, far lavede en sne fort for mig."

Charles fumbled for meaning in the excited chatter, and followed Ben's pointing finger. "Wow, Ben, that's fantastic!" His eyes traced the sculpted mound of snow set back from the road, sides smoothed and packed down. Crenellations marched along the top edge, with a round tower at each corner. "Your Dad's a clever man."

Across the road, a shallow escarpment faced the sheds. It was there, rather than the sheds, that Aaron steered.

A row of verandas, with glass glinting in the shadows, broke the slope of the escarpment like massive gun emplacements from a bygone century. Through a gap in the banked snow lining the road, a ramp led down to a tunnel under the nearest balcony.

In the gloom ahead, a roller door was already opening in the hillside to swallow them. The snow bank rose around and over them. Charles's breath caught in his throat.

They entered a subterranean garage, bare concrete, steel beams, cold and alien. And crowded. Ahead and to one side, vehicles faced them like predatory beasts crouched to pounce: two more battered trucks, headlamps and crash grilles snarling testosterone; a caterpillared snow cat, oily and orange; a family of snowmobiles, sleek and muscular.

The truck started turning on the spot, a slow, stately movement, but so unexpected it made Charles giddy. *They're living like troglodytes!* It was all Charles could do to stop himself from scrabbling for the door of the truck as daylight narrowed to a slit, and vanished.

Aaron turned in his seat and beamed. His chest swelled as his hand sought out Sylvie's. "Well, Professor, welcome to Johansinge."

A movement in the corner of his eye alerted Tin Man. Without thinking, he lunged for the portal. A residual flash of gold, and an outraged roar fading to a subliminal echo in the moment of its utterance, confirmed his instincts.

"Holy fucking shit!" Tin Man flung himself through two more quarantine layers before relinquishing his white-knuckle grip on his handheld. Still immersed in the online world, he flexed his fingers and rubbed his palms on his pants, but nothing could quell the trembling in his limbs as he processed what had just happened. *Tiamat was lying in wait!*

He mouthed a silent "thanks" to the Samurai's forethought in setting Typhoon's portals to admit the three gamers freely. No fumbling around with key codes.

Pink! Was she here already? Or on her way? About to run into Tiamat?

He reached to pick up the two-piece gamer handheld again and fumbled, knocking one of the grips off his lap. He cursed. Vision still locked in to the online feed, he slipped off the couch and to his knees, groping in the electronically-induced darkness. *There it is.*

Tin Man took three deep breaths and tried to forget his own narrow escape. *I just need to get a message to a friend.*

Fingers once more in control, he retrieved the handheld and slid back into his seat. He composed a brief message to Pink Marie, fervently hoping she chose to read it before venturing anywhere near Typhoon, and dispatched similar warnings to Moonshadow and Terry. Only then did Tin Man make his way into the now-familiar central hall.

Rain still hammered the distant glass, but the vast globe hung dark and motionless. There was no sign of anyone else.

Tin Man waited at their agreed meeting place for over an hour. He used the time to ponder how to make a safe exit. Typhoon would still not allow direct entry or exit from within its working zones, Terry had insisted on that. He would need to venture out through the portal before he could withdraw his avatar from virtual space.

On a positive note, it seemed that Tiamat couldn't pursue him anywhere inside Typhoon. Something about this zone was inimical to her. The recorders in Terry's trap had shown Tiamat vanish just as she had previously, despite the fact that it shouldn't be possible. She must have some serious hacks in her system. Maybe that interfered with the peculiar architecture here.

Tin Man filed that thought away for future reference. It was time to go.

He worked his way through the security layers, opening each portal with his heart performing an ever harder percussion solo in his chest. *Last one!* The portal opened. A flurry of wings and claws framed a vicious snout and those dead black eyes.

Despite his readiness, Tiamat's appearance nearly made Tin Man wet himself. He retreated back to the rain-lashed hall.

So much for that. Time for the backup plan.

Ever since Moonshadow had unhitched himself from his trapped avatar, Tin Man had been doing his homework. He'd surreptitiously sought out the less respectable gamers, those with more 'dangerous' reputations. Money and favors changed hands. Tin Man grimaced at the thought of what repayment might involve, some unspecified time in the future, but the tortuous trails finally led him to the handheld hacks he'd been looking for.

His paid work lay neglected. A stack of engineering papers sat in his online workspace waiting to be edited. To catch up, he'd have to pull a few all-nighters, and maybe call in some favors of his own, but right now he gave thanks that he'd taken the time to prepare properly.

He found a blank message board in Typhoon's workspace and scrawled a note in case anyone found him sleeping there: "Tiamat is watching the portal. I'm holing up here until I can exit safely. Leave me a note if you find me."

Using the newly-installed hacks he pulled his audio-visuals free from his avatar, leaving the connection dangling but intact.

Back in his apartment, Joseph Wong stretched and rubbed his eyes.

On legs like rubber, he staggered to the kitchenette. He pulled a ready meal at random from the larder and popped the tray into the oven.

Only then did he notice the discreet signal at the edge of his vision alerting him to waiting messages. Ones from his supervisor he ignored, but there was a note from Trudy Lundquist—Pink Marie—that had arrived while he was immersed online.

Joseph smiled. The note was brief: "Thanks for the warning."

Underneath, Trudy had scrawled: "Found this ..."

He scanned the attached clipping from a news page, and his appetite vanished.

"More on the Sydney pile-up. Crash investigators sifting through the wreckage say it will be days before even a preliminary report is ready, but unofficial speculation points to an unprecedented failure in vehicle guidance systems. Three vehicles, including an unmanned delivery truck, ploughed simultaneously and at high speed into a Sydney Transit bus with nineteen passengers on board. We have confirmation that there were no survivors from any of the vehicles involved."

"Are you all right, Dad?"

Charles opened one eye a crack to reassure himself that the truck had stopped its un-truck-like pirouette, then he lowered himself through the doorway and off the sill to the floor.

He gave Aaron and Sylvie a weak smile. "I don't travel well. All this novelty is a bit much for a frail old man."

Sylvie and Ben climbed down. "Come on, Dad, rest for a minute while Aaron parks the truck." She patted the hood of a snowmobile.

The gleaming skin of the snowmobile felt oddly warm to the touch. *Not metal, then. Plastic?* Charles leaned back, grateful for the support.

With a rumble, the truck glided back into line with its brethren, and Aaron emerged clutching Charles's baggage.

With the truck out of the way, the turntable, sunk flush to the floor, became clearly visible. Wide enough to hold even the hulking snow cat, it would allow vehicles to be maneuvered into their allotted space with a minimum of fuss and no wasted space.

"Very neat." Charles gave an approving nod.

Aaron grinned. "We think of everything." He hung the truck's key on a rack on the wall. "Come, Professor. You will want to clean and change. Come see our home."

Tin Man rejoined his trapped avatar. Someone had been here. The message board held a terse reply. "Who are you? And who is Tiamat? Bring answers tomorrow."

Strange. It had never occurred to Tin Man that this place would be used by anyone other than Terry.

Or his boss, whoever that was. Tin Man's scalp crawled. If this was Terry's boss, he (or she) clearly knew nothing about Terry's venture. He remembered what Terry had said about his boss's attitude to gamers. He could have been deleted on the spot.

He prowled the hall, checking up and down each aisle, and examined every corner looking for portals. This was the first time that Tin Man had taken the time to explore Typhoon in depth. Apart from this vast hall of displays, and the shells of security, there didn't seem to be much to it. Not that he could find, anyway.

Concluding that he really was alone, he returned to the message board. "I am working with Terry Quan. I was supposed to meet him but now I am trapped here. We need to talk. I will check back in at 18:00 mountain time tomorrow. If not convenient, leave an alternative time to meet."

This was becoming tiresome. Time to return to the real world. Work beckoned, before his supervisor got twitchy.

———•◆•———

The after-effects of the travel drug were wearing off at last, leaving Charles struggling with the alienness of his surroundings. He tried to detach himself and look on his situation as an object for study, for analysis. Despite his initial misgivings, living under a hill might not be such a bad choice after all. England had spent large fortunes trying to preserve its traditional buildings, and for what? Very little was left of Oxford, and nobody even remembered London any more, not since they'd abandoned the battle against rising tides and hurricane winds sweeping unchecked from the North Sea.

Charles wondered how the costs of hollowing out a hillside compared with above-ground shielding. Could they attract people back to keep his city alive? He frowned. He was neither builder nor businessman, but straight away he could see the flaw in his thinking: a lack of suitable hills.

He had to admit, though, Aaron and Sylvie's home was comfortable. He felt a pang as he pictured his dusty rooms in Oxford, with fading wallpaper older than this entire country.

After the stark underground garage, and the spotless adjoining workshop with its clean benches, and tools all lined up on labeled racks ready for inspection, a flight of stairs led them up to wood-paneled domesticity. Aaron had shown him into a high-ceilinged common room. Despite the lack of windows, it wouldn't have looked out of place in an old-fashioned Nordic lodge. A broad and heavy table looked large enough to seat twenty people. Charles wondered why a family home would have such accommodation.

He didn't get a chance to question that oddity before Aaron had ushered him back to the tiled hallway running through the depths of the house. A flash of daylight caught his eye through doors opposite the stairs, then they were padding across thick rugs softening the quarry tiles.

"Bathrooms here." Aaron pointed to a door. "Use as much hot water as you need. This side," indicating the opposite wall, "is our rooms. Sylvie and me and Ben, then Christian and Lise." At the end of the hall he pushed open a door. "This is for guests. Make yourself at home."

Now, refreshed, Charles ran a comb through what remained of his hair. His skin still tingled from the high pressure needle jets. He felt a guilty pang at the memory. Accustomed to a frugal daily sponge-down with a damp flannel, he had taken Aaron at his word and luxuriated in the unaccustomed extravagance. He reminded himself that these people had a whole freshwater sea on their doorstep.

He gazed out of the windows of the sitting room at the end of the guest suite. Two large tractors, trundling on double wheels taller than a man, churned the snow beyond the road and disappeared into the furthest of the row of blue sheds. Quiet descended once more. The darkening sky stretched impossibly clear above.

Charles glanced in a mirror and combed his hair once more. He knew he was procrastinating, but this was someone else's home and setting foot outside his door felt like an intrusion. Ah heck! He was here to spend quality time with his family and that was not going to happen holed up like a hermit. He threw the comb onto the dresser, took a deep breath and strode down the hall before he could change his mind.

Aaron met him at the door to the common room. "Good! I wondered if you were ready. We will eat soon." He ushered Charles in. "You remember my brother, Christian?"

"Of course." Charles hastily suppressed rather uncharitable impressions from their brief meeting years ago—conjectures of a mixed Viking and Neanderthal ancestry. Christian had been a man of few words back then, none of them especially cultured.

"Professor!" The stocky man stood, red hair streaming past his shoulders, beard bristling. "Please to meet my wife, Lise."

Charles started in surprise, both at the mannered tone and the fact that the ape had found himself a rather beautiful wife. "Sylvie has talked about you. I'm pleased to finally make your acquaintance."

The petite woman stepped forward from where she'd been leaning against a sideboard. Ice blue eyes pierced Charles from beneath a severe pixie cut. "Likewise, Professor." The tone matched her eyes.

"Lise," Sylvie's voice seemed unnaturally bright. "That chowder must be ready to serve, no?"

Lise sniffed. "I make myself *useful*, yes?" The blue eyes gave Charles a contemptuous once-over before she strutted through a door at the far end of the room.

With the sound of dishes clattering, Sylvie leaned over and whispered, "Lise is very practical. She has highest regard for the hard sciences."

Charles sighed. "My field of study is not popular. I resigned myself to that truth years ago."

Christian gave Charles a serious look, and nodded.

"I like to think, Professor," said Aaron, "that we have room for *everyone* here. Scientists and engineers, but also artists and ... academics."

"The world disagrees with you," said Charles, in little more than a whisper. "Life is tough. Life depends on the scientists and engineers. If I could turn my mind to those things to help people along, don't you think I would?"

"We have good homes, good shelter, water, power, and food. We have everything we need to live comfortable lives."

"One thing you haven't got," Charles said. "I went to catch up on the news. My handheld's dead."

"True, Professor." Aaron bowed with a theatrical flourish. "You uncovered our weakness."

"Doesn't it bother you?" Charles's chest tightened. "No storm warnings?" The weight of rock cloaking the house was now even more of a comfort. They would be well-protected in here, but who dared step outside without first checking the weather?

"This isn't England, Dad."

Charles gave Sylvie a weak smile.

Aaron said, "We have means of communication. Old technology, but more than enough for our purpose. Daily forecasts, of course. And to plan a season's planting we need quality data for months ahead, not quantity, not minute-by-minute."

The clatter of a tray next to him made Charles jump.

"Aaron is right," said Lise. "We have everything we need already."

Chapter 10

"Charles!" Aaron strode into the common room where Charles was draining a cup of tea. "Message for you." He skimmed a folded sheet of paper across the table.

Charles caught the paper before it slid off the edge of the table. "Thank you," he called.

Aaron had already turned and left, zipping up his jacket as he went.

Pushing aside a half-finished bowl of porridge, Charles flipped the page open. The handwritten note was brief and uninformative, just an instruction to contact the university. *Julia Chan.* Charles was torn between anxiety and curiosity. *What does the Junior Dean want?* It seemed unlikely that she'd have anything to do with Gwen's warning about Charles's project. She looked after welfare, discipline and procedure. *Has one of my students been causing trouble?*

Sylvie strolled in, dressed for the outdoors. She draped a coat over the back of a chair.

"Where's the nearest place I can get a service connection?" Charles fingered the handheld sitting uselessly in the bottom of his pocket. "Preferably somewhere with decent-sized screens for dodos like me."

Sylvie glanced at the note and laughed. "The downsides of latest technology. Useless as soon as you leave the comfort of mainstream civilization. Have you forgotten how people used to communicate?"

"Aaron mentioned old technology. I'm guessing low grade fiber, or maybe short wave radio?"

"Radio, out here. Fiber is coming, good for our needs but still nowhere near the bandwidth that modern handhelds expect. People take connections for granted, but they forget just how hungry their gadgets are."

"So," Charles mused, "technology divides the world into haves, and have-nots."

"We'll be plugged into the global net in time, but probably not for years. And what's the hurry? Virtual reality's a luxury when we have farms to build on soil that's never before seen a plough."

She poured herself a mug of coffee and sat at the table. "It's not so bad. We're not completely out in the sticks here. Krisgaarde is well connected, and there's a netcaf on the main street. They have booths you can use." She looked thoughtful. "I was hoping you could look after Ben this morning while I went in for supplies, but I guess we could all go. If he could stay with you it would help. I promise he won't be trouble."

"That sounds good. Then maybe you can show me what's new in Krisgaarde."

Half an hour later, they emerged from the underground garage and turned onto the snow-packed road through Johansinge.

Sitting up in the front seat, with a clear view of the road and their surroundings, Charles admired the casual skill with which Sylvie handled the big truck. Maybe he was getting used to the antiquated idea of fallible humans in charge of heavy machinery. A part of him wanted to revel in the sense of freedom, then he pictured the teeming roads of large cities and logic took over. This freedom was just a passing phase of the new frontier.

In Krisgaarde, Sylvie led them into a tiny café, greeting an elderly gentleman who tended a row of gleaming coffee urns against one wall. Booths lined the opposite wall, each equipped with a bench, a table, and a large screen. *Good.* A handful of tables and chairs in between littered the tiled floor in no obvious arrangement.

Warmth enveloped Charles as he closed the door behind him. The air was heavy with the smell of cinnamon and coffee. He noted beer taps alongside the urns, a reminder that European culture still held sway this close to North America. *Hmm. Maybe later.*

Benedict ran straight to one of the booths. Sylvie followed.

Charles nodded a greeting to the proprietor and slid into the booth nearest the door. The translucent polymer screen half-obscured his view of the street. He stared at it, wondering at the emptiness in his stomach and sudden foreboding. *It can't be about Typhoon. The council won't have met yet, and Julia has nothing to do with it anyway.*

In the booth behind him, Sylvie murmured something in Danish to Benedict.

Heaving a sigh, Charles pulled out his handheld and activated it. Visuals from the online world overlaid his view of reality. Shaking off his customary queasiness, he directed the visual feed to the screen, which glowed into life.

The café came back into focus. Benedict giggled to himself, immediately absorbed in whatever game Sylvie had found for him. It sounded like he would be happily occupied for a while. With a brief smile and a wave, Sylvie left.

For a few moments, Charles gazed across the room.

A large picture hung on the wall, above the urns and a counter laden with tempting pastries. Charles recognized the famous work, '2089' by Kristian Offa. It showed a series of photographs, taken at midday each day from the top of a hill somewhere near Isfeldt. Charles knew it took about ten minutes to go through a full cycle, from darkness back to noon midwinter darkness. Just now, the sun was creeping slowly up the sky. As the pictures dissolved, one into the next, snow retreated in fits and starts to the mountains on the horizon. Clouds appeared and vanished again.

Not for the first time, Charles marveled at the tranquility of the scene. *So few storms up here.*

The grey-haired barista chatted to a couple of customers. Charles could only pick out a word or two from the stream of Danish. He felt suddenly alone and isolated in a foreign country.

How long will Sylvie be? The thought was irrational. She'd only just gone. He quelled the urge to dash out of the door after her. All the same, the need to hear a familiar voice became irresistible.

Charles squeezed out Julia Chan's personal code. He waited, knowing that the messaging network would be tracking her whereabouts and checking whether she would agree to take the call.

The screen cleared. "Charles! Glad you got my message. I gather you are off-net this vacation."

"Hello, Julia." It occurred to him that she'd had to go to some trouble to reach him. Whatever she needed to discuss must be important. His stomach knotted.

"Visiting your family?"

"Yes." *Get on with it!*

She paused, chewing her lip. "It's Doctor Quan."

"Terry?" It had to be serious. The unaccustomed formality unsettled him.

"He hasn't been in touch with the College office for two days."

"You've tried contacting him?" Charles swallowed a brief glimmer of anger. *They would have, before interrupting my vacation.*

Julia nodded. "We need his end-of-term reports, and he promised to send in a schedule for next term's classes and lectures. I thought you'd want to step in before it reaches the Head of Anthropology."

"That's not like Terry," Charles lied.

"He's working for you." She chewed her bottom lip. "I thought you might have a way to reach him that's not on our files. Please get hold of him and get him to call in."

Charles frowned as Julia cut the connection. He checked the time. *What will that be in Alaska? Bit early yet.*

He checked on Benedict, got a coffee, and sat again, mulling over his first move.

Not calling in, that wasn't unusual. Nor was failing to file reports and lesson plans. Terry was notorious for his disregard for bureaucracy, and Julia had talked to him often enough about deadlines and paperwork.

But being unreachable?

Julia was right to be troubled. Charles realized there had been a sub-liminal tension in her tone and posture. He shared a growing dread that she'd chosen not to voice.

Shit! If I happen to wake him, the worst he can do is grumble. Charles keyed Terry's code.

And waited.

All too quickly, the response came: customer offline.

Not surprising. The office would have been trying that, but he was ever methodical.

Try looking in Typhoon? No point. To be there, Terry would need to be connected and reachable.

Rubbing his eyes, Charles pulled contact details from his handheld and tried calling the terminal in Terry's apartment.

No answer.

Okay, plans 'B' and 'C'?

Charles was composing a message to leave for Terry, when he paused. *Hmm. How's he going to reach me?* "... I'm not likely to be reachable, but you can leave a message at the Krisgaarde mailroom at ..." He looked up the correct address, "... and tell them I'm staying with Aaron Johansen at Johansinge. It seems they'll be able to send word to me. And please post a note to Typhoon's drop box telling me how I can find you."

There's a thought, just on the off-chance. Charles sent an instruction to an agent in his handheld to sign on to Typhoon and fetch any new posts that might be waiting for him.

While he was waiting, he called up the business directory for Fairbanks, Alaska.

Rental housing ... that's Terry's address ... owner ... no, property manager, that's more likely ...

Charles selected the contact details and placed a call.

A long while later, he got an answer: call refused.

Dammit!

He tried again.

Call refused.

One last time. You must be awake by now!

Finally, the screen cleared to show a frowning face, hair mussed, and cheeks red.

"This had better be good, pal. Do you have any idea what time it is?"

"I'm trying to reach Dr. Terry Quan."

The manager's expression melted from anger to visible apprehension. He swallowed and ran his fingers through his hair. "You a relative?"

Huh? "No, I'm a colleague at Oxford University."

The manager chewed his lip.

"And I'm also a personal friend. I've been trying to reach him. Has something happened to him? Is he in trouble?"

Before the man had time to answer, movement caught Charles's attention from the corner of his eye. Outside the window, Benedict was crossing the street.

———•◦•———

Hours before the allotted time, Tin Man once more explored the hall. Everything still seemed as it had been yesterday. There were no new notes on the message board.

Heck, it looked like he was in for a long game of message tag. When should he next plan to visit? It occurred to him that the game could be shortened by giving his own home address to call. He cringed at the thought. But these were university people, not gamers, maybe they could give *him* an address to call.

Tin Man struggled to compose a message. It was unnatural. He couldn't begin to think how to phrase such a request without giving deep offense.

He groaned and set the problem aside for a moment. It was pure avoidance, he knew, but he rationalized it as exploring other options. He began a more systematic search of the place, scanning each aisle with care. He paid exceptional attention to what seemed to be the boundaries of the hall. Like many virtual spaces, this one played tricks with geometry at its edges. Red brick walls were obscured by rows of columns—fluted wrought ironwork painted a glistening green. Shadowed alcoves hinted at spaces beyond. Only by patient exploration of every nook could he be sure they didn't lead into some spatially-impossible realm.

Satisfied that he wasn't missing anything obvious, he studied the corner where he and the gamers had first entered this room. The portal opened as he approached, but otherwise he would have been hard-pressed to tell that there was an exit there.

That exit led down to the under-layers, the wrapping that simultaneously connected this zone to, yet insulated it from, the raw computing infrastructure beneath. Regular users, he guessed, would never enter or leave by that route. There must be other ways into this place, equally concealed to anyone not recognized by the zone's strict security.

If Moonshadow were here, he'd have sniffed them out in minutes. Tin Man was no Moonshadow, but he did have a good set of illicit tools.

In a typical "habitable" workplace, ways in and out of zones usually showed themselves as their real-world analogues. Doors and openings, locked or otherwise, were designed to be visible to their users. Security-conscious zones like this were typically less obvious, revealing pathways only to authorized users, and often going to some lengths to conceal avenues that you had no business knowing about.

Even hidden portals left a subtle imprint on their surroundings. You just needed the right tools to peel back the display characteristics that usually fed your avatar's senses, and poke at the computer logic hidden beneath.

He closed the portal in front of him. The wall now seemed featureless.

First off, not holding out any hope, he tried a simple off-the-shelf probe. The sort of thing noobs used to find the main highways of the virtual underworld. Nothing. Okay, so it was actively hidden, not simply invisible by the omission of designed-in cladding. Not surprising.

More subtle tools probed for the kinds of logic typical of secured portals. No matter how well-hidden, there had to be *something* there to interact with. At last, Tin Man was rewarded by a white outline on the mock stonework.

He let out a deep sigh. This would be a slow process scouring the perimeter once more, but at least, now that he knew the protocols this zone used, he should be able to find other exits.

Whether he could unlock them, of course, was another matter entirely.

⸺◆⸺

Panic gripped Charles. "Damn!" He bit back more expletives as he realized the café's few customers were staring at him. Their English was likely better than his Danish.

He hurried to the door.

Outside, he looked around and slowed his pace, reminding himself how quiet and safe this town was. Sylvie was always telling him that they didn't live under the shadow of the lethal sandstorms that plagued most of England.

Benedict was on the far side, chattering to a woman. Charles blinked in disbelief. It was the same person he'd spoken to on the plane. *Dammit! What was her name?*

"Good morning, Professor."

"Hello again ..."

"Katrine," she said, smiling. "I didn't realize you knew Sylvie and Aaron. Of course, I knew her parents were English, and I saw her at Isfeldt terminal but I didn't put the two together. Now it seems obvious."

"Oh heck!" Charles said. "I'm sorry. I was in the middle of a call. Benedict, please come back inside with me, I promised your Mum I'd look after you."

"You go. Finish your call. I can look after Ben and bring him back in a little while."

Charles hesitated. *Benedict obviously knows her.*

The three of them moved closer to the side of the street at the approaching growl of machinery. Charles looked around, curious.

"Snow plough," said Katrine, following his gaze.

Charles gave her a wry smile. "I was expecting to see a sand sweeper. It threw me, because we haven't had a storm."

Katrine frowned. "I wonder what it's doing here. I thought they were all the other side of town to clear the roads up to the horticultural centre."

The growl became a thunderous roar, and the giant plough gathered speed. Charles caught a fleeting glimpse of whirling blades as it passed them and careered across the street and into the little café.

Katrine screamed. Charles mouthed an incoherent stream of random curses. *Most unprofessional,* a detached corner of his mind sneered.

A screeching, grinding din drilled his ears. The rotary plough was still running at full throttle, massive tires churning the hard-packed road as it chewed its way deeper into the wreckage.

Stinging on his face galvanized Charles. He touched his cheek and his hand came away red. Rubble and splintered wood rattled off the wall behind him. The plough's discharge chute spouted a torrent of debris high into the air. Charles swept Benedict off his feet and pushed Katrine out of the path of the deadly hail.

There were more people around them now, running and shouting above the racket.

At last, a hush fell. The sound of machinery faded with a final grind and metallic clatter.

Charles gazed at the wreckage across the street. Buildings had collapsed onto the hulking machine, glistening an oily yellow in the settling dust. There was nothing but rubble where the café had stood.

Realization hit like a sand storm. His knees weak, Charles sank to the ground unable to speak.

CHAPTER 11

"Look up."

Tin Man did, and ice tingled his spine. Where the vast globe normally hung, a round face gazed down at him.

"That one just leads to the archives. You can't get out that way."

Tin Man glanced back at the outline on the wall he'd just revealed, then turned to face the disembodied apparition. It was difficult to tell with the oblate distortion, but she looked young. Unlikely to be Terry's boss. "Are you the one who saw my message?"

"Not very informative, was it? And seeing as you're the intruder I think I'm the one asking the questions."

Tin Man blinked. The face gave the impression of rotating in space, like the globe before it had, yet staying perfectly still. It had to be an illusion. It made him dizzy.

"Let's start with who you are, and what you're doing here."

"I'm Tin Man—"

The face snorted. "Wizard of Oz meets Terminator?"

Tin Man frowned.

"Heck! Doesn't anyone watch the classics any more?" Giant lips pouted. "Sorry, keep talking."

"Yeah. Like I said." Suddenly his carefully-crafted avatar, modeled on The Assassin from the 2062 classic of the same name, seemed foolish. "I'm a gamer. We got in here by accident and Terry caught us. We were helping him trap Tiamat, but it didn't work."

"Wow. The questions are stacking up aren't they? Looks like this is going to be a long night."

In his apartment, Joseph Wong groaned to himself, careful to keep the subliminal sound from triggering his jaw implant.

"You said 'we'. Seem to have lost your mates somewhere along the way."

"Umm..." Tin Man wondered how to talk about Moonshadow and Pink Marie, but didn't get the chance to form words.

"Never mind, I'm more interested in this 'Tiamat', and why Doctor Quan was trying to trap him."

"Gamers always talk of Tiamat as female. Not sure why. She lives in the under-layers. There's a lot of rumors about what happens if you run into her."

"Under-layers?" the face muttered to itself. "And why would you run into her?"

"We play games down there. We landed up in here trying to get away from her, and found we couldn't exit." Tin Man bit back his line of thought. This girl didn't seem to know much about online culture. There was no need for her to know just how important the avatar was to a gamer. "We agreed to help Terry get a closer look."

"Why would he be interested? He usually deletes intruders on the spot. He'd probably expect me to do the same."

"Tiamat got into one of the outer zones, then something strange happened. I think Terry wanted to see if it was a threat to his security or something."

"You don't sound too certain."

"I know nothing about security. All I know is, the trap didn't work. We were supposed to meet up here again for another try, but Terry never showed up."

"Back up a bit. This could all be a load of tosh. I've only got your word for this."

"You can ask Terry."

"I will. Bye."

"Wait!" But the globe was back.

⸺⸳◆⸳⸺

Charles watched Benedict happily sketching at the dining table. Several sheets of paper were already covered in bright drawings of yellow machines with large teeth.

"He doesn't seem too bothered by it," Charles whispered to Sylvie. He nursed his third beer. That, and two large brandies, were finally starting to calm the trembling in his limbs.

"It was all just a big load of excitement to him," Sylvie murmured. "He hasn't made any connection to what might have happened. He's got no concept of mortality."

"Lucky him." Charles drained his beer. The glass beat a brief tattoo on the tabletop as he set it down.

Aaron silently reached for a pitcher and refilled the glass.

For a long while, the only sound was Benedict making brumming and crashing noises as he sketched.

At length, the sound of motors outside rumbled faintly through the walls.

Charles shuddered.

Sylvie looked around. She wiped a tear from the corner of her eye. "Come on, Ben." Her voice trembled only slightly. "Pack up now and get ready for bed."

While Benedict, grumbling and yawning, swept paper and crayons into a wicker basket, Lise threw her coat over the back of a chair and slumped at the table. She cradled her head in her folded arms for a moment, then peered up when Aaron poured her a drink.

"Thanks." She drained half the glass at one pull. "But no more. Christian will be hours yet. They make buildings safe, now people stay to help clean up. I come to find how are you doing, then I make hot food to take back."

"We'll be fine, Lise," said Sylvie. "I'll help prepare something. How many are still there?"

"I think we need a few flasks of soup. The big ones you take to the fields for lunch."

"I'll go find something," said Aaron. "You both rest."

"How's Katrine?" Charles asked. "I need to thank her. If she hadn't been passing by right then ..."

"And if the plough had veered the other way, you might have been killed at the side of the road instead of safe in the café." Sylvie's cheeks flushed red. "You can't play those games, Dad, you'll go mad with what might have been."

"Katrine is shaken, naturally," Lise interrupted, "but she is tough. Sylvie's right. What is past is past."

Charles paused, on the verge of arguing. He picked up his glass and swirled it around, studying the whirling froth. Eventually he broke the somber silence. "Any explanations?"

"Street crew can't explain it. They clear last night's snowfall around town and finish for the morning. All ploughs on automatic, returning to the yard. This one broke ranks. They are taking it apart trying to find why it took off like that. Guidance corrupted, we think."

"Did you pull anyone out?"

"A few from the bakery. Flying glass and falling shelves." Lise grimaced. "Hardware store was a mess. We were picking our way through when Olga turned up. Lucky she shut up shop for lunch."

"What about the café?" Charles asked.

Lise's face hardened. She shook her head.

———•◆•———

The face reappeared, startling Tin Man, who had continued his exploration and located two more portals.

"That took longer than I expected. Doctor Quan is usually online somewhere or other, but I ended up making inquiries through the university office."

"Did you find him? I've been trying to reach him all day. I need to talk to him."

"That'll be difficult. The office just got news. He died in his sleep last night."

The sunny voice was so at odds with the words that it took Tin Man a few moments to process what she'd said. His stomach lurched. Locked though he was in his avatar's senses, the room of his apartment and the chair beneath him seemed to spin. He dropped his handheld into his lap and gripped the arms of his chair.

How the heck did he get involved in this mess? He was tempted to cut all connection to his avatar and have done with it. No. Last resort only. If he could persuade this girl to guide him to an external portal he'd be gone. No looking back.

"Strange. I can imagine the Professor popping off any day, but the Doc's not that old."

Her dismissive tone surprised Tin Man, but then he was still shaken by what had happened to Moonshadow. "Did you know him well?" His voice was weak.

"Not really. He helped the Professor with Typhoon. I never had much to do with him."

Silence lengthened. Tin Man groped for his handheld.

"Trouble is, that leaves you looking like a common intruder with nothing to back up your story."

"Yeah, so if you're going to delete me, get on with it," Tin Man snapped, "otherwise let me out of this dump."

"You weren't this tetchy before." The mouth opened. "Oh! I'm sorry. Were you friends with Doctor Quan? I assumed not, he hates gamers, but I didn't really think..."

"Not friends." Tin Man sighed. There seemed to be a spark of sympathy there after all, and he didn't seem to have much to lose. "He held us hostage until we helped him. After the disaster with Tiamat we were going to tell him we were through. Especially after what happened to Moonshadow." He swallowed hard. "I never wanted to see that bloody Samurai again, but I didn't want him dead too."

"Too?"

"My friend, Moonshadow, died last night too. Sydney transit."

The face gasped. "I heard about that. Nasty."

"It's strange. I only ever knew him as a creepy medieval dude in a shabby cloak. I never knew the actual person, but it feels like I lost a friend." Another long silence. "Look, I'm sorry about Terry, I mean Doctor Quan, but all I want to do now is leave here and forget about all this."

"Well, I'm not stopping you."

Tin Man paused and thought. The bloated face gazed at him. "You don't use an online avatar, do you?"

The head shook.

"I don't know what you can see from up there. For me, it's like I'm standing in a big room, but there's no doors. I need to find a portal to an exit zone. Everything here must be access-controlled. They're there, somewhere, but nothing's visible to me."

"Why can't you leave the way you came in?"

"When I got here, Tiamat almost caught me again. Last time I tried to leave, she was still waiting. I'm not risking it."

"What are you afraid of?"

"Tiamat's curse." Tin Man laughed, but his heart wasn't in it. "It's a myth among gamers. People who get caught by Tiamat are never seen again. There are stories. Way too many stories, and always second or third hand. I just thought she deleted the avatars and people were too ashamed to talk about it."

"There's nothing real there, though."

"So I thought. But Tiamat had her claws in Moonshadow and Terry, and within two days they're both dead. For real."

CHAPTER 12

It was still dark when Charles felt his way to the common room. Sleep remained firmly out of his reach. In the dead of night, every creak and unfamiliar whisper teased his nerves.

A nightlight shed a glow over the coffee pot on the sideboard that seemed to be on permanent standby. He dropped a tea bag into a mug and topped it up with scalding water from an adjacent urn.

"Aaron is taking Ben down to the fields today."

Charles jumped, slopping weak tea over the sideboard.

"Sorry, I thought you saw me."

He peered into the gloom. Sylvie sat at the far end of the table, hunched over a mug. Charles mopped up the spill and left the tea to brew. "I can't help playing out what might have been. It's what I do for a living."

"It happened. The universe is a dangerous place, Dad, it doesn't owe us a living. Right now you're safe. Ben's safe. It'll take time to get over the shock, but then we need to get on with our lives."

Charles took an unsteady breath. "I live a safe and quiet life. Nothing like this has ever happened to me before. I was one outrageous coincidence away from being minced to a pulp. I don't like the idea of such a fragile hold on life."

Sylvie laughed, with just the slightest edge of madness. "Are you kidding? This, from a man who spends his life dodging sandstorms that can strip a man's flesh from his bones in two minutes flat?"

Charles gazed at her long and hard, then he grunted. "I see what you mean, but that's different. Storms are easy to handle, that's what the weather networks are there for."

"Dad! I know you. If the report says a storm is due in twenty minutes, you'll figure you have an easy fifteen minutes to reach the pub."

"And?" He cocked an eyebrow at Sylvie.

Her face grew serious. It was difficult to tell on the fringe of the yellow glow from the nightlight, but her red eyes seemed to be welling with tears once more. "I watch the news, sometimes. Every time a really big storm hits England, it scares the shit out of me."

Charles groaned. "Let's not get into this. Not now. Oxford is my home. It always has been. I'm not planning on moving."

"I know." Her voice was quiet. "That's not what I meant. Don't you see? You live a few minutes from death every day but it doesn't bother you. It's not the risk, it's how comfortable you are with it that counts."

Charles mulled over that thought while he fetched his tea. Almost strong enough to dissolve the spoon. Perfect.

"Katrine sent me a message last night," said Sylvie. "She can't work today, her supervisor insists on that, but she needs something to do. You need distraction too."

"And you don't?"

"Touché! Anyway, she suggested an outing, show you something of what us pioneers are building here. I thought that would interest you."

"Ummm ..." The last thing Charles wanted was more travel and novelty. He wanted to retreat somewhere warm and safe, but he could see that Sylvie needed to get out of the house.

"It's decided, Dad." Sylvie smiled. "You didn't think you were getting a choice, did you?"

She was right. They all needed a distraction.

———————

Joseph Wong shook the packaging off his new handheld. It was a low-end gaming model, the cheapest he could find, but it had still cost twice as much as his trusty MoveMojo Pro. He was happy to pay the outrageous mark-up in return for a working service connection with no unwanted questions. He'd registered it under a false name and the street address of a vacant lot he often passed on his way to the general store.

With fastidious attention to detail, he shut down his old handheld and double-checked it was completely disconnected before patching the new handheld to his implants.

Satisfied with the connection, he visited the guest zone on his personal account and collected the spare avatar he'd purchased. A crude off-the-shelf embodiment, he'd spent little more than an hour tailoring it, giving its skin a metallic sheen. Even this minimal effort was only to make him easier to recognize. Both the avatar and the handheld were expendable.

He looked at the clock—still an hour to go. He paced the floor. Time for a coffee? Gamer habit intruded. He never drank anything this close to going online. He sat again and tried making a list of priorities for dealing with his backlog of work.

His efforts were half-hearted. Unease nagged him. He teased out the worry. Ah, shit! If anyone saw him they'd think he was being paranoid, maybe even a coward, but he was alone, only himself to answer to, and he still had time. He thumbed the black market handheld to life again and installed the hack that would allow him to disconnect if needed. This time, he paid more attention to the original purpose of the hack—diversion. He set up a false trail of service providers between himself and his tacky avatar, terminating in a fictitious entry point at the unused street address. He let out a breath, suddenly feeling a lot better.

He was ready.

But was he? Really?

The handheld felt wrong in his fingers. It didn't sit correctly in his palms like the well-worn grips he was used to. He could operate this device perfectly well. That, he knew, was not the problem. The alien feel was nothing more than a reminder of his raw outward appearance. Despite the superficial tinkering, he was about to venture into the online world, *his* world, looking like some pre-teen noob. It was like wearing someone else's skin.

Joseph wondered if this would work. Serena, as the face had introduced itself, had offered to help him out. It was worth at least a bit more investment in time. It wasn't just the visible tailoring at stake, his avatar's profile held many functional modifications he'd accumulated over time. The thought of starting all over made his skin crawl.

He paused to wipe his palms on his pants, then took a deep breath and launched himself through the service portal.

Following the directions Serena had given him, he quickly found the public portal for the University of Oxford.

Standing in the entrance zone, gazing around at the constellation of signs hanging in mid air, he reassured himself that his ungamerly appearance was hardly out of place. A steady flow of avatars crossed the floor. Some were individualized with expert care, but many were embellished with nothing more than the simplest visual effects. There was even someone wandering around in the bare factory default produced by an unmodified handheld. Joseph's breath caught in his throat at the sight. This was so far removed from the dark and self-conscious virtual underworlds he frequented.

He shook himself, and looked for the way to the public research library. The portal led him to a circular atrium surrounded by doors, each labeled in luminous blue. It took just moments to work out the classification scheme. Each door led to a new room with a new choice of doors, offering ever-narrower slices of human knowledge. Such an arrangement would have been geometrically impossible in the real world, with many rooms doubling back and trying to inhabit the same physical space. Freed of those restrictions, it took a few steps to traverse what would otherwise have been kilometers of shelving.

Through a door marked 'Anthropology, Theoretical, Cultural Group Dynamics' Joseph faced a wall of densely-packed references: reports, media clippings, research articles. The titles were all alien to him, speaking in abstract jargon from an unfamiliar field, but the format and feel of the indexed and collated entries he knew well from his own work editing engineering journal papers.

The wall enclosed one side of a translucent catwalk; the other side lay open to a drop into unknown depths. Joseph walked to the edge and surveyed his surroundings. Above, below, and around him, similar catwalks swept into the distance. They formed a web of virtual glass and chrome enclosing a sphere of unimaginable proportions. Joseph couldn't see the far side through the forest of nested shells marching into the distance.

The door he'd emerged from hung in space. Other similar dismurated doors were strung out at intervals along this and other pathways. These, he guessed, were more exit points from the library's index that he'd just traversed.

"It's like a whole other world in here!"

Joseph jumped.

Serena sounded breathless. "Sorry. I'm not used to using an avatar. I can't get used to all this."

Joseph gave her avatar a quick glance. It looked untailored, a generic female shape with a face that bore a passing resemblance to what he'd seen watching him, but it was more than an average off-the-shelf rendering. This was a luxury product. Strange, for someone who never used it. "How did you get inside that room where you found me, then?"

"The university has a big office in New Boston. I go there and use one of their screens."

"Old school interface." Joseph gave a wry smile. "I heard that's how people always used to interact online. I'd forgotten about that."

"Come on. I just brought you here because I knew it would be a quiet place to meet up."

"Where to now?"

"Typhoon." Before Joseph could say anything, she continued, "That's the name of the research experiment where you're trapped."

Serena turned away, then stopped. "Oops! Almost forgot." She looked up and down the aisles. "I wanted somewhere quiet because I didn't want anyone to see me giving you this." She handed Joseph a token. "I borrowed this from another student. This should get you into Typhoon."

Joseph took the token, a standard kind of identification. He decided not to ask how Serena had 'borrowed' it, or who from.

"Follow me!" And she was off through the door.

Joseph cursed and hurried after her. Physics-defying navigation online was a blessing, but also made it way too easy to lose track of someone you were trying to follow. Unless you had the presence of mind to tag their avatar first, which he hadn't.

He just glimpsed Serena heading through the next door, and followed, finding himself back at the university entrance zone.

With a brief glance over her shoulder to check he was still there, Serena led him past a large opening for 'University Admissions', then into an adjoining hall marked 'Faculties'. A few steps later, through doors with signs that Joseph had no time to read, they were alone.

On top of a mountain.

Pink-tinged clouds stretched to the horizon. The summit was only a few meters across, with steep cliffs on all sides plunging to meet the cloud tops.

"Well, that obviously worked then."

Joseph glanced at Serena. "What?"

"This is Typhoon. The token worked."

Serena positioned her back to the orange sun hanging over the horizon, turned to her left, and stepped off the cliff.

Joseph blinked, shrugged, and followed her.

"This is the command room. You should find what you need in here."

Joseph gazed around. The mountain and clouds were replaced by a long room. He was startled to see his temporary avatar staring back at him from blue tinted glass walls.

Buttons and displays seemed embedded in the glass. They came into clearer view as he approached the wall, as if the glass were evaporating like mist. He walked along the wall with a sinking feeling. This interface looked more refined than the cobbled-together console running the failed trap, but he still couldn't make sense of anything. A large part of the near wall was covered by a complex web, a bit like a circuit diagram. Dense tables of numbers crowded the spaces between nodes and arrows.

"Found anything yet?" Serena watched him. Her avatar wasn't sophisticated enough to show facial expressions, or maybe she simply didn't know how to display them, but the posture suggested eager anticipation.

"This looks like something to do with the experiment itself."

Serena peered at the wall. "Yep. These are group dynamic models." She moved along a few meters. "Aha! Here's the free market influence chain."

Joseph narrowed his eyes at Serena. There must be a hundred meters of wall to investigate. On a hunch, he asked, "Are you familiar with what's in here?"

"Oh, yes. I've spent the last few days learning about Typhoon. I've not seen it quite like this, I view it on a screen at the university." She sniffed. "I don't see what all the fuss is about avatars. It's neat to feel like I'm standing in a room like this, but it's just the same stuff that I saw on my screen."

Joseph took a deep breath. "In your learning, did you come across some controls that you didn't know what to do with?"

Serena stopped and turned. "Now you mention it ..." She crossed to the other wall. "Must be somewhere ... around ... Here!"

"Okay, let's see." Joseph joined her. User tables, roles and assignments, branching hierarchies of zone assets ... this was more like it. His heart sang. The bizarre security in this zone enforced its rules with near-unbreakable rigor, but the rules themselves were laid out in a standard access control language.

His hands flew over the controls. He and his gamer colleagues had to be registered already, because Typhoon knew to admit them. There they were. And here was a list of things they were allowed to see. A few seconds later, and he had given himself, or Tin Man, rather more powers than Terry's boss would approve of, he was sure, but what the heck! As soon as he rejoined his real avatar, he was free.

Once more in the university entrance hall, Joseph turned to Serena. "Well, thank you." He paused. "I guess this is goodbye."

She hesitated too. "Yeah. I suppose so."

In the awkward silence that followed, Joseph glanced over her shoulder and his blood froze. "Exit." The word came out as a hoarse whisper.

There was something wrong with the willowy avatar sashaying towards them across the hall. The customization was phenomenal, but porcelain skin didn't quite hide the hint of golden scales. He stood, transfixed by dead black eyes.

"What?"

Joseph snapped back to reality. "Exit! Now!"

"I don't—"

"Just exit, while you still can." Without waiting to see if Serena was obeying, Joseph pushed past her and ran at the menacing apparition. He hoped this zone enforced physical rules about cohabiting space. He should be able to block the approaching danger while Serena escaped.

It seemed as if his eyes couldn't quite focus, or as if two avatars were occupying the same space. The tall and curvy blonde in a red kimono had initially caught his eye, but scales and fangs were coming into sharper focus. Claw-tipped fingers reached for him. Ghostly wings enfolded him.

The world around Joseph vanished. A woman screamed, a raw, hysterical scream that scraped Joseph's nerves. He fell, tumbling head over heels. The ground rushed to meet him, so real he could feel acid rising in his throat. He bounced. High into the sky. Higher. Higher. The sun reached for him, flares arching towards him. He screwed his eyes shut, but nothing could blot out the flames searing his brain.

Chapter 13

The road skirted a steep hillside. The land fell away alongside them into a deep ravine. For the twentieth time since meeting Katrine at Krisgaarde and setting off into the hills in her battered truck, Charles forced his fingers to loosen their death grip on the door handle. He didn't relinquish his grip altogether, though, and gave Katrine a weak smile. "It'll take a while to get used to all this manual driving."

"Auto guidance is good on your nice level European roads," said Katrine, "but look at what we deal with here." She gestured out the window with one hand while steering around a pothole. Charles's knuckles cracked. "I wouldn't trust my safety to a computer. They can't read the road conditions like I can."

"This is a frontier nation, as you keep reminding me, Dad," said Sylvie from the back seat. "The New Danish are too proud of their independence to be chauffeured around by a computer."

"It's just not practical," Katrine retorted. "And that's another reason why getting global coverage isn't too high on our priorities up here."

Charles hesitated as an unwelcome memory played out, but curiosity gained the upper hand. "What about that snow plough? Wasn't that unmanned?"

The mood in the truck sobered.

"Sure, machinery can move itself around the towns, and where the roads are good. But we're not so settled that everything can be run automatically, or even remotely. This is still wilderness, Professor, not tamed by centuries of civilization. To do any useful work, we still need people behind the wheel."

As Katrine eased the truck over the treacherous surface where ice still lay in the shadows, Charles appreciated her viewpoint. Seeing the skill with which she guided the vehicle, compensating for unpredictable bumps and skids, he wasn't sure he would trust such fine control to a computer either. Although the high speed mechanical ballet of a typical city centre was a feat to be marveled at, choreographed largely by the networked control systems of the vehicles themselves, their main task was to avoid each other and obstacles around them. They could rely on a well-maintained and predictable road surface for traction. But not here.

The ravine beside them opened out, and the road meandered through a bleak but less precipitous landscape. They rounded a corner, and the valley opened further in front of them. Nestled side by side in the embrace of encircling hills lay three warehouses, each the size of a football field.

Katrine guided the truck into a parking lot underneath the nearest building.

As they climbed out, a discreet signal appeared on the periphery of Charles's vision. "Oho!" he said. "My handheld's active again."

"What do you expect?" Katrine grinned. "This is an industrial plant."

"Hadn't thought about what to expect, really. It doesn't look like much from the outside."

The grin widened. "Wait till you see *inside*. My boss signed me off work but said nothing about showing visitors around." She turned on the spot, arms outstretched. "Welcome to my kingdom. And, unlike the roads, here is one place where we trust the network completely. There's a lot of complicated machinery here, and too much room for human error."

"All the same, I must be getting used to being out of reach of the net. In fact, I think I'm beginning to see some of the attraction." Charles sighed. "Looks like there's a pile of messages for me."

"They can wait," Sylvie said firmly. She waved a hand in front of his eyes, dimly seen through the ethereal list of messages hovering at the edge of his line of sight. "Let your handheld pick up any mail. You'll have plenty of time to read it later."

Worry tugged at Charles's memory, an elusive ghost of unfinished business, but he caught Sylvie's deepening frown and he shut off the handheld's display.

Katrine led them up a flight of stairs, through a lobby and cloak-room, and up more stairs. They emerged into a wide hallway, warm and softly-lit.

"This building is the control block. Garages and workshops down below. This level has the control room and some offices, but mostly it is living quarters for the engineers."

Through a double door near one end of the hall, Katrine ushered them into a bright room. "Hi Sean," she called. "Charles, this is Sean Cleveland, shift engineer, and Klaus Wenkel, control room operator. Guys, this is Professor Charles Hawthorne, Sylvie's father."

Two men stood from behind the horseshoe-shaped console that dominated the centre of the room.

Charles shook hands, with little more than a glance at the two of them. His eyes kept getting drawn back to the complex schematics covering the wall opposite. "I'm impressed. There's a lot more to this place than it seems from the outside. I hope you can make sense of all that."

"Aww, c'mon, Professor," said Sean. "It's not as bad as it looks."

Klaus glanced from one man to the other, bobbed his head, and turned his attention back to the console.

"I'm no engineer, but I thought geothermal plants were fairly simple. How is this"—Charles waved his hand at the wall—"simple?"

"The plant is based on a very simple idea. There's a magma chamber not far under us." He laughed at Charles's startled expression. "Not far in geological terms. There might be a volcano here in a few thousand years time, but for now it's quite safe."

"Aah. I feel much better."

"All the same, there's a lot of heat down there. We bring that heat up to the surface, make steam, and drive a turbine."

Charles peered at the schematics more closely.

"How do you bring the heat up?" asked Sylvie.

"We drill a pair of boreholes which meet at the bottom." Sean turned to her, while Charles paced the wall. "We pump mineral oil down one. It goes in cold, and comes back up the other at seven hundred degrees Celsius."

Charles whistled from the other side of the desk. "You could fry a whole haddock in about three seconds in that!"

"Trust a fellow Brit to think of that!"

"The idea is not complicated," said Katrine, "but as you can see, putting it into practice is challenging. That's what most of this control equipment here is about. There are thousands of sensors measuring temperatures, pressures, and flows all the way through the system. It's a constant balancing act."

Charles's eyes roved over the schematics. "So, hot magma here." He pointed. "Oil collects heat, and ..."

"Heats water to make steam."

Insight clicked in Charles's mind. "It's like an influence network." He gestured at the wall, eyes darting from one section to the next. "Ignore the fact that these are closed loops, the important flow is from one side to the other. I use diagrams like this to model how groups of people interact. Except here, your 'influence' is heat."

"Spoken like a true academic!"

Charles turned at the broad Scottish accent.

A newcomer strode across the room, clutching several meter-long rolls of paper. Tall and lean, he radiated vigor that belied his graying and receding hairline. "But the token of influence is better described as energy, rather than just heat. Heat energy at one end, electrical out the other." He tucked the papers under one arm and stuck out his hand. "Stephen Morrow."

"Aha! The elusive Professor Morrow." Charles winked at Katrine.

"Stephen is here to study the geology around us." Katrine gestured to a large map on the back wall of the control room. "We're planning to drill more shafts, and need to decide where to place them and how deep to go."

"How deep are you talking about?"

"The first two sets we started off with go five kilometers down. Last year we brought 'C-shaft' online at seven kilometers."

"It's a trade-off between geology and engineering," said Stephen. He dumped his papers on a table near the maps and started unfurling them. "The deeper you go, the higher the temperature, and you get a quicker and steadier supply of heat. But it gets more difficult to drill, to maintain the shafts, and you are dealing with much higher pressures in the circulation loop."

Katrine beckoned Charles towards a side door, forestalling more explanations. "I think you'll appreciate Stephen's work better once you've seen what goes on here. Sean, I'm going to give Charles and Sylvie a tour, the usual stuff, then maybe we can talk more over a coffee."

They left the control room and found themselves in an enclosed bridge leading from one building to the next. Through the windows, corrugated walls stretched away on either side, a narrow artificial canyon.

Charles noticed Sylvie craning her neck, her eyes mirroring his own curiosity. He gave her a quizzical look. "This seems as novel to you as it is to me."

"Playing the tourist in my own town. I've never had reason to trek out here, and managing the farm leaves no time for sightseeing."

The bridge took them into a cloakroom, with brightly-colored overalls and helmets hanging from the wall.

Katrine took a white helmet and a pair of ear defenders from a hook on the wall. "Put those on." She gestured to helmets hanging from other hooks. "Take the orange ones, for guests. It's noisy in here. Use your handhelds. We can talk to each other through the local station service."

Charles put on a helmet. Silence swallowed him as he pulled down the ear defenders. He could see Sylvie talking to Katrine, but no sound came. He found the communications channel Katrine had set up for them, and rejoined the conversation.

"You can both hear me?" Katrine double-checked the connection and waited for their answers before moving on.

They stepped through a heavy door, down a short hall, and through another door.

Despite the sound-proofing, Charles could *feel* the noise in the cavernous room. It seeped through his jaw and skull. It penetrated skin and muscle, setting the bones of his arms and legs thrumming like guitar strings. Charles realized he was holding his breath. His chest muscles unconsciously tightened to still the singing in his ribs. He forced himself to relax.

"Turbine hall," said Katrine. Her voice carried clear into Charles's mind.

They stood on a gallery running down one wall of the shed. It looked so much bigger inside than out.

Charles gazed over the railing at a massive piece of machinery. Apart from its size, it was almost anticlimactic. There were no moving parts visible, no spinning gears, no thrashing pistons or venting steam. Just a mound of rounded shapes huddled together and piled on top of each other. It wasn't even shiny, like Charles felt hi-tech machinery should be. It looked like someone had driven a pair of old-fashioned steam locomotives in, side-by-side, tenders and all, straddled them with a fleet of dump trucks, and then swaddled the whole lot with slightly dirty papier mache.

A few meters to the left, a duplicate arrangement lay alongside the house-sized pile.

The tableau was motionless, but the turbines thrummed with hidden energies.

Despite the size of the two turbine sets, the hall was almost empty. Katrine must have seen him looking around at the unused space, or maybe she was just used to this reaction from visitors. "We planned for the future when we built this plant. We can add more turbines, and we can install bigger sets than the two you see here."

A flight of steps led them down to the floor of the hall. They hurried past the turbines, the sound a physical presence around them, and through another door. Beyond the turbine hall, the third shed was mercifully quiet. Charles lifted his ear defenders and craned his neck to take in the curve of a polished steel cylinder set on massive concrete plinths.

"This is the primary heat exchanger," said Katrine. "The heart of the plant." She waved to the far side of the hall, away to their right. "Over there is the pump room for the heat transfer loop. It sends cool oil down the boreholes outside. The oil comes back up here hot and flows through the heat exchanger. Water goes in at that end, and is heated by the oil. It comes out here as superheated steam and is piped off to the turbines."

Charles studied the labyrinth of pipes that spanned the room. "Sounds simple, so why all the plumbing?"

"Lots of pumps and valves to help control the system. And obviously it's more complicated than I just said. Before the waste steam returns from the turbines it gets condensed back to water. That mess of piping at the far end is the condenser network. We draw water from the river as a coolant. And some of the waste is tapped off and circulated around the plant for heating."

On the far side of the heat exchanger, they came to a railing surrounding a pit in the floor that lay underneath a maze of pipework. Katrine climbed a ladder down to the floor of the pit. Charles couldn't dispel an overwhelming feeling that they were intruding. He glanced at Sylvie, who nodded in encouragement.

When they were all down she looked across the floor to where three engineers were working on a piece of machinery. "Wait a bit, please." She motioned them to one side of the ladder. "Hey Sean? We're down in the hot oil containment pit. Is this scheduled maintenance going on down here or should we clear out?"

Charles could only hear one half of the conversation with the shift engineer back in the control room. He and Sylvie waited patiently while Katrine listened. After a few moments she turned to them. "Okay, we're fine but we'll move down that end of the pit. The engineers over there are in the middle of a routine overhaul of one of the input regulators. They're on a strict time schedule, so we mustn't get in their way."

While they walked away from the ladder and the engineers, they passed a stepladder standing proud amidst a litter of tools and paint cans. Katrine frowned. "Someone needs to clear up after themselves, I think." She gave them an impish grin. "I leave the best until last. When we go back through the turbine hall, I show you my work area, the electrical switchgear. You see how a clean workplace should look."

Charles gazed around with a twinge of envy at Katrine's evident pride. Like Charles, and like Sylvie, she'd found her calling in life, her passion. The difference lay in how the world valued their usefulness.

They stopped a safe distance away, and he pulled himself from the depths of pointless introspection.

Katrine said, "This is one of two containment pits for the heat transfer loop. Pretty much all the valves and other bits we need to work on are suspended above our heads. If anything springs a leak, any spillage will be contained."

She pointed up to a meter-wide red-painted tube running the length of the pit, three meters above their heads. "This is what I wanted to show you. You can't see it properly from above with all the supports and pipes in the way. We call this the 'hot bus'. It collects heated oil from the boreholes and shares it out between the heat exchangers. This arrangement is what allows us to switch feeds and heat exchangers in and out of the system as needed. Exactly what those guys are doing right now, in fact. There's a similar arrangement next door for the cold oil return. Oddly enough, it's called the 'cold bus'."

"So what are the engineers doing, and why the rush?"

"Look right above where they're working. See the open pipe ends up there?"

A white pipe peered over the edge of the pit and angled downwards. Its flanged mouth glistened. An oily slick colored the floor below.

"That one coming through the wall is from 'A-shaft'. The other open end leads into the hot bus."

"Does that mean there's boiling oil in there?" Charles eyed the open pipes.

"Held back by redundant stop valves on either side. It's quite safe. There are valves all over the network to isolate sections and allow us to work on them. That section they've taken down right now is a pressure regulator. Gives fine control of the flow when the stop valves are open. That's why we rely so much on computer control. It's a complicated network, and you wouldn't want to accidentally crack open the wrong valve at the wrong time."

Charles relaxed a bit. This was something he understood.

"So back to the other part of your question. Obviously we've shut down 'A-shaft' while they work. But the circulating oil acts as a coolant down there, which stops the bottom of the borehole lining from softening and closing up. We can't keep it shut down for long. Matter of hours at most."

"What are all those?" Charles pointed to a series of valves and gaping pipe openings overhead.

Katrine pursed her lips. "Seems you have a nose for the important details." She gestured overhead. "Most people are interested in what's there, not what's missing. All those unused openings? More forward planning, and really the key to the plant's design."

"It's like at Johansinge, Dad," Sylvie said. "We built storage and processing sheds much bigger than we need, ready to expand."

"Exactly," Katrine said. "What do you think would run all the extra turbines we have room for? All the pipe network was designed with multiple connection points so we can add in new feeds or new units and switch over to them without ever shutting the plant—"

A bubbling scream interrupted Katrine's enthusiasm.

CHAPTER 14

It's not real!

Joseph swore. With trembling fingers he shut off the handheld, cutting all connection with his throwaway avatar. His eyesight returned in patches. Sunlight burned his vision and black dots wheeled through the air.

He yanked open the back of the handheld and ripped out the power receiver. For a moment, he stared at the dead unit with a pang of regret at the cost, then he steeled himself. Expendable. Anywhere it was active, it could be traced and was now a liability. He tossed it into the garbage.

Taking three quick breaths, he calmed himself. No harm done. He would wait a safe time before trying to escape with his real avatar, but he was starting to wonder if that would ever be possible. Tiamat had never been known to stay in one place long, yet she seemed to have developed an unhealthy interest in this particular plenum. He was now certain that escape through the under-layers would be impossible. But for Tiamat to show herself in a public zone? He'd never heard of it.

Damn that infernal Samurai!

To pass the time, Joseph worked on a few assignments from his growing backlog of papers, then scoured the larder for food. He'd been neglecting his housekeeping these past few days. He picked his way through the dwindling pile of tins and packages, but nothing took his fancy.

Well, it was still light and he could do with some fresh air. He grabbed a jacket decorating the back of a couch, a backpack from the floor, and headed out to the street.

After two blocks in the warm Yukon spring air, he felt better. He rounded a corner, and the feeling of peace evaporated. Emergency vehicles blocked the street ahead. As he approached, Joseph's unease deepened.

His pace slowed as he neared the cordon.

"Excuse me!"

A sweating fireman looked up from the hose he was busy rolling up.

"What happened here?"

"Gas main blew. Must have been a pressure surge or something, or maybe kids tampered with the shut-off." He turned back to his work.

"Anyone hurt?"

"A few cuts from flying rocks." The fireman straightened and wiped his face. "We were lucky it blew under an empty lot. A few meters further and those apartments would have been toast."

Joseph stared. The hole in the ground didn't look like much, but the chatter of onlookers nearby painted a picture of a geyser of solid flame roaring into the sky. The fire crews had managed to shut off the supply and damp down adjacent buildings before the heat did any real damage. There was thankful speculation on what might have been if there'd been a building here.

Joseph's knees weakened, his mind filled with his own private might-have-beens. There was no building here because he had chosen an unused address, *this* address, to register his black market handheld.

A jolt of adrenalin hit Charles like a jackhammer. Where the engineers were working, the oil feed from the borehole had opened up. Under high pressure, the golden flow looked solid. One of the workmen took the full brunt of the torrent. His overalls smoldered then flamed. Flesh sizzled. He collapsed into the pool with a short-lived shriek and a thunderous crackle.

An overpowering barbecue smell made Charles gag.

The other open end from the hot bus fountained more oil.

Sylvie swore and ran to the near side of the pit, edging her way along the wall. But she retreated with an angry shake of her head, clothing spattered with smoldering smudges. The deadly arcs of oil cut off their escape, and the floor was flooding fast.

The two remaining engineers backed away, shocked, on the far side of the spreading pool. "Fetch help!" Katrine screamed at them. They bolted for the ladder leading out of the pit.

Katrine yelled, "Help me with this." She grabbed the aluminum stepladder and closed it up.

"What good is that?"

"It extends."

Giddy with relief, Charles recognized the mechanism. With the two sides closed together, it became an extension ladder. He put his foot on the bottom rung while Katrine struggled to slide the upper section. Metal jammed on metal. Katrine's face took on a wild expression.

Painfully aware of his own near-panic, Charles grabbed her shoulder and shook. "Slow down."

Katrine gulped and pursed her lips. She jostled the two sections into better alignment and lifted.

"Come on guys!" Hysteria tinged Sylvie's voice as she shepherded them away from the creeping pool.

Charles pulled the ladder towards the wall of the pit. Katrine tugged in the other direction. For a second, they engaged in a bizarre tug-of-war, until Katrine reached between the rungs and punched Charles in the chest.

Surprised, he let go his hold.

"It's too short to reach the top of the pit!" She leaned the ladder against a horizontal I-beam supporting the hot bus. "Climb!"

Charles threw Sylvie at the ladder.

"You next," Katrine ordered.

Without questioning, Charles scrambled after Sylvie, who climbed up onto the beam. Before Charles could gain safety, Katrine leaped for the second rung. Oil swished below. A wash of heat bathed them.

The top of the ladder rattled against the beam, with only a few centimeters' purchase. Charles reached up to steady them. "Careful, we don't want to fall."

Katrine yelped. She pressed hard up behind Charles. He turned and cursed. One by one, the spare attachment points along the hot bus began to spew oil.

"Sean, what the fuck's going on?" Katrine had a connection open to the shift engineer.

Charles eased himself up another two rungs, keeping a firm grip on both ladder and beam. Katrine followed.

"What do you mean, everything's normal? The hot bus is flooding the pit. All the stop valves have opened up. Shut the system down!"

Charles blinked and rubbed his eyes on his sleeve. No. He wasn't mistaken. The ladder was slipping.

"No, I'm not joking. It's gone haywire. Your instrumentation can't be seeing it."

Charles climbed the last two rungs and straddled the beam, laying along it on his stomach. He reached down and grabbed Katrine's arm just as the ladder, softened by the ferocious heat, slumped into the rising oil.

Katrine dangled, feet almost brushing the surface. Charles grunted with the effort, wishing he'd kept himself in better condition, and tried to haul her up. He gritted his teeth. He didn't have the strength to bring her to safety.

Sylvie reached down for Katrine's other arm. "On three," she called. She counted, they heaved. Katrine's fingers grasped the bottom flange of the I-beam.

Charles and Sylvie adjusted their grip and hauled again. Katrine wrapped her arms around the beam in a desperate bear hug. Hair straggled across her face, sweat streamed down her cheeks. "I can't move," she sobbed.

"We've got you." Charles adjusted his position. Legs and one arm secured him. His free hand twined through Katrine's waistband. "All or nothing." His thighs trembled with the force of his grip.

Summoning every last ounce of desperation, he heaved again. His weight shifted off the edge of the beam to counterbalance hers. Katrine's legs swung up level with the beam. The heel of a boot raked Charles's calf and dug in. He bit back a cry, and pulled. He was winning. His arm screamed at him to release its load. As she slid around behind him his shoulder felt ready to pop out of joint. Only when he felt her weight on his back did he untwist his hand from the waistband. Her chest ground his face into rivet heads.

Charles groaned and clung tight, blinking back a wave of vertigo, as Katrine wriggled backwards. Her legs still pinning his in place, she helped him to steady himself.

"Come, we can't stay here."

A furnace heat clamored for attention. The surface of the oil still rose towards them, the whole pit a giant deep-fat fryer. Charles pushed himself upright, battling another wave of dizziness. Sylvie sat facing him, back pressed against an upright post that cradled the hot bus, her face an unnatural white.

"Sylvie, look at me!"

Unfocused eyes drifted his way.

Charles's heartbeat hammered in his ears. She was about to faint.

"Take slow breaths. Sylvie, listen to me! Squeeze the beam with your knees. Now relax a bit. Squeeze again."

At last, Sylvie responded. Charles saw her muscles work under her overalls. A tinge of color returned to her cheeks.

"Hang on a few more minutes," Katrine called behind him.

Charles looked up to see ladders already reaching from the lip of the pit to the suspended framework. Overalled engineers swarmed along the supporting structure to each valve. One by one, the deadly sprays dribbled to a stop.

Charles lingered in the doorway and glanced around the common room. A shower and a change of clothes had worked miracles on his appearance. Cuts and grazes on his face, now cleaned of oil and grit, would heal. But when he'd gazed deep into his own eyes in the bathroom mirror, he knew the ghosts lurking in their depths would take far too long to banish.

"Charles." Aaron stood, looking somber. "Come in."

Sylvie, swathed in an outsized sweater and curled up with her arms wrapped tight around her legs, looked as bad as Charles felt. Red eyes peered at him above her knees. Aaron returned to his seat alongside her, face twisting, fists clenching and unclenching in frustration. At the end of the table, Christian nursed an empty tankard. White froth speckled his beard. Next to him, Lise's fingers traced geometric patterns in lingering dampness on the tabletop.

Beer would help his mood. It always did. The company of strangers, though, he could do without right now.

A giant of a man stared across the table at him. Ruddy cheeks shone above a bushy beard.

Hesitant, feeling all eyes on him, feeling every kilometer of his distance from familiar surroundings, Charles crossed to the table.

"Charles," said Aaron, "this is Erik Thorsen, mayor of Krisgaarde."

Charles leaned across the table, hand outstretched.

Erik heaved himself half out of his chair, shaking Charles's hand briefly. "It seems you are a dangerous house guest, Professor." Despite his ferocious appearance, his voice was surprisingly mild.

"I can't help thinking that it can't be coincidence."

"Professor, I was joking! You English use humor in times of difficulty, maybe I leave it to the experts in future." Erik's mouth drooped at the corners. "I came to express my sadness at the experience you've had as a guest here."

"You may be joking, but I don't think I am."

"Dad!" Sylvie's eyes widened. Tears brimmed.

"Well, I've never been one for paranoia, but then I've never believed much in coincidence either."

"True enough," said Erik, "though you talk as if you are the reason. Why so? These accidents hurt Krisgaarde badly, and not everyone wishes us well."

A low growl sounded in the awkward hush. Erik gazed along the table. "Come, Christian, we all on the Northern Rim are meant to be friends, but the North Americans don't like us on their doorstep."

"Nevertheless ..." Charles sat down. He planted his elbows on the table and steepled his fingers, taking temporary refuge behind this flimsy barrier while he tried to swallow the tightening in his throat that had cut his words short. Silence lengthened. At last, he said, "Two events already make an unbelievable coincidence, but there is something else that makes me wonder."

He poured himself a beer from the half-empty pitcher on the table. "While we were at the thermal plant, my handheld picked up some files. I knew there was something bugging me, but I couldn't put my finger on it until this evening. In all the turmoil I'd completely forgotten about my colleague at the university, who I was trying to reach while I was in Krisgaarde."

"Terry?" Sylvie asked.

Charles nodded. "There was mail from my college office." His throat tightened again. He swallowed. "They'd been contacted by the authorities in Alaska. Terry is dead."

Sylvie gasped. Aaron and Christian gazed at the table, at a loss for words. Erik leaned forward, urgent concern in his eyes. "Did they have any more information? Did they say how he died?"

"Yes. Some details, anyway. The heating unit in his apartment went wrong and flooded the place with carbon monoxide. He died in his sleep."

"Too many freak accidents." Erik huffed, beard bristling. "I can understand why you are losing faith in coincidence."

"I don't want to believe this, in fact I can't see how this could possibly be true, but it seems to me that somebody out there killed Terry and is trying to kill me."

"Using remote-controlled machinery as a murder weapon?" Aaron's voice held a mixture of astonishment and awe.

"Have you any idea what you are saying?" Christian protested. "Someone would need an unbelievable knowledge of security."

"Well," said Lise, "they would need to track you. Not too difficult, I think. And I think too that domestic heating systems not much problem."

"But our road equipment?" Christian interrupted. "People all over the world trust their lives to guidance systems. And the thermal plant is secure. The control systems are life-and-limb."

"Exactly! I was getting there." Lise slapped the table, a fierce gleam in her eyes. "Those systems are designed and the hell tested out of them to stop from happening exactly what did happen!"

"But ..."

"No! Christian. Broken security? It's hard to believe yet to my mind it's possible. But accident? No, I don't believe that."

Charles gazed around the table, hands spread helplessly. "I'm open to other explanations."

Erik broke the uncomfortable hush. "This is a serious thing you are saying. Do you have thoughts on who could be behind such a thing?"

Charles snorted. "Academia is a surprisingly cutthroat business, but dons usually opt for character assassination rather than the physical kind." He gave a wry smile. "It hurts more." He took a deep breath. "But what you believe, what I believe, really doesn't matter. Maybe this is real, or maybe there is an innocent explanation. Thing is, I don't think I want to take that chance."

"What—" Sylvie started.

"Please bear with me for a moment. Just assume that someone out there is trying to get me." Ice settled in his stomach as he framed the thoughts that had been troubling him. "If someone *is* tracing my handheld, they must know who I am. It won't be much of a leap of imagination to track me down here. They don't seem to care who they hurt along the way. With the kind of machinery you have running around this country, do you think they'd hesitate to demolish this house, and everyone in it?"

Charles locked eyes with each person around the table, half daring, half pleading that they'd offer some killer rebuttal. The stunned silence was enough of an answer.

"I'd like to think that in a week's time we'll all be laughing about how foolish I was. But I'd rather be seen as a fool than take even the slightest chance with the lives of my family. I have no idea what I've done to upset someone, but if there is anything here beyond accidents and paranoia then they are persistent and resourceful. I can't see some-one like that stopping until they've succeeded. I can't come up with any other answer. Think of this as insurance ..." He paused, not really believing he was about to say something so clichéd and melodramatic. "I have to die."

⸺ ◆ ⸺

With blood pounding in his temples, Joseph tried to think.

First Moonshadow, then Terry dead. No evidence of foul play, and either alone would not arouse suspicion, but add the two together ... and then as soon as Joseph got caught, a lethal explosion at the address he had appropriated. Coincidence? Was he being paranoid? Keeping a sense of perspective, a sense of sanity, seemed impossible.

Come on! What was he thinking? Could anyone really engineer that kind of thing remotely?

Joseph couldn't imagine what kind of hacking skills would be needed, but he grudgingly admitted that it was possible in principle. Everything in this world was controlled by the vast global network. Goosebumps tangoed up his arms and across his shoulders. Whoever was behind Tiamat had shown hacking skills beyond anything he'd ever heard of.

He wandered the streets of White Horse in the fading light, inde-cision gnawing at him.

How well did he cover his trail? Was he being tracked even now? His regular handheld lay dormant in his pocket. He hadn't dared switch it on. Was there a risk? Was there anything to tie him to the throw-away device he'd used? He'd paid in cash, no identification given, false name and address, and that decoy seemed to have worked. All the same, Joseph decided he couldn't stay in his apartment tonight.

He directed his wandering towards home, passing his block twice before plucking up the courage to enter.

Everything seemed quiet. Muted conversations behind closed doors gave the place a neighborly feel that jarred with his heightened anxiety.

He eased open his door and threw a few clothes into his backpack. He was in and out in a matter of minutes, breathing more easily as he reached the street.

Now what? Joseph sat in a nearby park, at a loss. The town didn't feel safe, he had to get away, but where to? He needed a plan. Nothing came to mind.

He did need to warn Pink, though. Shit! Why didn't he think of that before? He scrabbled through his backpack for a pen and scrap of paper, thanking all the gods he'd ever heard of that he still kept such items as backup for the rare occasion when he needed an alternative to online messaging. He risked switching on his handheld for long enough to get Trudy Lundquist's contact information, then sought out a public call booth.

On the verge of placing the call, Joseph stopped and smacked his palm into his forehead. Idiot! Without thinking, he'd been about to pay through his online account. Was it safe? He didn't know. He *did* know that he wasn't going to risk it. He was already running from trouble and having to look out for himself. For him, the damage was done, but if the account could be traced, so could the call and it would lead Tiamat to Pink.

He fished in his pocket for cash. Nothing useable. His fingers ran along the edge of a slip of plastic, and his heart lifted. A prepaid call card! His emergency lifeline to a cab home if he ever got separated from his handheld. Not enough credit for an international call but it gave him an idea.

A brisk walk to the corner of the next block, Joseph found a newsagent. He bought a new call card, topped up from his account. That was safe enough, he reckoned. Once loaded, the anonymous card just held a cash value with no link to where the funds originally came from.

Finally, he tapped in Trudy's telecomm address.

He waited, shivering both from anxiety and from the biting cold sweeping the street in the early night.

Call terminated.

He tried again, wondering about the message—terminated meant the call either wasn't answered or couldn't be placed. Trudy hadn't refused it. Nobody was there.

Call terminated again.

Where was she? What time was it in Norway? Joseph wracked his brain. He had clients all around the Northern Rim, he should know this, but his mind felt numb. Europe. Maybe nine or ten hours ahead of him? Early morning. She should be home, dammit!

Unless something had happened.

Fingers shaking, he tapped in the address once more.

CHAPTER 16

Charles pushed away the remains of his bowl of fish, a rarity in his part of England but which seemed to be a staple dish in New Denmark. A warm meal had gone some way to restore spirits after his bizarre pronouncement, and they'd spent the last two hours talking back and forth around the problem.

The premise was simple enough. Someone wanted him dead. That same someone needed to be convinced they'd succeeded. Without actually succeeding. That was the tricky part.

He swigged his beer, only half listening to Aaron and Lise listing all the mechanical death-dealing opportunities in and around Krisgaarde. The table swam in and out of focus, then snapped into clarity like an ice-cold shower.

"Erik." Charles struggled to contain his excitement. "Your small mail planes are unmanned, yes?"

Erik nodded.

"But they do occasionally take passengers."

"Only as a last resort. And it's not a comfortable ride."

"But supposing I was in a hurry to get away from here and return to England, and couldn't wait for the next flight out of Isfeldt?"

Erik shrugged. "It could be arranged." His mouth twisted in distaste. "But if someone *is* after you, what would happen to that plane?"

A sly smile played at the corner of Charles's mouth. "If you're so sure this is all nonsense, then you have nothing to lose."

Erik started to protest, then stopped. "I see what you mean," he said, grudgingly.

"If I'm wrong, and I could easily be, then nothing happens and I collect my handheld when I return to Oxford."

"But if you're right ..." Erik paused, and chewed the inside of his cheek. His eyes narrowed. "Then an uncrewed plane and some mail seems a fair swap for God knows how many more lives here."

"So what do you intend to do?" asked Christian.

"All I'm planning to do is mail my handheld to myself in Oxford. If anyone's tracking it, they'll think I've boarded the plane."

Christian pursed his lips, then said, "No. Not good enough. We don't know what sources of information this mystery person might have. We need to convince them you also are on that plane."

Erik looked thoughtful. "I need to speak to some people and make some arrangements. I think I know how we can do this."

———•◆•———

A stream of gibberish assaulted Joseph's ears.

"Hello? Pink? I mean, Trudy?"

"Tinny?" The voice calmed instantly. "Do you know what time it is? I am a slow starter in the morning."

"Sorry. I didn't think ... I needed to talk to you, to check you're all right." Giddy with relief, the words tumbled out.

"Slow, Tinny. What's happened?"

Joseph recounted his meeting with Serena and encounter with Tiamat, and the explosion in the vacant lot. He waited, not daring to ask the question that most troubled him.

"What about Serena?"

"Serena?" Joseph fumbled for some relevance. Then it hit him. "Damn! I was so shaken I forgot all about her."

"Did she get caught too?"

"I don't know." He recalled his last moments online, picking through each memory as if studying frames from a video. The scream haunted him. He was sure it wasn't Serena. An onlooker, maybe? Who knew what people in the university hall had seen. Maybe nothing. Maybe the sound was just one of Tiamat's artifacts, designed to scare. Well, it worked. "I don't think so. And, I don't know how to reach her, other than through Typhoon."

"You're not going back there, are you?" Trudy sounded horrified.

Joseph heaved a sigh, head swimming. "So, you don't think I'm going mad then?"

"Define mad."

If this had been Pink talking, Joseph felt sure she'd have been lining up rejoinders to cut him to the core. He could imagine her waspish tone online, but the gentle European voice lulled him. "I feel ... hunted." He hesitated. Putting it into words sounded insane. He had suffered Pink Marie's scorn many times in the past and it was not a feeling he relished. "Please, if this sounds stupid then feel free to offer a better explanation." He gulped, and pressed on before he could change his mind. "It's as if Tiamat is able to reach past all the security and do things in the real world. She's a psycho. Run into her, and it's not just your online persona she trashes, she's out to get you for real."

He paused for breath, dreading the silence on the other end of the line. Dreading what she would say even more.

Eventually, Trudy spoke. "Do you think that's possible?"

"In theory." Joseph released the breath he'd been holding. "Everything's wired together and could be controlled remotely. Thing is, you'd have to be able to walk past layers of security like it wasn't there. I don't know anyone who could do that."

"So, it's not impossible. You just have to know what you're doing."

"Put it that way, yes. All the same, the knowledge needed would be superhuman."

"Do you think she really killed all those gamers who ran into her?"

"It makes sense, in a scary kinda way. Nobody's ever seen or heard from any of them. There's got to be other explanations, but it fits. I just can't understand why. Is she some psycho serial killer, topping anyone she catches online?"

"Or maybe you just pissed her off trying to trap her!"

"You were there, too."

The line went quiet.

"Pink? I mean, Trudy?"

"Yes. Still here. Sorry, that bit hadn't sunk in yet. But I think she needs to catch you before she can trace you, yes?"

Joseph thought. "Seems like it. She had Moonie and Terry. Nothing happened near me until she caught me. That gas main could still be a coincidence, you know."

"You want to take that chance?"

"Back to my question, does this sound mad to you?"

"Of course it does. But it also sounds real." Another pause. "Listen, Tinny, I kinda like you. Just remember, you're not the mad one. Tiamat is."

Thoughts came back into focus, as if an invisible, intolerable pressure had lifted from Joseph's mind. The outline of a plan took form, at least in the short term. "Listen. I'm going to stay off-net for a while. I think it's safer. Can you do me a couple of favors?"

"Whatever is within my feeble powers."

"First, round up the gamers. See if you can get Deacon onside. I think I'm going to need some expert help against Tiamat."

"I have some friends. Many people liked Moonshadow, some big-time hackers among them. Just depends whether they believe me or not."

"You have a good reputation." Joseph grinned. "And your tongue is a formidable weapon. You'll have no trouble."

"You make me blush. And your second favor, my metal friend?"

"Keep an eye on the news. Look out for any suspicious accidents in New Boston."

"Aah. Your student friend?"

"I don't think Tiamat snagged her. I hope she's safe, but no news is good news." He was about to break the connection. "And, Pink, don't run into Tiamat."

"Not fair, Tinny. That's three."

CHAPTER 17

"Remember, look nervous," Aaron muttered as they trooped into the airfield office.

Charles held his hands out in front of him. They fluttered like leaves in the wind despite his best efforts to hold them steady. "Won't need much acting." He cocked an eyebrow at Aaron.

Aaron grunted and led Charles to a desk inside the terminal building. He spoke to a clerk, a sandy-haired youth with a prominent Adam's apple.

The exchange in Danish flowed back and forth, too fast for Charles to follow. The many disbelieving glances the clerk threw his way suggested that a trip to a loony bin would be more fitting than what he was planning.

"You do know there's a scheduled flight in two days?" the clerk said to Charles. "The mail plane is automatic, not meant for passengers. This is most irregular."

"An emergency at the university." It was close enough for Charles to be comfortable with the lie. His anxiety was unfaked. "I must leave immediately."

More Danish. The Adam's apple bobbed.

At last, the clerk threw up his hands. With a roll of his eyes, he reached under the desk and pulled a thick pile of forms from a dog-eared folder. A printer spat more pages, which the clerk passed to Charles. "Your copy of the travel documents."

Charles keyed his handheld to life, and approved the payment which the clerk's terminal had already sent him.

"And this waiver." The wad of forms slid across the desk in front of Charles.

Charles gazed at the dense pages of type, in Danish. "Is all this necessary?"

The clerk shrugged. "It won't be a smooth ride and you fly at your own risk."

How much should I pretend to read this?

After a few more moments turning pages, Charles signed the document.

"And this form confirms that you know how to secure yourself in the aircraft."

"Which means, Charles, that they aren't even allowed to help you into the aircraft," said Aaron. "If they helped you at all, it could be seen as an admission of liability."

The memory of his last flight made Charles feel queasy, even knowing he would not be boarding the aircraft.

"Is he all right?" The clerk peered closely at Charles.

Damn! Can't have him deciding I'm not fit to travel! Charles nodded. "Just never flown like this before." He forced a smile. "As you say, it is most irregular."

The door behind him creaked open and banged shut. Feet stamped, and a babble of voices echoed in the otherwise deserted terminal.

The clerk craned his neck to see who'd come in.

"Can you remind me how long is the flight going to be?" Charles tried to sound casual.

The clerk returned his attention briefly to Charles. "Two and a half hours." He peered past again. Charles could hear people milling around, and more doors banging.

"And what are conditions like up there?" asked Aaron, trying to keep him distracted.

"Well, for a mail run I only bother checking alerts for the most serious storms. Certainly choppy. Make sure he's well-secured."

Erik loomed alongside Charles, effectively blocking the clerk's view, and plonked a large box on the desk. "I trust I'm in time to get this onto the mail run?"

"Come on, Charles," said Aaron, "last bathroom visit before Scotland."

The clerk was already busy scanning the label on Erik's box and making notes on the screen in front of him.

Charles and Aaron strolled over to the door to the washrooms.

Inside, Charles hastily unzipped his bright orange survival suit. Christian was already there, with a companion apparently standing far too close for comfort in a public washroom.

Aaron unzipped the jacket from Christian's companion, revealing nothing more substantial than a thin metal frame supporting a coat hanger and a dummy's head. He unclipped the snow pants dangling from the frame and handed them and the jacket to Charles.

Charles gazed at the jury-rigged contraption strapped to Christian's waist, and shook his head. "I can't believe that official didn't notice anything odd."

While Charles dressed, Aaron draped the survival suit over the frame, pulling the hood over the dummy's face. "You'd be surprised. He was busy checking in his unwanted passenger." He winked. "And now he's got a visit from the mayor. He won't be paying too much attention to a rowdy gaggle of farmers."

"But you can be sure he'll be counting the bodies passing through that far door," said Christian. "Seven go out, six come back in, leaving one on the plane. All is well."

Aaron adjusted the suit, and stood back eyeing it from different angles. "I'd be more worried about your mysterious stalker. Maybe he just tracks your handheld, but maybe he can tap into the cameras out there. Not likely a problem up to now, he would be watching your orange suit, not Christian, but we have to be more careful now. Stay close together."

Heart thumping, Charles edged out of the door. Erik was still talking to the clerk. Charles pulled the edge of his hood to hide his face should the clerk glance his way. He, Sylvie, and Lise loitered outside the washroom doors, forming a screen when Aaron, Christian and his skeletal sidekick eased their way out.

Aaron waved to the clerk as they left. Erik followed, clutching his box.

The plane squatted in a pool of light a few meters from the building. A moment of panic gripped Charles when he saw two maintenance crew loading the plane.

Aaron glanced back, and muttered, "Stay here a minute."

They huddled together, with Christian and the dummy well hidden. A whiff of kerosene tainted the clean air.

One of the crewmen called out something. Aaron answered. Charles caught only a few words of the exchange.

"I told him we'd stay out of the way until they're done." Aaron winked. "No question of liability."

Their breath formed clouds in the night. "Any cameras out here?" asked Charles, acutely aware that the dummy's breath was conspicuously absent.

Lise frowned. "Cameras inside, yes, but those on the roof are watching the runway. Safe enough, I think."

An agonizing five minute wait, stamping their feet against the cold, and the crew waved. They busied themselves at the rear of the plane, unhitching the fuel wagon and securing hatches.

From the foot of the steps, Aaron watched their movements and scanned the terminal building while pretending to talk to the dummy Charles. He signaled. Christian sidled up the steps, the survival suit trailing behind him.

Charles waited for a shout, or some sign that the blatant maneuver had been spotted.

"Smile and wave, my friend." Erik grinned as he scurried up, box in hand.

Charles followed and stood at the top of the steps, watching in fascination.

Grunting in the cramped space, Erik helped Christian undress the dummy.

Christian unstrapped the frame from his waist and dismantled it. "Aah! You have no idea how awkward that thing is. And it digs into your side where the harness attaches."

Erik bundled everything into the empty box he'd been carrying. "Well, we had to improvise, and at short notice. My ancestors used this trick to fool guards at a prison camp in the wars. Glad to see the simple ideas still work." He looked around expectantly. "Your handheld, Charles."

"Shit! Of course." Charles felt foolish. "Kind of defeats the object otherwise."

Erik dropped the handheld into the box and sealed it, then stowed the box behind cargo netting. "When this safely reaches Glasgow, my friend will send the suit back to me, and your handheld on to your Oxford address. And we can all get on with our lives."

After watching the sturdy aircraft disappear into the distance, Erik accompanied them back to Johansinge with an old-fashioned two-way radio set. His daughter provided them updates on the unmanned mail flight's progress from her home in Krisgaarde.

"Right now," Charles said, "with what's been going on, I'm glad you're off-grid but keeping in touch would be a lot easier if you had network coverage out here."

"We're managing well enough," said Sylvie. "We make a living. We eat well. We have warm and comfortable homes. That counts for a lot. Luxuries like being able to talk to someone in Australia or having the complete works of Mozart at your fingertips can wait a while longer."

Erik pursed his lips, his beard bristled. "Besides, coverage doesn't come cheap. Lots of infrastructure needed, and we are still spread so thin across this country."

"How will Ben manage his schoolwork?" Charles asked. "I don't know how elementary schooling is done these days but university classes are all remote. I'm not sure if Oxford even has a bricks-and-mortar classroom or lecture theater any more."

"We home-school for now, then we'll take him in to Krisgaarde." Sylvie looked thoughtful. "If there was one thing that would make me want us properly connected, that would be it."

"Not so much of a good thing as you may think," Erik grumbled. "My daughter spends all her time online instead of working. Believe me, you don't want the distractions."

"She's a gamer." Lise's lips curled.

"She's a grown girl now. I can't help who she meets online, but it does worry me, how long she spends and what she might be getting up to."

"She says they do no harm. They have their *code*." Lise spat the word. "But I tell her, you stay out of my systems and keep your friends out or there'll be hell to pay."

"I think Terry Quan would have agreed," Charles said. "He was always complaining about gamers upsetting our work. He spent half his time on security."

"And if she did anything to harm our community I'd happily help Lise." Erik's voice was stern. "Like I tell her, don't shit on your own doorstep."

The drive from Isfeldt, on icy and unlit roads, was scarcely shorter than the flight to Scotland. The lights of Johansinge had just appeared in the darkness, and Charles was starting to entertain a belief in coincidence, when the news came in: the flight had dropped off the radar just north of Scotland. There was no definite information, no news of a crash or sightings of wreckage, but the craft did not land as planned, and was nowhere to be seen.

"Welcome to the afterlife, my friend."

Charles grimaced at Erik Thorsen's attempt at humor.

———•◆•———

As soon as the truck stopped on the turntable, Charles leapt from the door. He almost tripped on the moving floor, and staggered to the stairs. In his room, he grabbed his travel bag and began stuffing clothes in, cursing as a fistful of shirts entangled themselves in their hangers.

Sylvie burst through the door. "Dad! What are you doing?"

"Isn't it obvious?"

"Where do you think you're going?"

Charles stopped, panting. He hadn't yet thought beyond removing himself and the danger he presented to his family.

Aaron appeared in the doorway behind Sylvie. More voices sounded down the hallway beyond.

Two and a half hours ago, this was nothing more than a schoolboy lark, fooling the lax airport security. They'd laughed in the truck on the way back. Now, the world seemed etched in black and white, real and unreal. The room around Charles, the people, were solid, bright, yet unearthly and irrelevant. He felt he could walk right through them and they'd vanish like pre-dawn dew. But out there, invisible in the darkness, something hard and real stalked him.

He yanked on the shirts. A sleeve ripped.

"Dad! Stop it!" The edge in Sylvie's voice pierced his rising panic.

"Shit! Sylvie! This is serious." Charles stared around at the people crowding the doorway. His breath whistled in his throat as he gasped, "Some fucker out there's trying to kill me."

"Calm yourself, my friend."

Charles tried to move, but his arm was clamped tight in Erik's grasp. He gazed into eyes of ice blue in a sea of straggly hair and bristling whiskers. His breathing steadied. The faces came back into focus.

Charles gazed at the floor and shook his head. "I can't live out the rest of my life in hiding, and right now I'm a danger to you all." He was surprised how clear and level his voice sounded. "I need to leave. Isfeldt is too risky. How else can I leave this country?"

"Next large airfield is at Thule," Christian said. He grunted as Lise punched him.

"Professor!" Erik's grip on Charles's wrist tightened. "Your plan worked. The trap is sprung."

"But nobody truly believed there was anything out there to spring it. Now we know different."

"Whoever is behind this thinks you are dead. Only we here know different. Remember also that we are off the net here. Invisible. Safe. We will work out a new plan, yes, but now is not the time for panic action."

Erik's words brought little comfort to Charles, though he turned them over in his head throughout the subdued meal that evening, and long into the night. Johansinge may be off the net, but new possibilities plagued him. The attacks so far had been ruthless, indiscriminate in terms of collateral damage, but accurately focused on his location. They'd happened while he'd been visible to the net.

Without his handheld and away from networked devices he was hidden, that much was true. But if his unseen assailant got one hint that Charles was still alive and living with Aaron and Sylvie, there were plenty of cruder ways to wipe Johansinge off the map. Less certain, maybe, with no way to verify Charles's exact location, but what if his attacker got impatient?

It didn't bear thinking about.

With the house sleeping around him, in the faint circle of his flashlight, the darkened garage seemed ten times as big as Charles remembered it.

He screwed his eyes shut for a moment and pictured the layout. Okay. Key rack to the right. He aimed the flashlight and awarded himself a pint of Norwegian at the sight of tiny metallic glints speared in the beam. *When I next reach a bar, that is.* Charles swallowed hard, then scanned the row of keys, thankful both for Aaron's passion for neatness, and for the fact that he could read Danish far better than he could speak it. He reached for a key from the meticulously-labeled rack.

"The cat would be a good choice in winter"—Charles cursed and dropped the key and the flashlight—"but you need the lighter sled to reach Thule in the thaw."

Pale light flooded the garage.

"Christian! You startled me." Charles fumbled for an excuse for being down here, at night, dressed for the outdoors. With a travel bag.

Nothing convincing came to mind.

CHAPTER 18

Charles gazed at Christian, leaning against the two-man snowmobile, legs crossed casually in front of him, and felt his cheeks burn as the silence lengthened. "I'm leaving." While the words seemed wholly inadequate, it occurred to Charles that Christian, too, needed to do some explaining. He'd been waiting in the dark. His thermal overcoat hung off his shoulders, unzipped to the waist.

"You think we'd let you kill yourself?"

"We?"

"Lise guessed you'd do something like this." Christian shook his head. "I said no. Too sensible, I thought. I saw boring professor. She saw Don Quixote."

"Please. You can't stop me. I can't stay here." Charles floundered for something more concrete. For a moment, he sized up the younger man, before dismissing the thought. Too many years, too little muscle. "Being off-net doesn't make you safe. If my stalker gets even a hint that I'm still here, he might decide to get a bit less subtle than downing a small plane. I can't have anything happen to Sylvie or Ben."

"I know."

"So ..." This wasn't quite the answer he expected.

"You drive these things?" There was the hint of a laugh in Christian's voice.

Charles examined the snowmobile. Brutally simple. Raw machinery. Like nothing he'd ever imagined driving. His knees felt weak.

"You have a map, I see."

Charles glanced at the map case poking out the top of his bag. He nodded.

"Useless. Can't just follow roads like England. Still snowed up. Have to improvise."

"Wait ... you're not trying to stop me?"

"I said, can't let you kill yourself." Christian zipped up his coat. "You need a guide. Besides, we need sled back in one piece." He pointed to a sleek orange sled sitting behind the snowmobile. "You stow bag in second compartment this side."

The sled had a hard top and a row of storage hatches down each side. Charles flipped open the second hatch and squeezed his travel bag into the cramped space. Curious, he opened other hatches at random.

Christian watched him, arms folded across his chest. "Food, water, medical supplies, fuel."

"All packed and ready, I see."

"The cargo sled is always kept ready, Professor. Dangerous country in winter. May need to help neighbors ... or lost travelers." He strode over and slammed the hatches closed, checking each one as it latched. "Heavy load. You help me hitch up."

"Does Lise know you're here?" Charles panted as he helped Christian haul the cargo sled to meet the snowmobile.

"I did not tell her." Christian seemed to be choosing his words more carefully than usual.

"That's not what I asked."

"I make sure that in the morning she can put hand on heart and say she didn't know."

"Plausible deniability." Charles gave the heavy-set builder a wry smile, and new respect. "So, Sylvie doesn't suspect?"

It was Christian's turn to smile. "You in big trouble when next you meet, I think. Snow plough is nothing next to angry Sylvie." He chewed his lip. "I think I spend time in Thule before coming home."

Christian picked a key from the rack, a silver cylinder on a short tether. He slipped the loop of the tether around his wrist and mounted the snowmobile, donning one of a pair of helmets dangling from the handlebars. He held out the other helmet to Charles, who climbed up behind him.

Christian reached for a remote control in front of him. The garage lights winked out.

Charles blinked. Velvet black swathed him. His stomach turned over and he felt giddy despite the solid seat between his legs, then a sliver of gray ahead widened to reveal snow and stars.

The snowmobile thundered into life, deafening in the echoing enclosure, and lurched forward. They crept along the entrance road, then Christian gunned the engine and they surged up the snow bank. Charles clung to the handgrip in front of him, heart racing. The bank was steep, surely they'd topple backwards. Then they were up and skimming across the snow.

"I don't think your plan is so secret now!"

The clear voice in his head startled Charles. "We can talk?"

"Wireless connection, helmet to helmet. Easier than shouting, no?"

White fields flashed by, an ethereal landscape in the growing light. Dawn tinged a range of mountains in the distance ahead, and flooded the plains with brilliance.

A few hours later, they stopped on a ridge overlooking yet another dazzling sweep of white. A brown smudge on the horizon to their left showed the edge of the snow pack.

Charles heaved himself off the snowmobile and massaged life back into his aching legs and buttocks.

Christian frowned at the horizon. "Snow clearing quicker than I thought. This could be tricky. We stay to higher ground. Longer, but we need good snow. He pulled a pair of red cans from the cargo sled and began refueling the snowmobile. "First compartment." He pointed.

Charles opened the hatch and found an insulated bag.

"Coffee, soup, fresh bread." Christian stowed the cans away and joined Charles, who was busy unpacking a nourishing snack. Mugs steamed in the crisp air.

Christian cocked a bushy eyebrow at Charles. "So, what next when we reach Thule?"

"I need to get to New Boston. There's a big university office there so I can visit in person, nothing online to give me away. If I can get someone there to contact people I know, people with resources, I hope I can find someone to help me." Charles frowned. "I'm still making this up as I go along. You were the one who mentioned Thule. It's the largest town in New Denmark next to Isfeldt, and it's just across the sea from New Boston. I assume there'll be planes running, or boats, maybe. You should be able to drop me off and get back home."

"Hrmmm," Christian growled. "Planes, maybe. Yet you want to stay off grid? To board commercial plane you need to identify yourself. Will be logged. Could be traced."

"Yeah, you're right. It's not easy getting around without leaving some kind of trail. I guess I'm looking for something less ... official." Another thought struck Charles. "And can I even use cash there?"

"Thule, no problem. New Boston, more difficult." Christian's beard wagged as he chewed on a hunk of bread. "Where will you stay?"

Blackness seemed to open up in front of Charles. Travel of any kind was new and uncomfortable territory, and the multitude of details threatened to drown him. "I'll figure something out before we get there."

Christian guffawed at Charles's evident discomfort. "Don't worry, Professor. Fifty-fifty chance we never make it as far as Thule!"

Christian's jest should have unsettled Charles, but a spark of anger drew his lips into a thin line. "We'd best get going, then." Ignoring the pains in his lower region, he swung back into the saddle of the snowmobile.

The day wore on, a monotony of searing cold up top, and vibration numbing the growing tenderness below. More and more often, Charles found himself easing his position in the saddle, trying to find a spot to sit on that didn't feel pummeled raw.

Many hours and two more stops later, with the sun low in the sky ahead, they rounded the shoulder of a hill and pulled up in front of a prefabricated shack.

Charles gaped as he slid off the seat. The bright yellow structure looked so out of place in this pristine wilderness. Steps led up to a wide porch sheltered by overhanging eaves.

Christian winced as he, too, dismounted. "A hard day's ride. I fear the thaw may beat us. It gives us reason for haste, and we travel further than I planned today." He gestured at the small building. "But our path brings us to better lodging than we might otherwise have enjoyed."

"Any chance of a hot shower?"

Christian bellowed with laughter. His beard quivered and the sound echoed from the slopes around them.

They hobbled up the steps and pushed the door open. Most of the shack seemed to be one large room, with bunks along one side, and a long table down the other.

Christian strode to the oil stove in the center of the room, gave two swift pumps of a handle and clicked the igniter. He grunted in satisfaction as blue flame lit the glass door. "Easy to start. Traveler could be near dead from cold and needs heat without fuss."

Charles rummaged in the cupboards, pulling a few tins from the neatly-stocked shelves. "What is this place?"

"Traveler's lodge," Christian answered. "There are places like this through the mountains. People stay as needed." He lit a pair of oil lamps to dispel the evening gloom.

"The owners don't mind?"

Christian stared at him. "We are the owners, Professor. This place, kept clean and stocked by the government. I will leave money for what we use."

Within half an hour, heat from the efficient stove had thawed the chill in the room, and Charles set a kettle and saucepan on the stove top. Soon, the rich aroma of a thick fish stew filled the air.

Christian brought in their depleted food hampers from the cargo sled. "Finish the bread while fresh. We will re-stock for tomorrow." He indicated a stack of vacuum-packed loaves in the larder. "Not as tasty as Lise's, but we have far to go, and no need to be hungry."

They ate in silence. As warmth seeped into Charles's limbs and belly, the unreality of his situation began to fade. He gazed at the darkness outside the windows. He had gone a whole day without once yearning for the familiarity of his study, the ancient buildings, the sun-baked earth. The unremitting cold here was so foreign to his experience, but, he reflected, these people knew how to make themselves comfortable.

Eventually, Christian broke the silence. "What is it you do, Professor?"

Charles groaned to himself. This was not a good time to get into an argument with someone whom he depended on for survival.

"What I mean is, I build, Aaron and Sylvie farm, these things are real." Christian's brow wrinkled. "Then there is Lise. She makes computers run our machinery. Her work I do not understand, but I know it's important." He waved his hand, as if to indicate the world around them. "Out there, many clever people do clever things to know the weather, where to get power from the earth, how to make better crops. Too clever for me, but I see how important it is. We need food, shelter, power. But you, I don't understand. You are clever, too. There must be meaning in what you do."

Charles studied the open face. He could sense no hostility, just curiosity. He sighed, and leaned back in his chair. "What do you think of the world right now? Your life here?"

"Life is good, and getting better each year. I do not understand."

"You live in a new country, one that is just emerging from the ice that used to cover it. This is a frontier nation, a growing land. I guess life *is* good, for you."

"So, what's the problem?"

"This is true for a small part of the planet. New lands are being settled that used to be uninhabitable."

"And that is good, right?"

Charles shook his head. "We're living in a connected world like never before," he muttered. "Access to the sum total of human knowledge, and yet, hardly a generation on from worldwide disaster it's barely a distant memory." He gazed at Christian. "What did you learn in school?"

"Computing, engineering, biology—"

"Practical subjects. No history?"

Christian looked puzzled.

"My home is dying. Oxford used to be in the middle of a green and fertile country. Now it's desert. Only a few thousand people live there now, and those only because it's a historic place that people with a connection to it are reluctant to give up. In reality, we only hang on at all because it's a major weather monitoring center."

"That is sad." Christian looked somber. "I can see why you are upset. But all told, we win some, we lose some."

"No!" Charles thundered. "We win *some*, we lose *lots*. Earlier this century, two thirds of the people on this planet died. For every acre of farmland you open up here, we lost a thousand this century to storms, floods, and deserts. What we do now, scratching a living on the margins, is not progress, it's little more than survival."

"So, the planet has changed." Charles wished he could borrow some of Christian's stoic acceptance. "What can we do about it?"

"We do what we *are* doing. Learn to adapt and survive."

They sat in silence for minutes. Christian looked puzzled. "So, you have no argument with what we are doing."

"No." Charles sighed. "My argument is with what we *did*."

"I still do not understand. What is done is done. What is it you do that matters today?"

"Those who do not learn from history are doomed to repeat it." Charles's tone was grim.

"The world warmed. That is physics, not history."

"Physics didn't get us into this mess." Charles held up his hand as Christian started to protest. "It was the mechanism, yes, but it didn't cause it. People did."

"Why would anyone do that?" Christian's eyebrows almost vanished into his red thatch.

"People, individually, are smart." Charles looked Christian in the eye. "Nobody wants humanity to struggle for existence, crops to fail, children to go hungry. We want hope for our children, for the future. And I bet if you asked anyone in the street, they'd say the same thing. But collectively," it was Charles's turn to gesture to the world at large, "people do some pretty dumb things."

"True enough."

"The world warmed because of people, and I'm convinced we could have avoided it. The science was well understood, even eighty years ago. Why would anyone want to bring this on themselves? And even if they had some doubts, why take that gamble with our only home? The stakes don't come much higher."

"Good question. If you are right, why did we let it happen?"

"As I said, individuals are smart. They're reasonable. But corporations aren't people. Governments aren't people. They're made up of people, but they are not the same thing. Crowds don't behave like individuals. They have a life of their own, behavior of their own. That is my field of study."

Charles leaned forwards, half out of his seat. "The thing that scares me the most is, what is to stop it happening again? Our *future* isn't just an 'engineering' problem, or a 'biology' problem. It's a 'people' problem. All the physics and engineering in the world won't help us if the collective lunacy of humanity gets in the way again. I want a future for my family!" Christian shrank back in his chair at the ferocity in Charles' voice. "And I will do whatever I can to secure it."

CHAPTER 19

Breakfast in the middle of New Denmark's wilderness was a subdued affair. At last, Charles felt compelled to break the awkward hush. "I shouldn't have raised my voice last night. Most people see no value in my work. You are not alone." He turned back to his porridge, wondering, as the silence lengthened, what to say next.

"Professor."

Charles looked up. Christian's expression was unreadable.

"Do you think about who your stalker might be?"

Charles pondered the question. "In the back of my mind, yes, but right now I need to stay alive and hidden. I haven't thought too much about it ... yet."

"Yesterday, I puzzled why someone would want to kill you. Making enemies that bad needs something big to fight over. That, I could not see in you."

"I know, I'm just an old Oxford don. An academic. How can I possibly have enemies?"

"Just an academic? Maybe. But last night, you showed passion. Anything worth passion can also divide. You believe your work is important. Others may also, but not in the same way." Christian pursed his lips and eyed Charles. "Now I see something that makes me believe you could be important enough to kill."

Charles sat back, stunned. He pushed the remains of his porridge around his bowl. "You know, I thought I was just going mad. Paranoid. For a man who relies on his mind, that's a terrifying prospect, but now I'm not sure which is worse: mad and safe, or sane and endangered."

Christian threw back his head and laughed. "Come, Professor. Finish your food. You need strength to fight another day."

Breakfast over, and provisions from the lodge safely stowed away, Charles eased himself onto the snowmobile, wincing at the contact with the frigid seat. Christian gunned the engine and swept away from the lodge, gathering speed in the milky light of dawn.

The morning started off much like the previous day. Within minutes, sore skin and muscles began protesting the motion and relentless vibration.

When they stopped at the top of a shallow slope, Charles sighed with relief. He climbed out of the saddle and stretched, then noticed Christian's expression. Puzzled, he followed the other man's gaze. The land below stretched to the horizon, unusually level. Dazzling white was struck through here and there with slashes of brilliant cobalt.

"This is not good, Professor." Christian pointed down the slope. "We leave the cargo sled here and investigate."

Charles helped him unhitch the sled, and Christian pulled a rod from one of the compartments. Without a word, he extended it to a two-meter pole which he handed to Charles.

Free of its burden, the snowmobile leapt forward as if exulting in its release. Christian picked a path down the slope and skirted the level plain. Keeping the engine running, he slowed, stopped, and peered at the snow. He edged forwards and stopped again. A hundred meters onto the flats, he took the pole from Charles and poked at the ground. The pole slid in half its length with no obvious effort.

Engine roaring, Christian swung the snowmobile around and headed for the slope. Charles looked back, and saw that in those few moments of stillness, the machine had left a sizeable impression in the soft snow.

With the sled once more in tow, they roared along the ridge, away from their previous line of travel.

"I hoped to join the road to Thule this afternoon, but the basin is thawing early." Christian's voice in Charles's helmet cut through the thunder of the snowmobile's engine. He gestured to the low lands to their left. "Too soft for us. Soon this will be water."

For an hour, they raced along the margins of the wetlands. The landscape unrolled endlessly beneath churning tracks.

"Where are we heading?" Charles asked. "Is there a way around this?"

"There is a rift under here. Hot springs near the surface, like at Isfeldt. The ground warms early every year." A long pause. "Should still be firm further north."

Something in Christian's voice gave Charles a chill. He decided to ignore it and place faith in his guide.

They had stopped for lunch, and were on their way again, when a change in engine pitch alerted Charles. He was about to ask Christian what he was looking at, but held his breath when he saw the tension in the set of the burly man's shoulders. They slowed and crawled forwards.

At last, Charles could see that the ground ahead dropped abruptly away from the endless level flats alongside them.

Christian stopped the snowmobile and turned to Charles. "Wait here." His voice was grim.

Without further explanation, he strode away to where the plains ended in a steep escarpment. He stood for long minutes, a tiny doll figure, fluorescent orange against the endless white, then turned and plodded back towards Charles.

Even at a distance, beneath his helmet and goggles, Charles could tell it was not good news.

"We continue north," Christian said. "Let us hope." He swung back into the saddle and eased the throttle open, picking a course that took them wide for hundreds of meters before angling back towards the lower ground.

Christian kept looking around to survey the terrain alongside them. Charles wondered why they were moving so slowly, but this didn't seem like a good time to be asking questions.

At last his patience was rewarded. They stopped. "Look back there."

Charles followed Christian's pointing finger. A slope of white rose to meet the plains they'd been following all morning, now thirty meters above their heads.

"Past that slope, remember all those hours we travel beside that soft snow? All that snow back there melts before the rest."

"The hot springs?"

"Yes. Soon now, it makes a big lake between the hills. That slope is a dam. The edge of the melt. I had hoped to cross there, but we are too late. It is too fragile. Even the sound of our engine could set it moving now. Soon, it will collapse."

Charles was suddenly aware of a sound so unfamiliar, he'd not been able to place it. "Is there water running nearby?"

"Many streams are already running beneath the snow, running under the dam, from the melt up there. Bad news. We will keep going and see."

Another half an hour of slow travel, with frequent stops while Christian surveyed the fragile snow, confirmed their fears. Deep ravines opened out to their left, revealing gurgling creeks. These joined and slowed. Soon, they found themselves on the bank of a sluggish river a hundred meters across. Startling blue water mirrored the sky, crusted here and there with drifting ice.

"Is there any way round? A bridge, or something?" Desperation edged Charles's voice. The cold seeped into his mind and filled it with frustrated hopelessness.

Christian stopped the snowmobile and turned in his seat. His arm made a sweep from left to right. "The land here is one hundred thirty kilometers from Indhav to Kane Bay. Goes from sea to tundra, which we cannot cross, to soft snow, to dam too fragile to cross, to river, to sea again. This is what I feared, Professor. Once the spring melt starts, this land is impassable for weeks." Christian seemed unmoved. Charles wondered what it would take to break that maddening stoic calm.

Christian looked all around, head tilted back as if sniffing the air. Turning his back on the river, he aimed for higher ground.

"So, that's it then? I need to find another way out of this country." Charles felt emptiness inside at the thought of returning to Johansinge. There would surely be other ways to get him safely away from his family, but after abandoning them in the night he couldn't face the thought of returning, tail between his legs.

They didn't travel far, and stopped just below the crest of a hill. The afternoon sun lit the shallow ledge Christian had chosen for their camp. From this vantage point, the hopelessness of the situation became clear. The river meandering below them broadened to a long lake snaking its way to the northern horizon. There was nowhere to cross.

Christian followed Charles's gaze. "Ways out of New Denmark ... Thule has airport, and big sea port. Plenty of traffic to North America and out to the Arctic." He frowned. "This side of the country, we have plane from Isfeldt, and we have the Norwegian Sea."

Charles pictured the scenes from the plane's window on his flight from Scotland, the churning cauldron of windswept slate that besieged Iceland.

As if reading his mind, Christian pursed his lips. "Boats do not go there."

Charles shook his head and focused on practical matters. He unpacked thermos flasks, still steaming from that morning. "Do you have tents or something there?"

Christian smiled. He opened a hatch near the front of the cargo sled, and twisted a handle. The hard lid of the sled split down the middle and opened out flat like a clam shell. Ribs supported a canopy stretching over the open halves. Christian unzipped the canopy at the front.

Charles peered inside. Each half of the lid lay flat, forming two narrow beds. "Very impressive." He looked back at the body of water barring their way. Anger rose inside him. The cobalt ribbon seemed to mock him. "Why did we stop here? There must be hours of daylight left."

"You in a hurry to return, Professor?"

Charles shook his head.

"We camp," said Christian. "I think."

CHAPTER 20

Stiff and numb, Charles eased himself out of the shelter. Christian was already busy with a camp stove, melting snow.

Breakfast over, Charles stowed the food back in its compartment, and watched in fascination while Christian folded the shelter away and closed the lid of the sled.

Fascination turned to puzzlement when Christian pulled out a backpack and filled it with the remaining full flasks and bottles. He turned to Charles with a grin and handed him the backpack. "We do things different today."

When he offered no further explanation, Charles settled the pack on his shoulders, donned his helmet, and mounted the snowmobile. He twisted around in his seat, in time to see Christian unhitch the cargo sled and haul out Charles's travel bag.

"You aren't leaving that here, are you?"

Christian stood alongside and peered close. "Professor, do you trust me?"

Charles studied Christian's earnest face, and nodded.

"I mean, trust me with your life? Do you trust that I know how to drive this machine?" The words echoed loud in Charles's helmet.

"Yes, of course I do."

Christian jammed the bag on top of Charles's knees and swung into the saddle. "Then, Professor, do as I say. Hold tight, grip the saddle with your knees. Whatever you do, whatever your eyes see, hold tight and do not move or you could spill us."

Before Charles could answer, the snowmobile roared and sped down the slope. Christian aimed straight for the water and opened the throttle. A high scream escaped Charles's lips as they hit the water.

Christian stood on the running boards, half out of the saddle. The nose of the snowmobile lifted slightly as they scudded across shimmering blue.

"Holy fucking shit!" Charles felt his knuckles crack under the pressure of his grip on the handlebar. Christian's words of advice were superfluous. Despite the burning ache in hands, arms and rigid thighs, a dozen men couldn't have pried Charles free of the snowmobile.

Spray sheeted out on either side with a hiss audible above the thunder of the engine. The machine tilted from side to side under Christian's guidance as they weaved between bobbing ice floes. Icy droplets stung the exposed skin of Charles's cheeks.

The far side drew nearer. The water around them seemed to be rising. Familiar kerosene tangs mingled with the damp mugginess of steam. Water lapped the running boards. The engine reached a new pitch as they scrambled for safety.

Once more on solid ground, Christian swung the snowmobile around and surveyed the hundred meter crossing. Fading ripples marked the course of their desperate dash. "Not bad," he said. "Never tried that with a passenger before."

Charles pounded on Christian's back. "You stupid bastard!" He staggered off the snowmobile, his bag sliding to the snow, and rounded on the younger man. "You could have drowned us!"

Christian gazed at him. "This from a man who has cheated death twice already?"

"I didn't put myself into those situations on purpose. I didn't ask you to join in the game of 'Professor Extinction.' "

"Think about it, Professor." Christian's voice sounded so reasonable, so level, that Charles felt the hammering in his temples subside. "If I had told you what I was going to do, would you have let me?"

"Not a chance in hell!"

"What if I told you this was a thing I know I can do with a snowmobile? Risky, yes, but not unusual."

Charles hesitated, picturing the raw terror he'd felt as they hit the water.

"And you are in danger and you need to leave this country. There is no other way to cross. In a day or two it will be even worse. How anxious are you to leave?"

"You have a point, but you should have warned me."

"But, Professor, if you knew what was coming, would you have been able to sit still? I could not give you time to think, or you would have drowned us both."

Charles stared at the river, now once more a placid, unbroken surface. Laughter bubbled up in his throat. At first it came in fits, high pitched, hysterical. Then it emerged full-bellied, echoing off the hills around. The madness passed. Charles sobered. "So, now what? All our supplies and shelter are over there. You going back to get them?"

Christian pursed his lips. "I hope I left the sled high enough up. When that dam breaks this valley will flood for days." He turned to Charles. "Now, we ride for Thule like the devil is at our heels."

Charles picked up his bag and swung back into the saddle. "Then we'd best get going." As Christian turned to start up the machine, Charles tapped him on the shoulder. "You're still a stupid bastard."

Christian put words into deeds, and the snowmobile, released once and for all from the cargo sled, swallowed kilometer after kilometer of rolling hills.

By midday, they had reached the road, which was little more than a narrow depression winding its way from one horizon to the other, flattened by the passage of vehicles.

Christian examined the road and sniffed. "We follow to one side. Smoother going." He angled the snowmobile back onto virgin snow and opened the throttle once more.

Charles noticed other tracks running parallel to the road, occasionally criss-crossing each other. "Why have a road if you don't use it?"

"There is a real road under there. Needed when the snow is gone. In winter, heavy trucks break up the surface, and it freezes again. Okay for trucks and suchlike with wheels, but it will be bumpy for us."

In answer to Charles's next unasked question, Christian added, "We need to follow the road through the mountains. It will guide us safe to Thule."

The sun had sunk low in the sky, when lights twinkled in the distance. Christian heaved a deep sigh. "I had forgotten how long this road was. Never gone this distance on a snowmobile before."

"Is this Thule?"

"Not quite, my friend, but we stop here tonight. Rest. Refuel. I will make inquiries about transport, and tomorrow you will be on your way."

Christian's idea of "Not quite" turned out to be another morning of bone-shaking agony before the rooftops of Thule welcomed them. They left the snowmobile on the outskirts of town, where hard-packed snow met cleared streets, and walked the two kilometers to the harbor.

Charles waited, stretching tormented limbs and marveling at the sea, a sight he had rarely seen in real life, while Christian pottered in and out of buildings along the wharf.

After the relentless drone of the snowmobile, new sounds penetrated the residual humming in Charles's ears. Further down the wharf, gulls mobbed a fishing boat unloading its catch. Frustrated cries sawed the air. Far off to sea, a single bell tolled in the rollers, slow and mournful. Salt and seaweed cloyed the air, adding to a disconcerting sense of unreality.

Eventually, Christian returned, a broad grin stretching his face. "Well, Professor, it is all settled. There is a freighter crossing to New Boston first thing tomorrow. They don't officially take passengers so they will not be too fussy about identification. I have paid the quartermaster and booked passage in my name." He winked. "Just brush up on your Danish."

Christian rummaged in his jacket and pulled out a wad of notes. "Take it," he insisted, when Charles started to protest. "Sylvie can repay me, when she forgives me of course. You need to feed and house yourself for heaven knows how long, and stay out of sight at the same time. Cash only, as long as you can manage."

He pulled out a scrap of paper. "Here is the address of a hostel. Directions, too. Not exactly the Ritz, but warm, dry ... and safe. No questions asked. Friends of mine here recommend it."

He gazed steadily into Charles's eyes. "I wish you luck, my friend, for Sylvie and Ben's sakes if nothing else. Find out who your stalker is and deal with him. Come back safe."

"Christian." Charles hesitated, not sure how stupid this was going to sound. "When you get back, make sure Sylvie and Ben stay out of Krisgaarde. Best for you and Lise, too. Stay off grid. Whoever is out there works through the network. I need time to get to the bottom of whatever's going on, then I'll be in touch through Erik."

Charles studied the New Boston branch of the university from across the street, fighting a sense of unease. This was so different from how a university should look that he'd checked the sign alongside the entrance three times in case he'd made a mistake. "University of Oxford," the sign announced. Underneath, in smaller lettering, "Administration, Library, and Faculties."

With a resigned sigh, Charles saw how his narrow and cloistered experience had thrown him off balance. He was used to the traditional seat of learning, centuries-old sandstone relics from a world long dead. But, like many surviving institutions, Oxford had become a global village. Branches around the world would naturally reflect the styles of their surroundings.

The low frontage occupied a whole block. Overhanging eaves and faded sidings blended in with the other weatherbeaten buildings on the street. It was hard to believe this town was barely thirty years old.

He grimaced. He'd thought that once he stepped into the familiar world of academia, everything would be all right. Now, faced with the reality, he had no idea who to speak to or what to say. Not safely, anyway.

His breath hung in the morning air. His hands trembled, but not from cold. He retreated to a corner coffee shop and took a seat that gave him a view of the university building's main entrance.

Charles ordered coffee and checked his wallet, his conscience, and his taste-buds in that order before handing over the extra dollars for the extravagance of a shot of milk. Tea he habitually drank black. Coffee was an acquired taste he was still working on.

The warmth of the oversized mug steadied him. He still had no idea how to proceed, but at least the problem felt once more open to analysis. List the questions to be answered. Separate them out. Divide and conquer. He sipped his drink. This was more like it.

Who was after him? And why? Too big a problem right now, those questions were what he needed help with.

Who could help? Or, a more manageable goal, who could seek help on his behalf without exposing him to the net and arousing suspicion?

He hesitated. Someone at the university. That's why he was here, but it felt too obvious. Emptiness yawned inside him when he thought how easy this question was ... how few options he had. Many of his colleagues had worldwide networks of contacts, meeting online and traveling in person. The conference excesses of the engineering faculty were legendary. Agricultural genetics came a close second. Heck, even the caustic Gwen Stoppard held some wild Christmas parties with her computational fellows.

At Christmas, he and Terry raised a lonely glass over the airwaves then went their separate ways.

Nobody held conferences in anthropology.

He shook his head. This was getting him nowhere.

How to make contact without revealing himself? That was the killer. Without that problem, he could stroll right through that door across the street, introduce himself, and place a call.

Once again, he broke the problem down further to analyze it, homing in on more tractable goals.

He'd asked Christian to make sure his family stayed off grid. All very well, but *he* needed the grid to reach anyone. So, what was he afraid of?

Obviously his stalker had been able to track his handheld. That was no longer a threat, but hacking into industrial machinery showed a superhuman ability to work the network. He had to steer clear of any-thing that needed his name or citizen identification. The stalker would surely be on the lookout for details like that showing up, even in a sup-posedly secure system.

If he announced himself to anyone at the university, whether from the building or from a public booth, he would have to provide identifica-tion. The skin between Charles's shoulder blades crawled at the memory of frying flesh. If a power plant wasn't safe, the university systems would be an open book.

So, this resolved into separate problems of transmission, and recep-tion. He needed access to some means of sending a message, and the recipient needed a way of knowing who it was from without using any regular identification.

His head hurt. He rummaged through his pockets for something to write on and with. It was hard keeping track of all these thoughts. He longed for the weight of his handheld in his pocket. Oh! To be able to subvocalize a few thoughts knowing they would be held until he needed them.

A flashing thundercloud and a muted alarm distracted Charles. Information rolled onto the screen hanging on one wall of the coffee shop.

A few chairs scraped. A few glances at the screen, even though the storm was a full ninety minutes away. Charles frowned. Strength two. He could stand up in that! They had it so easy on this continent. All the same, he drained his mug and made ready to leave. Rain he could handle. Hail didn't sound so friendly.

Outside, Charles checked the street signs over again to make sure he had his bearings. It wouldn't do to get lost on the way back to the hostel.

A group of students emerged from the university across the street, laughing and chattering. They went their separate ways in a flurry of farewells.

One girl, face almost hidden in a fur-lined hood, caught Charles's eye. She held back from the group.

He hesitated for a moment, and blinked. The coincidence was too much to believe, and he had nothing more than a peripheral glimpse of her face before she turned away, yet the sense of familiarity was overwhelming.

But if he was right, could he—dare he—involve one of his students in whatever was happening to him? Heck! Normal rules of civilized behavior had gone through the window with the snow plough, and what if the whole anthropology department was being targeted? Himself ... Terry ... maybe the students were already in danger. He cursed his indecision. She had already disappeared around the corner of the building, heading in the opposite direction he needed to go. If he was wrong ... Dammit! He strode after her.

Around the corner, she was no more than fifty meters away.

"Serena!"

The girl stopped and turned. She peered from beneath her hood, eyes wide. Blood drained from her cheeks. She screamed.

Charles stood, dumbstruck. It *was* her! It had to be.

She turned and ran.

He swore under his breath. He didn't want to attract attention, but he had no choice. "Serena! Wait!"

She slowed and glanced over her shoulder.

"It *is* Serena, isn't it?" Doubt gnawed at him. He ignored the curious gazes of the few passers-by and hastened after her, hoping to close the distance without spooking her. "I'm sorry to trouble you, if you aren't Serena then you must be her twin." He held up his hands and stopped, feeling stupid. "Please accept my apologies for startling you."

"Professor?" She pulled a strand of hair from her face and took a couple of hesitant steps towards him, frowning.

Charles let out an unsteady breath. "I thought I was going mad for a moment."

"I still do." The pain in her voice countered his own giddy relief.

"Serena, what's wrong?"

"Damn it, Professor, I thought you were dead!"

Insight hit Charles like a sandstorm. "Oh ..." He couldn't think through the sudden rush of guilt. "I mean ..." Try again. "I had to disappear. Fast. I never got as far as wondering who else in the world might care ... or even notice."

Serena's mouth hung open.

"Look. I'm in big trouble and I needed to drop out of sight. I still don't know what's happening."

"Trouble? Police?" She took a hesitant step away. "Professor, what have you done?"

Charles shrugged, his arms spread wide. "I don't know. I wish it were as simple as the police. I'm running, but I have no idea who from, or where might be safe."

Serena halted her retreat. By her posture she looked poised for flight at the first hint of a threat.

Fatigue overcame Charles. The rush of relief at so unexpectedly seeing a familiar face evaporated. He lowered himself to the curb. From his seated position he looked up at Serena. "Did you know that Doctor Quan is dead?"

She nodded, chewing her lip.

"I don't believe it was an accident."

"I heard that he died in his sleep." Serena's tone was oddly flat.

"Carbon monoxide. A faulty unit. But I believe it was engineered. And whoever did it is after me, too."

"You look ill."

"I'm not delirious, if that's what you mean."

"I didn't say you were. You need to tell me more about your suspicions."

"I'm not sure I should. People around me have died and I could be dragging you into danger." Charles wondered at the sudden intensity in Serena's stare. He glanced at the sky. "It's a long story. Is there somewhere we can talk?"

"When did you last eat properly?"

Charles struggled to untangle the non-sequitur. His mind had been already assembling the pieces of his story, which fell apart like a train wreck at the change in tack. A gust of wind tugged at his jacket, sending icy feelers across his chest.

"You look ill." The tone reminded him of Sylvie. "You've not been caring for yourself." Serena held out her hand. "Come on. There's a place nearby where we can wait out the storm."

———◆———

Charles wolfed a second bowl of vegetable chowder under Serena's disapproving stare. In between mouthfuls, he related his story, the incidents in New Denmark that convinced him he was being hunted, and his flight to Thule and New Boston.

As he progressed, and as his hunger abated, he took more notice of Serena's reactions. He'd been readying himself for disbelief, for pity, for a quick call to the local mental health services. Instead, she just listened more attentively, nodding from time to time.

He paused for breath, and stared out of the café's window. Natural dangers came in many forms. He found new respect for these coastal dwellers. They may not have ferocious wind speeds to deal with, driving abrasive sand and grit hard enough to flay exposed skin in seconds, but their weather didn't need wind power to be deadly. Hailstones, some as big as his fist, pummeled the empty street outside and hammered the roof overhead in a thunderous roar that made conversation difficult. A blow from one of those icy missiles could split a man's skull.

Now, Charles could see why the low buildings all had such broad eaves. Despite the wind howling down the street, hail fell in a near-vertical sheet of ice two meters beyond the window. It had turned the ground outside white in a few seconds. Driving stones now mashed the frozen blanket and sent sprays of fragments clattering against the sidings.

He mopped his bowl with a hunk of bread, and turned his attention back to Serena. "So, I still don't know what's going on, but I feel sure someone is after me. I had to get away for my family's safety."

"So, what do you plan to do?"

"That's what I was trying to figure out when I saw you. I don't want to involve you, but it suddenly struck me, what if someone's taken a dislike to the whole department, students included? You might already be in danger. You need to be careful, but I'd appreciate some help getting a message through to one of my colleagues, if we can figure out how to do so safely." He chewed the inside of his cheek. "At first, I thought I'd drop into the university and talk to someone. Then, I realized I'd have to identify myself, and it didn't seem like such a good plan."

"Just out of curiosity, because I think I know the answer, why not?"

"It looks like my stalker is able to monitor all sorts of things online. I don't know what he might be capable of, but it can't be easy to subvert municipal vehicles or industrial machinery, so I assume there's a deep capability there. I'm doing all I can to avoid attention. Most especially, I don't want to give my identity online anywhere."

"That makes sense."

Charles was taken aback by the matter-of-fact response. "The trouble is, I'm running out of time. I have a small sum of cash, which I'm using sparingly, but I'm going to have to show myself somewhere before too long." He finally teased out what seemed odd about her reactions. He narrowed his eyes at her. "None of this seems to surprise you. You've already heard something like this before, haven't you?"

The corners of Serena's mouth twitched upwards. She gazed into space for a few moments then glanced at the wall screen behind the counter. "The storm will be over soon. You're coming home with me. There's someone you need to meet."

J oseph Wong surfaced from his online foray, and stretched. He shivered, pulling his overcoat closer around him. He was alone in the open-sided shelter. Everyone else had fled the approaching storm. He welcomed the solitude. It freed him from distraction while he worked.

The ground around him glistened, a good hundred meters in all directions of level openness before the first storm-battered trees. He stood and watched the slate grey clouds recede. When it was safe, he stepped into the open, hail crunching underfoot.

In one of the towns on the north-west shore of Hudson Bay, he'd exchanged some of his dwindling reserves of cash for another bootleg handheld. Not a games model, he couldn't afford that, but it was an avenue to the virtual world and he could be confident that it hadn't been compromised.

No avatar, either. Joseph reawakened rusty skills in using more basic interfaces, less immersive, the kind that half the population still used to navigate the global network. For once, the lack of full immersion was a welcome benefit. The feeling of being hunted left him with a visceral need to be in control of his senses, with a view of the outside world through a ghostly veil of information.

That was also why he was shivering out here, rather than warm inside. It shouldn't be possible to trace the handheld back to him, but he didn't want to be near any machinery if his online wanderings caught unwelcome attention, so he'd come out here to the middle of a park.

Now his fingers could barely hold his handheld, let alone operate it. It was time to drop out of sight and return to the house. He used another trick he'd learned from gamer friends. As long as it was switched on, a handheld usually advertised its presence to the nearest online service provider. The hack he'd installed allowed him to keep it switched on, but invisible. He'd finished his online fishing expedition and could examine his catch at leisure, in comfort, and safety.

Burying his hands deep in his pockets, Joseph strode through the park. Surreptitious data mining at the behest of someone he knew practically nothing about was one hell of a way to earn his room and board.

Wary as ever these days, he sidled along the street, eyeing each passing vehicle for any suspicious deviation from its course. Traffic was picking up again after the storm. His eyes felt like they wanted to peer in five different directions at once.

He passed the house once, looking for signs of life or of menace, before doubling back and listening at the door. These kinds of precautions were second nature to Tin Man, accustomed to breaking into heavily-guarded corporate zones, but that was his online persona and this was the real world. Joseph had spent his whole gaming career keeping the two rigidly compartmentalized. That was the gamer code. Mixing the two worlds like this felt profoundly unclean.

Damn! She should have been back by now. He fished the spare key from his pocket and let himself in. He put on a pot of coffee, and prowled the kitchen, unable to settle. Only after checking over the house room by room did he finally sit, mug of coffee on the table in front of him, and return to his work.

A noise startled him. Despite his nervousness, he'd become engrossed in the files he'd collected that afternoon.

The door opened. Serena breezed in. "Joseph, glad you're back. There's someone I'd like you to meet."

Serena ushered in an old man wearing a grubby orange jacket. He looked like he'd trekked down from the mountains. The long jacket hung, unzipped, off his shoulders, revealing mud-crusted windproof pants. Days-old stubble roughened his skin.

"Come on, Professor. Get those winter clothes off and make yourself comfortable."

"Your Professor?" Joseph's eyes widened. "You mean, the guy who built all that ..."

"Typhoon. Yes."

Joseph wondered why Serena looked so smug. Had she ratted on him to this guy? "Oh shit. I mean, Professor, I'm sorry. Surely Serena told you we didn't mean any harm. I don't think we did any damage or anything—"

"What the hell are you blathering about?"

The old guy's acid tone stung Joseph. He blinked, then felt a tingle of relief. Clearly this Professor didn't know about the gamers' intrusion. "I visited Typhoon—" Under the Professor's sharp glare, Joseph wished he hadn't started down this path. He improvised hastily. "—With Serena. I'm helping her with some research." Well, that part was actually true. Now.

He was relieved to see the scalpel stare turned to Serena. She returned it with a smile of disarming innocence.

"Hmmph. Yes." The Professor's eyes lost their laser-like intensity. "Full marks for initiative, Serena, enlisting the help of colleagues. But Typhoon is a sensitive experiment. In future, please check with me first."

"Maybe I would have, if I hadn't thought it would require the services of a medium."

The Professor winced. "Well met. And again, I'm sorry for that deception."

"I'll forgive you, eventually." She turned from the Professor to Joseph. "Professor, this is Joseph. Joseph, Professor Charles Hawthorne."

The Professor grunted and held out his hand. "We're off campus. Please call me Charles."

"Right, gentlemen. There is some method in my actions here." Serena's manner became brisk and commanding. "You each have a story to tell. Professor, you start please. Tell Joseph what you told me. Joseph, I am keen to hear what you think."

While Serena fetched hot drinks, Charles talked of his experiences in New Denmark. When he spoke about Terry Quan, his face sagged. His tanned skin looked grey under the stubble.

Joseph's throat tightened. *This must have been after we set that trap.* His stomach churned. He kept quiet but wondered how he was going to explain Terry's death. *The Samurai forced us to help him,* Joseph reminded himself, *we had no wish to disturb Tiamat.*

After a long pause, Charles frowned and gave his head an irritable shake. "I've been so caught up in my own troubles I haven't thought of Terry in a long while."

He continued with his story. Joseph jerked upright when he heard about the snow plough.

Serena set a mug of coffee in front of him, and gave him a 'told you so' look. Joseph opened his mouth, then silenced himself when she shook her head.

Charles must have seen the exchange between them. "You don't believe me, do you?"

"Sorry, Professor, I mean, Charles. I'm just a bit floored. You don't seem the type to be caught up in all this."

"What do you mean by 'all this'?"

"You'll see. I have my own story to tell, like Serena said." Joseph glared at her. "But I would like to hear the rest of what you have to say." When Charles hesitated, Joseph said, "Believe me, this all makes sense. You'll see."

When Charles described the accident at the geothermal plant, Joseph whistled. The story of the plane decoy made him laugh out loud. "Okay, I know this is serious, but that was a move right out of a spyfic."

"Hmmph." The tone was dismissive, but a hint of a smile played at the corners of Charles's mouth.

Joseph swallowed. "I suppose it's my turn then. You'll probably be angry, but I hope it'll answer some questions at least." He wondered where to start. Feet first. No point skirting the issue. "I'm a gamer."

Charles frowned. Joseph hurried on. "I run with a group in the network under-layers. We found ourselves in Typhoon by mistake. Well, what I mean is, we were looking for somewhere to hide, it didn't matter where it was as long as it had some layers of security."

"Typhoon has that, for sure. Terry made sure of that." Charles looked like he'd bitten into a lemon. "What could you possibly be hiding from? Online police?"

"No such thing. Corporates have their own security, but the under-layer is wide open. That's the whole point of the global net, openness." Joseph eyed Charles. "Now it's my turn to wonder if *you're* going to believe *me*."

Charles sniffed. "A week ago I wouldn't have believed what I just told you."

Unsure whether or not to be encouraged, Joseph continued. "There's a peculiar avatar that roams the under-layer. We call her 'Tiamat', but nobody knows whether she's an artificial construct or whether there's someone behind her. Anyway, gamers run from her."

"And you ran into Typhoon."

"And Doctor Quan caught us. He's got some security measures none of us have ever heard of before."

Charles sighed and nodded.

"When we told him about Tiamat, he decided to trap her. He forced us to help him."

"How?" The fatigue seemed to wash from Charles's face. "Surely he didn't know who you were, he had no hold over you."

"He managed to trace our real world accounts, and he held our avatars hostage." Joseph wondered whether or not to elaborate, but Charles's mouth hung open, eyes turned to the ceiling.

"Aah! A vital icon of popular subculture. Hold power over the icon, you hold power over its worshipper."

"Huh? I don't worship..." Joseph broke off at Charles's glare.

"So why not leave it there," he snapped.

Okay, the old goat did have a point.

"And your avatar's still there, isn't it? That's why you're helping Serena."

Well, that saved Joseph another headache. He'd been wondering how much he could tell without letting on that his avatar was still trapped. But the Professor didn't have it all his own way. "I'm helping Serena in return for a place to stay. I'm on the run, just like you."

"Hmmm." Charles settled back in his seat. "Perhaps you'd better finish your story."

Joseph told him about the failed trap, about the subsequent deaths, and his own brush with the wrath of Tiamat.

"I see," said Charles, when Joseph had finished. "So you think Tiamat is also behind what happened to me?"

"Death by out-of-control machinery? It's too much of a coincidence." It seemed blindingly obvious to Joseph. Why was the old man even questioning it? "The thing that ties us all together is Typhoon. Tiamat seems to be staking the place out, and going after anyone who goes near there. Terry, Moonshadow, me, and you, Professor."

"What about me?" Serena asked.

Joseph puzzled over that. "Tiamat needs to get a hold of you, I think, before she can trace you. My friend, Pink, was with me but never got caught. She's still safe. You don't use an avatar. You go to the university and sign on directly. I guess that path isn't visible to her. She seems to stick to the immersive online zones."

"Just one hole in the theory." Charles's voice was quiet.

"What?"

"I don't have an avatar either, and I haven't been near Typhoon since leaving Oxford."

Chapter 23

Grey dawn crept across the kitchen floor, a pale reflection from the polymer-coated sidings of the house opposite the window. Charles paused at the threshold, mapping out the locations of kettle, mugs, and tea in the dim light.

A coffee pot bubbled on the counter. Charles scanned the room again, and finally spotted a shape hunched in the shadows cloaking the table.

Gamer. The thought left a bitter aftertaste. Although the deeply-immersive online world was foreign territory to Charles, Terry had always talked about them in contemptuous and angry tones. Parasites. Pests to be controlled and expelled at all costs. It was strange to see the human behind the mask. Joseph looked like a normal twenty-something, and gave the impression of being conscientious and hard-working. Hardly your archetypal parasite. And then there was Erik's daughter. Charles hadn't met her, but she sounded normal enough over the radio and Sylvie had talked of her in positive enough terms. A bright kid, ready for College. How many of Charles's own students were gamers behind the scenes? He'd probably never know.

Charles ran his tongue over his lips. Tea beckoned. Joseph hadn't stirred. "Don't tell me you've been up all night!"

The shape moved and grunted.

Charles snapped on the light.

Joseph blinked and peered up at him, eyes red, face white. "Any idea how many days I've been hunting down freak accidents around the world?"

"Accidents? You mean like the ones that happened around us?"

A frown played across Joseph's face. "It's been a long night. Can't remember how much I told you. How much did I talk about the gamers?"

"I rather think you were trying to avoid the subject." Charles was rewarded with a flicker of guilt in Joseph's expression. "Don't worry." He glanced at the coffee pot, then sucked his teeth and filled the kettle. He tried to keep his tone reassuring. "I have more serious problems to deal with than an intruder in my experiment."

"Tiamat has a reputation amongst the gamers," said Joseph, after a long pause. "She chases us when we're out in the under-layer. Anyone she catches disappears, but nobody has ever known for certain what happens to them."

"Disappears ... you mean, from the online world?"

"Sure, why would we think anything different? But with what happened to Terry, Moonie, and me, Serena's got this hum in her hand-held about gamer disappearances. Trying to prove something, I guess." Joseph grimaced. "Now, I'm not so sure I want to know."

A memory from another life nudged Charles. "In my experience, Serena has an uncanny knack for following her instincts along unlikely but fruitful roads. What's she got you digging up, and what have you found that you don't want to know?"

Joseph heaved a deep breath. "Serena told me to go through this whole long list of gamers we know who vanished. We, I mean Moonie, Pink, and me, put the list together for Terry to help work out how to give us the best chance of bumping into Tiamat. He had it all mapped out with locations and so on. I guess she must have found it stashed somewhere in Typhoon."

"Dr. Quan kept meticulous records." Serena's voice from the doorway startled Charles. Joseph's head jerked up. His eyes twitched.

"Everything about the trap, and the method for luring her in. I found it while you were on your way here."

"Good morning, Serena," said Charles. "I hope we didn't disturb you."

"There had better be coffee, that's all." It was hard to tell if Serena's ominous tone was entirely in jest.

Joseph waved towards the pot on the counter. "Anyway, I've been scouring local news feeds around the world for reports of unexplained machine or systems failures leading to fatalities, and then seeing if they correlate to these online encounters with Tiamat."

"He's been amazing, Professor. A proper investigator." Serena pouted and fluttered her eyelids. "I could use a good research assistant."

"When anthropology becomes a lucrative field of study, I'll think about it."

Joseph snorted. "You couldn't pay me enough. This was like a needle in a haystack."

"Except, first you had to find the right haystack." Serena grinned.

"Hey! Who's doin' the talking here?"

When Serena made a 'zipping' gesture across her mouth, Joseph continued. "Our list had dates and times, online locations but no geo-graphical information. Gamers only know each other by their online personas. Real world info is taboo. We never discuss it, so we never know where anyone is from. So my net had to be global, and it pulled up lots of possible matches. Too many."

"For each disappearance on our list, we usually had several acci-dents within a two day window. Statistics is my part of the bargain." She gave Joseph a pointed glare when he seemed on the verge of protesting at another interruption. "And there were no peaks or anything around a disappearance. The list of accident reports was just a continuous random stream. There was no correlation of any significance."

"I did notice something odd, though, about some of the reports." Joseph took a gulp of coffee. "I edit technical journals, and I did a stint on the promotional side of things, working with the media. I know the publishing business, and how news reports are indexed and circulated. Some of these articles were surprisingly hard to find."

"They're all hard to find," Charles said, "unless you know what you're looking for."

"I know. That's just regular needle in a haystack stuff, but usually the right search terms will dig them up. What I'm talking about takes obscurity to a new level. These articles that caught my eye would be so far down *any* search that they may as well not exist."

"So, how did *you* find them?"

"I was coming from a different starting point. I was looking for records of suspicious deaths. These coroner reports are public record and reli-ably indexed. Not dependent on automated search crawlers. Often they link directly to related media coverage. Search ranking doesn't matter, but unless you know exactly where to look, and follow a direct link, the media reports I noticed are effectively buried from sight."

"Let me get this straight." After days on the run, it seemed an effort to Charles to kick his analytical mind back into action. "Out of all the reports you pulled up, just some of them seemed to be trying to stay hidden?"

Joseph nodded. "Most reports had the usual entries in the major search engines. Then there was this handful that had been tampered with."

"Tampered? How do you come to that conclusion?"

"I can't see how this can happen by accident. Someone deliberately suppressed these reports by stripping out metadata and adjusting their search ranking. It's way more subtle than deleting the records themselves. They're still there, and anyone who knows they're there and pulls them up by any direct means will find them, so no suspicions aroused. But unless you already know about them, they are invisible to the world at large."

"Hmmm." Charles glanced at Serena, but her expression was intent. No hint of disbelief. "I'll have to bow to your knowledge here."

"This is where it gets scary." Joseph drained his mug and held it out to Serena to refill. "Now I had a pattern to look for, I spent all night working through the latest refinement. I've singled out all the accident reports that fit this publicity profile. When you know what to look for, the tampering is highly distinctive."

Serena sat at the table and leaned forward, face set in concentration.

"It doesn't take a statistician to analyze this." Joseph's voice cracked. He accompanied his words with staccato waves of his hands. "Every disappearance on our list is followed, within two days or less, by one of these ghost accidents. Our disappearances are far enough apart in time for the pattern to stand out." A tear dripped from the corner of a red-rimmed eye. "Tiamat didn't just freak out gamers she caught. She killed them for real, and then covered her tracks."

CHAPTER 24

Serena gazed out the window. She seemed preoccupied with something on the wall opposite, but Charles recognized that vacant look. "So, what we have is a global epidemic of mechanical murder over at least two decades." Her calm tone jarred with the ghoulish discovery. "But they all look like freak accidents, and each incident is so isolated that anyone who knows about it will assume it's a local one-off. There's nothing to bring these as a whole to anyone's attention, to allow them to connect the dots."

Her voice trailed off into silence. Charles held up a finger when Joseph looked like he was about to say something. At last, his patience was rewarded.

"Joseph, new line of inquiry." Serena's voice had a distant, dreamy quality. "Can you recognize this tampering well enough to search for it?"

Joseph frowned, scratched his head, then slouched over to the sink and splashed cold water over his face. He absently grabbed a tea towel and sat again, deep in thought. "You mean as a primary search term, don't you? No other qualifying criteria?"

With a roll of her eyes, Serena snatched the tea towel from his hands before he could mop his face with it, and swapped it for a hand towel. "If that means, sniff out any old news articles out there that have been tampered with in this same way, then yes."

"What are you looking for?" asked Charles.

"Not entirely sure." Serena chewed her lip. "I just wonder if there might be other kinds of incidents that maybe didn't get reported as a fatality, but might be related."

Joseph ground his knuckles into his eyes, then shook his head. "Dammit. I think I can do it—I *think!*—but have you any idea how big a search you're asking for?"

Charles put on his best lecturing voice. "Regardless, young man, I strongly suggest that you follow this line of inquiry." An idea struck him. "But before you get started, there's something else you can help me with."

He caught Serena's puzzled look.

"I need to call in reinforcements," he said. "I've been wondering how to go about that without identifying myself online."

"What do you need Joseph for, Professor? I can do that right now!"

"Dammit, Serena, haven't you been listening? There's a killer out there, and she ... he ... whoever, seems to have taken a dislike to anthropologists as well as gamers. I want you to stay offline as much as possible."

"But that's why you ran after me in the first place. You wanted my help to contact your colleague."

"I did so with great reluctance because I fear it might be dangerous, but at that point I didn't see an alternative."

Serena opened her mouth to respond. Joseph forestalled her. "Umm, I hate to say this, but I think the Prof may have a point."

Serena glared daggers. Joseph shrugged. "An active handheld is easily traceable. I suggest you keep yours switched off as much as possible just on general principles. And definitely stay away from Typhoon from now on. Even contacting the university might be dodgy. We just don't know."

"But do you think you'd be okay?" Charles asked.

"I'm using a handheld and account that has no connection back to me."

Charles did a mental calculation. "It must be early afternoon in England. As good a time as any to give it a try."

"Whoa! Even with a supposedly clean handheld I'm still taking precautions." Joseph drained his coffee and stood. "Grab your coats. We're going for a walk."

The walk turned into a bit of a meander. Joseph seemed to be picking his route with care, and he jumped when Charles touched him on the shoulder. "You seem to be worried about the street cameras." Charles gestured to the end of the street where a bright yellow box stood atop a pole.

Joseph shrugged. "I can't get rid of the feeling I'm being watched."

"Is that a serious possibility?" Serena eyed the camera. "The civil protection network. I've always thought of them as old friends."

While they skulked along the shelter of the covered sidewalk, Charles said, "Presumably they can be hacked, just like anything else on the network?"

Joseph grunted.

"Even so," Charles said, "is there any reason anyone would be looking this way, right now? If you were trying to find someone, there's got to be easier ways than watching thousands of camera feeds for hours on end."

"They might not need to," Joseph muttered. "These cameras are designed to identify storm damage ... things like floods and landslides, fallen trees, collapsed roads and buildings. They have software that recognizes threats and brings them to public services' attention."

"So?"

"That's new tech, built on the new network, but way back when, similar algorithms could pick out a face in the crowd."

"Anti-terrorism." Ice ran between Charles's shoulder blades. "The turn of the century was rife with government-sponsored fear-mongering. Any chance that technology is still in use?"

"Who knows?" Joseph glanced around the next corner and waved them across the street. "Tiamat seems to prefer the modern parts of the network. She only seems to notice immersive avatars and never bothers other users. This kind of thing has no practical use in today's world. It's old. Hopefully forgotten."

All the same, Charles thought, it's got you worried.

After a few blocks, Joseph led them across a park to a picnic shelter. Six sturdy carved totems supported a steeply-sloping roof. Joseph perched on the edge of a picnic table. "Okay, Prof, what's this colleague's code?"

"Aah, well," Charles said. "Slight problem. That information was all on my handheld, last seen disappearing into the sea somewhere between Iceland and Scotland. I'd hoped to look up her internal account from the university network."

"Well, instead we're out here, freezing our butts off, with the public index to play with. Surname?"

"Stoppard." Charles spelled it out for him.

"Okay, time for some more old school crap," Joseph grumbled. He gazed into the middle distance, fingers working his handheld. "So, that's Stoppard, Professor ..."

"Gwen," said Charles. "Gwendolyn. Professor of Computation, Oxford University."

Joseph muttered to himself. His breath formed clouds in the morning stillness. He snorted in exasperation, then muttered some more.

Just as Charles felt his patience stretching thin, Joseph smiled. "Hah, got it. She seems to value her privacy." His eyes came back into focus. "I had to trawl a few unlisted directories to find a contact code."

"Unlisted?" Charles frowned. "I can't remember off-hand how many years I've known Gwen. She's always been reachable to me, to colleagues, to students. Strange. Never thought about beyond the university, but it fits with what I know of her. Yes, she does value her privacy."

Joseph rubbed warmth into his hands. "I'm ready to try giving her a call, but you'll need to tell me what to say."

"You do realize I'm making this up one step at a time, don't you?"

"That always worked for me."

Charles chuckled at Joseph's deadpan expression. "So help me out here. I haven't figured out what to say to identify myself to Gwen without giving the game away to any potential eavesdropper. She thinks I'm dead. If a stranger calls up and says I'm not, she'll need convincing. Assuming she doesn't bite your head off first."

Joseph leaped to his feet and paced back and forth across the shelter. "She'll need something to convince her, something private between the two of you. But that's the 'proof' part. Initial contact and ID is the first thing. How to name a thing without using its name." He tapped his teeth, deep in thought. "How does she talk to you? I mean, are you something other than 'Professor Hawthorne' to her? Something less obvious, but something that would be meaningful to her?"

"I hate it, but she always calls me 'Charlie.' "

"Hmm. Bit generic. Might not be unique to her. Can you do better than that? You've known her for years. Close friends?"

Charles nodded.

"So, how about something more ... intimate? Nicknames? Pet names?"

"Well ..." Charles felt his face reddening. "When she really wants to get my goat, it's 'Charlie Boy.' "

Joseph's grin was maddening. "That's good enough to be getting on with. Should at least stop me getting the door slammed in my face. Once I've made contact, we can wing it from there. Some sort of challenge-response kind of thing, until she's convinced I really have got the mad old Prof with me."

Cheeky pup! Charles struggled to frame a retort, but Joseph already had his handheld out.

Minutes passed. Joseph's grin had slipped within seconds of starting work, and his mouth now twisted in frustration. Eventually he scowled and swore under his breath. "Not only is she unlisted, she's surrounded herself with the most damnable barriers and filters."

"Can you get past them?" Serena asked.

"That's what I was trying. Then I poked at them with a few ... aah ... tools of the trade ..."

From the discomfort evident on Joseph's face, Charles decided the details were best kept in the 'need to know' category. He waved Joseph to continue.

"I recognized the signatures of some of the filters she's using. High end privacy stuff. Nobody's getting through unless they meet criteria that she's set. Criteria that we don't know how to meet."

"Let me understand this," said Charles. "You're saying that you can't even place a call to Gwen's account."

"On my own, here and now, that's about the size of it." Joseph glanced at Serena. "To answer your question, there are ways to hack past filters like this, but I need the tools and know-how of some of my clan. It'll take time." He grimaced. "I really need Moonshadow."

Charles felt a pang at the pain in Joseph's voice. "Let's keep that path in our back pocket for now. You mentioned criteria. I think we're not as much in the dark as you assume. I've never heard of anyone having trouble contacting Gwen from *inside* the university network."

He looked at Joseph, then Serena. "We passed by a café on the way here. Time for some breakfast, then I think we need a Plan B."

CHAPTER 25

For the twentieth time, Charles glanced at his reflection in a passing window. After a shower and shave, he looked respectable for the first time in a week. He'd left the stubble in place around his mouth and chin, and now sported the beginnings of a goatee, but he still looked too recognizable for comfort.

"Pops, this city only has a low-grade street cam network." Serena nudged Charles in the ribs, jolting him back to reality. "The best way to be conspicuous is to look like you're trying not to be." Her light tone couldn't quite hide the edge in her voice.

"Joseph's zealous paranoia is somewhat infectious." Charles allowed himself a twisted smile. "Even for someone they really are out to get."

He tried to put Joseph's surveillance concerns into perspective. On a practical level, he decided that this was a risk outside his control. If Tiamat could deploy face recognition through the city's cameras, he would probably have already been spotted. If not, then scanning camera feeds by eye would be a shot in a million.

Besides, she thought he was dead. There was no reason she would even be looking for him.

"Just remember what we agreed," Serena whispered, as they approached the entrance. "Stick close by me, especially when we go through the card-locked door at the back of the lodge. If anyone asks, you're my grandfather, Pops." She grinned, an impish curl of the lips. "Act confused and let me do the talking."

A wave of panic swept over Charles. He was not used to sneaking around; surely there had to be another way to get him into the building without some kind of identity check. But that obstacle was what had held him back in the first place.

Before he could say anything, Serena was striding through the door. Charles cursed to himself, feeling like he was being pushed off a precipice. He caught the door before it closed, and hurried to follow.

He hesitated inside, bewildered. What Serena referred to as the 'lodge' was not what he'd expected. He'd assumed he would be able to hurry past a tiny window, maybe with the porter's view half-obscured by Serena ahead of him. Oxford college porters were more sharp-eyed than people gave them credit for, but they rarely questioned someone walking through with enough self-assurance.

Charles felt his last shreds of self-assurance desert him. The room inside was wide open, with a broad desk to his right. He felt fully exposed to the piercing gaze of the grey-haired woman behind it.

Serena was already half-way across the floor.

Erik Thorsen would be proud of you … not! Charles swallowed, and scanned the room like he owned it, careful to avoid eye contact with the woman. He clasped his hands behind his back and marched towards the door Serena seemed to be heading for.

From the corner of his eye, he saw the woman's face register disbelief. He reached the door just ahead of Serena. "Allow me." The door unlocked to Serena's pass. Charles opened it with a flourish.

"Hey! Wait!"

He ignored the shrill call and slipped through the door.

Footsteps clacked overhead, echoing down a flight of stairs alongside them. "Change of plan." Serena pointed down stairs leading to the basement level as she whispered, "Stay quiet. I'll meet you in the reading room. South corner."

Charles hurried to obey. He ducked out of sight just as the door behind clicked open. He slowed his pace, hardly breathing.

"Was that man with you?"

"Who?"

Charles stifled a laugh at Serena's vacant tone. She had that innocent act perfected.

"Are you blind? The one who opened the door for you." The wasp voice shrilled in frustration.

"I think someone went up the stairs." The voice seemed to come from another planet. More footsteps overhead seemed to confirm the lie. "Sorry, did you have a message for him? You might catch him if you hurry."

A snarl of exasperation answered her.

Charles didn't wait to hear any more. He slipped down the rest of the stairs and emerged in a corridor dwindling into the distance on either side. A sign on the opposite wall announced 'Stacks' to the left, and 'The Pantry' to the right. Which way was south? Voices clamored down the stairs behind. Doors in the distance on the right banged open to the sound of laughter. Charles turned left and strode away with as much apparent confidence as he could muster.

With a hollow feeling in his gut, he realized he had no idea where the reading room was. At least the stacks sounded bookish. Did they bother to keep hard copy books on site here?

His footsteps sounded like gunshots on the tiled floor. A group of students appeared from a side door and passed Charles, eyeing him curiously. He forced his pace to remain steady, fighting the impulse to glance back. Muted conversation murmured behind him, secretive whispers. The skin between his shoulder blades crawled under imagined scrutiny.

Without thinking, Charles turned down a side passageway, not caring where it led, as long as it was away from curious people. His pace quickened. He had no idea how many students might work here in person, but if it was anything like his home town they would likely know each other by sight. A stranger would be conspicuous, especially wandering alone down here.

Panicked, he ducked down the next side passage to put himself out of sight of that main thoroughfare. This area had an industrial feel to it, painted concrete walls, harsh lighting, and a tangle of pipes overhead. No signs of movement but he couldn't stay here. He paused to gather his thoughts. How long had elapsed since he and Serena had parted ways? Only minutes, he was sure, but she would be waiting for him soon.

The reading room. Where the heck was that? And would it matter if he knew? His sense of direction, bad enough above ground, was hopelessly confused in this subterranean labyrinth.

Should he ask for directions? That would be a natural thing to do, though it might beg unwanted questions. He could still use the fiction of being Serena's grandfather, and claim they got separated when he went looking for a washroom. The cover story wouldn't stand up to scrutiny by the hawk at the front desk, but there was no reason why anyone else would question it.

Unless the old biddy had raised the alarm. The place could be crawling with people looking for him by now. Shouts and more laughter echoed around the corner, sending a shudder through Charles.

Crap! It just sounded like student high spirits. This was a university, not a high-security facility. Besides, there must be a steady stream of visitors on legitimate business. The porter was probably just offended that he didn't check in first.

Charles *belonged* here. He repeated it over and over to himself. This was *his* world. He squared his shoulders, and retraced his steps. When he reached the main hallway, he turned left, in the direction of the stacks. This was *his* world, and no-one could make him believe otherwise.

The hall was busier now. Charles felt a pang. His own college must once have resounded with clattering feet and chattering youth like this. Now it was largely the ghostly preserve of a few die-hard dons dispensing wisdom and learning to remote populations.

"There he is!"

Charles's heart climbed up his throat. Feet sounded closer behind him. A young man, with more than his fair share of simian ancestry, peered into Charles's face from beneath a shaggy mop of black curls. An elfin blonde appeared at his other shoulder.

"Come on," the gorilla said, "Serena's waiting for you."

"Don't look startled, silly. Just follow us." The elf linked arms with Charles and steered him around a corner, avoiding the glass double doors leading to the stacks. "Scruff, let Serena know we've found the errant grandparent."

"Already did."

"You're friends of Serena's?"

"She's got a few of us scouting out for you, before Attila the Bun catches you."

Attila ... an image of the woman at the entrance frowned from beneath severely-tied grey hair. Charles almost choked suppressing a laugh.

"This way," Scruff muttered. "Bandits descending from the library."

"How ... ?" Charles bit off the question as his arm was almost wrenched from its socket. "Never mind. I see."

"Double back to the second staircase." Scruff's eyes had a slightly glazed look. He kept one hand on Charles's shoulder while the elf guided them.

She grinned up at Charles. "Our spies are everywhere."

Another turn, and Charles was hopelessly lost again.

"Wait up." Scruff whispered. They paused at the next corner. Footsteps sounded, receding, slow and measured. "Quick and silent." They tiptoed around the corner.

Charles froze at the sight of a jacket stretched far too tight across muscled shoulder blades. The owner maintained his steady pace away from them, glancing left and right into doorways, but not looking back. The elf high-fived a loitering dreadlocked youth and tugged Charles onto the stairs.

They slunk up one flight, and scampered up the next. "Keep going," said Scruff.

They climbed to the second floor. Charles blinked in sudden sunlight. The elf led them along a wide and airy gallery overlooking a grassed quadrangle. Along the inner wall, in between doors and openings, benches and circles of armchairs sat under portraits and landscapes from another era. Groups of students sat, some talking, some with faces blank to the world of physical reality. A few glanced their way with knowing smiles.

The gallery led them to a second quad, much smaller, which they circled. Their surroundings faded in stages from rich comfort to threadbare austerity. Bare floorboards lay worn underfoot. Paint peeled in hard-to-reach corners.

Scruff grunted. "Navigation's up to you now, Tammy. Don't think I've ever ventured back here into Humanities."

The elf, Tammy, shrugged. "You chemists need to get out a bit more. Live dangerously."

"I thought I was supposed to meet up at the reading room." These two seemed harmless enough, but Charles felt a twinge of anxiety as he thought how completely he was at the mercy of his guides.

"Relax. That was only a rendezvous and it was too obvious anyway. Serena shouldn't try to make things up on the fly like that. Good job she rallied the troops when she realized you'd get lost."

Another staircase twisted up into a dingy and windowless hall. From the outside, Charles only noticed two floors all the way around this sprawling building. They must be up in the angle of the roof.

Light glimmered ahead.

In a narrow alcove, Serena looked around from a wall screen. "Thanks Tammy, thanks Scruff. Can you keep watch for a bit?"

The two escorts vanished into the gloom. Serena's cautioning hand held Charles back as she returned to the screen. "Professor Stoppard, please remember what I said, first names only. We've gone to a lot of trouble to avoid identities being revealed online."

She's found Gwen! Charles stepped alongside Serena.

"Ch— I mean, no, it can't be you."

"Would a pint of Norwegian convince you otherwise?"

She cackled, then sobered. "Your student said you were in big trouble. I assume you are staying away from the All Seeing Eye."

Charles nodded. "Has she told you what happened?"

"No time. I assume it wasn't easy to arrange for this meeting. She'll get me the details in due course. More important right now, I'm relieved to see you're still with us. What do you need from me?"

Charles hesitated. He'd been so busy fretting about step one, making contact safely, that he'd given little thought to step two. "This is going to be hard to swallow, Gwen. We'll get some evidence over to you somehow, but even with what we've found, you're going to think I'm a few trees short of an orchard. I thought so myself, except others have had similar narrow escapes."

Talking things through out loud helped him to think. But where to start? Over the last day, things had become more complicated than he could imagine. "There's something strange afoot in the global network." Charles picked his way through a maze of words and half-formed thoughts. "I guess you know how online gamers roam the network—"

Gwen hissed. "Tell me about it. It's a full time job keeping them out of our plenums and clearing up the damage."

"I see." Charles flinched at the unexpected venom in Gwen's voice. "And I thought Terry was just taking it all too seriously."

Gwen's lips curled back, baring her teeth. She shook her head.

"Well, what would you think if I told you that someone was giving you a helping hand?"

"More power to their elbow! I've always said the service providers should find a way to police network activity outside of the managed plenums."

"Okay, but what if I told you this was more vigilante style, involving summary executions of offenders."

"Wait up." Gwen leaned close. "What do you mean by that last bit? What does a 'summary execution' look like online? Delete their avatar? Trash their service account? Serves 'em right, I say."

Charles pressed his lips tight. His head shook, just the slightest of movements, but Gwen's eyes narrowed. She grew very still.

"I'm talking about very real murder. Accidents happen to people. Real people in the real world."

The silence dragged on. Gwen chewed the inside of her cheek, her expression unreadable, while Charles wondered just how stupid he must have sounded.

"I'm having a hard time with this." Gwen ran garish fingernails through spiky hair. "But you mentioned some evidence, I'll let that speak for itself. All the same, assuming this is for real, and not some aberration or artifact, why would anyone go to such extremes to deal with a few gamers?"

"I don't think it's as aimless as you make it sound, Professor." Serena's voice quavered, but she swallowed and pressed on. "We've mapped out the online activity, and it's not totally random. It's as if someone took a map of the network, drew a boundary around a big chunk of it, and put up 'keep out' signs around it. In anthropological terms, it's classic territorial behavior."

"I agree," said Charles. "Someone's trying to hide something down there, and is prepared to deal harshly with intruders. This kind of ruthlessness feels like big time organized crime. And," he gave Gwen a stern look, "it's not just 'a few gamers', it's hundreds!"

"Where do you come into all of this? Unless you've been leading a double life, the person I knew had trouble with a handheld, let alone an avatar."

Charles grunted. "Good question. Let's start with what happened to me. Remember, this was all before I knew anything about any gamers, that's something I just found out about yesterday."

He rapidly recounted the incidents in New Denmark, including the mail plane decoy that led to his official death. He found it easier to talk about this time, distanced by repeated telling. In fact, the whole thing was starting to feel like some bizarre fiction until Serena intervened.

"You'll want to check up on these accidents, of course, but if they are related to the gamer deaths then I suspect you'll find the news reports hard to track down." Serena's eyes took on a distant look, and her fingers twitched and shifted on the grip of her handheld. "There. I've sent you *direct* links to the news journals that ran articles on those incidents. I bet you a month's worth of essays in a subject of your choice that you will not be able to find them through any regular search."

Gwen gave a twisted smile. "I always knew you anthropology types were a bit loose in the logic department. Are you in the habit of betting on impossibilities?" Her smile inverted when Serena sat back, arms folded, with a defiant pout. "You're serious, aren't you?"

"Deadly," said Charles. "And yet I have no idea why I was targeted. As you say, I'm not exactly known for my online presence. All the same, someone out there has it in for me and I assume it's related. For some reason they've turned the spotlight on Typhoon, and anyone associated with it."

"Hmm. That may be a non-issue soon. With you and Terry gone, the council has agreed to delete Typhoon."

"Delete ... ?" The room seemed to tilt. Charles staggered, and gripped Serena's chair back.

"Charlie! Your use of the cloud has risen tenfold in the last month. There was no way that could go unnoticed."

"That can't be right." Someone else seemed to be talking, as if in another room. "If anything, we've been taking it more slowly while we sort out glitches." The arguments, lines of logic, assembled themselves in the distance while Charles's world reeled. Delete Typhoon? All that effort, a career devoted to this modeling approach, gone? And they were so close, too.

Gwen sucked her teeth. "That's not what last week's invoices say."

Anger boiled against the reefs of despair. It was disrespectful. Terry was dead. He was supposedly dead. All major research experiments, even incomplete ones, usually got archived for posterity. Deletion? That was an act of dismissal.

Gwen must have read some of the emotions crowding Charles's mind. "Listen, Charlie, you've got to report in. You've been keeping your experiments too close to your chest all this time. The university has some patience for blue-sky research but it needs some idea what the point is. Only *you* can make that case."

"I can't." Misery dulled the anger. Gwen was right. "I'm damned close to reporting something bigger than I ever imagined. Maybe I've got enough to convince the council, but if I show myself now I won't live long enough to make that presentation."

"You really do believe that, don't you?"

Charles nodded. "From the incidents I've seen, the people behind this are shockingly quick. It's superhuman." He shivered. "If I can be identified online, my life is probably measured in hours."

"Then we'd better work out how to keep you safe."

"What about Typhoon? Can you stall them?"

"The one thing stopping them from blowing the whole thing away is they haven't figured how to. Yet." Vividly-patterned fingernails drummed a distant tabletop. "That thing has some highly irregular roots into the infrastructure, and they don't think they can untangle it without damaging other plenums in the cloud."

"Good for Terry." The words stuck in Charles's throat. "So, what happens next?"

"Malachi has a team trying to break in through your damnable security." Gwen's lips quirked. "I've never seen him so frustrated."

"Uh-oh." Serena glanced up at Charles. "Looks like the search is heading our way."

"How long do you think it'll take?"

"Hard to say—" Gwen started.

"Two minutes," Serena cut in.

Both Charles and Gwen stared at Serena.

"Gwen," Charles said, trying to sort out a thousand thoughts competing for attention. "I need to stay off grid, can't let the authorities here know about me. I need your help. It will mean going against Malachi, and it could be dangerous if you catch their eye. I don't know where this might end up. I'll understand if you say no ..." He trailed off, feeling helpless.

She chewed her lip, then nodded. "Providing your evidence stacks up. Otherwise I'm putting in a call to the funny farm."

"Understood. I'll get Serena to drop off more details later, meanwhile do you have any students you can trust? I don't want anyone placed in the line of fire, but there's a lot to figure out that might take computational skills. One more thing," Charles hastened to add, under the intensity of Serena's glare. "Please get hold of my other students and warn them to stay away from Typhoon."

Without waiting for an answer, Serena cut the connection and shooed Charles out of the alcove. He started heading back the way they'd entered, then stopped when Serena hissed. She stood, eyes unfocused, then beckoned in the opposite direction.

A few paces along, Serena froze, and held a finger to her lips. "I think they're just patrolling the second floor. Unlikely to come up here unless they hear something, but footsteps will sound like crazy on these boards."

They waited, ears straining, for ten minutes before Serena moved again. "All clear on this wing, but we'll have to leave by the back gate. Main lodge is being watched."

"Why the heck didn't we come in that way in the first place?" Charles grumbled. "We could have saved a lot of fuss."

"Exit only. Only staff cards will open it from the outside. We can leave by several different gates, but everyone has to enter through the lodge."

They tiptoed to the next staircase and descended. Serena paused on each landing, to listen and to check reports from the handful of friends watching the movements of security staff.

When they reached the ground floor, Serena leaned up to murmur in Charles's ear. "Not far now, but absolute silence. I don't have anyone watching this level. Anyone loitering is too obvious." She slipped into a stone-flagged corridor. Charles followed.

As they approached a corner, Serena pulled a short tube from her pocket. It looked rather like a flashlight, but the business end swiveled on a ball joint. "Pocket camera," she whispered, seeing Charles's curious look. She twisted the camera lens at right angles to the hand grip, and poked it around the corner. The fingers of her other hand worked her handheld. "Shit," she muttered, as she withdrew and pocketed the camera. "Campbell's lurking near the gate."

"Need some help?"

Charles jumped at the low voice. Scruff grinned over his shoulder.

Before he could say anything, Tammy sauntered past. "I've got this one."

She disappeared around the corner. Charles's pulse hammered in his throat. He strained to hear dainty footsteps receding. "Hello, Mr. Campbell," a sunny voice called. A few seconds later, a chilling scream cut the air.

"That's our cue," whispered Scruff.

They crept around the corner. Charles glimpsed the back of an over-stuffed jacket vanishing at speed around the far end of the corridor.

"Oh! I'm sorry to startle you, Mr. Campbell." Breathless words floated back as they slipped into the alcove leading to the outside world.

"I watched *Vapor* last night, and I'm all of a tizz today. I felt a draught on my cheek and it made me jump. It's nothing, really."

"I'd better see if I can help." Scruff smirked. "That was a good scary vid, too."

Serena blew him a kiss, and pushed Charles through the gate.

Joseph signed off, disconnected his handheld, and tried to soften the scowl masking his face. His demeanor was scaring the locals. A young mother with a stroller looked at him with wide-eyed alarm and positioned herself between him and her children as he passed on the sidewalk. Her hand slipped unobtrusively into the top of her shoulder bag.

Joseph mumbled, "Excuse me," doing his best to appear unthreatening, and walked on with a tingling sensation between his shoulder blades. Did people still carry weapons this side of the country? And did he really look that bad? His reflection in a nearby window confirmed the worst. He straightened his shoulders, held his head high, and sought a happy place in the turmoil of his mind.

It had been days since he last spoke to Pink. He'd checked in with her briefly when he reached New Boston to let her know he'd found Serena safe, and he'd been buried in his research ever since. Research that he almost wished he hadn't started. What he'd uncovered scared him witless. Online damage was one thing, but, in his supposedly harmless ventures, how often had he come close to an ugly end?

At least Pink had stayed safe. After this morning's revelations he felt giddy relief at the sound of her voice. Not for the first time, he wondered what she'd be like to meet in real life. Her soft voice, so unlike the sharp tones of her avatar, gave him a warm glow.

The scowl crept back as he reviewed their conversation. Deacon, the unofficial leader of his gamer clan, wanted nothing to do with Tiamat. Without Deacon's support, they could expect very little help.

Even knowing the true extent of the danger, which they discussed at some length, Pink had been dubious about talking Deacon around. "He's obsessed with the gamer code," she'd repeated yet again. "Online is the only reality that matters. Any mention of the world outside will dig him in even further. He'll shut me down before I get two words out."

"Then you'll have to work around him. Spread the word to people you can trust. The clan needs to know about the danger."

"I can't do this on my own, Tinny. You're so much better at getting people to help."

The pleading in her voice tugged at Joseph. This was so unlike the fearless, reckless, Pink Marie he knew. But he could understand her fear only too well. "I've tangled with Old Red. You haven't. She doesn't know you and I'm doing my best to keep it that way. You should still be safe as long as you don't meet her face to face, but I have to be more careful."

"You've managed to stay out of her way. You can drop out of sight and move towns to stay hidden. I don't have that luxury," she whispered. "My world is online. Pink Marie can look after herself there. Out here in the real world, it's a different matter. I'm just not that person."

"I understand, but I'm depending on you, Pink. This isn't a game any more."

"No, Tinny, you *don't* understand." She'd sounded sad as she cut the connection.

Joseph sighed, and paused to get his bearings. His musings had distracted him from his real world wanderings. He scanned the street, the low buildings, peeling paintwork, and sidewalks sheltered by deep overhanging eaves. An antique bookshop caught his eye, a distinctive store front. He knew where he was, and was glad to see his autopilot had brought him close to home.

Two blocks further on, Joseph spotted Charles and Serena. He hurried to catch up, wondering at the daft grins they wore. "Good news then?"

The grins slipped.

Charles recounted his conversation at the university.

"How long did this Professor Stoppard reckon they'd take to break into Typhoon?" Joseph struggled to force the words past a knot in his throat. How the heck was he going to get his avatar out?

"Gwen says Malachi has his students working on it."

"And?"

The grin returned. "One or two of *his* students are also *her* students."

"Aah." The knot loosened. Joseph reminded himself that the Prof had far more to lose than he did. "Before I forget ..." he dug in his pocket. "A gift for you, Professor."

Charles took the proffered handheld and turned it over in his hands, studying the worn grip. He snuggled it into his palm, but kept his fingers off the controls.

"Well done, Joseph," said Serena.

They stopped at Serena's door. Charles looked from one to the other while she ushered them into the house. "You two been conspiring to bring me into this century?"

"Serena thought it might be handy for you."

"I'm trying to stay hidden, remember?" Charles held the device at arm's length as though it might bite him.

Joseph sucked his teeth, an exaggerated expression. "Well, it's a good job this is registered to a Mr. Tom Cobley, residing at a street address that would put him about three miles offshore." He took the handheld from Charles. "Let's get this baby linked to your implants, then I'll show you some of the features I've installed."

Serena fetched beers from the fridge. "I hope you didn't spend all morning shopping!"

"What?" Joseph looked around, distracted. "Oh, you mean my other assignment. I configured a search, and rented time at a netcaf downtown to set it running. I told you it will take a while. I'll drop in tomorrow to pick up the results."

Charles and Serena exchanged glances. "Just because you're paranoid ..." she said.

"Doesn't mean they're not out to get you," Charles added.

"You've dodged snow ploughs and boiling oil." Joseph's voice was low and level. "You, of all people, should know better."

Serena giggled, a helpless and infectious sound.

Despite the shock of Gwen's news, Charles smothered a chuckle. "Sorry, Joseph. We've just spent the morning sneaking around the university like secret agents. I'm still pumped with adrenalin, and it's a bit difficult to take things seriously when you've been chased by Attila the Bun."

J oseph leaned on the moss-clad wall surrounding a viewpoint in the middle of the park. Serena in particular had grumbled at being dragged outdoors again, but Joseph had insisted.

"Have you got everything ready?" Charles asked Serena for at least the tenth time.

Joseph wished Charles would calm down. It was a beautiful day. The chill air was clean and bracing. It reminded him of winter in the Yukon.

Serena gave Charles a pitying look. Joseph wondered how she did it. Her round and pale face would normally put a professional poker player to shame, yet she could mould her features into remarkable expressions when the occasion demanded.

Charles stopped pacing the stone slabs of the viewpoint. "Don't get smart. I fear Joseph's right to be cautious. We need to ration our communications and make them count."

Now he agrees!

"I've got the files with all our searches," said Serena, "and Joseph's analysis of the tampering. Now, question for you. Do you think Professor Stoppard will pick up my call?"

"She knows you now, and she's expecting to hear from you ..." Charles cocked an eyebrow at Joseph.

Joseph shrugged. "As long as she's added your account to her filters, we're good. If not ... Well, only one way to find out."

Serena chewed her lip. "It's getting late."

"And only you students aren't tucked up with a bedtime cocoa beyond nine o'clock?" Charles softened his withering tone. "Don't worry, Gwen's scary, but she's reliable."

The three of them linked handhelds into a private conference while Serena called Professor Stoppard.

Joseph scanned the horizon from their vantage point. In the distance, through thickets still waiting for their spring green to appear, the roof of the shelter they'd used previously was just visible. The only sound from the real world was a muted hum of afternoon traffic. It was difficult to imagine any danger here, but still he stayed alert.

"Dammit, Serena!" An acid voice broke the expectant hush. "Have you ever tried operating a handheld with wet nails?"

Serena blanched. Charles threw back his head and roared with laughter; a tinge of color returned to her cheeks. "I'm sorry, I was admiring those nails yesterday. They're works of art. I hope they aren't smudged." Serena's voice was exactly the right blend of admiration and contrition.

Joseph eased the tension that had crept into his shoulders.

"Listen, Professor Stoppard, before you say anything, we've decided on some protocols to help protect the innocent."

Joseph studied Charles's face with interest. He reckoned this bit of paranoia would be too much for the old man to swallow, so he'd only discussed it with Serena. She seemed tickled by the cloak and dagger elements.

"We want to avoid certain names triggering any kind of monitoring going on. You and I are probably okay, and we're already identified by our accounts, but your beer-drinking friend is henceforth known as 'The Norwegian'—"

Charles spluttered. His face reddened. Joseph grinned.

"Our mutual winged friend is 'Old Red', and the place slated for demolition is 'Area Fifty-One'. Have you got all that?"

"Oh! You kids."

"I think you'll see some sense in it when you read what I'm sending you."

A pause, then, "Got the files. Thanks. I'll look into it as soon as we've finished here. Meanwhile, aah, Norwegian, what can I do to help?"

"Not sure." Charles's voice was quiet. "Ideas mainly. We have to be careful with our online access, you can work more freely. I want to find out who's behind this. Maybe there's some kind of trail leading back from these reports, or some other evidence surrounding the incidents." He shrugged, even though the distant professor couldn't see him. "Not much to go on, I'm afraid. If you can come up with any other angles that would be great. I don't fancy living the rest of my life as a fugitive."

"One other angle does come to mind. Old Red herself. Has anyone investigated her directly?"

"Yes," said Joseph.

"Who's this?" The tone could have curdled milk.

"I'm, umm..."

"Terminator," said Serena, with a sly grin. "A friend of mine."

"Thanks, Serena." Joseph shot her a poisonous look. "Anyway, The Norwegian's colleague tried to catch her. There's a set of recordings in Area Fifty-One."

"Right. I'll need access."

Charles paled. His mouth worked with indecision.

"You realize what it means if the wrong person gets access?" Serena seemed to be speaking as much for Charles's benefit as Professor Stoppard's.

"I'm asking for something that Malachi would sell his soul to get hold of." Professor Stoppard spoke with surprising gentleness. "I know how much this is to ask. You'll have to trust I'll be careful."

Charles heaved a sigh and glanced at Serena. Serena sent the encrypted token containing Typhoon's access key.

"While you're at it," Joseph said, "maybe you could look into what it is about Area Fifty-One that Old Red doesn't like. You'll see what I mean when you examine the records."

"Anything else your obedient servant can do for you while she's at it?" The Professor's voice was honey-coated razor wire.

Goosebumps crept up Joseph's arms, but he held his voice steady. "Yes. Can you do something about your filters in case we need to reach you from another account?" A glow of satisfaction warmed him when Charles gave him an approving nod.

After a long silence, Professor Stoppard answered. "Seeing as we're playing cloak and dagger games, address messages to 'Madame Claw' in the salutation, and I'll make sure they get through."

Joseph skimmed the news reports he'd spent the last few hours sorting and cataloguing. The three of them hunched over a table in a crowded coffee shop, steaming mugs in front of them, sharing Joseph's documents with their handhelds linked into a conference.

"I delved back in time to see when this all started. The accident reports seem to start about thirty years ago, which I guess makes sense because that's when the new generation of immersive interfaces became popular." He studied Charles's expression as he said this, and was rewarded with a flicker of a grimace. "But there were other kinds of reports that had been doctored. It's not just accidents Tiamat's been hiding."

"Oh?" Charles showed interest.

Serena gave Joseph a smug look.

With a sinking feeling he realized she already knew that. Why else send him on this hunt in the first place? The Prof had said something about intuition. "One group caught my eye, because it's kinda my field of interest." *And I wonder just how far her intuition stretches.* "Ever heard about some new invention that you felt sure would take the world by storm, only to see it vanish without trace?"

Serena frowned. *Looks like she wasn't expecting this.*

"I edit engineering journals, so I see a lot of cutting-edge research. Much of it never gets taken any further. Some of it is plain old practicality, or economics, but some discoveries are so obviously brilliant, it's hard to explain why they never make it."

Charles and Serena pored over the list, neatly grouped by fields of endeavor. After a few minutes, Charles whistled. "I don't pretend to understand the details, but I get a feeling that if even a fraction of this work was developed further, we'd have licked our energy and food shortages twenty years ago."

The Prof was quick. Joseph pursed his lips. It had taken him half an hour to reach the same conclusion. "It doesn't stop there. From what I've seen so far, advances in computing technology are a mixed bag. Raw power is advancing, but buried in here are radical new information architectures that could have leap-frogged us into the next century. Why would anyone want to stop that?"

"Vested interests."

Joseph puzzled over Serena's sour tone and persistent scowl. She must have been fishing for something else. Then he thought about what she'd said. "That makes sense. Or rather, it doesn't, but it fits the facts. It's as if Tiamat is deliberately holding us back. We advance just enough to feel like we're making progress, but anything that would make a real difference gets squashed."

The frown deepened. "And you're sure it's the same work?"

Joseph squinted at Serena. "Are you doubting my competence?"

"Oh, I didn't mean—"

"Relax. Just teasing," Joseph said. "Yes. The way the reports were doctored fits the same profile. That's what I was searching for, remember?"

She shrugged. "I'm surprised they go so far back, that's all. If this is the work of one person, they've been bloody persistent."

"And exceptionally long lived," said Charles. "However, I don't see that as an issue. I had my doubts that all those accidents could have been arranged by one person. This has to be the work of an organization. Something ruthless, with reach and staying power."

Joseph's spine tingled. His eyes tried to take in the café's clientele without being obtrusive. Loud laughter behind startled him. Every word, every glance, suddenly seemed directed towards them, loaded with menace. "You mean, organized crime?" His voice barely carried. It didn't need to. His words, though only subvocalized, were picked up by jaw implants and carried loud and clear to his compatriots.

"I don't know." Charles seemed to have thrown off half his weight in years. His posture was like a cobra coiled to strike. "Crime, corporations, government. We need a motive. There must be something linking these themes together. What else did you find?"

"Well, those caught my eye because of my line of work, but that's not the biggest cluster I found. This lot here," Joseph pulled up a new list, "from even earlier on in the century really puzzles me. Seems a lot of climate reports and studies got the treatment too."

Charles spluttered. Joseph looked over in alarm, but the Professor wasn't choking, just struggling to form words.

"Joseph," Charles finally managed to say, "where was that netcaf you used?"

"The only reason to tell you that is to make sure we go somewhere else." Joseph had developed an almost fanatical determination to not spend too much time online in any one spot. "There's another one two blocks away. Why?"

It was Serena who answered, with a smile like a cat with a canary. "I think the Professor has found what he's been looking for."

"Let's not jump to conclusions." The words were cautious, but the Professor's face radiated suppressed energy. "But Serena's right. This *could* be the missing piece of the puzzle. An influence we knew nothing about, that could explain why the simulation keeps diverging from reality. We need to get into Typhoon."

"Whoa! What?"

"No avatars. Old fashioned screen work, that's how I work anyway, but I do need a big screen to play with."

"Hold on a moment." The edge in Serena's voice chilled Joseph. "I've forwarded this latest information to Professor Stoppard and picked up a message from her. We've got a problem. Ty—, I mean Area Fifty-One's gone."

CHAPTER 29

Charles's jaw hung open. He looked like he'd just been sentenced to life for jaywalking.

"Slow down," muttered Joseph. "You just pushed the Prof into coronary territory. Just how 'gone' do you mean? Let's have facts only, please, no speculation."

Serena's face went blank. "The message reads, and I quote, 'The portal to Area Fifty-One has been deleted. I checked with another of the Norwegian's students …' I guess she must mean Michael or Lauren, '… and they confirmed they can no longer find it.' "

"Yeah. Thought so. The turn of phrase says it all. That's a long way from gone. And it's the first thing I'd have done, too, with something I wanted to get rid of."

"You mean Typhoon might still be there?" The look of hope on Charles's face was both comical and tragic.

"Dammit, Professor, remember the protocols." Joseph swallowed his frustration. How could someone so clever be so damned dumb at times? "And, yes, I reckon they've just blocked up the front door. I've seen the security your friend had in there, and I doubt if some group of students will have broken past it yet. Moonshadow had trouble, and he was a scary talented hacker."

Charles scowled. "Those students are bright."

"It takes more than brilliant minds and theory, Professor. Have any of them wormed past Homeland Security defenses without getting caught? That takes practical experience and superhuman cunning." Joseph felt cold inside as he thought through what needed to be done. "Serena, let Madame Claw know we might be able to let her in another way. I'll give you directions to pass on, but I need to check a few things and make some calls of my own first."

Joseph screwed his eyes shut and reviewed the hectic afternoon of calls and preparations. It was hard to dispel the haunting feeling that he'd overlooked something in his haste. He mentally shrugged and tried to settle himself on the hard plastic and tubular steel bench at the back of the netcaf. A faint whiff of bleach hung in the air. Serena had led them to a shining and clinical establishment, all polished surfaces and lights, for two reasons: it was mercifully quiet, and it sported booths with unusually large screens for the Prof's benefit. Comfort hadn't factored into it.

He wiped sweat from his palms and looked at the other two. "Ready?"

"As ready as I'll ever be." Charles frowned, and jerked his head towards the screen. "How safe is this?"

Joseph bit back the retort on his lips, and hesitated. "You didn't ask, 'is this safe?' "

"Clearly it isn't, so what would be the point of such a question? I ask in relative terms, not absolute."

Joseph shook his head, bemused. The old buzzard had some bizarre attitudes to risk. "My old handheld might have been compromised if Old Red made a connection between the temporary avatar she caught and my real account. Unlikely, but no way to tell for sure."

"And you can create a secure portal from Area Fifty-One that we can sign on to here?"

"That's the least of my concerns. I'm more worried about the university folks who are going through the back door in immersive mode. I tried to talk them out of it, but they insisted." *As I knew they would*, he added to himself. If these students were anything like gamers, they'd hardly know how to work online without their avatars.

Charles shook his head, eyes downcast. "We've done what we can for them."

"Look. I need to get to work." Joseph rubbed his hands fiercely on his pants one last time. The grip of his gamer handheld felt strange after so long using black market models, but it soon snuggled into his palms like an old friend. Without giving himself time for second thoughts he launched into the virtual realm and woke his metallic avatar. He was Tin Man once more.

The faux railway station looked unchanged, except the rain had stopped and glimpses of blue shone through the grey clouds above the glass vaults. He double-checked the chat lines he had open, a three-way conference with Serena and the Prof, and a private line to Pink Marie. "I'm in. It's still here." His voice was a whisper, as if speaking aloud might break the fragile spell that held the simulation together. Past the audio implants, Joseph heard three sighs of relief.

Up in Typhoon's control room, he found the security console. Back with his gamer avatar and its accumulated stock of illicit tools, it was a matter of minutes to open up a direct portal into an unused corner of virtual space and secure it from intruders.

"Here's the address." Joseph reeled off a long sequence of numbers and letters for Serena to copy, and waited patiently while she double-checked them. "Go straight there from the booth, and you should be in. The only way someone can trace this is if they stumble directly over one of the end points." The nape of his neck prickled. "Remember, I'm blind. I trust one of you is keeping an eye on the outside world?"

Joseph was hardly reassured by the excited muttering alongside him. Serena and the Prof seemed too eager to bury themselves in their theoretical work to worry about such mundane things as personal safety. "Not so fast, Serena. Are you in contact with the tech-heads?"

An elbow dug him in the ribs. "All eager and waiting. Snap it up please, Terminator, we want to get this show moving."

"Okay," he murmured. "Pink? You're up."

"On it, Tinny. We're in the under-layer now, almost reached the back door to Typhoon." A long pause. "Yep. Tiamat's still camped out here. The crew's going into action."

"Thanks for doing this, Pink. Be careful."

"Hey! I passed on your instructions verbatim, from the maestro of prudent cowardice himself. These are all disposable avatars run from bootleg handhelds registered to fictitious nonentities. And we've loaded ourselves up with hacks to mess up her audio-visuals real good."

"All the same ..." Joseph murmured to himself. He was relieved to hear her devil-may-care attitude return at last. When he'd first talked to Pink about this plan, she'd freaked in a most un-Pink-like manner. Somewhere the other side of the world, a very frightened woman sat behind the brash persona. Well, he could understand a certain healthy measure of self-preservation, but if things went badly they could easily hide off-grid, or switch identities. There were lots of small, remote settlements on the northern fringes of the Old States, for example, where pioneers were reclaiming habitable land just like the Prof's family was doing up in New Denmark.

Frustrated, he listened to Pink directing the small band of gamers closing in on Tiamat. They were out there, just beyond the boundaries of Typhoon, so near in virtual terms. He wished he could join them, but he couldn't afford to compromise his avatar and handheld. He had his own work to do. He tried to picture what was happening just from Pink's audio feed.

"Grover, stay out of reach, she's on to you. Vixen, close in a bit, left flank. Dewdrop, Mustard, Sherlock, close in. Keep the circle tight."

His private chat line only included Pink so he wouldn't get distracted by the group's chatter while he was working earlier, but now he could only hear one side of the action.

"She's confused, picking a target ... get ready to— Crap! That was quick." Pink's voice rose to a shriek. "You okay, Vixen? Nice hit Grover, that must have hurt."

Joseph squirmed on the hard bench; the tubular steel back rest dug into his spine. Next to him, Serena and the Prof were already deep in conference. He elbowed Serena. "Don't get too caught up. Be ready for my signal."

Without waiting for an answer, he turned his attention back to the virtual world and directed Tin Man through Typhoon's long rows of monitors and displays. Above his head under the glistening glass vault, the giant globe, dark for so long, lit up once more. The continents and ice caps appeared, and orange lettering wrapped around the equator: 'July 2000, pop. 6.1 billion'.

He paused alongside the portal leading down to Typhoon's back door, wishing there was some way to see what was happening in the under-layers beyond. Instead, he gritted his teeth and tried to calm the thudding in his chest. He couldn't afford to get caught up in the dog fight that was still going on.

"Next phase," Pink's voice shrilled over the chat line. "Mob her, and be ready to split."

The next words disintegrated into incoherence. Had Pink Marie dropped into her native Norwegian? She'd never live that down if anyone else had noticed. His chest tightened. What was happening? The yelling reached fever pitch with just the occasional word discernible.

Pink screamed. Joseph froze, then realized the yell was not pain or fear, but exultation.

"Hey, Tinny, we've got the beast by the tail. The road is clear."

Joseph released the breath he'd been holding, and passed the signal to Serena. He hurried outwards through the layers of security zones. With caution born of habit, he opened the last portal.

No wings beat, no claws reached.

Avatars appeared.

A black cat stretched. Shining fur gleamed around deep green eyes. Leather clad human legs unfolded, a leather bodice strained. *She should meet Pink!*

"Terminator?"

"Tin Man."

"Easy mistake." The cat laughed, a brittle sound that sent a shiver between Joseph's shoulder blades.

He cursed Serena's impromptu naming.

"Magic." She bowed. "Although I do rather like the sound of Madame Claw." The cat gestured to three figures hovering behind her. "The most I could round up in the middle of the Easter vacation. Basalt, Greybeard, and Sticks."

Joseph relaxed a bit. This was more like it. They used their online names. His kind of people. He cast an appraising eye over the professionally-tailored avatars: a troll, a pirate, and a neon glowing skeleton topped with the surreal porcelain perfection of a geisha's face

He motioned them through the portal and led them into Typhoon and up to the control room.

"Hello, Gwen." Charles and Serena peered down at them from high on the wall, seeming to float in the blue glass enclosing the room.

"That's 'Magic' to you, or are you forgetting your manners?"

"My zone, my rules," the Prof retorted.

The cat stuck out a pink tongue.

Next to Serena's image, Joseph caught a glimpse of his own shoulder where it impinged on the netcaf camera's field of view. He shuddered and edged his physical body away out of sight, gamer's sensibilities violated. Real and virtual worlds were not meant to be mixed up like this. He gazed around the room. The students were already at work, dismantling one of the consoles to examine how Typhoon was constructed. His throat tightened. The way they opened up seamless walls and spirited glowing machinery out of thin air reminded him of Moonshadow.

"There's another makeshift control room through there." He gestured. "That's where we tried to trap Tiamat."

The cat sent the troll off to investigate, then turned her attention back to the console's innards.

"Okay then, looks like you've got everything you need ..."

The pirate grunted without looking up from his work.

With a last look around the zone that had imprisoned his avatar for so long, Tin Man slipped out through the security zones one last time, and into the underworld. He hadn't mentioned this part to anyone, but he wasn't needed here now and it was too good an opportunity. Free from Typhoon at last, he exited.

With his avatar safe at last, Joseph blinked as his senses readjusted to the real world once more. He stretched.

Serena looked around as he pocketed his handheld. "You're back."

"They're digging. Not much I can do to help."

Serena grinned. "Make yourself useful here, then. Fetch coffee." Within seconds, she was head to head with Charles again, engrossed in the collage of symbols and figures crowding the large screen.

Joseph shook his head with a faint smile, and slipped off the end of the bench. Looks like he'd need to keep watch, too. Even without avatars, these two were as immersed as he'd ever been.

For half an hour he tried to make sense of their discussion before giving up, baffled. The words were English, well, most of them, but the meaning eluded him.

He signed on again, old-style interface, and pinged Pink. "Busy? Or okay to talk?"

"We're good, Tinny."

He breathed a deep sigh. "Glad to hear it. Did anyone get caught?"

"Tiamat got her claws good into Dewdrop. She dropped the connection and picked up another handheld. She's fine." She hesitated. "Well, her hearing will come back, eventually."

Joseph pondered. "Tell her to stand down and lie low. Once is enough, don't want to give Tiamat too many chances."

"Already done, Tinny. She's well pissed but I told her she already had bragging rights for taking a hit like that and living to tell the tale. Tiamat seems to have disappeared. We must have hurt whoever's in the driver's seat."

Joseph squirmed inside as he thought what a risk he'd asked those gamers—and Pink—to take. He bit his lip. He still had other responsibilities to worry about. "I don't know how long those academics are going to take in there."

"No worries." Pink's usually acerbic manner was remarkably mild. "We'll be ready to clear the way again when they need to leave."

Joseph changed the subject. "Any progress with Deacon?"

The answering silence failed to cheer him.

"Pink?"

"I think Deacon is best left out of the picture."

"He won't help?"

"I tried to sound him out again, without letting on what we were up to."

"I guess it didn't go so well."

"He's one step away from shunning us altogether."

Joseph's heart hammered. "We're screwed then."

"I'm going behind his back." Pink's voice was small, frightened. "Recruiting gamers I can trust. I figure he hasn't actually ordered anyone to back off yet, so I'm not giving him any reason to do so."

"What the eye don't see ..." Joseph murmured. "Good work, Pink." He wondered at her uncharacteristically subdued tone. The thought of being shunned was scary enough, but he got the impression she was risking far more than he could comprehend. Her life online meant far more to her than he'd realized.

They chatted for a while until, feeling exposed, Joseph surfaced and resumed watch over the café and the professor and student working feverishly at his side.

Sweat slicked his palms as he pocketed his handheld. He wondered what online life would be like outside the clan if they crossed Deacon too far. There were other clans, he knew, but a member expelled from one was rarely welcome into another.

Joseph's reverie was broken by an excited cry. "Professor, it worked." Serena beamed at Joseph. "Dammit, it only bloody well worked!"

"What worked?" Joseph tried not to feel immeasurably stupid.

"The simulation!"

"Typhoon has finally proved itself," Charles said. Joseph wondered if the Prof had feline blood in him. He hardly moved, just sat up a little straighter, yet he seemed to be preening himself.

"Shit, Professor!" Serena moderated her volume when she noticed disapproving stares from the handful of other patrons in the netcaf. "This is it. You've got to publish your results now."

"Yes, Serena, it would seem so." His face darkened. "As soon as I can do so without risk of fatality. We still need to deal with Tiamat, or whoever's behind her. The group profile you used should give us more clues as to what we're up against."

Excitement subdued for a while, the two of them busied themselves again with arcane charts and symbols.

After a few minutes Joseph acknowledged the proprietor's pointed glances at their empty mugs, and fetched more coffees. As he deposited the gleaming mugs on the table Charles blinked, stretched and gave Joseph an inane grin. "I think something stronger is needed to celebrate this evening."

When Charles didn't immediately resume his conference with Serena, Joseph ventured, "Any chance of explaining what the excitement's all about?"

Charles sipped his coffee and grimaced. "What did you learn in the course of your trespassing in my experiment?"

"I saw nothing there that looked like the hard sciences. I think I'd recognize jargon from engineering, physics, chemistry ... or meteorology."

"So?" The Prof's expression hardened.

"And Serena talked about anthropology ... which all makes me wonder why you got so excited by doctored climate reports."

"Aah." The expression softened again and Charles nodded. "You have indeed pinpointed the key elements." He sat bolt upright, eyes glinting. "You're quite right. Typhoon has nothing to do with the 'hard' sciences, as you like to call them, the sciences the world finds *useful*. Typhoon models human behavior. Not individuals, you understand, but groups. Whole populations on a global scale."

Joseph kept his puzzlement to himself, hoping things would become clearer in time. He smiled to the Prof in encouragement, but the old buzzard didn't look like he needed it. He was now in full stride.

"Large groups have their own dynamics, their psychology. They have a life of their own. They live in an information ecosystem and react to threats and opportunities. That is what I've been modeling. The course of human history."

He paused, clearly expecting Joseph to say something.

"Where does the climate come into it?"

"Come on! Don't be dense," Charles snapped. "Older history was all about power, territory, resources, economics, but what single factor has dominated our history this century?" Before Joseph could answer, he continued, "But it's far from a one-way street. What do you think has been the biggest influence on the climate in the past two hundred years?"

"The climate and people are linked."

"The two influence each other. We had amazing success with Typhoon right up until the turn of the century, then something strange happened. History went off track. Terry and I went nearly mad trying to figure out why. Now you've unearthed a factor we never had in our models, a group we knew nothing about but which steered us into irreversible climate change. Serena and I just added this influence into the model, and Typhoon finally mirrors the catastrophe that unfolded." He sat back looking like the cat that got the canary, then his expression soured. "Now we need to figure out who that group is."

"All this happened decades ago. You don't think they're still ..." Joseph hesitated. "They are, and they're still guarding their privacy."

"With deadly effect."

"Professor." Serena drawled the word, thoughtful, a million miles from the booth where they huddled. "I know I still have a lot to cover in the group psychology module, but ..."

"If you have a thought, spit it out."

Charles's waspish voice grated on Joseph. Did he talk like that to all his students? But Serena seemed unfazed.

"Okay, take a look at these motivational profiles. These are the parameters I homed in on to get the simulation to run its course."

Charles's forehead wrinkled. "How did you arrive at this?"

"The actions we've seen show willingness to embrace violence. I started off with the usual things that might lead to extreme inter-group violence, such as deep-rooted ideology or religious belief. From there, I tried adding in factors that would explain a willingness to consign the whole world to misery."

"Did you try willful stupidity?" This whole game sounded too far out for Joseph.

"Of course." Serena gave Joseph a withering glare. "But the thing that took me closest was profound psychopathy. Complete uncaring of human suffering in pursuit of goals." She chewed her lip. "I had to play around with other factors too, just to get it to work. I was desperate by then, and you can see why." She gestured to the screen.

Joseph grunted. "I assume you're only talking to the Professor when you say that."

Serena ignored him. "But it makes no sense. I must be wrong." For the first time, Joseph noticed that she was deeply upset by what she'd found. "This is just ... alien. Inhuman."

"What the heck is going on?" Joseph was used to being at least able to follow a technical discussion, even if the participants knew far more than he did, but this was unnerving.

"This profile works," said Serena, turning to him at last. "But there might be other profiles that would also lead to the same historical results."

"Like an equation with multiple solutions," Joseph ventured. This sounded like something he could understand.

"Exactly." Charles gave him an approving nod. "Serena hit on a solution by experiment, not by deduction, and she doesn't like the look of the solution." He leaned back and rested his chin on steepled fingers. "She has a valid concern, but I think it is likely to be irrelevant."

"How can you say that? This is pure trial and error."

"But it works. Terry and I already tried throwing rogue groups into our model, stakeholders based on typical group motivational patterns, in our attempts to replicate historical events. We tried a long list of parameter sets based on known human traits. None of them came even close to working, so we gave up on that line of inquiry."

"Surely there has to be a better answer. This can't possibly be right."

"Right or wrong doesn't alter one troubling conclusion. Even if we find another solution to fit the model, I believe it will be just as bizarre as the one we have before us."

"So ..." Joseph turned the thought around in his mind as he spoke, afraid to appear utterly foolish. "You're saying that the intelligence behind Tiamat is not human."

"Scorpion." The word escaped Charles's lips as a hoarse croak.

"Huh? Sorry, Professor, I didn't have arachnids pegged as beyond-human intelligence."

"No!" He pointed to the screen. Down in one corner, insignificant alongside the overwhelming mess of charts and diagrams, a cluster of postcard-sized panels showed avatar views of Typhoon. In between the rows of animated hoardings in the monitoring hall, a green scorpion stalked with measured tread.

Fingers trembling, Charles fumbled with his handheld. "Gwen!"

"Here, Charlie Boy."

"Who uses a scorpion as an avatar?"

Gwen's response dropped into their minds like venom. "Malachi."

CHAPTER 30

Like a gunslinger of ancient times, with scarcely a shrug of his shoulders, Joseph's handheld appeared in his grasp. His fingers squeezed out the launch sequence even before it was properly in his grip, and Tin Man re-entered the underworld. Wire frame rooms and halls flashed past his eyes. His pulse pounded in his ears, not quite masking a furious shriek in the distance.

Tiamat!

Tin Man didn't care. He was too fast for her. Through the portal he flew, Typhoon recognizing and admitting him without a pause.

He reached the monitoring hall to find the scorpion at the far end, confronted by Gwen and her students barring the portal leading up to the control room.

The vast globe hovering over the rows of displays wore the faces of Charles and Serena, distorted like reflections in a Christmas ornament.

"Professor!" Joseph shouted. "Can't you shut him out?"

"I wish I knew how." Charles's words sounded strained. "But I fear he has already locked me out. All we can do from here is watch."

The scorpion reared up and bowed to the pirate, a mocking, theatrical gesture. "My thanks, Greybeard. Your first class honors is assured. I wish all my students showed as much loyalty." The voice turned grim. "I'll deal with you others later."

"They're working for me." The cat stood, paws on hips, defiant. "As far as they were concerned, this was a security assignment."

The scorpion laughed, and gave his sting an airy flick. His carapace gleamed with an oily sheen in the light streaming down from the glass vault. "Nice try. But I might be lenient if they step aside."

The troll and the skeleton glanced at the cat, who jerked her head to one side. They scurried away, shooting poisonous looks at Greybeard slinking down the opposite side of the hall. Sticks, the skeleton, made a flickering hand gesture, almost too quick to be seen. Joseph recognized it from gamer culture: *I'll get you later.*

The cat stayed put. Her paws silently extruded bright red inch-long claws.

"This is pointless, Gwen. Your career is already on the line for this. Why are you helping this loser?" A pincer waved at the globe.

"There's more going on here than you understand." The cat's voice was low and urgent. "Charles has uncovered something bigger than both of us."

"Pah! How can you have been duped by this charlatan? One last time, stand aside."

The cat seemed to grow to twice her original size. "I can't let you shut down Typhoon. Hundreds of people have died because they got too close to what Charles has unearthed here. We have to get to the bottom of this." She crouched, tail swishing.

Tin Man's eyes widened. He'd been involved in avatar combat, but had always seen this as young person's territory. If the situation had not been so serious, he would have relished the chance to see how two old professors managed. If nothing else, this would be highly entertaining.

Concern edged the thought aside. Gwen was no gamer. She'd already made her contempt known and, although she was clearly comfortable with an avatar, she lacked the casual fluidity of movement that characterized seasoned users.

The scorpion, on the other hand, looked mean and competent.

A movement caught his eye. Greybeard seemed to be trying to edge back to the control room portal. Tin Man sidled between two rows of displays. If the cat and the scorpion were busy, he might have a chance to sneak past and expel the unwanted intruders. He wished he knew how Terry had managed to freeze his avatar all those ages ago.

The scorpion lunged. The cat blocked his way. So, this zone did enforce basic physics. Good to know.

There was no trial of strength. Strength had no meaning to avatars. You simply could not inhabit the same virtual space, so whoever held it couldn't be moved aside. All the cat had to do was avoid getting out-maneuvered.

Keeping half an eye on Greybeard, Tin Man watched for an opening, wishing he could enjoy the spectacle. He loved seeing noobs try to fight, seeing their frustration as they realized the subtle differences between real world and online physics. But he had to get to that control room.

The scorpion's next move revised his plan. The sting lashed forward, and a violet bolt of lightning struck the cat in the chest. Tin Man didn't recognize the hack, but he sensed a momentary distortion in the virtual space around him that signaled some sort of sensory dump.

The cat doubled up into the fetal position. Gwen's scream echoed in Joseph's mind.

Rage overtook Tin Man. This scorpion must have experience, but Tin Man would never deal that kind of punishment to a noob. He threw an attack of his own, nothing harmful—yet—but Malachi should be getting dizzy watching blinding lights whirl through his head.

Tin Man used the distraction to position himself in front of the portal. "You've got *me* to deal with now, old man."

"Hah!" The scorpion glared at Tin Man and reared up on its hind legs. "You don't know what you're dealing with, young pup."

Shit, he recovered fast.

The sting lashed again. Tin Man braced himself. Sound and light exploded around him. Readouts on the edge of his vision told him that this would have exceeded safe limits, but his defensive hacks dispersed the worst of the onslaught. He felt a pang for Gwen. If the scorpion had used the same assault on the acerbic professor, she'd have a monster headache for hours.

Pity congealed to cold fury as he turned his attention back to the scorpion. Dammit, how the heck did Malachi make a scorpion *smirk*?

"That the best you got, old man?"

The scorpion stepped back, appearing to contemplate him anew. "I see you're not as new-minted as your shiny hide would suggest." He vanished.

Slightly disappointed at the amateur move, Tin Man augmented his senses with a deeper view of his online world. The scorpion's digital presence showed itself as a glowing outline, edging to one side of his view.

Tin Man puzzled. He seemed in no hurry to sneak past. Was he planning to attack again with the advantage of surprise? Tin Man gazed straight ahead, to where the scorpion was last seen. When he finally drew level, at the last moment, Tin Man leaped to block his way.

With a snarl, the scorpion reappeared, backing off a few paces. His pincers clacked in a mockery of applause.

"I'm not letting you through to that control room."

"I don't need you to," the scorpion sneered. "The damage is already done."

Tin Man whirled on the spot. Greybeard was nowhere to be seen.

"Greybeard has turned zone control over to me. All it takes now is a gesture ..." A green pincer waved, "... and this waste of resources will burden me no more."

Tin Man launched a hack designed to override implant safety cut-offs. The target would hear a piercing siren wail loud enough to cause crippling pain.

Too late.

The room dissolved.

What happened to your avatar when the zone around it got deleted?

He was about to find out.

Instinctively Joseph squeezed his eyes shut, knowing the gesture was pointless. Whatever sensations he was about to experience would bypass such physical barriers.

He needn't have worried. His avatar was still responding. Typhoon simply vanished around him, leaving him and the others back in the network under layer.

The avatars belonging to Gwen and her students looked around, bemused. The scorpion staggered in a daze. Tin Man's attack must have hurt.

A harpy screech jarred him. Tiamat was still lurking, and now there was nowhere to hide.

"Run! Exit! Now!" Tin Man roared. He span around to see a flurry of golden scales and beating wings almost on him. He lunged desperately out of Tiamat's path. A claw reached and missed. One dead black eye regarded him for an instant, then she was past and reaching for another target.

The other avatars leaped to safety, leaving the bewildered scorpion in Tiamat's path. One by one, they winked out of existence.

With shaking fingers, Joseph keyed the exit sequence that would return him to reality. His last sight, as the virtual world around him faded, was of gold and green bodies twined together thrashing in the void.

CHAPTER 31

The room whirled. Charles groaned and ran his fingers gently over his scalp, trying to dislodge the construction crew hammering at his skull.

He shut his eyes. The room still whirled. He opened them again.

A glass came into focus, clenched in a white hand and holding an evil-looking creamy concoction. "Drink this," Serena said.

Charles squinted at the glass and eased himself into a sitting position on Serena's couch. The construction crew brought some heavy drilling equipment to work.

Fragments of the previous night surfaced. A bar. Bourbon. He never drank bourbon.

Weakened fingers clutched the glass. He closed his eyes and downed the contents, trusting to student folklore. He gagged, but the drilling eased.

Why the heck did he get drunk? He was borderline alcoholic, thriving on a steady and unhealthy intake, but never getting drunk. Recollection hit him, and he groaned again. Typhoon. Really gone this time, not just the portal. Joseph had confirmed it.

Speaking of whom ...

"Ah, the big man's awake." Joseph peered in from the hallway and gave Charles a cheerful grin.

A night of oblivion gave Charles a remarkable perspective. He may not have Typhoon any longer, no evidence to publish, but after a lifetime's search he had answers. He knew what had happened all those years ago. Exactly what to do with that knowledge eluded him, but right now he had more urgent things on his mind. "Breakfast," he croaked.

Steamed windows blurred the street outside the bustling café. A heavy frost had settled overnight. The brisk walk from Serena's house cleared some of the cobwebs from Charles's mind, and the artery-clogging plateful in front of him was slowly setting the rest of him right. Bacon! An unattainable luxury in England, it seemed to be a staple part of the diet here. Maybe there were other parts of the world worth living in, after all.

Across the table from him Serena jerked upright. "Conference in! Professor Stoppard just pinged me, she sounds upset."

"So she should be," Charles muttered. "She chose those students. One of them wasn't as trustworthy as she supposed."

Serena pursed her lips. "It's not that. Sounds worse."

Joseph whipped his handheld out in one slick movement. Charles fumbled his from his pocket, feeling like he'd sprouted more than his fair quota of thumbs, and joined the conference.

Serena's view of the online world filled his mind. Gwen was talking, but Charles didn't hear her. Serena had pulled up a news feed. Charles scanned the report, feeling numb. A massive storm hit Oxford that morning. Nothing unusual there, except that the weather networks had failed to report it. Forecasts were for hours of clear skies and calm. For the first time in decades, people were caught out in the open when the storm howled in from the coast on wings of silicon death.

Pictures whirled through Charles's mind, images from the news feed. The Radcliffe Camera stood proud amongst the low-lying relics of surrounding buildings, Charles's favorite haunt and the last bastion of the accumulated learning from centuries of human studies. The polymer shielding, installed before funding for the soft sciences all but dried up, had been of little use. The storm found the shutters open. It blasted doors off their hinges and windows out of their frames before wreaking havoc on the priceless interior.

"Charlie!"

His name brought him back to the conversation.

"Malachi is gone."

Through the translucent veil of pictures hovering in his line of vision, Charles locked eyes with Serena and Joseph. Serena mouthed the word, "Tiamat."

"What happened?" Charles tried to keep his voice level, battling a turmoil of emotion. Whatever he may think of Malachi, and despite Gwen's frequent disagreements and acts of defiance, he knew Gwen had always held grudging respect for the old man.

"I spoke with him this morning ... yelled at him, more like. I was still fuming for what he did yesterday. Thought I'd beat some sense into him." She paused. "He was meeting one of his cloud management cronies at the Swindon center. He went to tell her in person about the slice of cycle time he'd managed to save her." Gwen's voice carried a bitter edge.

"In person?"

"He was bloody terrified of going back online, Charlie. I don't know what happened yesterday, but he could barely bring himself to pick up a handheld long enough to place a call."

Charles tensed. "Details, Gwen. This is important."

"He was caught out in the open on the Abingdon Plains."

Charles winced. His mind's eye painted a picture of the desolate and uninhabited wastes outside of Oxford. Miles of rolling, hard-packed dirt. No shelter anywhere. "What about his vehicle?"

"This was a strength seven. Some of the pieces probably got carried all the way to Swindon. Charlie, I checked the forecasts for him. *I* told him it was clear. *I* sent him out there."

Charles could hear the tears choking her. "Gwen, there was nothing you could do."

Gwen's voice rose, verging on hysteria. "This is *her*, isn't it? Old Red?"

"Joseph?" Serena's voice seemed distant. She was thinking. Piecing things together. "Can you check the stored files for this news report?"

"What do ...? Oh. Good thinking."

"Gwen," Charles said, "I know this is scary. I still have trouble with it, but this is what we've been dealing with all this time."

A minute later, Joseph grunted. "Metadata's being cleaned up even as we speak."

"This should be national, even global news," Serena said. "But I bet we won't find mention of it outside of the Oxford area, and maybe the university channels here and other places we've got offices."

A whimper was all Charles could hear on the other end of the chat line. "Gwen, she had Malachi's avatar. That's how she locates people. Traces it back to a real world identity. You managed to get away clean, didn't you? And your students?"

"I ... I think so."

"Listen, I know this is a lot to ask." Charles's pulse pounded in his ears. "Did you get anything at all from Typhoon? None of us will be safe until we deal with Tiamat. We need all the clues we can get, and Typhoon was the best link we had."

"Dammit, Charlie! I'm scared shitless! I'm signing off and going dark, like you did. I don't want to go within a million kilometers of that damned project ever again."

"Gwen!"

"Not a fucking hope in hell!"

CHAPTER 32

Charles broke the connection and let his handheld clatter onto the café table. He sat, staring at it, pain lancing through his temples.

"Professor?" Serena peered at him.

"Death by sandstorm." Charles pushed his half-empty plate away and screwed his eyes shut against the pain. "Feels like almost biblical judgment."

"Come on, she didn't create the storm. She just did what she does best, manipulate information."

Charles groaned, and eased himself to his feet. "People depend on those forecasts. Who the heck would mess with them? It's inhuman."

"Severe and inhuman psychopathy, remember?"

Charles squinted at Serena. "A strength seven storm is rather a blunt instrument."

"But too good a chance to pass up," said Joseph, "if you don't care about collateral damage."

"Some of us *do* care." Charles stood and staggered to the back of the café, ignoring protests as he squeezed past crowded tables, and slipped into an empty booth. Audio-visual immersion and hangovers definitely didn't mix. How did his students cope?

He flicked the screen to life, and located the University news feed. A master index listed damage reports from across the county.

Many buildings were caught with their defenses down and suffered damage from sand blasted through unprotected openings.

The Radcliff Camera once more caught his eye. He felt a pang for the irreplaceable manuscripts, on show in glass cases on the library floor, that had been shredded when the storm tore through.

The nearby covered market was gutted. Its wide-open gates and narrow alleys funneled the wind like an air compressor. The wrecked stalls had been busy when grit and broken glass scythed through.

Joseph sat next to him. His face sagged as he took in the grim scenes. "In all the gamer killings, I've never seen anything like this."

Charles felt sick as he remembered the people in the coffee bar in Krisgaarde. "She doesn't work by our values. She has a target, anyone else gets in the way, it's too bad for them."

"All this, to get one man?"

"Or maybe her target was broader this time," Charles muttered. "The university hosted Typhoon, this will hurt. Surely there's no way Tiamat can cover this one up."

"Let's try the local news." Serena shoved Joseph along the bench, and perched on the end. "See if anything pops up."

"Why bother?" said Joseph. "We already know how thorough she is."

Serena looked down her nose at him. "But in science, we *never* assume. If we have a theory, we test it. Right, Professor?"

Charles gave her a weak smile. Bacon, eggs, and hash browns dueled in his stomach.

He let her take over the screen, and closed his eyes. Would he ever see Oxford again? He had to keep reminding himself that he was still on the run. Sooner or later, he would have to confront Tiamat. The thought chilled him, but until he did he would never be safe returning home.

If there was a home to return to. The city of Oxford clung to the wastelands of southern England through sheer weight of history. An anachronism. There was no practical reason for it to still be there.

The university was under pressure to remove itself to more habitable parts of the world. Most of the staff and students were already dispersed across the globe. All classes and lectures were held online. Only a few die-hards clung to their geographical roots. The city might not survive this onslaught. The damage could be repaired, but would anyone bother?

"Hey, Professor, isn't this where your daughter lives?" Serena pointed to a headline on the screen. " 'New Denmark embraces 21st century.' Bit insulting isn't it? I thought they were well set up there."

Charles touched the screen, which cut to the report.

"After a mysterious corporate benefactor stepped in, the northern reaches of New Denmark will soon join the world network with service to every household. A pilot scheme will test the infrastructure in the region of Krisgaarde and surrounding communities, starting this week-end. A telecom spokesperson said that if they can achieve full coverage here, they can do it anywhere."

Stills from around the town filled the screen. Charles felt a familiar pang. Something he'd only ever felt for his beloved Oxford.

"Mayor Erik Thorsen told our reporter that this is a dream come true for the remote community. 'The town of Krisgaarde itself is well-con-nected,' he said, 'but we have a dispersed population crying out for cov-erage.' "

"Great," said Joseph, "have they run out of real news now?" He caught Charles's eye. "No offence, Prof, but how is this world news?"

"It's not, goofball, this is the local New Boston site." Serena peered close. "Are you all right, Professor?"

The room seemed to darken around Charles. He slumped back on the bench. "Tiamat knows who I am. Don't ask me how." He glanced at Joseph. "You say she needs to grab your avatar, but I've never even *had* one. Yet here we are. She knows me so she knows where my family lives. It's a matter of record. They're safe right now because they're off grid." He buried his face in his hands. "This means that in three days time Tiamat will be able to reach them."

"We won't let that happen." Joseph's voice was firm and reassur-ing. "There must be a way to get a message to them. You said so your-self, right? Well, I can get one of the gamers to warn them. There'll be enough steps in the chain that nothing will lead Tiamat back to us."

"Hmm?" Charles realized that Joseph was right. There would be places they could stay safe, and plenty of time. His reeling mind calmed down, but something else nagged at him. Something in what Joseph had just said.

"I'll talk to Pink. She can pass on a message. Best through a third party, just to be safe."

Charles racked his brain. *Think, dammit!*

"Professor?"

Charles jumped. "What?"

"I said, you need to tell me how to reach them. Did you say there was a mailroom somewhere?"

"Wait. Let me think, please. There's something wrong here. Why the heck would someone offer to connect up a remote community like that?"

"The report mentioned a benefactor," said Serena.

"Corporate," said Joseph. "They must see some profit in it eventually."

Charles snorted. "I've been there. There's no profit, they are barely scratching a living. And I've talked to Erik Thorsen. They're in no hurry to extend coverage. They can't afford it, and don't need it." A growing sense of dread crept over Charles. The thought was on the edge of his mind, but he needed to test it before giving it the substance of words. "What's even stranger, Serena." The words seemed to belong to someone else. They were too calm for the hammering in his chest. "When did your local channel ever report on anything more than fifty kilometers away?"

Charles gazed at them without seeing. He couldn't bring anything into focus. "Joseph, is there someone you can call in your home town? See if they've heard this story."

Half an hour later, Joseph turned, puzzled, to Charles. "I've tried contacts everywhere I can think of. This isn't global news. Nobody else is running this story." He paused, thoughtful. "Let's try another angle. I'll need your help, Serena." More telecons, and puzzlement turned to worry. "It's not even local news. We've tried places up and down the coast. This is only showing in New Boston."

He stood and stretched. "Could be a glitch? Someone in a news distribution center dropped the story in the wrong folder?"

"Or someone put it here deliberately." Charles swigged the dregs of his coffee, long ago gone cold. He craved a beer to steady his nerves. "And I've given up believing in coincidence."

"Okay, you've lost me now."

"I think remote controlled killing may be a relatively new development. Tiamat is falling back on something she excels at, something she's been doing far longer. She manipulates people through the media. We just saw that with the Oxford storm. This message is aimed at us. She wants us to panic and reveal ourselves."

Joseph's eyes lit up. "So you think this story's a fake? Your family is not in danger?"

"I wouldn't say they're not in danger, but I don't think they are about to be revealed to the online world."

"But," said Serena, "that means—"

"Yeah," said Charles. "She knows where we are."

CHAPTER 33

They abandoned the café in haste. Every corner seemed to hide unseen dangers. Every passing vehicle held unspoken threat.

Even indoors at Serena's house, Charles didn't feel safe. He twisted the top off a beer bottle with unsteady fingers. "If this story is fake, it means it's bait. It was designed to catch my attention."

"Which it did, obviously, but there's more to it than just mentioning your family's home."

Dammit, Charles hated it when Serena reversed the role of professor and student like this.

"The name of the town caught your eye, but what made you freak out?"

Charles thought back, reliving the shock he'd felt as the story unfolded. "The idea of them being in reach of the global network."

"That only makes sense because we know how Tiamat kills."

"So, for her to use that as bait, she must know that we know." Charles was having trouble seeing exactly how this knowledge helped them.

"Wait up, there's no 'we' here as far as we know," Joseph protested. "Tiamat tailored this for the Professor, nobody else."

"Fair enough," said Charles. "Regardless, this story only appeared in New Boston, which means she knows—"

"Or maybe only suspects!"

"—That I am alive and well, and residing on the northern shores of Nunavut." He rubbed his eyes. "All well and good, but how does this help?"

"One!" Serena counted off on her fingers. "You are no longer safely dead. Two, she has an approximate geographical location."

"I much prefer the 'bad news or good news' version," Joseph grumbled. "This all sounds bad to me."

Charles grinned. "Okay, the good news is, three, she hasn't tracked me down exactly, or she'd be working on killing me, not just scaring me."

"Spoilsport!" Serena punched Charles on the arm. "But we do have to be careful. The bit about knowing we know how she kills is important. I glossed over that part. I think she must have picked up on Joseph's searches. Sniffing out all her doctored news reports."

"Oh crap!" Joseph looked like he was going to be sick. "That means she's monitoring network traffic somehow." His face paled. "Lucky I always wander around outdoors to do my snooping. That's why she hasn't tied anything back to this house."

"And you thought you were just being paranoid."

A ping in his ear woke Charles from a doze. Without a second thought, his fingers sought out his handheld.

After the shocks of the previous day, they had talked through the problem long into the night without making any headway. For all the insights they'd gleaned about Tiamat's working methods, they seemed no closer to understanding who—or what—she was, let alone how to stop her.

This morning, at Charles's insistence, they set the problem aside. Sometimes the best way to solve a problem was to forget about it for a while. It had often worked for him in the past.

Food helped, too. A visit to a corner store had secured a ham, potatoes, and a selection of vegetables. They sat down to what seemed like their first home-cooked meal this side of eternity.

"Aha!" Charles felt his faith had been rewarded.

Joseph and Serena looked around from the kitchen table. Stomach full, warm and comfortable, Charles had drifted off to the sound of their voices picking through endless reports.

"Gwen left me a message. I knew she'd come around eventually."

"Hold on." Joseph's voice was dangerous. "How did you get a message, here, just now?"

Charles looked down at his handheld. Joseph's eyes followed his gaze. "Oh, come on!" Charles exploded in frustration. "You said this handheld was safe, nothing can possibly tie it back to me. I don't see

how Tiamat can pick one ordinary citizen going about his online business out from all the millions of others doing exactly the same thing,
right now."

Joseph's tense stance relaxed a little, but he still looked troubled.
"You've just been using the flat interface? No online immersion?"

Charles snorted. "I've never even owned an avatar. That's what I
keep reminding you."

"Okay, so where did you pick up a message from?"

"My university mailbox."

"Tiamat knows you. She could be watching your mailbox. Or, at
least, we have to assume she is."

"You said the old-style interface was okay, that she needed to grab
your avatar to trace you." This level of paranoia was starting to anger
Charles. But, he reminded himself, Joseph knew the online world and
its possibilities. In this vision of suburban normality, it was hard to stay
alert to the very real dangers still out there.

Charles sighed. "Look, I'll switch it off. I didn't even sign on directly.
I sent an agent to collect my mail, that's all. From now on, this thing will
only be on while I'm away from ..."

Joseph's face drained of color.

"What's wrong?"

Joseph sagged back in his chair. "You sent an agent ..."

"Something Gwen taught me years ago, and in this case I though it
best to keep my distance."

"Professor, an agent is nothing more than an avatar on autopilot.
Agents have their presentation aspect set so they are invisible to regular
avatars' visuals, and they don't interact with your audio visuals in the
same way, but they are the same technology. And they can be snagged
and traced, just the same."

CHAPTER 34

Charles staggered to his feet. He took two deep breaths to steady himself and dispel sickening vertigo. Adrenalin kicked everything into heightened focus. Joseph and Serena were pushing back their chairs, seeming to move in slow motion.

"Bags. Now!" Charles rasped. For once, he was thankful for Joseph's eternal paranoia. They all had travel bags packed and waiting, ready for a hasty exit.

Joseph was already on his way to the door. Serena was slower, but after a momentary look of incomprehension her expression settled into scared determination.

"Where are the street cameras around here?" Charles asked, as they peered from the back door into the alleyway outside.

"Thought you said they weren't a problem," Serena said.

"That was automated face recognition," said Joseph. "No other way you could hope to pick someone up out of thousands of feeds of random streets when you've no idea where they are."

"But a whole different matter if you already know where to look," Charles added.

Serena's face screwed up in concentration. "Mostly on the main intersections. We'll start off in the back alleys, shouldn't be a problem until we're a fair way away."

"Then she'll have more ground to cover." Charles gave an approving nod.

"Split up, just in case," said Joseph. "We don't know how many of us Tiamat knows about. If she gets a visual, it would be better to have separate targets to try to keep track of." He glanced at Charles. "Is your handheld still on?"

"Bugger!" Charles's heart sank.

He was puzzled when Joseph grinned. "No! That's a good thing. You've got to leave it anyway. It's compromised. It'll be traceable any-where. Leave it here, switched on. Gives the impression that we're still here."

Charles tossed the offending device onto the kitchen table.

"Joseph, you go that way." Serena pointed right. "Keep straight for a block, hang a left, then double back and pick us up on the corner of the park." She linked arms with Charles. "Pops and I will head the other way. Together. I've seen his sense of direction."

Serena's house backed onto a lane, little more than a strip of open ground between two rows of houses. Upper-floor windows gazed down at them from the shadows of deep eaves, giving the impression of frown-ing disapproval. In the main street beyond, a truck roared by. Charles's scalp crawled until it was safely past.

Laughter sounded from the next house. A child squealed in delight. What did Tiamat have planned? What means of destruction would she improvise? Charles shuddered at memories of the indiscriminate attacks he'd seen. He had to warn them ...

As if sensing his line of thought, Serena shook her head and tugged on his arm. At the end of the lane, she stopped in the shelter of the covered sidewalk. "Camera about fifty meters down to our left." She glanced up and down the road. "Stick close to me when I move."

A high-sided delivery truck trundled past towards the unseen camera. They darted out behind it, momentarily shielded from view, and scurried across the street. Serena yanked Charles into a hardware store and led him through to a parking lot behind.

After two more turns, Charles was thankful Serena had not sent him off alone, because the street was unfamiliar and he now had no idea in which direction the park lay.

They emerged from another narrow alley, glimpsing trees ahead, and crossed the intersection. Joseph loitered in the shadows and swag-gered off across the grass before they reached him. They followed.

Half way across the park, the sound of sirens filled the air. One, faint at first, then another. More joined the chorus. It was hard to tell which direction they were coming from. A few meters away, steps led up to the fenced-off viewpoint they'd used previously. They climbed the steps cut into the rocky outcrop. Lights flashed through a forest of bare branches on either side of the park, and raced past the corner they had just left.

"Shit," Serena muttered. "Looks like they're heading for home."

A pit yawned in Charles's stomach. "What's happened back there?"

"What do you mean, Prof?" Joseph panted.

"Come on." Heck, what was wrong with youngsters these days? "You think this is coincidence?" He could see the mental gears whirring.

"Silly boy." Serena had that dreamy sound to her voice again. "We got spotted. We scrammed. Because we *expected* something bad to happen." Her voice broke. "I *liked* that house. What do you think Tiamat's done?"

"Dunno," Charles muttered. "All I see is police. No ambulance. No fire trucks."

They waited. The sirens stilled, and unnatural hush blanketed the park.

"Oh, the clever bitch." Joseph chuckled. "Don't you understand? She hasn't done *anything*, yet. I bet she's just called the cops in. Anonymous tip-off, hostage, guns, drugs, something like that. Should be easy to do, some faked message."

"What good would that do? We'd be released as soon as they figured out there was nothing to it."

"But we'd be helpless while they held us, figuring it out. Think about it. Is it easier to shoot a deer running free, or one that's trapped in a pen?"

Charles shivered. "We'd better disappear, then. Serena, anywhere else we can hole up?"

———◆———

"Come on," Serena grumbled. "It's nearly evening, *someone* should be home." She leaned on the doorbell a third time before putting her ear to the door once more.

Bicycles littered the fronts of the townhouses along the street. Beneath the defiant grandeur of imposing frontages and ornate wood-work, the neighborhood was a faded shadow of past affluence. Music and voices drifted from windows nearby, colliding in a vibrant melting pot of sound. A battered twin cab stood lonely guard by the curb.

Charles puzzled over the contrast between this, and the relatively up-market district they'd left behind. This seemed more fitting for student accommodation. What was Serena doing in a detached house, all by herself?

Was Oxford like this, once? The student population had once lived in the city. He tried to picture bustling streets where sand dunes now marched, and college and faculty buildings teeming with life, like the university building here.

An elfin face peered out at them and gasped. Tammy, Serena's friend from the university, threw the door open and yanked her inside, peering up and down the street as she did so. Charles and Joseph followed.

"What's up?" Serena asked. She grimaced at Charles and Joseph and turned her attention back to Tammy. "What have you heard?"

Cold knots of apprehension churned inside Charles.

Breathless, Tammy half-dragged Serena up creaking stairs. On the third floor, she paused and glanced at Charles. " 'Scuse the mess, Professor. Wasn't expecting company." She bumped a door open with her hip, still holding Serena's hand. "Promise me you won't freak."

Charles followed them into a spacious living room. Windows overlooked the street, letting in the last of the afternoon sun. Clothing littered the floor and backs of chairs, while mugs, plates, and stacks of papers concealed any hint of useable horizontal surface. He resisted the urge to wrinkle his nose, and guessed that the 'freaking' had nothing to do with the state of the room.

Tammy ran across the room and flicked the wall screen on, leafing through a list of news feeds. "There," she panted.

Serena groaned. Her face gazed back at her from the screen, accompanied by a police report.

Charles glared at the report. "So, I am supposedly wanted in connection with the death of my colleague in Alaska, despite being six time zones away at the time."

Joseph scanned the screen intently. "Tiamat's trying out new tricks. No mention of my name, though. I'm guessing you're still the main target, Professor, and the link to Serena is through the street address."

Charles glanced at Serena. "I suspect I'll be spending the rest of my rather short career apologizing to you for that. Do you regret harboring such a dangerous felon?"

Serena ignored him "Do the others know about this?" she asked Tammy. "Will they say anything?"

Tammy looked shocked. "Turn you in to the cops? Not a chance."

"All the same," Charles said, "now that Old Red's got human eyes helping her, it's not just a matter of staying out of the online world. We're a danger to you. There are worse things than just the police at work here."

"Prof," Joseph murmured. "We'll need wheels. Wonder whose truck that is outside."

Tammy must have overheard. Her pale face turned grey. "Are you serious?"

"Joseph," Charles said, "stealing a truck would make us more conspicuous than ever."

"I don't fancy our chances of hiding out in town. We need to get out altogether. Any better ideas for transport?"

He had a point. Charles chewed his lip. He was sure of one thing: he was not going to endanger any more students. Less sure—what to do about it. Did Joseph know how to hack a truck's guidance system? If it had one. This one looked old enough to be a manual drive.

"Listen." Tammy gulped. "The truck belongs to Colin. He's stopping over at his girlfriend's tonight, I don't think we'll see him until tomorrow."

She looked earnest. "You didn't hear me say anything about the keys in a dish on the worktop in the kitchen. He lets us borrow it from time to time. If he misses it, in the absence of any other information I would assume Scruff took it to get provisions." She frowned, and fiddled with her handheld peeping out of the kangaroo pocket on her sweater. "Make a note to speak to Scruff."

Serena hugged her. Tammy looked startled. "Just bring it back in one piece, okay? And there's food in the kitchen. Not much. Bread, cheese, juice. And I didn't say anything about blankets and sleeping bags in the closet, second door on the right down the hall. If anyone asks, you slipped out while I was having a shower."

———— ◆ ————

Charles unfolded himself one protesting limb at a time from the corner of the truck's cab. The cold night had been filled with fragmented memories of their drive from New Boston miles down the coast of Nunavut. They'd pulled off a winding side road and hidden as best they could behind a bank of brambles. In the deepening chill, their breath quickly fogged the truck's windows as they wedged themselves into various corners, Joseph in the front, and Charles and Serena at opposite ends of the back seat.

Conversation stalled. Charles had felt too weary to kick his mind into gear. Besides, there was nothing they could do that night, and their problems would wait until morning. Joseph seemed lost in thought, and Charles felt guiltily thankful that the darkness hid Serena's sullen anger.

The drive itself had been remarkable only for glimpses of the iron grey waters of Baffin Bay past precipitous cliffs, and a white-knuckle ride along unlit roads until Joseph announced that they were out of range of any service connection. Charles's dreams, though, were haunted by screaming sirens and rampaging snow ploughs with baleful eyes for headlamps.

Now, returning circulation breathed fire into numbed flesh and aching joints. Joseph was already outside, stamping life back into his feet and hauling a canvas bag onto the hood of the truck. Charles tried to untangle himself from a pile of blankets and ease his door open without disturbing Serena, but she stirred and peered at him with reddened eyes. He gave her a weak smile and tumbled out, barely catching himself on the door handle.

"Joseph." Charles stretched the knots from his back and studied the bleak landscape of dark rock, tough grass, and patches of snow. "I sense that you're more accustomed to this running from danger lark than I am. Where to now?"

Joseph looked up from a map spread out on the hood. "Right now, I'm wondering how far they'll stretch the hunt for you and Serena. I think we need to stay clear of large towns."

Charles glanced at the map. "Looks like that won't be much of a problem, but I think the smaller populations will be even more danger-ous. Strangers stand out more. What about further away? Lose ourselves in another city?"

Joseph gaped, then rolled his eyes. "I guess North American geog-raphy isn't your strong suit."

"I thought there were large towns all around Hudson Bay." Charles frowned. "Surely we could reach one of them?"

Serena plodded around from the other side of the truck, rubbing her eyes. "Is this guy for real?" she mumbled.

With a maddening grin, Joseph said, "Geography one-oh-one, then."

"Oh, spit it out," Charles muttered. "I never was one for traveling."

"Those cities are a thousand kilometers away," Serena said. "I don't think you've got much sense of scale. It's not like England. More to the point, we can't drive there. Up here, we're cut off from the American mainland. The only way off is by boat or plane."

"Well," Charles said, "I don't intend to live out my life like this, and we can't tackle Tiamat from off-grid."

"I know," said Joseph. "Problem is, you don't have a handheld. Serena, was the house in your name?"

Serena grimaced and nodded.

"So, that's how your face got into the news. Your identity is compromised also, and you'll be tracked the moment you use your account." Joseph gave her a sharp look. "It *is* switched off, isn't it?"

Serena nodded again, miserably, and glared at Charles. "Unlike some."

Joseph shrugged. "And I don't want to use my spare, the one I used to do all that research. That's probably what gave Old Red clues about New Boston, so that account is suspect."

Despair clutched at Charles.

"My old handheld should still be good, though," Joseph continued. "I escaped clean from Typhoon and I'm fairly sure there's nothing to link me back to anything that's happened so far."

"Fairly?"

"Fairly." Joseph eyed Charles. "Get used to it. You Humanities folks deal with uncertainty all the time."

"All the same, any online access has to be handled with extreme care now." Charles grimaced. "One good handheld between us."

"Two," said Joseph. "I have one last bootleg spare that I haven't used yet. I got myself another spare when I got yours."

"Paranoia rules!" Charles felt his spirits lift, just a little. "We're still in the fight. Question is, how to proceed? I only got a glimpse of Gwen's message, but she had something important for us and it's on the handheld I left behind."

"I thought she was out of the picture." Serena frowned.

Charles chuckled. "You don't know Gwen. She reacts on gut instinct. She was rattled by what happened to Malachi, and she always needs time to come to terms with things that upset her world, but I've never known her run from a fight. We need that message."

"Serena," Joseph said. "It's safe to switch on your handheld while we're out of service range, so conference in. I need Madame Claw's address from you. I'll set up a new account and ask her to re-send her messages there. If she's clean, and my account's clean, should be safe enough."

Charles scanned the craggy horizon, the crests of barren hills towering over them. "What chance of getting service out here?"

"Us, here." Joseph pointed at the map. "Two small towns down on the coast. Hydro-electric plant. Radar station. Weather stations here, here, and here. Other infrastructure scattered along the coast, they will all have service for their own use and be providing public access. Anywhere within five kilometers of any of those spots."

"Then what are we waiting for?"

With Charles and Serena keeping anxious watch up and down the road, Joseph made his brief foray online to relay instructions to Gwen. The tiny settlement across the glinting water, just a couple of buildings keeping a lighthouse company, nevertheless afforded a service connection for passing travelers.

The road hugged the foot of steep cliffs, nowhere to run if they were discovered. Charles felt dangerously exposed and could see his fear echoed in Serena's wide eyes. They both breathed shaky sighs of relief when Joseph announced that he was done.

Now, sheltered under a stand of stunted pine a few kilometers inland, and comfortably out of sight of the road, Charles struggled to contain his impatience while Joseph leafed through the messages Gwen had sent him.

"Professor Stoppard rounded up more of her students. She's had teams of them working through the night picking through what they scavenged from Typhoon." Joseph read more. "Sounds like they've been following up on my research, too."

"Professor." Serena's voice was tight. "Do they realize the dangers?"

"Gwen knows what happened to Malachi." Charles blinked away an angry tear. *And to my beloved city.* "And she knows the network. She'll be taking as many precautions as we are, if not more." He nodded to Joseph to continue.

"The records from the trap were interesting." Joseph fell silent, eyes flickering as he scanned his inner world. "No offence, Professor, but I'm going to have to translate this stuff. It's raw tech-speak."

Charles sighed. He should have guessed.

"Everything online has a digital footprint." Joseph seemed to be choosing his words with care. "Avatars, agents, zones, including your simulation, are all just chunks of code and data."

Charles screwed his eyes shut, trying to visualize what Joseph was saying.

"All the different types of things you see online all have distinctive architectures—"

"Now you lost me. What does that look like?"

"Slow down, Joseph. Let me try." Serena puckered her lips. "Okay, Professor, what is this?" She slapped the hood of the truck.

"Assuming this isn't a trick question, it's a truck."

"No trick. Correct answer. Next question: how do you know?"

"I think I know a truck when I see one." Charles couldn't quite keep his irritation under control. Where was this leading?

Joseph hastened to take over. "That's exactly my point. You recognize this as a truck because it has wheels, a chassis, a cab, and other bits arranged in a certain way. That certain way is what makes it a truck, rather than, say, a plane or a coffee machine."

"Okay."

"You don't need to know all the gory details, just trust me that code and data are nothing more than the computing equivalents of wheels and engines and body parts. How they're arranged tells me what kind of beast I'm looking at."

"Got it," Charles lied.

"Thing is, the students looked at Tiamat's footprint in the trap to work out what we'd caught."

"And?"

"They have not a freakin' clue!"

Charles and Serena exchanged frowns.

"The only thing they can be sure of is that Tiamat is not a directed construct." Joseph gave them a triumphant look, as if he'd just concluded a career-making thesis presentation.

Charles looked blank. "In English, please."

"Sorry." Joseph deflated visibly. "Means it isn't being controlled by a real live person."

Charles glanced sidelong at Serena, hoping the confirmation of her insight might lift her out of her sulk. Then his mouth hung open and he turned his gaze back to Joseph. "Hang on. You mean *nobody* is trying to kill me? Us?"

"Not necessarily. I mean that Tiamat is an automated and independent agent. She might just chase avatars and report details back to someone at base later."

"No," said Serena. "What you've said up to now makes perfect sense, up until that last sentence. Remember, Professor? The motivational profile was clearly not human. That profile applies to whoever is giving the orders, no matter whether they're controlling directly or at a distance."

"So ..." Joseph chewed his lip. "Tiamat must have been built, given some kind of rules, non-human rules, to drive behavior, and then set loose in the network."

"Is that possible?" Charles wondered. "I didn't think we'd got anywhere near that level of artificial intelligence."

"That's the problem." Joseph looked glum. "We haven't."

———◆———

"Come on, Professor. If you're going to help me at all, you've got to get used to a double handheld."

Charles groaned. He knew Joseph was right, but it seemed too much to take in.

"It's all we've got left," Joseph said. "And we've got no big screens out here. When you get used to full immersion it's better than any size screen."

"So Terry kept telling me."

"And it means you can join in the conference with Professor Stoppard."

The pleading in Joseph's voice quirked the corner of Charles's mouth into a hint of a smile. "What? Can't you handle Madame Claw on your own?"

Serena stifled a snort and glanced at Joseph, one hand hastening to cover her mouth.

"I'm just some gamer scum to her. At least you two belong to her world. You talk the same talk."

"And that's another thing I'm not happy about. Just how safe is it, letting Serena join in? Her handheld is suspect, you said." Charles hated feeling so out of his depth. His contribution to Typhoon had been the theories, the models of human behavior, motivations, cause and effect.

All the computational aspects had been Terry's domain. Now he was firmly in alien territory and he didn't know what part of it might turn out to be important, possibly fatal.

Joseph rolled his eyes. He looked like he was about to spit out a snarky reply, then thought better of it when he caught Charles's glare. He sighed. "While we're out of range, it's safe to switch hers on. While we've been out of reach of the network, I've hacked it so she can keep it offline like I did with yours, remember? But she can still connect direct to mine, handheld to handheld, and share my view. When we get in range, it'll be like we were both sat in a netcaf booth on one end of a chat line. She can join in, but we're using only my account, not hers."

Charles shook his head. It *sounded* safe enough, but this online world had already surprised him far too often. Ah, heck. This was Joseph's world. "Just make double sure of the settings or whatnot. Make sure she's not connected accidentally."

⸻ ◆ ⸻

Charles's head ached. He wondered why the hell he'd agreed to this. The controls confused him. He'd spent decades getting comfortable with one-handed control and light immersion, now he needed to co-ordinate both hands to move and express himself. Every wrong move wracked him with nausea as his viewpoint shifted out of step with his inner ear.

And, to cap it all, he could barely follow, let alone take part in, the conference.

Joseph, on the other hand, seemed to be in his element, picking through the findings the computational students had unearthed under Gwen's guidance.

With a grunt of exasperation, Charles let his avatar freeze and extracted his senses, taking a deep breath and drinking in the welcome stability of the distant horizon. A fishing village nestled in a bay, boats bobbing like toys below their vantage point.

"Professor?"

Charles jumped at Serena's voice. How long had he been gazing at the iron grey ocean, lulled by the crash of surf?

"We wondered if you were okay. I'm not a techie either, and all this avatar stuff is new to me, too, so I persuaded the tech-heads to sum up in English."

"Do they know the meaning of the word?"

Serena rested her hands on the railing that separated the roadside rest area from a precipitous drop. "Glad I wasn't the only one feeling stupid. Professor Stoppard's scary enough anyway, but on her own turf she's a total dominatrix."

A laugh bubbled up through Charles's throat. "That isn't helped by the leather get-up."

Below them, a gull screeched, fending off an intruder from the precarious nest it was busy building. The last of the boats was making for the breakwater where people scurried like ants, tiny specks in the sun.

Charles glanced over at Joseph, reclining in the driver's seat, still in intense subvocalized conversation. "I suppose we'd best rejoin them."

"Welcome back, Charlie Boy." The black cat sauntered around the private conference zone she'd opened up in the university plenum. Her right hand absently twirled the end of her tail.

Maybe he was starting to get the hang of this. Charles found his movements fractionally smoother, resulting in less of an urge to vomit. Only slightly less, though. He gave Gwen's feline avatar a sour look, and tried to ignore the gaggle of simpering acolytes behind her. "Just keep it brief, please. What have you found?"

"Ever heard of emergent phenomena?"

"The whole is more than the sum of its parts." Charles wrinkled his nose, both hands too busy to deal with a distracting itch. "Human organizations show emergent behavior all the time, things you couldn't predict just from studying how individual people behave. I'm more than familiar with it, Gwen, you know that."

"Just opening your mind."

"To what?"

"To the idea of fully autonomous computer-based intelligence. And I mean *fully* autonomous. Not directed by or dependent on any human agency."

"Artificial intelligence?"

"Artificial implies man-made. This was neither devised nor intended by human beings. The Faculty of Computation"—she gestured to the students around her—"has concluded that we are dealing with some-thing that emerged spontaneously."

"Tiamat? You've got to be kidding! That thing is showing something like human intelligence. Never mind the chances of something like that appearing out of thin air, any idea how much computing power it would take?"

She speared Charles with an emerald gaze. "Yes. Have you?"

That stumped Charles. He had spent so long studying the infinite ramifications of the human mind, the idea of a machine with the same capabilities was hard to swallow.

"My stooges have trawled the theory on AI," Gwen continued, "including computational intensity and infodynamics. A human-like level of intelligence would take a significant, but manageable, slice of the total global resource."

"That's insane."

"But theoretically do-able."

"In whose estimation?"

"The *pure* AI buffs"—the depth of contempt in her voice startled Charles—"got excited back in the thirties when they realized that the global network had long since passed the theoretical level of complexity needed to support human-level intelligence."

Curious, Charles asked, "Why wasn't it followed up?"

"Apart from the fact that, after decades of trying, we still had no clue how to go about making it?"

"But you said—"

"I said the power available was computationally equivalent to a human brain. That's a theoretical calculation. Doesn't mean we know how to actually do it. Besides, when the climate collapsed, we had more pressing matters than pure research. Who the heck can afford that kind of power now? We need all kinds of specialized applications to help solve real world problems. Lean, mean, focused. General AI research is a wasteful extravagance."

Like anthropology, Charles thought, sadly.

"But, somehow, we seem to have wound up with a general AI anyway."

"I get the conclusion," said Joseph, "but you said it needs a 'signifi-cant slice' of the global network."

Gwen shrugged. "Theory only. Who knows if that's right?"

"If it is, how, exactly, could that go unnoticed all these years?"

Embarrassed silence answered Joseph, then, "Typhoon," Charles blurted. He paused to tease out the thought that had just hit him. "Gwen, you said something about our usage going through the roof. I knew that couldn't be right."

"So?"

"She manipulates information. Usage reports, invoices, never heard of creative accounting?"

Gwen smacked her forehead. "Everyone thinks they're using more than they really are, and she creams off the difference."

"All very well," said Joseph, "but surely she'd show up somewhere on someone's scope?"

"If she can rig cloud usage reports, presumably process logs and suchlike are no problem."

"All the same, there's got to be some core processing going on some-where. Even if this emergence is globally distributed, surely there'd have to be some kind of a virtual network to tie it all together or it would simply fall apart. You can't just hide something that big."

"Ummm ..." Serena held her hand up. "Anybody? What about that big hole in the middle of the network that Tiamat's guarding? Everyone's spent decades happily overlooking *that*. We assumed she was just keep-ing people away from some plenum used to host criminal activity."

"Which doesn't make sense now, though, does it? No people to hide."

"No, it's not crime or anything like that. It's Tiamat herself. It's her nest."

"Uh-oh."

The tension in Joseph's voice sent a tingle through Charles.

"We've been jawing too long. Exit. Now."

CHAPTER 36

As Joseph spoke, Charles noticed the weather warning icon in the corner of his field of vision. After a lifetime living in the shadow of some of the most lethal storms on the planet, how did he miss that? Normal vision returned, and he scrambled for the door of the truck.

Serena clambered in behind him, shoving him across the seat. Her eyes still looked unfocused, hooked into Joseph's world. "Ten minutes. Maybe fifteen."

"We have to get under shelter." Joseph gunned the engine to life. "Did you see how big?"

"Strength five. Wind, hail, it's set to last for hours."

The truck rumbled onto the road.

"Where the hell are you going?" Charles asked.

"Town." Joseph jerked his thumb towards the valley as he swung down the hill. "No choice. We can't be out in the open in that."

Town meant people, and police. Charles gripped the seat back, knuckles cracking, while Joseph flung the truck around switchback bends. He wanted to urge more caution, but bit his tongue. A momentary view down the valley and out to sea revealed tumbling clouds blotting the sky. Tufted grass alongside the road whipped in sudden gusts.

"Professor." Serena nudged Charles. "You need to scout ahead. We need somewhere to stay, and fast."

Charles swore. Joseph was driving. Serena couldn't afford to go online. He had no choice, and Serena was right—they had no time to lose. A flurry of rain attacked the windshield. Big, angry drops with icy teeth.

"Just keep it steady, Joseph." Charles gritted his teeth and swallowed. Information clouded his view of the world outside and fuddled his balance yet again. "There's a bridge over a river before we reach the town. Let me know when we reach it."

He cleared his vision for a few moments, giving his rebelling stomach a chance to subside, before diving back into the local business guide. This was clearly not a tourist destination. On the plus side, he didn't have to spend long searching for somewhere to stay. "Looks like it's either the hostel, or the hostel."

Joseph glanced over his shoulder at Serena, then turned his attention back to the road. A gust caught the side of the truck, shunting it almost across the road before he wrestled it back under control. "Hope there's room at the inn, then," he muttered. "Don't know what you're used to, Serena, but it could be rough."

Charles thought back to the hostel he stayed at briefly in New Boston. "Probably used by fishing crews, itinerant workers. Joseph's right, not going to be the Ritz."

◆

The wind was rocking the truck, and pummeling it with plum-sized hailstones, by the time lights appeared ahead. Joseph wrestled with the wheel, cursing his stupidity. He'd been too engrossed in the technical discussion. Heck, his head was still whirling with the possibilities. He gritted his teeth and drove, more by instinct than by sight as the fierce-driven flurries intensified.

"There's the bridge. Where to?" He hoped the Professor had managed to stay online through their fairground descent.

"Take the second turn on your left. Should be Fifth Street."

"Got it." The wind slackened off in the lee of the buildings. Before the Professor could give further directions, Joseph spotted the sign for the hostel on his right. He eyed the seedy building with misgiving. Looking on the bright side, it didn't look like the kind of place where they'd ask too many questions.

"Off street parking on the next block."

"I see it." Joseph slammed the truck through the deserted intersection, anticipating the vicious thrust of the gale whistling past the corner. "Shit! I should have dropped you two off at the door."

"Bollocks to that!" The Professor startled Joseph with the antiquated expletive. "We stick together."

Joseph was relieved to find the storm-proofed parking lot almost empty. He skidded to a stop in the nearest space and they piled out.

"Wait," the Professor called above the rushing wind. "A few seconds more won't make much difference." He hauled out their travel bags, flinging them at Joseph and Serena. He picked up the bag containing the last of their provisions.

Joseph nodded. "Let's go."

Out in the street, the wind snatched his breath away. At least the covered sidewalk offered some shelter.

They reached the intersection, where the storm screamed up from the sea.

Joseph peered around the corner and was immediately blinded by driving rain and stinging pellets. "Can anyone stand in this?" He blinked to clear his eyes, and brushed ice from his eyebrows. His fingertips came away tinged with red. The far side of the street seemed impossibly far away through a horizontal torrent.

The Professor pursed his lips. "Hold your bag to shield your face, like so." He threaded one arm through both straps of the bag and clenched the straps in his other hand. The bag nestled tight against his shoulder, with its base pointing into the wind and shielding his head and hands.

"Now, we stick together and support each other." He positioned himself windward, and motioned Joseph alongside him, then Serena.

Together, they edged into the teeth of the gale. Almost immediately, the Professor staggered into Joseph. On his other side, Serena pressed close, helping him fight the force of the wind.

One step, then another. Hail pounded their legs and beat madly at their improvised shields. Joseph felt his feet slide on the crusted road. Serena steadied him. He, in turn, shored up the Professor who was taking the worst of the pounding.

Another step, and another. How wide was this bloody road? His bag angled across his face, and Serena's pressed alongside him, obscured his view. Joseph gritted his teeth and shuffled one foot in front of the other.

A shadow cut across the sheeting hail. The sidewalk.

They staggered into shelter and hurried along the block to the hostel's entrance.

Joseph pushed on the armored door. A dim light glimmered through a heavy perspex fanlight, offering little promise. He groaned, the door was locked.

"Allow me." The Professor reached up and released a second latch that Joseph hadn't noticed at shoulder height. "You don't get the winds where you come from, do you?" Before Joseph could answer, he continued, "Storm latch. Won't open if the outside pressure's too great. Makes sure the door will only open if you can push it closed again."

The door swung inwards, with the Professor in tow, and they hastened inside.

"Mind you shut that door good," a woman's voice echoed from the depths of the building.

Joseph blinked in the yellow light, and put his shoulder to the door to help the Professor. The bite of disinfectant battled with steam and stale sweat. Serena wrinkled her nose.

A woman rolled, rather than walked, down the hall to meet them. "Now, what you be doin' out and about in this? It's a fierce wind out there." The voice seemed jolly, but her lips pressed thin and her eyes glinted as she studied them, cold and calculating.

The Professor said, "We got caught by surprise on the road."

"English, is it?"

Her sudden interest made Joseph uneasy. "Common mistake, isn't it, Uncle James?"

"Umm, yes."

"A lot of folks in White Horse migrated up from BC mid century." Joseph didn't offer any further explanation, and fervently hoped the Professor would refrain from elaborating. He dared not risk a glance to warn him off saying anything more.

Joseph counted off heartbeats while the woman surveyed them, clearly hoping for more information. The Professor, thankfully, said nothing and just grinned like an idiot. Serena found a sudden interest in the pinboard hanging on the wall, with sparse and faded leaflets announcing the few local attractions for those unfortunate enough to stay here a while.

Eventually the proprietor sniffed and pushed a damp strand of grey hair out of her face. "Youse lookin' for a bed for the night?"

The Professor, nodded, still grinning.

"Yer in luck. Most of the lads're down the docks securin' the boats. They'll hunker down there and not be back 'till sunrise now."

Her eyes took on a distant look. She quoted a cost for the night and gave the Professor a hard stare. "Prepaid."

The edge in her tone alarmed Joseph. In his experience, hostelries never settled up front unless they had good reason to fear their guests wouldn't be there in the morning. "I'll settle this," he said. "Good job one of us remembered to grab a handheld from the car." He glanced at the other two, glad to see they weren't arguing with his lead.

———◆———

The storm still howled outside the shuttered windows. A distant thunder hammered the roof above them. A basin of warm water and a shave had worked wonders for Charles's demeanor. Joseph was clearly worried about the proprietor's interest in them. The Goblin, as Charles had instinctively named her, made him uneasy too, but he set aside those worries for now. Nobody would venture outside for the next few hours at least.

Joseph toweled his face. "Better." He grinned.

Charles handed him a shirt. "You're the technical one here. What did you make of Gwen's analysis?"

"The conclusion's pretty astounding."

"Seems to fit the facts, though, from what I can see. Did you have any better ideas?"

"How did they decide on an emergent AI, rather than designed, or remote controlled? I'm keen to see the details of their work." Joseph sniffed. "Trouble is, it'll probably be way over my head."

"I think you underestimate yourself," Serena said, swinging her legs where she perched on a creaking counter top. "And those computation students aren't half as smart as they like to make out."

"Thanks. If the conclusion's right, though, I'm itching to know just where Tiamat came from. How did she emerge? And why is she so bloody murderous? I mean, what did we ever do to her?"

Good question. Charles frowned at the mildewed curtains offering the only privacy in the hostel's communal bathroom. "We already decided we can't judge her motivation in human terms." What did a burglary or mugging victim ever do to their aggressor? He'd seen an incident in the Head of the River once where a guy had glassed a complete stranger just because he'd 'looked at him funny.' Humans were perplexing enough. What did *he* ever do to Tiamat?

He doubted he'd ever get answers to that. Best for his own sanity to put it out of his mind and steer towards safer shores. "While we're into questions, I'm more curious as to why the heck she messed around with our climate early on in the century."

"Technically, *we* did the messing—"

"You know what I mean, Serena. She weighted stories left, right, and centre. All the public heard was Skeptic propaganda, doubts and scientist conspiracy theories. It was a clear manifesto for business as usual."

"Hell," said Joseph, "she even played up some crackpot theories that said a warmer world would be good for business."

"Exactly. But why?" Charles scratched the stubble itching his chin. He was still cultivating a goatee in half-hearted disguise. "I can't see what it gained her, and if technological society had collapsed, where would that leave Tiamat?"

"You know," said Joseph, "you talked about understanding motivation. Ever wondered what the world might look like to her?"

Serena gave him a doubtful look. "Not sure where this is going, or how we can possibly imagine it."

"Think about it. We live in the world out here. The global network is alien territory to us—"

Charles bit back a heartfelt affirmation.

"It's something we only dimly experience through screens and avatars. Even then, we have to interpret the online content using software to render it into something our senses can grasp."

"Okay ..." Serena screwed her face in concentration.

"For Tiamat, the situation's reversed. She emerged in the network. That is *her* world. What can she possibly understand of ours?"

"Obviously enough to know how to kill people," Charles spat.

"Fair enough. You know all about models, Professor. Well, a lot of the real world is modeled in the network. All those personal accounts, governments and corporations, and all the remote sensing, data constantly streaming from one place to another. It's all there, to be read and manipulated."

"So what are you saying? Can she make sense of our world, or not?"

Serena's eyes lit up. "The model is not the reality! We know that, don't we, Professor?"

"Exactly!" Joseph high-fived Serena. "She's a part of the network. All that data flowing through her hands. Who knows how she perceives it, but clearly she can manipulate it—"

"And the level of manipulation is scary."

"—But she can never *experience* weather, heat, cold, winds, drought. It's only something she gets to know about through streams of data in the network."

"You talked about motivation." Charles was growing impatient with all this talk of networks and data. "What conclusion is this leading to?"

"We see the effects in terms of lives and hardship, and we struggle to understand why someone would want to do that. But what if concepts like life and suffering don't even register for her? When she messed with all those news reports and sites, she might not have even realized what she was doing."

"Are you saying the manipulation, the climate change, was accidental?" Charles struggled to keep an incredulous screech out of his voice.

Serena shook her head. "It was calculated and purposeful. Very deliberate. But the Professor's right. What good did it do?"

"I don't know." Joseph seemed unfazed by their reaction. "But I am saying that if we want to understand Tiamat, we have to get away from the decades of struggle she caused us. Stop trying to rationalize the human cost and look for explanations that would make sense to Tiamat. Explanations where human lives are simply irrelevant."

Some time in the night the storm had passed on as quickly as it arrived, and an eerie quiet blanketed the hostel. Joseph stirred from restless sleep, unease still nagging at him after the proprietor's manner last night. The Goblin, as the Prof called her, brought images of spiders and webs to Joseph's mind, but even without her unwelcome interest he felt an urgent need to be well away from anywhere populated.

His stomach growled, reminding him they should stock up on provisions while they had the chance. He checked his handheld, looking for a nearby grocery store. A Handi-Mart three blocks away advertised early opening hours.

He nudged the others awake. "I think we need to get out early." Serena and the Professor blinked at him, then came alert at the urgency in his hushed voice.

"I'll get food and see what our chances are of sneaking out. I'd like to get out without Her Creepiness noticing. You get packed and wait 'till I tell you it's safe."

Serena cocked her head to one side, brow creased. "If you make it out, how will you let us know?"

Good question. His mind raced. "Hook your handheld into mine, like we did before. We're only on the second floor and near the front of the building ..." Joseph screwed his eyes shut, trying to picture the turns along the hall and up the stairs. "I think."

"Should have enough range to reach the street, you mean." Serena nodded. She fumbled in her pocket. "Here, this might be useful."

She handed Joseph a tiny pocket cam. Quality model. "Nice," he said. *And just where the heck did you get a piece of hardware like this?*

"Of course, it's linked to my handheld ..."

"Not a problem, as long as I'm in range I can tap in through our link."

Joseph cracked open the door from the eight bed dormitory. Stepping as soundlessly as he could manage, he tried not to look furtive. He kept the camera palmed, feeling his way in the muted glow of night lights shining down the hall and to the top of the stairs. The lens nestled between outstretched fingers gave him sneak views around corners.

The way stayed clear.

He slunk down the main hallway, wondering how quietly he could open the front door. He needn't have bothered. The proprietor seemed to have acute hearing and no use for sleep. As she appeared in a doorway, face scrunched into a scowl, Joseph pocketed the camera. He had a fleeting vision of her hanging upside down from the rafters waiting to pounce on unsuspecting prey.

He gave a friendly wave. "Do you have kitchen facilities? I need to pick up some provisions for breakfast. We were planning on being back in New Boston last night until the storm caught us."

The woman's eyes kept flitting to the entrance door. Joseph's heart thudded. He tried to keep the hammering pulse out of his voice. "Are you expecting your other guests back? Just wondering if you need us out of here in any hurry."

She smiled, a hunter baiting a trap. "No rush, dearie. There's a kitchen through there." She gestured to a door across the hall. "Take all the time you need. I reckon youse be needin' a good fry up, now. The full works. That'll set youse up for yer trip."

Joseph thanked her. His scalp prickled as he slipped out into the street. It was obvious she was expecting reinforcements any minute. If Serena and the Prof tried to leave now, they'd be lucky to reach the truck, and even if they did Joseph doubted they could shake off a close pursuit. As long as the Goblin thought they were in no hurry to leave, Joseph hoped she'd wait for him to return. That would give him some time to think.

Treading carefully on crusted ice in the patchy glow of sparse street lights, he headed back to the main road, away from where they'd parked. Around the corner, he hurried one block then sought a shadowed alley a safe distance from the hostel.

Joseph fumbled with his handheld in the depths of his pockets, reluctant to expose fingers to the pre-dawn frost. He took a deep breath and rehearsed the steps he'd roughed out on the way out of the hostel.

He wouldn't have long if he was to avoid arousing suspicions. That woman was just too darned creepy. Wonder who she's been talking to?

The online world engulfed him. Tin Man, hacker-in-training, opened liquid metal eyes. The hunt was on.

The town's business directory gave him enough details to identify the hostel's owner, and her own site told him the service provider she used. Nunanet. He grimaced at the corporate play on words. He could have easily hacked the hostel's account, but he was pretty sure it was the owner's personal account he wanted. He was also willing to bet she used the same service provider. Human laziness ruled supreme.

Nunanet's defenses, as befitted a network provider, were better than an average commercial site. Tin Man was sure he could have taken them, given time, but he didn't need to. The gamer network routinely published details of corporate site weaknesses for its members' information. Gamers had breached Nunanet recently and left again undetected. The breach was still there.

And there was the creepy hostel owner. Same service provider. Same street address on her account. Tin Man grinned. Did these people know nothing about online safety?

Armed with her account handle, Tin Man started work in earnest.

Voices interrupted him. Joseph froze his avatar and glanced down the street. Two men came into sight, heads bowed, shuffling through the treacherous hail drifts clogging the sidewalk. Their breath hung in the air as they grumbled about the storm keeping them from warm beds and hot food.

They passed. Joseph released his breath, trying not to let it whistle through teeth clenched against chattering. He flexed cramped fingers and resumed his online assault. The cold gave him fresh focus, and he deployed the most incisive tools in his arsenal, discarding subtlety and caution. This old biddy might be a shark in the real world, but her online presence was childishly naive. He need not fear the booby traps favored by corporates or fellow hackers.

There. He was in. Tin Man shared the owner's online world, an invisible fly on the wall.

Oh, you sneaky old bat! Tin Man understood now her supernatural ability to appear when least wanted. A camera feed gave her a constant view of the entrance hall. That was going to make a clean exit tricky.

He set that problem aside for now. Her call history was a mess. It seemed she liked to talk, but none of her recent contacts leaped out as law enforcement. All personal calls, and meaningless to Tin Man. Not without a lot of digging, anyway, which he didn't have time for.

Joseph emerged from full immersion, but kept a small window visible into the hacked account. He hurried on down the street to the grocery store, relieved to find it open after last night's storm.

As he entered, a wash of warmth engulfed him carrying a distant whiff of rubber and fish oil. He took a few moments to orient himself to the rows of shelves. Beige metal racks standing on a green-painted concrete floor gave the store a military feel.

A hawk-faced woman peered at him over an old-fashioned counter to one side of the door. She returned his smile with a surly grunt, and disappeared through a door behind the counter.

Hospitality must be a casualty of Atlantic life, Joseph decided. He grabbed a sturdy shopping bag from the stack by the door and set off down the nearest aisle.

Within seconds, he jumped at a voice inside his head. The account was active.

"Mary, you can relax, he's here."

" 'Bout time too. Thought he'd done a bunk."

"Must have gotten lost on the way. Looks gormless enough to lose himself in his own front yard." Joseph clenched his teeth at that, and only just stopped himself glaring in her direction. "You sure they're the ones?"

"Jeez, Brenda, New Boston police put out descriptions for 'em. Been looking all up'n'down the coast. Gave me some blarney about White Horse and New Boston, but it's got to be them."

Joseph's hands shook as he realized how right his suspicions had been. As he stacked cans of fruit and cooked meat in the bag, a transponder in its rim tracked the electronically-tagged items and built a growing tally in his handheld display.

"Ah, well. Brad'll sort out the truth. You called him?"

"He'll be waiting to pick them up as soon as the lad gets back."

Joseph fumbled a can, and barely saved it from hitting the floor. He took a few deep breaths and tried to focus. Better make this shopping spree count. Who knew when they might be able to get food again?

Feigning a casualness he didn't feel, Joseph took his time filling up two more bags. Rather more than he could explain just for a quick breakfast, but suspicions were already aroused, and would be confirmed anyway when they skipped town in a hurry.

Now, about that ... Who was Brad? Law enforcement? Or some local thug in the pay of the hostel owner? Any plan of action involved knowing which it was.

Joseph dropped the bags on the counter and keyed his handheld to confirm payment for the groceries. The storekeeper glanced out from her office and nodded. Keeping the snooping channel open in case the two witches exchanged any more useful information, Joseph balanced his groceries in his arms and left.

With the first glimmer of dawn pinking the sky, he headed two blocks away from the main street and approached the covered parking lot from behind. As a last resort, he could stay out of the way. From the outside, with his handheld and some gamer help, he might be able to spring Serena and the Prof before Tiamat got to them.

He dropped two bags in the truck and lightened the third, keeping hold of a random collection of goods for appearances. With his lighter load, he peered down the street. He grinned. An unmarked truck sat across from the hostel and down the street in classic surveillance position. Discreet ... only to the overconfident occupants.

He had a plan but he needed help.

Chapter 38

"Hey, Pink?" Joseph lounged in the back seat of the truck, hidden from outside view behind tinted glass and mercifully warm after the icy hike to and from the store.

"Wassup, Tinny?" The voice was subdued, cautious.

"Glad you're here, but haven't you ever heard of sleep?"

"Tried it once. Overrated."

"Need a favor."

"Oh boy, Tinny, the tally's growing. Are you ever going to owe me for all this."

Despite himself, Joseph smiled. "Listen. We need a distraction." He quickly recounted their latest plight. "There's a cruiser waiting along the street right now. They didn't spot me, they're watching the hostel, and too busy trying to look casual."

Pink snorted. "Hick town cops."

"They're waiting for me to turn up, then nab all of us together."

"You want me to draw them off?"

"Could do with a report of some sort. Something they'll have to respond to." Joseph thought back to the way Tiamat had almost trapped them in Serena's house.

"I can't hack into the police network." Pink's voice was plaintive. "I'm not Moonshadow. Even you'd be better at this."

"Can't," Joseph muttered. "I need my eyes in the real world right now. Besides, no need to get that extreme. Find a business nearby and hack that. Place a call, or set off an alarm." He thought. "Wait. You got me on a map there?"

"See it. Hah! Which of the town's two streets are you on?"

"Funny. Look, I think there's a weather station about five klicks north of us. Should be unmanned. See if it's got an alarm system."

"Got it." Pink sounded uneasy. "Doesn't feel right, messing with a station like that. You know we leave infrastructure well alone."

"Needs must, Pink. Sorry. Besides, they'll *have* to check it out, and I'm hoping they're the only ones around to respond."

While Pink Marie set up her diversion, with a great deal of muttering and a few choice phrases she clearly didn't learn at charm school, Joseph worked on a diversion of his own. He hesitated only a moment before assembling a package of fighting hacks. Gamer protocol made it hard to use things like this against a civilian, but, as he'd just reminded Pink, needs must. Besides, the hostel owner had become a combatant the moment she'd ratted on them.

With his software agents ready to deploy, he sat back and waited.

"Almost there, Tinny."

Joseph held his breath. Should he dive in to help? There was nothing more he could do now.

"Gotcha! Alarms at the weather station now showing a break in. I'll give it a minute and then start sending a few damage reports. That should light a fire under their butts."

"Thanks, Pink!" Joseph clambered down from the truck and peeked along the street. Come on, guys. A cold hand gripped his chest. What if this wasn't regular law enforcement? They behaved like dim cops on a stake out, but could he have misunderstood? Another minute passed. Joseph retreated from view, pondering his options.

A screech of tires in the street made him jump. For a second, he failed to process what was happening, then he realized that the roar of the engine was fading. He stepped onto the sidewalk in time to see the unmarked truck swing onto the main street. A siren began its mournful wail.

Keeping his balance on the still-slick sidewalk, Joseph clutched groceries in one hand and worked his handheld with the other. At the intersection before the hostel, his link to Serena came alive again. "Hey, Serena, you there?"

"Affirmative, captain!" Her voice lifted his spirits. "What kept you?"

"Long story, no time. Are you all packed up and ready to go?"

"Sure. Professor? Professor!"

Joseph's heart sank. "What's he up to? Not online, is he?"

"He says he's picking up mail, old school only. No agent, no avatar. I reminded him his account's likely to be watched."

Joseph sighed. "Okay. Don't mean to be twitchy, but ..."

"They really *are* out to get you," Serena chimed in.

"No kidding. Listen, the hallway's being watched. I need to clear the way. Be ready to run for it when I say so."

Pulse thudding in his throat, Joseph swung open the door to the hostel. He saw himself in the camera feed. He paused in the entrance, sure the old lady would be watching like a hawk.

That's right, eyes on me. Really look close. He squeezed his handheld. His connection to the hacked account cut off, and the logic bomb he'd introduced to the camera feed clicked into life.

A shriek of anguish echoed down the hall, tearing at Joseph's conscience.

"Now, Serena!"

Feet clattered down the stairs.

A shadow appeared at the back of the hallway. Joseph's heart stopped for an instant, then he saw the shadow stagger, hands alternately clutching at eyes then ears.

He beckoned Serena and the Professor.

Serena shot a startled glance at the proprietor, and stumbled as the Professor shoved her towards the door. He steadied her, sidestepping the old woman who gazed at them with panicked and sightless eyes.

"What the heck did you do?" Serena's voice came out in a squeak as they hurried to the parking lot.

"Used her own spy feed against her." Joseph swallowed, those cries of pain echoing in his mind. Did he go too far? "You think gamers just play games, don't you?"

Serena's wide eyes mirrored his own across the hood of the truck. She shrugged.

"Things can get nasty. I kept my attack inside safe limits, no permanent damage, but you wouldn't believe some of the things we can do with audio visuals."

"That woman?"

"She'll have spots in front of her eyes and ringing in her ears for"— Joseph hesitated—"a few hours." He tried to sound casual, but her cries haunted him. He hadn't been too careful in setting up his attack. He'd been in a hurry. He'd been angry ... and scared for his life.

———— ◆ ————

Charles munched bread and cold meat, fumbling to work his unfamiliar gamer handheld with one hand. He cursed to himself and stuffed the rest of his food into his mouth. This was the first opportunity he'd had to review the messages he'd picked up that morning, and he was damned if this confounded technology was going to get in his way.

His head ached from too much time spent online, but this reading was gentle relief compared with the intense concentration of the morning. Joseph had turned the wheel over to Serena to help Charles with scouring online maps. Rather, Charles did the scouring and navigating for them while Joseph foraged online and copied every piece of cartography he could find while they still had a useable service connection. They were heading off grid again, and needed to be able to navigate away from any possible pursuit.

The usual maps only showed a handful of roads piercing the mountainous wilderness away from the coast, but with some frantic digging, Joseph had found large scale surveys detailing a network of service and logging trails. The going was slow and rough, but since Joseph explained their close brush with the local law, they all agreed they needed to be doubly careful now using anything connected with civilization.

Here, camped under a stand of dense fir, Charles felt happier knowing they'd charted useable escape routes in three different directions rather than being trapped on a single lane road to nowhere. He swallowed his mouthful and washed it down with a draught from a half-empty canteen. For now, he tried to ignore nagging questions of whether the police interest might have registered on Tiamat's awareness.

Serena's eyes followed the canteen, which gave a hollow gurgle as Charles set it down on a tree stump alongside him. "This may be a silly question ..." Her tone said she felt it anything but silly. "I saw Joseph had picked up lots of food, but we're nearly out of water."

Joseph cocked an eyebrow at her. "*You* try lugging enough overpriced drinking water for three people, on foot, at five in the morning."

Serena's face fell. "You grabbed armloads of food, but no water?"

With a deadpan expression, Joseph said, "I only think on a full stomach." He winked at Charles, who struggled to keep a straight face at Serena's evident distress.

"Put her out of her misery, Joseph." The same question had already occurred to Charles, used as he was to desert conditions in England, but after a morning immersed in every detail of the surrounding landscape he figured he knew the answer.

"Oh, all right." Joseph pouted. He reached through the cab window and rummaged inside, pulling out a round bottle which he rattled at Serena. "Steritabs."

Serena's eyebrows furrowed.

"Never roughed it in the wild?" he prompted.

She shook her head.

"Dunno about you," Joseph said, "but *I'm* not packing drinking water into a rainforest, when it's flowing free out here for the taking. It's probably good to drink straight from the stream, but these will make sure."

Serena's expression darkened, and she punched Joseph in the ribs.

Charles chuckled, then he sobered. "Let's get serious. We all come from different backgrounds, so what seems obvious to one might be a revelation to the others. Remember it. There's no such thing as a stupid question, and from now on we share information freely. Our lives might depend on it."

He looked from Joseph to Serena, whose eyes sparked. Joseph met his gaze. His smirk faltered, then he nodded.

"So, Serena, link in and I'll pass you the package of information Gwen sent me last night. Joseph's already had a chance to dive in. I copied everything to him while we were on the road."

"Dive? Skim, more like. I was interested in the analysis of Tiamat, but there were loads more messages I haven't looked at yet."

"Well, I skimmed that part and looked for the bigger picture. It takes a bit of piecing together from a stream of notes. I think Gwen is aware that time is of the essence, and she's just forwarding findings and supposition as soon as they discover them. It makes for a rather confusing stream-of-consciousness reading, but I think I can sum it up in two statements."

Joseph grunted. "You're streets ahead of me, then."

"Statement one." Charles held up a forefinger. "The good news is, they think they know how to deal with Tiamat."

Serena's eyes lit up. "Really? That's awesome! How? Does that mean we can go home?"

"Slow down." Joseph didn't seem to share Serena's enthusiasm. "I think that's maybe a bit of a stretch, from what I read."

"I did say 'they think,' and you, Serena, should know by now how much store I place in precise choice of words."

"Yes, Professor," Serena sighed.

"But I was only judging from the gist of Gwen's summary. So, Joseph, what did you make of the analysis from her students?"

Joseph puckered his lips like he'd just eaten a lemon. "Told you it would be over my head."

"Never mind the details, did you get any notion of what they were on about?"

"They tried picking apart her architecture, except there wasn't an architecture to pick apart."

Serena rolled her eyes. "I'm no expert, but that doesn't make sense. You said yourself everything online has its own architecture."

"Exactly. That's what showed them we weren't dealing with any-thing constructed."

"Emergent." Charles's voice raised a notch. "I bet as soon as they looked too close, she just dissolved in front of their eyes."

"They put it a lot more technically than that, a whole lot of chaos and complexity theory, but that kinda sums it up. I don't get it. It's just so much mumbo-jumbo to me." Joseph looked quizzically at Charles. "How did you guess? You said you skimmed the detail."

"Ever look at a mosaic? A picture on a wall or a floor, made up of different-colored tiles?"

"Or an old-fashioned raster display?"

"That's a good example, especially those antiques with the red-green-blue dots." Charles smiled. This kid knew *some* history, at least. "The picture is clear from a distance, but if you look closely, all you can see is the tiles."

Serena's eyes widened. "The picture isn't there at all. It only emerges at a distance."

"Emergent *behavior* is more complex." Charles chewed the inside of his cheek. "The best example I can think of is how corporations behave, or mobs. They show their own patterns of behavior that you'd never imagine just from the individuals that make them up. So, according to Gwen, something about Typhoon spoiled the way Tiamat emerges from the chaos."

"Professor Stoppard's notes said something about temporal coherence being critical."

"Temporal ... we put a lot of effort into temporal integrity in Typhoon," said Charles. "The theorems we were trying to model assume millions of actors working simultaneously, but they needed to be kept together in our simulation's timeframe. The trouble we kept hitting was when some parts of the process ran faster than others because they were running in different parts of the cloud. Terry put weeks of effort into tightening up the timing."

"That was good for your simulation, but bad for Tiamat. Seems like she depends on some randomness, some noise, to exist."

"Okay, that explains what Gwen's on about here. She reckons her students can come up with something that will kill her off for good." Charles took a deep breath, then held up two fingers. "Statement two. The bad news is, there's no way to put it into practice."

Chapter 39

Joseph could understand the Professor's pessimism. To someone so clueless about the online underworld it would sound like an impossible task. Certainly not for the faint of heart, nor for the law-abiding. He was neither, and he'd spent the last hour studying the reports in more detail. "It means effectively hacking past the security of major nodes in the network and infecting them with a virus."

Serena was aghast. "We can't infect the whole network!"

Joseph eased himself into a more comfortable position leaning against the truck, and grinned. "We don't need to. We only need to take out a few key points."

"How can that work? Surely she'll just use the rest of the network."

"That's the thing about emergent phenomena. They need a certain level of complexity, a certain critical mass, to show themselves." Joseph quelled a hint of smugness on seeing Charles's appraising expression. *Yes, I've read up about emergence.* "Break up the global net with enough zones that Tiamat can't live in, and there won't be enough connected chunks left to support her."

Serena looked dubious.

"It's happened before," the Professor said. "In the real world." He gestured to the trees around them.

Joseph felt a tingle of irritation. Trust the old man to throw him off his stride. "I don't follow."

"You need to read more history, young man. A century ago, this planet teemed with life. Millions of species, many of them with their own special habitats. People started noticing that some species weren't doing so well. They had plenty of habitat left, more than enough to support them, in theory, but it was broken up into pieces too small to support a viable population."

"So they died off?"

"That's right, Serena." To Joseph, he said, "This sounds like it might work ... in theory."

"So what's your problem?"

"Although it's only a small percentage of the global network, we'd apparently need to hack over five hundred major centers and deploy the virus, all within a matter of minutes."

Joseph looked incredulous at the Professor. Then he laughed. "Only five hundred. Is that all you're worried about?"

The Professor nodded, looking at Joseph as if he was finally cracking under the strain.

"Have you any idea how many thousands of gamers my clan could recruit? Top class hackers? They may not all be like Moonshadow, but they've probably already breached most of these systems in the past." And we keep and share records. "Pink Marie's been recruiting. I haven't checked in with her in a while, but we have something concrete to do now. We need an army to take on Tiamat. All the gamers need is an excuse to have some fun."

<hr>

Charles gazed up through feathery evergreens at the mountain hulking dark above them. Dripping cliffs towered into cloud. Somewhere up there an air traffic beacon guided planes into New Boston ... and offered a connection to the global grid.

He stretched the kinks out of his aching body. They'd chosen this spot because they would be in range of the beacon's public service broadcast while still staying well hidden. Better still, they could reach it from where they'd camped using only an obscure and disused forest trail. The downside to paranoid skulking was a battered coccyx. And shredded nerves. Never mind that the truck was designed for off-road, the trail was narrow, overgrown, steep and nearly impassable in places. The snow-packed roads around Krisgaarde that had terrified him in a previous life seemed like a distant nirvana in comparison.

With a scowl, he pulled the gamer's dual handheld from his pocket that Joseph had configured for him, and regarded it with distaste.

Joseph looked at Charles, worry creasing his forehead. "It's a lot to take in. Not just the controls for your avatar, it's the whole online culture I'm worried about. Gamers have their own rules. The outside world doesn't exist. Most important to remember, down there I'm Tin Man, not Joseph. Say the wrong thing, and it could wreck any chance of a deal."

"Human culture is my life's work," Charles snapped, "and I've been doing my own homework about your gamer etiquette. It's the bloody avatar I'm worried about."

"All the same, Professor, please, let me do the talking until I say so, okay? I need to get their attention before you present our findings."

Joseph flicked his own handheld to life. His eyes took on a faraway look.

Charles glanced at Serena.

"Good luck," she said. She gave what Charles guessed was intended to be a reassuring smile, but anxiety clouded her eyes.

He grunted and fingered the handheld. He was still reeling from the crash course in immersive interaction, mind brimming with new codes. Until their conference with Gwen, he'd only ever got to grips with light immersion, enough to work with, to access public services and lifesaving information. This was a whole new world.

And this time, his audience would not be friendly.

His breathing grew ragged.

Whiteness engulfed him. Not quite sterile, hospital white. This was blue-white like the inside of a lightning bolt. His surroundings were invisible, just blinding light with no source.

Tin Man stood alongside, metal skin gleaming dark against the stark backdrop. He turned.

Charles followed, and stumbled, gripped with vertigo at the sudden shift in perspective. They stood on a road suspended in mid air. Side roads led off every few meters. He doubted he would ever get used to this world. How did youngsters cope?

Tin Man led him down a nearby turn-off, which ended in the clouds. Charles had to will himself to step off the end, following Tin Man's lead. He blinked. They were in a dark alley dripping with moisture.

A large drop splashed on Charles's forehead. He jumped. Without thinking, he wiped the dampness away with the back of his hand and reeled as his viewpoint cartwheeled in response to his hand movement.

It took a few moments to regain his balance, battling to separate conflicting sensations from the real and online worlds.

"You okay, Prof?" Tin Man peered at him, but it was Serena's hands he felt on his shoulders, supporting him.

Charles stood stock still and took a deep breath. The world steadied. He recounted the ground rules like a calming mantra. Vision and hearing came from his avatar. Everything else—touch, smell, balance—belonged to the real world around him. He had to blot those out. Deliberately, without moving his head, he made his avatar nod. "I'm okay. Let's get moving."

Onwards they hastened through disjointed scenes: a glass-lined hall, a room full of advertising hoardings, a grassy meadow. Tin Man seemed to know where to find doors and openings that Charles couldn't see.

In a cavernous space filled with tangled pipes like a giant oil refinery, Tin Man paused on a high gangway. "Nearly there. You okay?"

"As okay as I'll ever be." Charles wished he could release his handheld long enough to rub his pounding temples. This space reminded him too much of the geothermal plant.

Tin Man pointed down a ladder. "You need to climb down three rungs, then step off. Only the third rung will work. Any other, and you'll fall."

He swung himself down, pausing on the third rung to glance up at Charles before stepping backwards and vanishing.

Charles sighed. So what if he fell? There was nothing real here. Was there? He followed Tin Man and found himself in a circular room, about thirty meters across, lined with unmarked doors. Looking behind him, it seemed as if they had emerged from one such door.

Avatars of all shapes and sizes crossed the space, entering and leaving.

Tin Man gestured. "Here we are. You ready, Professor?"

Charles swallowed and nodded, then remembered to make his avatar nod. "How do you know which door is which?"

"One of the secrets of the clan." Tin Man winked. "We have our ways. An intruder would be lost."

A purple unicorn paused to give Charles's unmodified avatar a contemptuous once-over before prancing through a nearby door. Past her swaying buttocks—it could surely only be a 'her', Charles decided—he glimpsed an endless vista of rippling grass, sprinkled with patches of white and blue flowers. The patches formed a huge checkered pattern, like a giant chessboard. And was that a rook-shaped cloud floating in the distance? The door shut.

Tin Man opened the adjacent door.

Charles followed him through, instincts telling him he should see the unworldly chess game. Rational thought reminded him these worlds obeyed no kind of physical geometry.

The space beyond felt small, cozy, like the firelit snug of an English pub. When he looked hard past Tin Man, Charles blinked. Tin Man was lit by a warm yellow glow against a background the color of oak-paneled shadows, but there were no panels, in fact no discernible walls. He glanced down, and hastily looked away. They seemed to be standing in mid-air, surrounded by a velvety, clinging nothingness.

A tabby cat strolled into view. A pink tutu and bodice strained to contain a biologically-improbable bust.

"Professor," said Tin Man, "this is Pink Marie. Good to see you, Pink."

"Hey, Tinny." Glowing eyes regarded Charles. "Surely you could have dressed him?" She sounded uneasy.

"No time. And the Prof insisted on sticking with off-the-shelf."

After a moment's confusion, Charles realized Pink Marie was referring to his untailored avatar. "There's no way I can pass for one of you," he said. "Better not to even try."

"The clan won't like it," Pink whispered. "Be ready to exit if things get ugly."

More avatars appeared while they talked. Some greeted Tin Man and Pink Marie. A few gazed curiously at Charles. He gazed back, smiling like an idiot before he remembered that his facial expressions would not be reflected by his avatar. He tried to maintain his composure and quell a mounting sense of nakedness. He reminded himself that this was not real. He was standing, safe and fully clothed, by the side of the truck. *I am a professor of anthropology. I have nothing to fear from these children.*

Charles forced himself to stay detached from his virtual surroundings. He studied the growing throng of avatars, shapes and vibrant colors glowing stark against the emptiness beyond. People, animals, mythical creatures, animated machines, filled the space, some drawn with unnerving realism, some cartoon-like. All were exquisite works of art.

He noticed that the snug space ballooned as the crowd grew. More and more avatars appeared and took their place in an expanding amphitheater, arranged in ranks so that at all times he had a perfect view of each one. A growing murmur of conversation enveloped him.

A metallic peacock strutted past. It cocked a beady eye at Charles, and recoiled with a sharp hiss. The hiss lowered to a steady exhalation. It was joined by others, here and there at first, then more from all sides. The sound grew, like a distant waterfall.

"Told you this could get nasty." Pink Marie moved slightly closer to Charles. "Stick close to me if anyone makes a move."

"Don't say anything," Tin Man hastened to add. "It'll be broadcast to the world. We've opened a private chatline to you. We can choose who hears what we say, but I don't think you've mastered that kind of control."

Charles bit back a reply. Tin Man was right.

The crowd, and the boundless space they inhabited, still expanded. Charles grew dizzy trying to take it all in. There had to be at least a thousand of them there now, and more arrived every moment. At least the angry hissing subsided. Charles guessed it was designed to provoke a reaction and, having failed, the instigators lost interest.

A hush fell. Expectation weighed like an approaching storm.

"Here comes Deacon." Pink Marie sounded like she wanted to be elsewhere, but suddenly, without seeming to move, the three of them stood on nothingness at the center of the vast arena.

A figure approached. Rather, he seemed to stand still while space, standing equally still, adjusted around him. Charles blinked and shook his head, reminding himself that his eyes were hostage to whatever tricks the gamers chose to play in this world.

Deacon stood in front of the trio, a drab monk's habit topped by a gleaming, polished skull. Vacant eye sockets regarded Charles, seeming to look through him, or past him, without acknowledging his presence.

Deacon shifted his sightless gaze. "Tin Man." He drawled the words, with a subtle and insolent emphasis on the first.

Charles bristled, but kept quiet. The academic in him reveled in the chance to study this new culture up close, while the dinosaur floundered in the queasiness of sensory immersion.

"I find myself bemused and short on patience," Deacon continued. "You convene a meeting of the clan. You claim to have something of importance to discuss, and you violate these hallowed halls with this ... this *beerbump*."

"Ouch," Pink Marie whispered in Charles's mind. "I guess you don't know just how badly he insulted you. Don't answer. Best not to react."

Charles had already decided that stoic immobility was the best strategy, for now.

"Why do you insult us so?" Deacon still addressed Tin Man, apparently ignoring the thousands surrounding him, but Charles was sure he was playing to the gallery.

"I brought him here because we need your help. He crossed Tiamat and now he's being hunted. You can see for yourselves, he doesn't belong here." Joseph gestured at Charles's conspicuous avatar.

Privately, Pink said, "Okay, you win, I see why you stuck with off-the-shelf."

"Who is he to us? Why should we care?"

"You don't. But I am also being hunted and I call on the clan to help. I brought him here to bear witness to my claims."

Charles wondered at the stilted speech. Mock medieval? Hierarchical society, he decided. So, they needed this Deacon's blessing. That made sense.

"This noob couldn't bear witness to his own reflection!"

"Says he who lectures on the dangers of looks alone."

Verbal sparring? Charles wracked his brain for memories that might help him here. Prior to last night's hurried cramming from hastily-downloaded documents, he'd read a paper on gamer cultures a few years ago. He wished he'd paid closer attention then, but the paper had included a large immersive component to it, which he'd elected to pass on.

"Does the outsider have a tongue?"

Deacon still faced Tin Man. Charles decided that he, the outsider, was still a silent third party in this argument and the butt of another insult.

"That depends on the will of the clan."

Deacon hissed, "In this arena, I *am* the clan."

So, Tin Man had just tried to bypass Deacon's authority. But was that an edge in Deacon's voice? A vulnerability?

"With this man's help, I have uncovered matters of importance to *all* members here. Am I to be heard?"

"We cannot help this outsider." The reply was flat and emotionless. A sigh like surf on a beach swept through the encircling throng.

Charles had had enough. He stepped between Tin Man and Deacon, pointedly turning his back on the latter. "We're wasting our time," he said to Tin Man. He poured as much contempt as he could manage into his words. "I told you this candy bandit wouldn't be up to it."

CHAPTER 40

Tin Man's heart stopped beating. Beside him, Pink gasped, then silence pressed around him a tangible weight in his mind.

What the hell was the old git playing at? Did he understand what he'd just said? And where had he picked up that gamer insult anyway?

The Professor turned and looked Deacon up and down, a slow and measured movement. Tin Man wasn't sure if the slowness was lack of experience with the handheld, but the effect was of open scorn.

His mind raced, wondering how to rescue the situation. There was no way to get Deacon onside now. This was scarily close to all-out war, and Deacon had some dangerous weapons to play with.

Before Tin Man could say anything, the Professor spoke. "Your world is under attack. Tiamat is picking you off, one by one, and you cower here in your hidey-hole too scared to face her. You're full of fancy talk, but that robe's just an empty bit bucket."

This time, the collective intake of breath surrounded Tin Man like wind in a forest.

Deacon stepped forward, polished skull pressed close to the Professor's expressionless face. "You have no idea who you are dealing with, old man. You think you're safe, driving this remote-controlled puppet from a distance? I can reach into your mind and visit nightmares on you that will keep you in therapy for the rest of your miserable life."

"Moonshadow is dead," the Professor retorted. "My friend and colleague is dead. My home town was ravaged and dozens are dead."

He stepped forward. Deacon staggered a pace back.

"Tiamat has driven a snow plough at me. She's thrown boiling oil at me, and crashed a plane I was aboard. I am still here. What possible harm can *you* visit on me that I haven't already faced?"

"Impressive breadcrumbs, old man," Deacon sneered. "So, you tangled with Tiamat. So what? This world and the outside world don't meet."

"This is no *game!*" the Professor bellowed. "I *am* talking about the world outside." He ignored the gasps and cries of outrage. "That is the world your bodies inhabit while your minds are here. You can't have *this* world without the real world out there."

"We don't talk about that here," Deacon hissed.

"Try saying that while your apartment floods with carbon monoxide from a remotely-sabotaged heater." It was the Prof's turn to face Deacon, eyeball to empty socket. "*This* is what Tiamat does to you when you cross her path." He gestured, and a cloud of newscasts filled the space.

The old man learned quickly, Joseph noted with grudging admiration. He'd taught him that trick barely an hour ago.

"She doesn't delete you from virtual space. She doesn't scare you off to go crying in a corner. She drives a vehicle at you. Burns down your home with your family still in it. Drops the elevator you're riding. Fills your prescription with a lethal cocktail." The multitude of accident reports fluttered like wind-blown leaves. Each one detailed a gruesome death, each tagged with a gamer's name. "She kills you."

Words had deserted Deacon. All around the meeting hall, gamers reached for the drifting reports, picked them up. A rumble of conversation swelled, disbelief, anger.

Finally, the Professor held up his arm, three more reports clenched in his virtual fist. "These were aimed at me. I am a dead man walking. Each time I go online I risk my life, yet here I am. I came to warn you— and to seek your help." He paused for breath. "I am Professor Charles Ainsley Hawthorne, and Tiamat fears me."

———•◆•———

"Why are you doing this?" A cold voice hissed into Charles's mind. Deacon's eye sockets swiveled towards him.

He's scared. He needs a way out. Charles guessed he was the only one in the throng who could hear Deacon's words and wished he could answer as privately.

The voice sounded again, a frustratingly one-way conversation. "You cannot seek to displace me. You are not one of us."

"You lead these people," Charles said, choosing his words carefully, knowing they would carry to the entire congregation. "Their safety is in your care."

Deacon spread his arms—Charles noticed they were empty sleeves, no hands—and the four of them were suddenly alone. "Words are like swords in your hands. I think it best to keep such sharp implements to ourselves."

Charles spun around. The space was once more small and intimate.

"Yes, we can talk privately. But be quick. The clan won't wait long and, thanks to you, my hold on them is now measured in minutes."

Charles gazed at Deacon. "I'm not trying to challenge you, you already pointed out that isn't credible, but my life is in danger, my family is in danger. I will do whatever it takes to end the threat."

"I cannot, I *will* not, order the clan into danger."

"They are in danger already!" Tin Man said. "Gamers come, gamers go. With all that movement amongst a membership of thousands, we don't notice one every month vanishing for good. But now we know, ignorance is no excuse. Tiamat is a danger to all of us wherever we go, and she will be until we get rid of her."

While Deacon pondered this, Charles said, "We don't need you to order anything of the sort. I don't pretend to understand half of what's going on, but the plan is not to confront Tiamat directly."

"There's no time right now for the details," said Tin Man, "but we know she's not man-made, not a construct. She's an emergent property of the global network. She evolved in the open architecture, and"—he smirked—"we know how to poison her."

"Pah!" Deacon spat.

"It doesn't take much to disrupt whatever emergent processes make up her intelligence. That's why she's so hell-bent on killing the Professor. His experiment tightened up temporal connections between threads, and the space he created destroys her."

"I can't claim the credit. I'm just an anthropologist. Terry did all the messing about that she took exception to."

"We can't poison every plenum on the network!" Deacon's eye sockets widened in disbelief.

Tin Man spread out his hands. "There's a threshold. She needs a huge contiguous slice of the network just to exist. Without that, the emergence collapses. All we need is to fragment her ecosystem." He shot a furtive glance at Charles. "We need gamers to do what gamers do best. Break into some of the major nodes and infect them with a small modification to the kernel code's configuration."

"Tin Man." Deacon drew himself up and squared his nonexistent shoulders. "This is folly. It will draw unwanted attention to our clan. We'll be shut down."

Wishing he knew enough controls to give his avatar facial expressions, Charles rested his hand on Tin Man's shoulder and did his best to stare down his nose at Deacon. "Your clan is about to desert you. You said so yourself. I thought you gamers were all about adventure, about thumbing your nose at authority." He paused to let his words sink in. "For those who want adventure, we're offering the chance to slay a dragon. The question is, are *you* going to give them that opportunity, or are you going to leave it to Tin Man?"

CHAPTER 41

"Professor?" In the darkened cab of the truck, Serena's voice had that distant quality again, but with an uncharacteristic edge of excitement. "You wondered about the media manipulation? Why push the Skeptics' agenda when it could have wiped us out altogether?"

"And Tiamat with it," added Joseph. "She was on a suicidal course."

Despite the mind-sapping damp and cold, Serena's tone kindled a spark of curiosity. "In between hiding from cops, it *has* been bugging me." More than a bit. Solving one mystery seemed to have left an even more puzzling one, but without Typhoon Charles had suspended any thought of answering it.

"Well, I think you forgot one important bit."

Charles hesitated. He'd seen Serena's insight at work before, and tried to guess where this was leading. Frustrated, he resigned himself to taking her bait. "I've run through your work in my mind a thousand times. You modeled it perfectly. I've spent a career trying to fathom how we came down this road, despite the science and the know-how."

"Turn of the century science?" Joseph's tone dripped with scorn.

"Weather forecasting was pretty random," Charles conceded, "but climate models were starting to show some predictive worth." Impatient, he nudged Serena with his foot, where she huddled at the other end of the back seat.

"I only had time to model the climate change part," she said. "The bit that showed us running off the cliff. The bit you were never able to recreate."

Okay, rub it in!

"But I never got to the next part, and keep your stinky feet to yourself if you want me to put you out of your misery." Her silhouette shifted in the dark, a shadow against the watery grey beyond the window.

"Next part?" Charles said slowly. It sounded like maybe he *had* missed something. He pulled his feet closer in, trying to find a comfortable position curled up against the door.

"In that pack of doctored reports, we focused on the ones that bolstered the Skeptics and rubbished the science." She paused. Charles had a feeling he knew what was coming, but he let her have her triumph. "We never got around to looking at the tail end of that set. There were a few from the thirties that suggests she also engineered the backlash."

"A few?" Joseph sounded puzzled. "There were thousands of pro-Skeptic slants. She put a lot of work into that. I assumed that handful of others were just mistakes. Maybe swept up in the search, not even Tiamat's work."

"I only saw a few. There may be more, but once the climate started to get really wild, it only took a tiny nudge to reverse the whole set-up. A few scandals of doctored data." The glee in her voice was unmistakable. "She even exposed some of her own media rigging."

Joseph whistled. "Neat! Nothing like evidence of conspiracy to turn the tide."

Charles looked from one shadow to the other, his mouth hanging open. "Do you realize what you're saying? If this swing was as deliberate as the first, what level of control that would take?"

"She pushed us down a path, then pulled us back. Too late to save the climate, but just in time to save civilization." Serena hesitated.

"She railroaded us!" Joseph whispered.

"But I see what you mean, Professor," said Serena. "We came damned close to reverting back to the stone age."

Silence lengthened as they pondered the implications. Eventually, Joseph said, "This is nuts. She almost destroys us, then does an about turn. Why?"

Charles's voice was grim. "I think we can safely say she didn't have a change of heart. Human lives have no value."

"So," said Serena, "the question is really what did it gain her?"

More silence followed.

Joseph spoke first again. "Could she have realized she was pushing herself off the cliff too?"

"Bullshit." Serena sounded too tired to be polite. "Doesn't explain why push us there in the first place." She yawned, a plaintive sound in the dark. "She must have known all along she needed us to keep her going."

Charles drew a blanket closer around him, puzzling over motivations, cause and effect, and the course of history. He was getting nowhere, going round in circles and battling exhaustion from their precarious road trip and online foray. Carefully-rationed bread, cold meat, and tinned fruit barely satisfied hunger pangs, and cold seeped into his core. He longed for the luxury of a cup of tea.

He was drifting off into fitful sleep when his eyes flew open. "Dammit! Think how the world changed in those thirty or so years." His heart beat wildly.

"Ummm ..." Joseph murmured sleepily. He would never cut it in one of Charles's classes.

"Billions of people gone," Serena cut in. "Populations displaced. Water wars."

That was more like it, Serena, but ... "Never mind the human aspect," Charles prompted. "Think how science and computing shifted."

"Needs must," said Joseph, suddenly fully awake.

"Huh?" It was Serena's turn to sound lost.

"I mean, everything became about survival. Science focused just on what we needed to stay alive."

"Exactly." And the non-essentials, like me, vanished.

"The engineers became the saviors," said Joseph, "and we needed every ounce of computing power to keep things going. We became slaves to a networked world like never before."

"And look at us now," said Serena. "We know to the nearest few minutes when a storm is brewing, where it will hit, and how badly. We can forecast how many weeks the growing season will be in any part of the world, and how hot or wet it will be, so we can plan what crops to plant. But our survival depends on ever more powerful computers to keep the world running."

"And we're still building up our infrastructure." Joseph sounded excited, as he completed the train of thought that had startled Charles out of his doze. "Genetics and materials sciences are still in their infancy. They reckon we need to double the capacity of the network before they can make the breakthroughs we need in crop genetics, superconductors, and solar arrays."

"It was a risky strategy," Charles said, "but history and evolution are full of examples. Nothing brings on technological advances quicker than wars and adversity, and in nature organisms under stress either die or grow stronger."

"Holy shit, Professor. She tricked us into building her nest."

————————

Sleep was hard to come by after that revelation, but Charles drifted in and out through a night troubled by visions of computers run amok, of red blinking eyes, of wires snaking out of the ground to snare him.

When grey light tiptoed through steamed windows, it was clear that Joseph and Serena had fared little better. Their eyes held haunted shadows as they breakfasted in silence.

Charles checked the time. "We need to get moving. Gwen's expecting us to rendezvous, and it'll take us at least an hour to get back into position under that beacon, assuming you plan to pick up service at the same spot."

"That's the closest," said Joseph, "and I like that we can reach it without going near a marked road."

"Assuming we make it in one piece," Serena grumbled. "At least you have a wheel to hold on to. We rattle around in the back like popcorn."

Once more in the shadow of the mountain, its peak today standing stark and clear against dazzling blue, Charles blew life into fingers cramped from gripping straps and seat backs. Joseph had taken it as easy as he could but the ride was still numbing.

"We'll have to head back towards a town tomorrow," he said. "This terrain is hard on fuel consumption."

Charles grimaced. "Let's worry about that later. Right now, let's hope Gwen has something for us."

Online once more, Charles followed Tin Man through a virtual labyrinth to the university conference zone. Gwen prowled the room, sleek fur and leather glistening ethereal power. There was no sign of her students.

Gwen's tail twitched. Charles's heart sank. She must have bad news. Before he could ask, the room seemed to shimmer in his mind. He blinked, and leaned back against the truck to keep his balance. When he looked up again, Gwen and Tin Man were in conversation.

"That's all there is to it?" Tin Man twirled a tiny golden disc in his hand.

"We picked apart what Terry did in Typhoon. Given all those months of work, it turned out to be remarkably simple."

"You mean you did it?" Relief flooded through Charles, washing away the aches, the cold, and the hunger.

"Did you really doubt me, Charlie Boy?" To Tin Man, she said, "I give you Operation Buckshot. My students packaged it up into a self-installing, self-replicating package. You just need to deploy it in the cloud management layer to infect a zone."

The meeting room flickered again. The pristine walls turned grainy, then reappeared firm once more.

"Professor Stoppard, we're having trouble with the connection."

"Not surprising. That's the other bit I wanted to warn you about. The network's collapsing."

"What?"

"I don't know what's going on, but here's some news reports you should check out. The elevator summary is there's a global shortage of computing power, and every big user is blaming everyone else for hoovering up the capacity."

"And I'll bet there's an untraceable tangle of usage reports that make it impossible to tell where the power is really going."

"How did you guess?" Gwen hissed through a screen of static. The room whirled and steadied again, then disintegrated around them.

With a hollow feeling in his stomach that had nothing to do with hunger, Charles said, "Tiamat is up to something."

Joseph leaped into the truck. "Come on. I've got to reach Pink. The service is too patchy down here. We need to get closer to the beacon, or another service point."

The truck bumped along the trail. "Take it easy!" Charles struggled to keep his fingers steady on the handheld, tracing a path through the maps Joseph had downloaded. "Another two kilometers and there should be a fork. Head right."

Trees gave way to scrubby grass. The beacon appeared in the distance, still high overhead, a skeletal framework silhouetted against the sky.

"Should be close enough." Joseph sounded uneasy. Charles sympathized. He felt far too exposed out here. Would they have any surveillance?

"Stay offline, Professor. It'll help if there's only one of us using up bandwidth." Without waiting for an answer, Joseph launched himself and started subvocalizing.

He was immersed for an age. Charles scanned the empty road and barren hills around them, senses alert for the flash of lights and sound of sirens.

Wind moaned around them. No sirens howled.

Joseph's face turned white as he cut the connection. "I think I've got an answer to the network shambles. To put it bluntly, we're screwed."

Charles gave him a blank look.

"Pink is going frantic. The whole under-layer is turning into a no-go zone. Tiamat is everywhere, and gamers are dropping like flies."

"Wait, what do you mean, everywhere?"

"I never gave it a thought. I've always assumed there was only one Tiamat, but just because we can only control one avatar at a time doesn't mean she can't run more."

"Tiamat ..." Serena breathed heavily. "It must take power to produce her avatars and give them intelligence."

"The media, and all the big public bodies, are blaming the spate of accidents on the resource shortage. There's been big city-center pile-ups, gas explosions, chemical leaks, all sorts. It's fucking indiscriminate, but you can bet there's a gamer or two caught up in each one. Not that anyone will ever put two and two together."

"Or realize that the resource shortage is the result, not the cause, of the accidents."

"Trouble is, Deacon's called an embargo on all ventures, and Operation Buckshot is off limits."

They stared at each other, stunned, before Joseph thumbed the truck back to life and turned back down the service road.

"So," said Charles, "we've got our silver bullet, but lost our army."

A few kilometers down the mountainside, they came to a regular road winding through the valley. Joseph chose a direction at random. "We'll recruit them back again. This can't last forever, Tiamat surely can't hide her tracks like this for long. There'll be tech crews picking through the network already. She'll have to go back into hiding."

"It's still only the under-layers that are dangerous, isn't it?" Serena seemed close to tears. "I mean, can't you use the regular parts of the network, where everyone else goes?"

Joseph sighed. "To get close to our targets, yes, but we need to go under to break past zone security. That's where she'll catch us."

"If you don't get caught first by one of those techs you said would be swarming around the place," said Charles. "I wonder if that's part of the game? Make it hard to sneak around?"

"We need a diversion," said Serena. "Wonder what would hold her attention?"

Serena was right, but Charles was fresh out of ideas. Maybe Joseph would come up with something. He seemed to be uncommonly devious. As he usually did when faced with a problem, Charles sought out distractions. He leafed through the sheaf of reports Gwen had passed him before the connection broke.

"These snippets from Gwen confirm it." Charles came up for air and gazed out the window at the valley rolling past. "The world out there is going to hell. Makes me glad we're so far removed from it."

"Wonder if this means the cops will be too busy to bother with us."

Charles laughed, brief and brittle. "Always looking on the bright side, Serena?"

He turned his gaze inwards once more, appalled at the destruction overcoming the world beyond their horizon. Not for the first time, he gave thanks that his family was so far removed from the global network.

"It looks bad, Professor." Serena was also studying the files he'd shared with her and Joseph. "When you see it all listed out like this, it's a lot to take in. But spread out over the world it's a drop in the ocean really."

He sighed. Serena was right. Civilization wasn't collapsing around them. Tiamat was too careful for that. It was just the work of a dispassionate serial killer keeping her territory clean.

Then he froze. His fingers trembled on the handheld, palms slick with sweat.

One message looked different from the others. It was like nothing he'd ever seen before. The envelope gleamed ruddy gold, with a subliminal shimmer of scales.

Tiamat had sent him a message.

CHAPTER 42

Charles stared at the glistening envelope, dreading what it might hold. *Clues*, a small voice whispered. Besides, he was offline, what harm could it do?

Bracing himself, not knowing what to expect, he opened the envelope.

Most messages opened into a page of information like an old-fashioned paper letter, not that anyone remembered those any more. Some simulated real paper, or parchment, or vellum. Some, reflecting the idiosyncrasies of the sender, looked like beaten gold, or brushed aluminum, or shimmered like water or smoke. They contained writing, still or moving pictures, sound. But most messages were sent by people following normal social conventions.

This envelope disintegrated with a hiss into a swirl of golden scales that engulfed him in a dizzying vortex. Charles jumped, barely containing a yelp of surprise. One of the scales grew until it filled his vision. Its surface twinkled and cleared like morning mist to reveal a news report. The snow plough at Krisgaarde.

It slid to one side and another took its place. The geothermal plant. More images paraded silently in front of his eyes. He shivered. There were no words, but a clear message. *I know you.*

Finally, a new image wafted into view. It showed a regular mail message, correctly formatted, perfectly normal.

It was addressed from him to Sylvie.

It was time stamped this morning.

Goosebumps crawled up Joseph's arms at Charles's anguished yell behind him. Frantically, trying to look in every direction at once, he scanned the road ahead and behind for signs of approaching danger. He craned his neck to take in the bare hills towering on either side, feeling perilously exposed away from decent tree cover.

A squeal from Serena brought him back to reality, and he grappled with the wheel to bring the truck back onto the road. He pulled over, puzzled why the Prof hadn't reacted to their wayward lurching, and twisted around in his seat.

The old man's jaw twitched and his gaze was unfocused. He was blind to the world outside so whatever had upset him was on his handheld.

Joseph's spine tingled with ice as he conferenced in with Charles and Serena. A simple mail message lay open in their shared workspace. "Dear Sylvia," he read aloud. "I've been hiding in New Boston while I sort things out. All is good now. I'm coming home, flight IA2737 landing in Isfeldt at 13:25. Please meet me. Charles." It took Joseph a few moments to digest the message, and a few more for the implications to sink in. "It's another trick. It has to be." He fumbled for words to calm the Professor. The beads of sweat and frantic eyes suggested he was not having much luck.

"Dammit! Of course it's a trick! But this time, I'm not the one she needs to fool."

Joseph's stomach lurched. He hardly dared breathe the words. "You think the message itself is real?"

"We've already seen she can learn," Serena said. "And she's shown she can create original content."

"I'll contact Pink again." Joseph tried to sound more reassuring than he felt. "She can contact your daughter and warn her." He cranked the wheel of the truck over and began to turn on the narrow road. "We just need to get back to somewhere with decent service."

"Too late. Sylvie can only be reached through the mail room and she must have already left. You'll never reach her. She'll drive right through Krisgaarde and on to Isfeldt."

Joseph cursed. Even under duress, the old goat's logic seemed perversely compelling. "What do you think Tiamat has in mind?"

Charles's face sagged. "Who knows? She uses whatever machinery is close to hand. Traffic guidance seems to be a favorite. All I know is Sylvie will be within reach." He checked the clock on the truck's console, and frowned. "That flight lands inside an hour, and she'll be there to meet it."

"All the same, what does Tiamat hope to gain? Your daughter lives mostly off-grid. She's never come into contact with Tiamat, as far as we know, anyway."

"Bait. Just like that faked news report. We've managed to stay out of Tiamat's reach, and this is meant to flush me out."

"She must have been tracking your mail," said Serena. "We set up this meeting time with Professor Stoppard through your mailbox. She doesn't have a handle on our immersive accounts to hunt us through, but she knew we'd be talking again and guessed you'd check for mail at the same time."

Another thought entirely struck Joseph like a trip hammer. "Let me check your handheld." Heart thudding, he pulled out a diagnostic toolkit and set to work. A few minutes later, he returned to the real world, puzzled. "I'm sure she's up to something. There's stuff going on in your handheld that I can't decipher. Something so alien it must be Tiamat's work, but I've no idea what it is or how to stop it."

"She infected you, Professor."

Charles cursed. "Thanks for the summary, Serena."

"You need to stay out of service reach. I wouldn't trust my offline hack to keep you out of sight any longer."

Charles pulled out the map, suddenly brisk. "Check my thinking. That side road up ahead leads to this hydro plant, yes?"

Joseph glanced over, trying to orient himself and watch the road at the same time. "Looks like it. Should be able to pick up service, but the plant is likely manned. Don't want the truck to be seen."

"Stop at the end of the road, and go on foot. I reckon the plant will be out of sight, and I should be safely out of range, but climb the hill a little way and you should be able to make contact."

Shit, it sounded like the old man was starting to think tactics like a gamer.

Joseph pulled onto the verge just past the turn off. "I'll be as quick as I can. Pink might be able to get someone at the mail room to flag them down on the road." He stepped out of the truck. There was a signal, but weak and patchy. Not enough even for a proper handshake.

He started up the hillside, relieved to see the connection strengthening as he went.

Finally, with his breath rasping in his throat, Joseph judged the signal strong enough to place a call. One of these days, he thought to himself, just when I need her Pink will be out shopping or washing her hair or something. He wept in relief when she answered.

Gulping chill air in between sentences, Joseph told Pink about Charles's message.

"No worries, Tinny, I'm on it." She signed off.

"Hey, Joseph!" Serena's ragged shout interrupted his train of thought. "The Prof asked me to rush this up to you." She clutched a folded piece of paper, fluttering in the keen wind. "Urgent," she gasped in between heaving mouthfuls of air. "He didn't want to leave the truck."

Joseph took the paper and unfolded it. A rumble of machinery distracted him. Down the hill, too far off to reach in time, the truck lurched away down the road.

"Shitfuckingdoublecrossingtraitor ..." The stream of incoherence tailed off to be replaced by worry. "Serena, has he ever driven before?"

They both watched the vehicle's halting progress. It gathered speed, veering from side to side, around the shoulder of the spur that guarded the valley.

"Stupid bastard. He'll kill himself."

"Misguided maybe," said Serena, "but I don't think 'stupid' is the word you're looking for."

Snarling in frustration, Joseph glanced down at the paper crumpled in his fist. The note read, 'Seek help. Stay safe.'

Serena's voice was hushed. "I think the bait worked."

"I said 'stupid,' " Joseph spat, "and I meant it. He's trying to distance himself, to stop himself being a danger to us. Doesn't he realize that physical distance is meaningless? I'll follow him online anyway, and head him off, whatever the fuck he thinks he's doing."

Joseph launched himself back online. Tin Man opened up his full arsenal of illicit software. Some of these tools he barely knew how to use, he'd only ever seen them in the hands of experts like Moonshadow. Well, nothing like learning on the job. "Okay, Professor," he murmured, "where are you?"

After a few minutes searching for Charles's online signature, Tin Man chewed his lip. "He must still be driving. Shit, I hope he hasn't stacked the truck or some such dumbfuck thing."

"Nothing we can do about that one way or another." Serena sounded strained. "I know physical distance doesn't matter online, but I'd still be happier if we were nearby. I think he assumes Tiamat can't do any physical harm out here, but I want to be near to help him if needed."

Joseph grunted, returning to the real world. "She's resourceful, we know that, but there's nothing out here she can control." He scanned the barren and windswept hillside. "Is there?"

"There's a hydro dam up there. What's to stop her flooding us?"

"Hmmph. Point taken." Joseph cast an anxious glance up the valley. In the distance, a line of grey concrete cut across the skyline above them. "We'll have to follow on foot, no other choice, but I'll be tied up with my avatar trying to keep the old goat out of trouble." He thought a moment. "Serena, do you still have that pocket cam on you? Conference in, give me an audio-visual window. I'll be in deep immersion and you need to be my eyes in the real world."

One of Tin Man's trackers pinged. "Got him! He can't have gone far in that time. Probably only a couple of kilometers. Let's see if I can trace his physical position."

"Hurry!" The pleading in Serena's voice cut across the wind sighing through tough grass. She really was fond of the old man.

Joseph realized he was, too.

"Listen, you're right, we need to get closer. I can keep half an eye on what he's doing without too much trouble. Can you steer us and stop me from doing a face plant?" Tin Man pulled up an online map and marked their position for Serena. "Not got a good fix yet, but he must be somewhere along that road, so let's cut across the hill that way. Take us uphill so I don't lose the signal."

With only part of his attention on the ground under his feet, Tin Man stalked the conspicuous avatar through the virtual underworld. This was too easy. Tin Man had made himself invisible, and the old man's halting progress was child's play to follow. It mirrored uncomfortably their own stumbling steps in the real world.

Trusting Serena's guiding hand on his arm, he risked focusing entirely inward to keep tabs on Charles's virtual progress at the same time as refining his real world communications trace. Still not precise, but good enough to tell they were headed the right way.

The Professor stopped, seemingly in thought, then opened a maintenance portal that Tin Man hadn't noticed.

Tin Man stood for a moment, stunned. Then insight hit. *He's following a map.* Feeling slightly sick, Tin Man pulled out the schematic they'd made of the global network core. "Serena, I thought the old man had no sense of direction. He may be slow, but he's navigating the under layer like a fucking pro."

Serena stopped. Joseph lost contact with her and felt momentary disorientation as he tried to separate real and virtual movements. The feed from Serena's camera showed the back of his own head. The feeling of disembodiment nauseated him.

"Well, that's interesting." She grabbed Joseph's arm and started walking again, new urgency in her steps. "You're right, he's hopeless in real life, but now I think about it he never had the same problems with artificial, logical structures. He just seems to have the kind of mind that makes sense of it." Almost as an afterthought, she added, "Where's he going?"

Joseph swallowed. "You really don't want to know." He gazed at the blank hole at the heart of the network. An old world map from early explorers might have labeled the uncharted space 'Here be dragons.' Those old timers had it more right than they could possibly understand.

— ◆ —

Joseph's throat burned raw as he tracked the Professor while shuffling up an increasingly steep bank. In the camera feed from the corner of his eye, the grey wall of the hydro plant's dam loomed across the valley above them. The Professor had positioned himself near the brow of the hill above the lake, in range of the plant's service broadcast but apparently out of harm's way.

The Professor's avatar made halting but unerring progress deeper into the network. Where was Tiamat? Maybe it wasn't too late.

"Hey, Professor!" Tin Man made himself visible.

"Don't know how you did that, but I should have guessed you'd find me eventually."

"I don't think Tiamat's spotted you yet. Exit, please, while you still can."

"If she hasn't seen me, then I'm clearly not doing the right thing."

"What do you mean? What do you think you're doing?"

"Did you get a message through?"

"I spoke to Pink. She'll get through to Krisgaarde."

The Professor grunted. "You've done what you can, but I can't leave it to chance. Tiamat's using them as bait to get to me. Well, I'm done running. If it'll keep her happy, she can have me."

"Dammit, Professor! You might save your daughter, for now, but what about the rest of us?

"From what I've seen, you're better at looking after yourself than I am. You'll be okay."

This was so wrong. The old man had gone batshit. "You're abandoning us? I could understand that before, when it just seemed to be someone out to get *you*. But now we know the truth. Tiamat has humanity by the balls. What future is there for your family in a world like that? We're so close to nailing her for good. You can't leave us now!"

The Professor's avatar froze for a few seconds. Tin Man guessed he'd dropped out of immersion to scan his surroundings. "I don't see what she can do to me up here. I guess she'll find something, but I need to stall her long enough to be sure Sylvie's safe."

"Professor!"

"You need to stay away from me, do you hear? I don't know what Tiamat's going to do, but I don't want you or Serena anywhere near." He turned away. "I need to save my family. You need to survive to save everyone else."

Tin Man stared at the Professor's retreating avatar. "Pink!"

"Here, Tinny."

"We've run out of time. The Norwegian's decided to be heroic."

"Are you kidding? With everyone running scared, I've barely got a tenth of the recruits we need."

"Not good enough. We need Operation Buckshot mobilized now. Like within half an hour."

Pink swore.

"On the bright side, I think Tiamat's going to be too preoccupied to patrol the under layers. Let's make the most of this diversion."

"We need all the gamers on board to have any chance. Only Deacon has the full clan mailing list. And Tinny,"—her voice sounded panicked—"we don't even know it'll work."

A chill swept though Tin Man. "Do your best. I've got to stop the Professor from getting himself killed."

Chapter 43

The virtual world around Charles grew dark. He took a few deep breaths to steady his heartbeat and settled his sweat-slicked grip on his handheld. Nothing more than a glowing green grid hanging in space gave him any frame of reference. He knew he must be close, but was momentarily stumped. Their maps of the network only outlined the gamer disappearances. Like brief summer rain on a driveway where a vehicle had been parked, the marks on the map showed a void where his avatar now stood. There had to be something special about this place.

As if on cue, the floor yawned open. Green-yellow light streamed up.

It looked like Charles was expected. The father and grandfather in him gave thanks, while the stay-at-home university professor quailed.

Without giving himself time to consider, he strode to the glowing gash and jumped in.

He fell, though there was no physical sensation in this unworld. Gossamer strands whipped past his face, growing thicker the further he went. His fall slowed. He tried moving an arm but the strands clung to his avatar like cobwebs.

He was stuck.

The eerie glow dissolved around him and his virtual viewpoint shifted. He was in an airplane, or rather, clinging to its underside. A sliver of glistening metal arcing across the top of his view reflected green and tan from the ground below.

He recognized the outline of the Indhav in the distance, and the approach to Isfeldt airport far below. He blinked as a wisp of cloud whipped past. This could have been a recording from any of a thousand flights in the past year, but Charles knew it was real, right now, sent to him in real time from over a thousand kilometers away.

This was the plane he was supposed to be on. *And I am!* He struggled to contain irrational laughter. Is this what Tiamat meant? His own actions had made her words true, in a sense.

The view changed again. With cold dread, Charles recognized the inside of the airport terminal. There, walking through the door, was Sylvie, with Ben and Aaron in tow. Tears of despair couldn't hide the images projected straight into his mind. Sylvie wore the same red jacket she had met him in two weeks and a lifetime ago. Although it was absurd, he fancied he could smell the perfume she always wore.

Shit. Pink Marie hadn't got through in time. Did she have the presence of mind to contact the airport too? Charles looked for the administration desk behind the gathering knots of people, hoping to see a clerk hurrying over with a message.

A thought struck him. He could call them himself!

His knuckles cracked from his desperate grip on the handheld as he tried to control the shaking in his hands. He snarled at himself. Calm down. Panic won't help. Icy determination flooded him, reclaiming control of his quivering body. He brought up the New Denmark directory and found Isfeldt Airport Administration.

He placed a call, but slashes of light cut through the directory page. A message appeared, a mockery of the standard network message: call refused. The letters dripped grey ooze, then exploded into a thousand droplets which clung to the cobweb strands ensnaring his avatar.

"No!" Charles tried again to bring up the network directory, but his handheld wouldn't respond.

More letters formed in the air in front of his eyes. "Welcome to my world, Professor Hawthorne."

"So, what now?" Charles wondered whether or not Tiamat could hear him.

Silence answered him.

He hung there, trapped in the strands streaming through an endless, glowing space.

"Professor? Don't answer. This is a private chat again, but you'll broadcast anything you say."

Joseph! Or rather, Tin Man. Charles's heart leapt. "Pink didn't get through in time. They're at the airport."

"Shit, Professor—"

"Joseph! I tried to call the airport but I'm being blocked."

"I'll try. Or rather, Serena can while I free you from this mess. Don't say anything else."

Tin Man appeared alongside him, standing in mid-air. The sticky strands brushed him, coiled around him, but couldn't stick to his gleaming skin.

"Tiamat may be emergent, but any time she wants to interact with our avatars she has to build constructs that follow our rules. These are things I can deal with." Tin Man reached towards Charles. His hand sliced through the entangling strands. He worked up and down Charles's virtual body.

Charles could move again.

He was falling again, down through the immense web. Tin Man followed.

In the real world, a hand touched his arm. He jumped and staggered, disorientated, on the tussocked hillside invisible underfoot.

The unseen hand steadied him. "Don't panic, Professor, it's us."

Gratitude battled with guilt in his mind. "You can't be near me," he whispered. "Even out here on top of a mountain, Tiamat will find a way to reach us."

"You didn't seriously believe we'd stay away, did you?" Serena's voice, her real voice, not through his audio implants.

"Professor," said Joseph on his other side. "Pink is rounding up the gamers. She just pinged me. Deacon's nowhere to be seen and they've had enough of this crap. You must have made more of an impression than we thought. Seems you have some fans out there and they're networking in as many other clans as they can reach. We need to keep Tiamat distracted to give them a chance. Before you ask, I don't know how long. Maybe ten minutes, maybe longer. We just need to keep her attention on us, and stay alive."

The skeins of cobwebs thinned. Charles's breath constricted in his throat. He'd stopped falling, though there was nothing visible to support him. He reminded himself that physical laws meant nothing here. They were only obeyed by design, not by default.

Curtains of glowing webs arched above, forming the inside of an immense dome, distance both meaningless and impossible to gauge. They were in the heart of the nest.

Below, an ocean stretched into the distance all around. This was no clean, watery ocean though. The surface heaved and bubbled, a viscous oily goop. Multicolored in sickly hues, Charles wouldn't have been surprised to see maggots or orphaned body parts broaching its surface.

After the stillness of the swaddling webs, the sound down here was an assault. The sea below hissed and sucked. Bubbles detached from its surface with a slurping pop. In the distance, storms of sound raged unseen. Clangs and screams, cracks and moans, like a bedlam of tormented souls heard from behind glass doors.

"Professor!" He could barely hear Serena's voice through the maelstrom. "I can't reach the airport. The call is connecting, but nobody's answering."

The sound reached a crescendo and the surface below Charles boiled.

A veil of milky mucus streamed in front of Charles. The surface showed two images, side by side. His family still stood, facing the doors to the runway with joy and expectation. Alongside, an aerial view of the distant airport chilled him. He knew little about air travel, but he was sure the plane should be lining up its approach along the runway, not straight at the building.

"Dammit! It's me you want! You don't need them. Come and get me!"

"Professor!" Serena's shriek cut through the seething din in Charles's mind. The feed from her pocket camera edged into a corner of Charles's awareness, a window to the real world outside.

A pilotless ground attack drone thundered across the lake towards them. Charles glimpsed dull olive skin, stubby wings, and weapons pods unfolding into strike configuration.

How the fuck did that get here so fast?

"I know how you work," he called. "I've seen it. You've been so clever up to now, but you can't divert a military craft without raising awkward questions."

"Shit!" Joseph's voice had lost its calm. "Some of those fuckers have nuclear capability. D'you think that bitch has the launch codes?"

Charles ignored him. If Tiamat could hack the Alliance military net, who knew what else she was capable of?

"You need to stay hidden." Just raise enough doubts. Stall for time. "If people out there ever so much as suspect what you are, your world will disappear. All they have to do is pull the plug on a few clouds and you will cease to exist."

A thousand kilometers away, the distant plane pulled up and skimmed the Isfeldt terminal building. It climbed and banked in a lazy circle.

On the mountainside, the drone slowed and also circled. The sound was muted beneath his internal clamor, but the hot wash from its exhaust buffeted Charles. The cloying reek of burnt oil filled his nostrils and caught at his throat.

"Your only hope is for people to keep blaming themselves, or faulty technology, for the deaths you cause. This time you've screwed up. This can never be mistaken for an accident."

The drone hovered fifty meters away, its deployed weapons still menacing.

The inner world of the nest wheeled and convulsed. Great gouts of sickly liquid fountained towards Charles with a bubbling slurp. The immersive world gave no sense of smell, but the vision of rotting excrescence was so compelling that he gagged on imagined stench.

He could feel Serena's hand on his shoulder, trembling with fear, but concern evident in the way she squeezed. He wanted to tell her he was okay, but held silent, knowing that the slightest whisper would be relayed to Tiamat.

Now was not the time to disturb her. Something he said had hit home. She was thinking.

The heaving mess subsided to nothing more than a witch's brew. A glistening bubble detached from the surface and drifted towards Charles. In its depths, a news report screamed of a horrifying accident, a small tactical nuke detonated on a remote mountaintop.

"Small," whispered Joseph in his ear. "Half a kiloton. Incinerate everything within a couple of hundred meters. Don't say a word, Professor," he added as Charles opened his mouth.

"She can't see us, can she?" Serena breathed in his other ear. "Her whole world is online, she can see our handhelds, but she can't see *us*."

"Hence the nuke," said Joseph. "The drone with a human operator could have gunned us down, but she needs to make sure. But surely she'd have the camera feeds—"

"But maybe she has trouble with images. She has the raw data, but she doesn't have *vision*. Not in the way we understand it."

Charles fought back the urge to add his views to the speculation. The youngsters could be right. Who knew how an intelligence born in the depths of the network would view the world outside? But how did this help them?

More bubbles floated into view. Beneath their yellow-green shine, half-completed incident reports wallowed on military headed paper. Mail messages and voice transcripts, flight logs and launch clearance instructions grew before Charles's horrified eyes. A sentence here, a paragraph there, all cross referenced and time stamped. Tiamat was building a false trail implicating officers in a botched drill. They would protest ignorance, of course, assuming they were allowed to live, but nothing would counter the damning evidence she was fabricating right there in front of him.

So why show him? Was she teasing him, or maybe not quite sure of herself? This was new territory. Until today, Charles had only ever seen evidence of her slanting reports people had already written. Hiding some, promoting others, in the endless race for fickle attention spans. Now she was producing sophisticated content of her own. This was leagues beyond faking a short message to a worried family member.

"Very impressive." Charles's voice sounded supernaturally calm above his hammering heart. "But crude. I've seen how you manipulated history, steered the course of the planet. You can do better than this."

The words in the bubbles stopped flowing.

"You fear my creation, my Typhoon, because it hurt you. When you strayed into its zone it destroyed your presence. But you don't know what Typhoon does." *Did!*

The visceral cauldron in the depths of the nest calmed. The sense of expectation weighed like a sodden blanket.

"Typhoon could show you how to *really* control people. Imagine it. Whole populations enslaved and building ever more powerful computers to house you."

"Professor! What are you doing?" Serena's horrified words broke through the immersive shell.

Charles held up his hand to signal her to be quiet. Unable to see whether or not she understood, he pressed on. "Typhoon spotted your influence. It knows how people in large numbers behave, and it was good enough to see the discrepancies and work out what you look like. Imagine being able to predict the effects of your manipulations? Being able to try out different tactics to achieve your goals?"

Come on! How much longer?

"I can show you how. Leave my family alone and I'll help you."

"I see what you're doing, Prof," Joseph murmured. "Keep it up."

"With that kind of power, you could have the population working for you like never before. No more wasting time and resources trying to better themselves. All efforts could be directed to building your network, and they'd never know the difference."

The inner world darkened. Silence fell. Long seconds passed, then a roar split his mind like a melon. The cauldron below him exploded. Rips appeared in the gauzy nest above, spilling blinding light into the heaving pit.

A vast bubble detached itself and flew towards him. Charles ducked, realizing as he did so that it made no difference. As he watched, the bubble slowed and seemed to frost over, losing its shine. The surface cracked like midsummer desert earth.

Someone dashed the handheld out of Charles's hand. He stooped to pick it up, but fingers yanked at his sleeve, dragging him away.

"Run, Professor!" Serena's voice pierced a feral hissing that blanketed his mind.

"The drone's going to attack!" Joseph yelled in his other ear. "I hope to God she's targeting the handhelds."

The nest wheeled. Charles stumbled on unseen tussocks. Hands guided him up the hill. Another bubble floated in his vision. Through obscuring patches like scratched glass he could see the Isfeldt airport terminal from the circling aircraft. The building looked like a toy, far below, but it hovered front and center in his line of sight and grew at a sickening rate.

"No!" He staggered and fell. "Sylvie!"

Vivid blotches of pustulence rained around him. The mind-numbing hissing, like a thousand angry serpents, modulated from blank evenness. Contours emerged in the sound, rising and falling.

Charles's breath rasped in his throat. His feet scrabbled for purchase on the unseen grass, while arms at his side half-guided, half-carried him up the slope.

The hissing pulsated in his mind, rhythmic hate. The soundscape morphed again, sharpened into a metallic clanging, and resolved itself into one word. "Die!"

Behind him, the drone's engines dwindled and changed pitch. A staccato hammering sounded above the inner racket.

"Cannon fire," Joseph yelled.

"But her aim's off," Serena added. "She's firing blind."

"Die. Die. Diediedie ..."

"Down!" Joseph's hand thrust Charles to the ground. He screwed his eyes shut against unseen daggers of wiry grass raking his face. A hornet swarm whistled past his ears, felt rather than heard, and the ground drummed against his cheek.

Hands lifted him once more. He stumbled forward, expecting at any moment to feel shells rip through his back. Behind him, the drone's engines roared and faded as it weaved back and forth. Bursts of gunfire pounded the hillside in a frenzy of destruction.

Vertigo gripped Charles as his inner viewpoint plunged towards the airport.

Abruptly, the hail of gunfire stopped.

Joseph swore. "She's breaking off to launch the nuke."

"How long do we have?" Serena's voice carried more clearly through the din in Charles's ears. They must be nearly out of range of the handhelds.

"The drone needs to launch from a safe distance, or the missile won't arm and can't detonate," Joseph called. "Nearly there!"

Charles wasn't sure whether that last yelp was alarm or reassurance. This was pointless. Could they really run from a nuke? He didn't care. The terminal building rushed at him. Helpless tears streamed down his cheeks.

The bubble collapsed into sticky blackness. Writhing, decaying strands of Tiamat's nest fell around him, drifting past his vision but fading fast. Flashes of blue sky emerged. Real sky, not simulated. Patches of real landscape, rock and wiry grass, intruded on his inner hell.

The ground at his feet dropped as they crested the hill. He fell. Unprepared, his feet jarred and skidded. He tried to keep his balance, almost toppling Serena at his side. The downward slope came into sharper focus as the connection to the handheld weakened. He guided his steps more surely, wondering how much time they had left. The roar of the drone had dwindled to nothing.

They slipped and slid down the steep brow. Joseph tugged, angling them towards a solid outcrop broaching the slope like a whale.

The sky lit up. The hill behind them cast the valley into impenetrable dusk. Charles screwed his eyes shut against the piercing light above, but his eyelids seemed little more than pink gossamer blotting out a car's headlamps.

He opened his eyes. The pink nothingness was still there. "Can you see?"

"Only shadows," said Serena.

Joseph just moaned.

Moments later, the ground bucked, sending the three of them sprawling.

Still blinded, they scrambled to where Charles guessed the outcrop protruded. His hands met a boulder, then a lichen-crusted face of rock. Serena and Joseph's hands were still on him. He hauled them into the lee of the cliff. They pressed themselves into the angle between stone and turf.

A giant fist squeezed the air from his lungs. Heat raged. Through Charles's clearing vision, a shadow loomed, blotting out the afternoon sky. Rock and soil whipped silently past their meager shelter.

Charles gasped for air—air which seared his lungs. On one side, Joseph curled up against the rock face in a fetal position. Serena buried her head in his other side, her body wracked by convulsive sobs.

Charles blinked, trying to moisten eyeballs parched by furnace air. The looming cloud overhead resolved into an ochre rain of ash and pumice. Glowing pellets hissed around them, scorching grass. The hairs on the back of his hand crisped.

Although he could still hear nothing, Charles was sure he was screaming.

CHAPTER 44

Lights. Voices. He could hear again.

Memory surfaced, unbidden.

Sylvie! Ben!

A band of fire tightened across his chest.

"... losing him!" Frantic shouts, distant, unintelligible.

Darkness.

Peace.

Lights again.

How many times had they glimmered amongst the night terrors, only to vanish again in pain and grief?

A new voice this time. Familiar. Beloved.

Charles opened his eyes a crack. He squinted past the blinding brightness. His eyes burned, but his ears could not be mistaken. "Sylvie?"

A hand brushed his face. A shadow blurred the brilliance. He breathed a familiar fragrance.

"Is that really you? Where's Ben? Where am I?"

"Too many questions, Dad. You must slow down or they'll put you out again."

Charles tried to speak, but Sylvie shushed him.

"Let me talk. You rest. You've been held in a coma for three weeks. They tried to bring you round but your body wasn't strong enough. You kept crashing. I thought you'd never wake up."

His chest tightened once more at the tears in her voice, but that voice was a tonic to Charles. "She sent a message," he croaked. "A trap. I thought she'd got you. I thought you were gone."

He squinted, defying the burning in his eyes. He had to see her, to be sure. Was this another trick? But Tiamat couldn't fake this, the touch, the smell. Images solidified, still limned in painful intensity. Pastel ceiling and walls, people, Sylvie's tear-streaked cheeks.

He reached to touch her face, movements hindered by a thicket of tubes piercing his forearm. The mottled pink on the back of his hand startled him. Memory flooded back. "Dammit, that bitch nuked me, and I'm still here."

"Well, well, you are a tougher old bird than I imagined." Erik Thorsen strode through the door, batting aside two flustering nurses.

"Erik, what happened? Isfeldt?"

"That message smelled bad from the start. Christian didn't like it. I didn't like it. More important, Ingrid didn't believe it." His brows arched in response to Charles's puzzled look. "My daughter. The one who plays games?"

"Oh," said Charles. Then, "Oh!"

"She was in that group you spoke to—"

"She says you gave quite the performance, Dad," said Sylvie. "It was such a relief to hear you were still alive."

"We spent that night scratching our heads thinking how to help you without getting you caught."

"But I saw the plane crash into the building," said Charles. "I saw Sylvie there, waiting."

"That first part happened." Erik nodded, beard bristling. He looked sad for a moment, then his chin jutted. "No matter. We needed a new building." He laughed. "I spoke to my counterparts in New Boston and Isfeldt. Both plane and terminal were empty. We fed old camera feeds into the system. Played that bitch at her own game."

Charles gaped, then realization hit. He laughed. His chest tightened and monitors at his side bleeped. Nurses scurried. He fell back onto his pillow, wheezing.

———•◆•———

Next time he opened his eyes, the room was dim. Curtains screened the windows.

A shadow stirred in the corner. "You awake, Professor?"

"Joseph?"

"Here."

"How are you? Where's Serena?"

"I'm doing okay." The shadow heaved itself upright, and hobbled forward using a pair of sticks.

"Shit, what happened to you?" The absurdity of the question didn't occur to Charles.

Joseph laughed. "What, apart from standing in the way of a half-kiloton nuke? I'll say again, I'm doing okay. Legs got a little overdone. The skin's still tight, hence the props." He gazed down at Charles. "Have you any idea what kind of bragging rights this earns me down in the game world?"

"I thought you never talked about the world outside."

"Times change."

"Serena?"

"Daddy whisked her off to a private clinic before I was awake. Heard she's doing well, too. She lost her hair, but came out of it well, all things considered."

"Daddy?"

"Big time shipping magnate." He chewed his lip. "Explains a lot. She seemed rather better set up than the average student."

Charles thought about this. Yes, it did explain a lot. He realized how little he knew of his students' backgrounds.

Finally, he asked the question he'd been avoiding. "Tiamat?"

Joseph grinned. "Gone. Operation Buckshot worked. Thought they'd have told you that already. Or you'd have worked it out from the fact that you're still alive, amongst all this lethal technology."

Dammit, Charles hated having the lecturing tables turned on him. But he didn't have the fight left in him to find a sharp riposte. Instead, memories beckoned, emerging from the mists of pain. "The nest looked like it was falling apart."

"She was clinging to what scraps of the network she could. It wasn't enough. The emergence collapsed."

"She still tried to kill us."

"You kept her occupied enough. Half the targets were infected before she even noticed, and then she didn't have enough power to deal with the gamers and you at the same time. Guess who she chose? You should be proud."

Joseph's face turned grey. He eased himself back into his chair.

Guilt washed over Charles. "She may yet have succeeded. How long were we out in the open? Before they picked us up?"

"Too long for comfort."

"I'm too old to count." Charles felt sick. "Sylvie says I should have been put out to grass years ago, but you and Serena ..."

"Don't know what sort of dose she got, I think she was more under cover. We were sick as dogs for a week or so. I can keep solid food down at last, which is an improvement, and I'll be on tumor watch and pre-emptive chemo for the rest of my life."

"Oh, Joseph, I'm so sorry. I didn't mean to drag you into all this."

"You seem to forget I was already in it up to my eyeballs. This is better than being fried in a gas explosion or something." The cheeky grin returned. "Besides, I always planned to live fast and die young."

Charles returned the grin. "So, do I glow in the dark?"

Joseph stared, then started to laugh.

Charles laughed, too. Hot knives scored his chest and the laughter collapsed to painful gasping. He subdued his ragged breathing before the monitors at his side could summon the nurses. "Important enough to kill," he mused. "Shame no-one beyond a handful here will ever know." Another memory surfaced. "Am I still a wanted man?"

"I understand mayor Thorsen has convinced the Alaskan authorities that you were the victim of a set-up, and confirmed your alibi. It wasn't too hard a sell. The network's awash with evidence of organized misinformation right across the globe."

"How so?"

"The official story is that a bunch of gamers accidentally wrecked a crime syndicate that's been siphoning off computing power."

"How did they explain a tactical nuclear explosion?"

"They found scraps of the audit trail Tiamat was building. Evidence of the conspiracy. The crime bosses trying to kill us off to stay hidden."

Charles chuckled. "Somehow, I doubt they'll ever bring those crime bosses to trial."

Joseph dragged his chair closer to the bed and stretched out his legs. They both rested in silence for a long while. Eventually Joseph asked, "What now, Professor? You have some serious research to publish, if you can piece together the evidence."

Charles pondered this. What about his research? Did he even have a post to return to at the university? He could never recreate the work that he and Terry had spent so long on, even if the university allowed the funding. And they would never do that without a solid grant proposal backed by some evidence.

Somehow, it seemed unimportant. He had found the answers he was looking for, even if the rest of the world didn't care. And what good would it do them? The menace was gone, and his own experiments repeatedly showed that people, left to themselves, had the wherewithal to figure things out.

And he could do a lot worse than New Denmark for retirement. At least they had decent beer.

Joseph Wong paced past the house a third time, indecision corroding his resolve. The mountains cradling Tromso reminded him of his native Yukon.

Scars on the back of his hand itched, and his legs ached like a bitch. He felt foolish, standing in the middle of an empty street, clutching a small bouquet of flowers he'd stopped to buy on the way from the airport.

Ah, heck! He hadn't come half-way around the globe just to turn back now. He strode up and rang the doorbell.

Almost at once, he backed away. This was stupid. It violated every ingrained tenet he'd held dear since his teenage years. Ever since the Samurai had forced him to abandon cherished ideals, he'd had some practice mixing the real and online worlds. He had been in the thick of it, and it no longer felt quite so strange. He wondered if Pink Marie would see it the same way. The thought of her withering scorn, the tongue-lashing she could so readily dish out online, made him tremble.

Too late. The door opened.

A young man, maybe in his thirties, stared at Joseph.

Joseph's heart sank. Oh, this was so stupid. He hadn't even considered the possibilities of Pink's own life outside of the virtual realm. Who was this? Boyfriend? Husband? This is why we keep real life out of the online world.

Joseph floundered for an explanation. Did this man even know about Trudy Lundquist's online persona? How would he react to someone from the gaming world dropping in out of the blue?

"Hei," said the stranger.

"I—I'm sorry," Joseph stammered. "I don't speak Norwegian. I'm looking for Trudy Lundquist."

"Hvem er det," called a husky voice from the depths of the house.

"En ung mann," the man replied, over his shoulder. He gazed at the flowers in Joseph's hand, and smirked. "An admirer, I think," he added in a heavy accent.

He stepped aside and waved Joseph up the steps. Without a word, he pointed to a door lying open to one side of the narrow hallway.

Joseph stepped warily through the door. A woman sat near the window, grey hair pulled back into a neat bun. The skin at the side of her neck sagged where her head lolled to one side. A flat panel screen on the table next to her beeped softly to itself, a reassuring heartbeat matching the row of pulsing graphs and figures.

He looked around the room, expecting to see a nurse or companion. There was no-one else there.

She turned. Rather, her chair turned. With a start, Joseph saw she was in a motorized wheelchair. A mottled hand deftly tweaked a joystick on the arm of the chair, and she glided towards Joseph.

A top-of-the-range gamer handheld lay in her lap, grips burnished through long hours of use.

"Trudy?" he breathed.

He smiled.

Finally, he understood.

Clear blue eyes gazed back from a crows-nest of wrinkles. "Hello, Tinny. So pleased to meet you at last."

The end

9 780099 372422